DRAGON'S
JUSTICE 9

D1528333

CONTENTS

CHAPTER 1

I turned my hand over, creating a curved wall of ice that stopped the geist from being able to run. The sun had set, but with my shifted eyes, I could make out the glimmer of magic.

The geist had created faint barbed wire out of magic all over the woman's body, cutting into her as it controlled her.

I rubbed at my forehead as the paranormal looked left and right, trying to figure out a way to escape.

"You need to leave her body." I told the geist.

"No!" It wailed and made the windows in the alley rattle. "I will not. She's mine."

The barbed wire tightened further, and the woman bled all over.

A terrifying image was thrown into my head, but clearing that attack was nothing compared to resisting demon and fae glamor. I pushed the nightmare out with a thought.

"Oh. Are we going to do that? Let me try." My draconic aura blasted out of me.

I'd gained more control since I'd accidentally sent my aura out into a crowd, making them all panic. The biggest problem I had now was that the intensity of my aura could easily just kill the human host the geist was using if I wanted to attack it.

But make it afraid? I could do that relatively safely.

"No!" the geist screamed, becoming distracted enough that I could summon a glowing gold ball of summer fae magic.

I targeted the barbed wire and geist with the light. It tried to dodge out of the way, abandoning its host, but I was getting better at using my abilities. I opened a portal right in front of the geist, delivering it into the ball of summer fae magic.

The undead didn't even make it all the way out of the portal before it turned into a fine glowing powder that fell into the alley.

"Goldie, can you help me pick that up? Best not leave anything around if we can help it." I walked over to the human woman and carefully picked her up.

My phone started ringing. Goldie picked it out of my pocket and held it to my ear since my arms were full from carrying the wounded woman.

"We lost you." Maddie came over the phone. "Frank blacked out for a minute there when it got angry."

"We were dealing with a ghost. Well, a geist, but it's like a rabid ghost. Ghost-like things are absolutely the worst. Track my phone; I'm walking out of the alley."

"Did you kill the woman?" Maddie's tone was grave.

"No. I didn't kill her, just the geist. Carrying her in my arms right now, if you want to swing the van around. Let's get her a sedative and get her patched up before we drop her back at her place."

"That place was a pit." I could hear tires screeching in the background as Maddie talked. "She's going to be very confused when she wakes up."

"Yeah. Someone will probably chalk it up to a mental break or something. She'll get therapy and go on with her life like everyone else," I grumbled, wishing I could just tell the woman that she'd been attacked and possessed by a geist. "At least she isn't dead. And the geist won't bother anything else."

Maddie's van passed the alley and then hit the brakes so hard that the back lifted up, then the entire van jerked to a stop.

This van wasn't Morgana's van, it was Frank's. Frank, likely with Sabrina's help, had been enchanting a beat-up old junker. They'd been slowly replacing all of the parts as they got paid in gold with Silverwing Mercenaries.

The vehicle looked like a piece of junk, but I knew they had put a couple hundred thousand into it. By now, it would probably survive an RPG or a troll collision. There wasn't much difference between the two, if I was honest.

"Get in. Fuck, she looks terrible." Frank spotted the woman in my arms. The back of the van had been emptied out, and a plate of steel ran along the floor now. "Hold on. I've got some sedatives. Close the door. But Maddie, don't you make me stick a needle in someone while you drive like a bat out of hell."

Maddie turned around, leaning between the two front seats. "Vampires aren't from Hell, even if they got mixed up with the demon of gluttony."

"Uh huh," Frank muttered, not sounding convinced. "You all drive like crazy people."

"It's the super speed," I told him, setting the woman down and letting Frank administer the sedatives while I pulled at some of the death in the woman's body to help it heal. "When they can run faster than they drive, they just don't take driving seriously."

"I do take it seriously," Maddie retorted. "It's just a lot easier now."

"Reaction speeds," I responded. "You feel a lot more in control and are comfortable doing wild things. Trust me, I've ridden with Morgana enough to know that, despite how wild she drives, I'm more at risk of being thrown out for not wearing my seatbelt than her actually hitting anything."

"How is Morgana?" Frank asked.

"Very pregnant. And very hungry. And vampires only have one pregnancy craving." I stared at him.

Frank glanced at Maddie and swallowed. "I see."

"Don't be scared. I don't take too much, and we supplement with bloodwine. Besides, it'll be hundreds of years until I could get pregnant. Not everyone is a walking giant magical battery." Maddie glared at me.

I shrugged. "I am what I am."

"Alright. We are all done, but take it—" Frank grabbed onto the side as Maddie shot off into the street.

Goldie shot out like a sudden explosion of bubblegum and suspended the unconscious woman, Frank, and I in the back of the van to prevent us from being thrown.

"—slow," Frank finished, rolling his eyes.

Maddie gave him a guilty smile in the mirror. "I knew Goldie or Zach would have you guys. Besides, I only have two speeds. Stopped and full throttle. So, how are all the pregnancies going, then? Everyone is okay?"

"Top of the line care from our own in-house dragon doctor," I answered. "But we've had to make a few adjustments. We now have a new freezer in the kitchen that a nymph is in charge of keeping stocked with ice cream. We go through milk like no one's business, and someone keeps eating Nyske's pickles."

"Why doesn't she just buy more?" Frank asked.

"She asked everyone if we needed extra. Supposedly no one said they wanted pickles stocked. Yet every week, someone eats all her pickles and even drinks the juice. That's her favorite part," I sighed. "She's not even pregnant."

Maddie chuckled. "Then tell her to just buy more."

"We are. We are up to eight times the normal pickle purchases, and they keep running out. No one seems to know who's eating the pickles, and it's driving Nyske crazy. At this point, she thinks someone is pranking her and keeps threatening to buy a second fridge she keeps, put a padlock on it, and stock it entirely with pickles."

"Seems like quite the pickle." Maddie couldn't help herself, snickering at her own joke.

"Funny," I muttered dryly while Frank chuckled in the back. "So, to answer your question, the pregnancies are fine. Life is just normal, manageable chaos in a giant harem."

Frank sighed. Maddie was still adamant that they remain the two of them. Though, a few nymphs had tried before being scared off by Maddie's fangs.

Honestly, I was fairly certain Frank didn't mind anymore. But he continued to press the topic because he enjoyed getting a reaction out of Maddie.

"Live vicariously through Zach and his lovely mansion. Just no touching," Maddie replied. "Otherwise, I'll have to kill one of them, and it won't be pretty."

The roads were fairly empty, but Maddie twisted hard on the steering wheel as something clipped the side of our van. Thankfully, Goldie kept us from flying about in the back. There was a shudder, and the faint hum of several of Frank's enchantments kicking in.

"Uh. Problem up there?" I asked.

Maddie was craning her neck to look above us. "I think that was either the largest bird I've ever seen, or that was an angel."

"Insanely hot with a penchant for angry sex that she totally doesn't have with Zach here?" Frank hooked a thumb at me. "What'd you do to piss Helena off?"

"I didn't get a good look. It just sort of came out of nowhere, swoo—"

Gunfire rattled against the exterior of the van, and several of Frank's enchantments were glowing hot with magic.

"Probably not Helen," I stated the obvious. "Also, there's more than one." I picked out at least three guns firing above us.

Frank tried to move, failed, and then waved at Goldie. "Move me over to that panel. The wards won't hold off this much sustained gunfire. I need to swap a few things out. Maddie, can you get us under an overpass?"

"Working on it," she growled. "Nothing for a good stretch, though."

"Goldie, can you?" I asked.

Goldie punched a hole in the top of the van and made a sleek arrow shaped canopy above us that caused the van to lurch and get a moment of air.

"My van!" Frank cried out.

"I bet I could get it to fly again. Might be its first and last flight, though," Maddie admitted.

"I'm heavy enough to hold us down," Goldie replied. "There was just a moment of adjustment." She melted out of the bracer on my arm to sit in the back with us, the movement not bothering the gold elemental at all. "They've stopped firing."

Even though she'd made a humanoid form of herself, she was still connected to the bracer on my arm by a thin thread. She never left my arm anymore.

"Can you get them?" I asked.

"No. They are too high in the air. I believe this is what the new rules around your honor guard are for." Goldie gave me a broad grin.

She wasn't wrong.

I had been spared having two constant tag-alongs with a very clear rule. Two of the dragons were always on duty, but I was supposed to call for them when help was needed.

I looked out of an uncovered part of the back window and opened a portal. Two figures shot through the portal the second I opened it. Both of them hit the road behind me, and then two much larger figures shot into the night sky a moment later.

Polydora and Amira had shifted and taken flight. They would spot the angels and deal with the threat. Lightning crackled high in the sky above us. Goldie retracted herself to thinly coat the van.

"I wonder when I will get to that level of badass wizard." Frank was peering over my shoulder, wanting to get a look at the action above us.

"Huh?" I asked.

"I mean, that was like a 'Summon Dragon Spell'. Pretty fucking badass." Frank's voice switched into an infomercial voice. "Got a problem?" Frank snapped his fingers. "Just summon some dragons! Problem solved."

More lightning lit up the clouds above us, and I could feel my marks on both of the dragons as they fought the angels above us. Having fought Polydora on more than one occasion, I pitied the angels.

With the angels under control, I glanced back at the human woman I had saved from the geist. I kept pulling death from her wounds and letting her body's natural healing do the rest of the work. I still wasn't as good as the other dragons at healing, which was clear to anybody who looked. I created bruised patches as I managed to close the wounds.

"Yeah. It is pretty convenient." I agreed. "Let's bring this woman straight to the hospital rather than to a healer. I think I can patch her up enough."

Her wounds were fairly shallow by that point, and I was going to pull at the injuries on her face to minimize the visual scarring. As much as we didn't want to admit it, a few big scars on someone's face did change their lives pretty severely.

"So... What was with the angels?" Maddie asked.

I shrugged. "No clue. Knowing Poly, she'll take one alive if she can and we can find out more." I paused, feeling both of my mates break from the tumbling fighting and form a straight line towards me.

Sensing where they were, I put a portal a good chunk ahead of them. In the night sky, it would be hard for them to miss the new portal. It would take them back to the mansion.

They both circled the portal a few times, likely looking for any additional threats, before both of them went through.

"Well, they are back at the mansion, so we'll head there after we drop the nice lady off." I held onto the side of the van as Maddie careened off the highway to the closest hospital.

"Let's not kill her on the way in, honey," Frank told his girlfriend.

"I didn't even take that one too sharply. Tell him, Zach," Maddie protested.

"My mates would argue that I am absolutely the last person you should ask for safety-related advice." I looked out the window, keeping an eye out for any more angels that might be in the sky. With my eyes shifted, I would likely be able to see their mana, even if I couldn't see their actual forms.

"You are absolutely no fun. Is this what happens to friends when they become fathers?" Maddie asked.

I rolled my eyes. "Yes. We think about safety. Eyes on the road."

"Yes, Dad," Maddie sighed and drove no less recklessly all the way up until a few blocks from the hospital. "Here we are. Want me to wait on you?" Maddie asked.

"Nope. I've got this." I pulled out a wooden block on a chain and hung it from my neck. It looked ridiculous, but they were still just a prototype. They were made out of wood for convenience until we got it figured out.

"Can we get Detective Fox to pull the recording tomorrow?" Frank asked hopefully.

"Ask Scar, but probably." I got out of the van as Goldie retracted herself completely into the bracer, bringing the woman with us and gently laying her in my arms.

The woman looked like she'd been through hell, but that was mostly the torn clothing covered with blood.

I winced at the idea of showing up to the hospital with a woman like this in my arms. It just wasn't a good look for a big man like me to be carrying around an injured woman, much less one that was bruised to hell with blood on her clothes.

Invisibility spells were far from perfect. Up in the sky, they were great. Down on the ground, too many people noticed the ripples of light the spell gave off. Frank's enchantment around my neck was supposed to work like one of those reflective outfits that celebrities wore to ruin photos. It gave off a lot of IR light that ruined image capture if I was around.

As for my face, it shifted with a shimmer of purple, gold, and silver magic as all three fae aspects were part of my glamor. I gave myself a generic face as I strode quickly to the hospital, put on a panicked expression, and hurried to the front doors of the emergency room.

The doors opened and I rushed forward to the attendant's station. "Help. She's been hurt." I let some genuine pain at seeing what happened to the woman seep into my voice.

The attendant was almost bored with my performance. I was clearly one among many after her years of working in the emergency room.

"Grab a clipboard, fill out the paperwork," the triage attendant mumbled before picking up a radio. "Stretcher to ER waiting room." She turned to her computer, not even looking up as she spoke. "We'll get her comfortable until the doctor can get to her."

It wasn't the first time I'd brought a victim to the emergency room, but the detached tone got me every time.

Before the stretcher came out, a group of four cops exited.

The one in front was half turned around, cracking a joke to the ones behind him, but when one of them stiffened in my direction he whipped around. None of them put their hands on their guns, but they tensed when they spotted a big guy with a bloody woman.

While I had pulled off distressed, I wasn't a sobbing mess. It must have made me look like a psychopath.

"Sir. Is something wrong?" One of the officers stepped forward.

"No, officer. Just found a friend in a sorry state and brought her in. We live around the corner."

"Uh huh. Please, would you mind letting us have some time with her?" The officer stepped forward and one of the ones behind him placed his hand on his gun.

"Not at all. But she's unconscious. The nurse sent for a stretcher." I kept myself calm. The last thing I needed was for Goldie to lash out.

"Wonderful."

The doors behind the officer bumped open as someone wheeled out a hospital bed.

"Put her here." The nurse pointed at the bed.

I carefully deposited the woman and squeezed out a smile as the officers clearly pressed in around her to 'help' push the cart and separate her from me.

"Why don't we have a talk?" The lead officer remained with me.

I knew he was well intentioned, but I did not want to deal with whatever bullshit he was going to bring.

"Sure." I had no intention of talking, but it would get me out of the building. "We were supposed to meet up for bowling night, and then when she was late. She wasn't answering her phone, so I went to her place and found her like that." I was not the best liar.

"Uh huh." The officer clearly didn't believe me, but that didn't matter once we got outside.

I made a portal on the other side of a big pillar and just walked around, stepping right through and closing the portal behind me.

My job was done.

I blew out a heavy breath, but I had another stop I needed to make. I portaled myself back to the apartment complex where we had gone to hunt the geist down.

We'd known where to go because the woman's boyfriend's boss was a paranormal and had heard that she'd gotten very weird all of a sudden. The paranormal network in Philly was quite large, and when a friend of a friend passed the tip along to the council, it was a simple check in with Maddie and Frank that had led to the discovery of the geist.

Morgana had then wanted me to help them deal with the geist. Neither Frank nor Maddie were well equipped to deal with that particular variety of paranormal.

"Why are we here?" Goldie asked.

"Because she's been possessed by a geist for a week, if not two. Her life is about to be flipped upside down, and you saw her place. When she gets out of the hospital, it will be like a slap in the face." I walked up the stairs to the apartment complex for the second time in the night.

"And?"

"We are going to clean it. Well, if I'm honest, you are going to do most of the heavy lifting. I'm just going to make a portal to the local dump. The place was like a hoarder's wet dream."

Goldie squeezed my arm. "This is a nice thing to do for her."

"It's the kind of thing that should be done." I got to the woman's door and opened it up, greeted by flies and the smell of a fridge that had gone bad. "Let's get to work."

CHAPTER 2

I popped open a portal and went through as my three nymphs followed me into the large chamber that still smelled of stone dust from the driders' sculpting. They had made the entire space out of stone.

"We are a little early. With you getting a handle on your portals, we really should stop scheduling so much travel time." Fiona tapped on a tablet.

"But then it gives me a little time to chat after or before. I like the moment to sit down and breathe." I sat on my throne.

The throne was a giant ornate piece that had a dragon clawing its way up to the heavens and setting flight above. There was a crown that someone had made, but I just let it hang off the back.

I was in no way interested in wearing a crown. For one, they were far heavier than I'd imagined. But I also didn't need to flaunt my power. Time had made me comfortable with being a dragon, and that made me more kingly than any crown.

"I need to add cushions." I leaned back into the hard chair. Several of the other chairs already had cushions added.

Ikta's cushion was a big, fuzzy material that had a bunch of swaddled babies on the print. She's really gone off the deep end into a baby craze after the two weeks in the hot spring with me.

While I sat, Goldie spilled out of the bracer, coating the throne and creating a buoyant cushion under me that formed around my body, holding it in place.

"Thank you, Goldie."

"No problem. I like these moments, Fiona. They let me spend time with my Zach."

Pixie gave me a look, one that communicated a conversation we'd had several times but I didn't want to broach again.

Goldie had been 'born' not that long ago. Yet she had consumed the knowledge of thousands of demons, giving her a new maturity, some of which was focused on me. I was conflicted about what that meant for her and me, to say the least.

The nymphs took their seats by me.

The room was split up into multiple sections. One was for the fae, where Summer, Maeve, and Ikta all had their seats. Their thrones were the same size as mine, with their own decorative flare. But they represented the fae part of my power.

Then came the paranormals. Jadelyn, Scarlett, and Kelly. They remained on the Philly council and represented me there.

Hell had a space in the room. Sabrina, Leviathan, and technically Goldie used that area. Though Goldie would only send part of herself over, preferring to stay as close to me as possible. Even if I wanted to, I doubted I could get rid of Goldie with her current strength and her amorphous form.

Lilith kept her distance from me, saying she very much wanted to seduce me, but all the fun would be over after it happened and she'd move on.

Talk about a bad decision.

The dragons had elected three to sit on the council. Polydora, Amira, and Regina would take their seats eventually.

Elena Wallachia, Yev, and Tyrande held another set of three thrones to represent the global forces of the paranormal. Though, if I was honest, we probably needed to broaden that group.

The FBI had a spot that they were welcome to use. Someone had even installed a little light that they could turn on for me to make them a portal.

The rest would just use one of the portals in my home that had become my own little dimension. The mansion seemed to be increasingly connected, and apparently was helping ground the other worlds. Sabrina had taken to studying the situation and came to the conclusion that the mansion was working like a keystone to stabilize multiple planes.

The last area in the room was held by Silverwing Mercenaries. Morgana, Maddie, and Frank joined when they were able.

My three nymphs sat around me or often on the sides of my throne, representing their support. The nymphs, now our largest force among the family, had more power than they realized. Thankfully, they only exerted their power for small things, like getting in on Ikta's two weeks.

"Goldie, if you would move him to a lying position, there isn't a reason that I shouldn't get to work on his shoulders. He keeps all his stress there." Nyske stood up, having finished whatever correspondence she was working on her tablet.

"Huh?" I asked, trying to replay what she'd just said.

But Goldie flowed over me before I'd fully processed, flipping me over and wrapping me at the hips as she became a table, while a little strand of gold shot off to the side and became Goldie's humanoid body. In her more human form, Goldie was a thin woman made of gold that stood six feet tall. She had several shades of gold to try and make her skin different colors than her 'dress'.

"Yes. I will work on his legs," Goldie replied happily.

Nyske gave me a knowing smile, and I only shrugged, helplessly.

"We are just getting back into everything. Let's not go crazy. I'm not that stressed," I groaned as Nyske pushed into my back with more strength than a nymph should have.

Nyske, due to a strange event with my father, was a type of fae-dragon never seen before.

Goldie enveloped my legs, and it felt like dozens of massage rollers were going up and down my legs from every angle. The pressure was enough for me to press my face into the headrest and grit my teeth.

"Go easier. I understand your desire for efficiency, but if you make him tense, then it does him no good," Nyske chided Goldie.

Nyske and Yev seemed to understand Goldie better than some of the others, so they were given the task of working to coach Goldie. Goldie's thoughts could be very foreign at times.

Yet the two of them working me together had me falling into the Goldie massage table like a dripping puddle.

"Portal to Georgia's office, please," Pixie spoke up.

Without needing to think too hard, I snapped my fingers and spotted the light from the portal in my peripheral to summon the new Special Agent in Charge of Philadelphia's FBI field office.

It wasn't until the stern woman's voice came through that I realized she'd entered. "Wow. Your nymphs really are full service."

Surprisingly, she didn't sound upset.

"My Zach needs to relax, and he has little time for it," Goldie defended me.

"What she— said," I grunted as Goldie pressed hard into a knot in my calf.

"So it seems." Georgia's heels clicked on the stone floor. "Where are we?"

"Zach's dimension," Rebecca Till's voice announced her entrance, and I heard the flutter of Helena letting her wings out, telling me that she was also present.

"Welcome to my court. Please enjoy the show." I waved off to the side.

"At least he's clothed and someone isn't sucking his cock," Agent Till spoke up, letting out a sigh as she got off her feet. "Could someone call for some coffee? It's been a long couple of days."

"What have you been up to?" I asked.

"Babysitting," Helena grumbled. "The six new recruits started their first paranormal cases, and we've been watching them." Her beautiful face came around the bottom of my massage table. "Some of us do actual work."

"Hey now, I caught a geist last night. Healed the woman and then picked up her apartment. I went above and beyond."

"Uh huh." Helena was unconvinced. "Maybe we should talk about it after."

"Yeah. I'll convince you later." I smirked, knowing that later would likely involve a lot of ruined furniture.

Agent Till snorted. "You don't have to hide it. We all know you two angry-fuck behind closed doors."

"What about my husband's angry sex with the angel?" Scarlett's voice carried over the group.

"Goldie, I think it's best for me to be back in the chair so I can see people coming."

"He makes it sound like another orgy," Fiona joked, not looking up from her tablet.

Goldie planted me back in my throne, with a few less knots in my back.

The rest of my court were filtering in. The ladies seemed familiar enough with the place, and their nymphs moved behind them. Some brought food, others drinks. They all immediately got to work staging the spread on a nearby table.

"This is far nicer than I expected a fae court session to be," Georgia commented, taking her spot between the two FBI agents.

"It's nicer than my court sessions," Summer agreed. "Though, mine are at dawn."

"Even more reason for food." Kelly was piling food on her tray at an alarming rate.

"You'd think you were a dragon when you eat like that," Morgana teased her.

"Says the woman who sticks to our man like a leech if he gets near you," Kelly shot back.

Elena Wallachia sighed and glanced my way, licking her lips.

"Don't get any ideas. Your whole people owe my mate an apology before he gives you anything," Morgana growled.

"The Wallachia family has exacted their pound of blood from your true enemies. Some vampires just want to grow closer with the Dragon King." She still looked at me like a bloodbag that she wanted to suck dry.

Ikta took that moment to fall through a portal in the ceiling, stopping a few inches from her plush, ridiculously decorated throne.

"Ah. My baby daddy. How are you darling?" Ikta didn't land on her throne. Instead, she skipped over to mine, her eyes filled with adoration and possibly a bit of insanity.

"How are the little ones?" I put a hand on her stomach.

She giggled. "The eggs are all sewn up and have twenty-four seven guards. No one is going to touch the egg sacs."

"Sacs, plural?" Pixie asked.

"There are eight in all." Ikta mimed wiping sweat from her brow. "Honestly, we will single-handedly repopulate the dragons."

Pixie gave me a raised eyebrow look. "I thought you didn't have time for more."

I pointed vaguely at Ikta's direction. "This is why. But I'm told they grow quickly?"

"Oh yes. They'll all come out as wild fae and be fully grown in five years. So, we'll have a year or two before they can tap any dragon in them and start shifting. Unfortunately, many will die those first few day," Ikta stated the fact as if it weren't incredibly traumatizing.

"Wait, what?" I turned to her, shock rippling through my body.

"That's how it goes." Ikta shrugged. "You have to let them fight among themselves. That's how you get the strongest ones out of the bunch. It's before their brains are even developed. They have no lingering trauma; it's just instinct. We don't give them names until after that."

I blinked at her. "This makes me very uncomfortable."

Ikta did a sad shake of her head. "Then that means you don't get to know where they are being kept. This is part of my people's culture and I will not have you interrupt it, or they won't develop properly."

"If they didn't do this, they would overrun all of Faerie and the mortal world." Summer sat in her throne. "Not that they are pests per se, but there is a certain resemblance."

Some of the wild fae culture started to make a little more sense if they started life this way.

"Don't you start. You only pretend to be all sunshine and rainbows. Then you smite people with golden fire." Ikta rolled her eyes and found her way back to her throne. As she sat, her spider limbs came out and promptly started knitting little baby hats in front of her.

"Alright. So, let's get me back up to speed. How's the de-escalation of the war in Faerie?" I asked Maeve and Summer, wanting to move on from this conversation.

"I've received eight requests for casus belli." Maeve rubbed at her temples. "The fighting is going to turn inward if we stop completely. They are legitimate grievances, and I can't deny them all."

"My experience has been similar." Summer shook her head. "Their blood is too hot, telling them to pack up their swords and go home is not a solution. Instead, I'd like to have them push directly into the Wilds. I propose we resume the Wild Hunt."

Ikta pursed her lips. "Dragons are off limits."

"Then you should take care of your children better," Summer challenged.

"What's the Wild Hunt? Do you go rampaging through multiple planes?" I asked.

"No, they push the borders of the wild fae territory." Ikta seemed unperturbed by the concept. "The Wilds are unknowingly large. Even I don't have the whole place mapped out."

"Would you come into direct conflict with either of them?" I asked.

"Unlikely, at least at first. The Wilds have expanded since they last held Wild Hunts."

"It sounds like a good use for the current tempers, but we need to see what we can do so that we decrease how much we have to go out on these hunts. Maybe we give allotments and pull them back over time." I thought it sounded like a decent plan.

All three fae queens nodded with me, so I shifted my attention to Leviathan. "Things going well in Hell? Have they stabilized?" It seemed that court had officially began as everyone settled in.

"Yes. Though, you should spend more time in Hell. Make your people fear you."

"Pass. I have enough going on." I glanced at Sabrina who just shrugged. Sabrina wasn't concerned, and Lilith hadn't passed on any signs of disturbance.

"Philly Council?" I turned to Jadelyn who twirled a finger in her platinum blonde hair. No doubt her mind was working on multiple problems at once.

"Moving along. Reminder that the swamp troll migrations are coming up again in a few months. They've asked for Silverwing Mercenaries to help once more," she reported.

The reminder of the swamp troll migrations was a blast from the past. When I was just starting to learn about my paranormal status, I'd helped Morgana take care of the troll situation.

"Of course. We'll have people on it." I glanced at Morgana's belly, which was now showing to the extent that she'd given up on her usual corset. I really did not want her tangling with trolls at that moment. "From the business side?"

"The shipping lanes to Sentarshaden are doing wonderfully. So are the ones to Faerie and Hell." Jadelyn clicked her tongue. "I know you are busy, but a word from the Dragon King to try and open one in Yangzi Valley would be a big help. That, and we could maybe talk to Eldorado during your trip?"

"My trip?" I tried to replay what my nymphs had told me about my schedule, but no trip was lining up.

Jadelyn glanced at Helena, who shrugged helplessly. "Ah. I think that's a later action item."

"The FBI has permission to go into Brazil to take down some of the cult," Pixie stage-whispered. "Silverwing Mercenaries are being requested for aid."

I rubbed my chin at the thought of Eldorado, a city of gold. "That would be a very interesting trip."

"He's thinking of the golden cities, isn't he?" Kelly laughed, rolling her eyes.

All of my wives nodded along.

"How does that look from the outside, Tyrande? Anyone on the global scale upset at me?" I asked.

"Your deeds in Hell and Faerie have been getting around. I'd say more people would be willing to bend over for you now. No one is moving against you, at least publicly," Tyrande reported.

"Except the angels that hit us last night." Maddie crossed her arms. "Stupid angel won't talk."

"You were attacked by angels yesterday?" Rebecca finally stopped making out with her coffee. "Why are we just learning this?"

"Because the interrogation was unsuccessful." Polydora's nostrils flared. I knew she took the fact that she couldn't crack the angel personally. "We killed four. Captured one, but he cut out his own tongue. We had to bring in Trina to stop him from dying on us."

"This information should be shared with us. Waiting this long is unacceptable." Georgia set her jaw.

I gestured around us. "Welcome to my daily court session. It's made to manage the now multiple planes that I rule. Gosh, that made me cringe. Is there a better way to say that?"

"It's not untrue." Jadelyn smiled. "Maybe we should just send you into Heaven."

I shook my head, not willing to admit that seeing Servil turned into the Silver Slave still haunted me. "I won't go on the offensive here. But what about Brazil?"

"State Department has issued a mission for us to go poke around and work with some of their resources to see what we can find and fix. Not everyone is in the know, though," Georgia reported.

"So I have to be sneaky. I can be sneaky and subtle," I answered confidently.

The room went quiet.

"What? I can." I narrowed my eyes on all the women suddenly not making eye contact with me.

Pixie patted my hand. "It isn't your strong suit, that's for sure."

"When are we going?" I asked Georgia.

"Two days. We'll be flying," she told me.

I made a face. "I assume you mean in a plane?"

"Is that a problem?" Georgia asked.

Wrinkling my nose, I shook my head. I'd deal with it, but airplanes just didn't feel very sturdy anymore. I sighed. "I'll manage. Give Pixie the time and we'll take it from there."

"Thank you." Georgia gave me a nod. "We are still getting the grips on this paranormal division. Your help is invaluable."

"His help really is invaluable." Jadelyn rubbed her fingers together. "I really think we should talk about raising his price so that it isn't so easy to send him away so often."

Kelly sat behind her, rubbing her belly; she was showing with the twins. "He's going to have more responsibilities soon."

"Lots of them," Ikta agreed.

"We aren't there yet. Besides, I'm going to be an awesome dad. When I throw my kid into the air, he'll actually touch the sky."

"Don't actually do that." Pixie patted my knee. "I like my kid with two feet on the ground. Preferably two hands on the ground too, at least for a while."

"We'd like to get a look at the angel you captured, if that's all right?" Georgia asked. "We can even bring some of our own resources. While I'm sure you are all very effective, we've made interrogation into something of a science."

"Not against angels you haven't," Helena disagreed. "You should see what they do to young angels and cherubs to make them into zealots. It won't be as easy as you think."

"Still, we have to try. Any new information before we head to Brazil could be vital," Georgia countered.

I nodded. "Let them have access. It can't hurt. Keep the angel where they are, and bring the FBI to them. Don't let them know where they are going."

Georgia pursed her lips but nodded. "These people will be in the know. Our little department is budding."

I wasn't sure if that growth was a good or a bad thing. But for now, I was handling problems as they arose. Managing multiple planes meant there was always something.

CHAPTER 3

I closed my office door behind me as Helena pulled at her top button. Her white hair was still cut short, kept in a sharp bob that made her otherwise heart-shaped face seem severe. It didn't help that she wore her white dress shirt and pencil skirt like a second skin.

I knew other men probably had dreams about being arrested by a woman like her. And while I was definitely tempted to go for another round of wild sex, I wanted to try something different.

"How do you feel about dinner tonight?" We'd been doing the fight and fuck dance for months without taking it a step further.

Helena paused on her second button and arched one of her white, manicured brows. "Does that mean nothing right now?"

Damn. I swallowed, struggling to turn down that offer. "Yes. With the idea of an interrogation up next, I'm not that interested. Rain check for tonight?" I quickly made an excuse.

Helena abandoned the second button and went to close the top one with a long pause. "Fine. I'll meet you at your place at seven."

Internally, I was pumping my fist, but I knew better than to show too much excitement and scare her off. "Of course."

Helena agreeing was a huge step for us and for her.

She watched me carefully.

I desperately needed a change of subject before she changed her mind. "So. Brazil? Ever been there before?"

I had traveled more in the last year than I had the entire rest of my life, but I'd never been to South America.

"Yes, actually, I have. I traveled quite broadly for the church when I worked for them." She wrinkled her nose. "They have quite the presence in South America. I would say a very dominant presence."

"Got any friends down south?"

"Not any more. Cutting ties with the church wasn't a smooth process." Helena let out a sigh that alluded to more frustration than regret.

Truthfully, I knew very little about Helena beyond some memories I'd once seen. She had a terrifying mother who had manipulated her with magical angel love magic. She'd worked through the church more out of fear than loyalty. But when Morgana had absconded with the portal to Heaven, Helena's fear of her mother was quelled long enough for her to cut ties.

Based on what I'd seen, I didn't blame Helena for wanting distance. Helena's mother could make anyone love her as the Archangel of Love. What she'd done to Helena had been nothing but abuse of her emotions.

Helena had vanished for a bit before showing up as a new FBI agent working on the Beelzebub case, where I'd met her. And in the process of fighting a demon, I'd seen into her memories and ended up marking her.

Only after a while had she finally, angrily, admitted that she wanted to have sex. Which so far, had always ended up violent and delightful.

"That couldn't have been easy. If you are having—"

"I can handle myself," Helena cut me off.

She was also stubbornly independent.

"You know what, maybe we should just fuck and get it out of our systems," I challenged.

Helena smirked. "No. You already told me to wait. I'm not going to bend over for you now like one of your love-stuck mates. But if you get to ask me all these questions, then I get to ask you a few. How are you holding up with the thousand kids about to be in your house? Do you even have a place for all of them?" She leaned back on the desk in my office, straining the front buttons of her blouse.

"Plenty of space. It was buying all the monitors that was a problem. And with all the portals and magical interference, they seem to struggle to really work in the mansion. At this point, there's a room that's just a big bank of baby monitors. One of the nymphs set it up. There's also a sort of daycare rotation being set up. Honestly, it's a lot. But we are determined to manage the flood of children."

Helena's expression softened. "You are going to be a good father."

"Damn right I am. Might have to slow down on running across the globe and getting into fights with big nasties, but then again, there aren't that many big problems left. So, I hope to spend some time with the kids when they come, in their various shapes and forms." I shrugged. I'd love them all.

Helena searched my face. "Wait until after we've finished this trip to jinx it. You are going to be buried up to your eyebrows in diapers."

I chuckled. "The nymphs are really into having kids. It's going to be hard, but I think they'll help make it work. I know I'm going to be putting in plenty of time being a father."

I wanted to dig more into her past, but my phone rang. Maddie was calling. "Sorry. I need to take this. Maddie, what's up?"

"Zach." Gunfire sounded in the background. A lot of gunfire. "Got ourselves into a bit of a pickle."

"Where are you?" I asked.

"En-route to the field office with the angel. Got a bunch of big buff dudes with little cupid wings," Maddie grunted. "They are doing a number on my van."

"Cherubs." I glanced at Helena. "Turn your camera on. I'll portal to you."

Helena flicked her wrist and twirled the large silver spear that appeared in her hand with a head shaped like a heart.

"Helena is coming with me," I clarified.

"Oh yeah. Bring her. She can soak up lots of bullets."

"I can hear you. And I do not 'soak up bullets'. An angel is a planar being, so being born on the prime plane connects me to it, which steeps me deeply in its magic, making me very durable with a large amount of self-healing," Helena clarified.

"Right. Sounds like the person we want shot to me, but who knows. I'm just a baby vamp." While Maddie was taunting Helena, she switched the call to video and showed me the broken window of her van so that I could see out and get a view of the road.

Fixing the location in my mind, I snapped my fingers and opened up the portal. At the same time, I felt Goldie flow over my body to protect me from gunfire.

The purple ring of magic for the portal appeared in my office. Helena was through the portal first, her wings coming around to shield her as gunfire switched and started targeting her.

I came through next, letting Goldie manage the bullets for me.

The cherubs had picked a somewhat isolated spot, which at least would make cleanup easier. It looked like they had run Maddie off the highway and into their trap.

She was completely surrounded by dozens of cherubs who weren't holding back as they continued to unload their magazines into Helena and me. But Maddie's van was now spared from the attack. We were considered the bigger threat.

I scoped out the van, taking in the damage. It had seen better days. Its windshield and windows were gone, and the metal was dented to hell and back.

"Just going to stand there?" Helena had her wings out and wrapped around her.

"These jokes aren't much of a problem." Bullets hit Goldie, who was still wrapped around me. The hits left little dimples that quickly faded away. Goldie could feel sensations, but not pain. "What I'm wondering is what they have in reserve."

The angels couldn't be stupid enough to attack Silverwing Mercenaries and not expect me to come out, so what did they have to take care of me?

Helena snorted and stepped forward, lashing out with her spear at the closest cherub. The tip of her spear sliced clean through the muscular angel's throat, but she didn't even pause as she turned to skewer another.

"I don't care much for being shot at." Helena pulled back her arm and threw her spear straight through the chest of another cherub before the spear reappeared in her hand a moment later.

Not to be out done, I reached for my winter fae magic and let the cold chill of the frozen norths of Faerie spread out along a line of the cherubs.

The cherubs, who looked like they had done a few too many steroids, were locked up under the frozen chill. I didn't want to kill them all; some would answer questions after we were done.

Helena wasn't the type to take hostages or accept surrender, so her spear continued to reap the cherubs better than a scythe ever could. The death all around them didn't seem to bother the remaining cherubs, who shifted their formation back while keeping up the fire.

Maddie poked her head out of the van's back. "Finally, you two came."

"Stay down." I was concerned about what else the angels were going to bring out.

Sure enough, I didn't have to wait long. The rumble of jet engines roared overhead as a wing of fighter jets bore down on us.

"Fucking kidding me?" I was highly concerned that any activity like a stolen jet, or even flying one over Philly, could bring down military scrutiny in a way that none of us needed.

"Goldie, shield the van." I moved to get closer to the vehicle so that she could shield me too. I knew what Goldie would pick if she had to choose.

Helena threw herself to the cover with a flap of her wings, reaching it right before the jets opened fire.

Clouds of dust kicked up everywhere, amid splashes of blood as the large rounds tore through any remaining cherubs. Even those that I had frozen were wiped out.

Goldie's shield dented repeatedly, and a few even broke through her barrier but with significantly reduced force. The van held out against the stray bullets, but they collided with the van with a loud thud.

As quickly as it started, it was over. The jets roared past and climbed higher into the sky.

"Is the military after us now?" Frank asked. "Because what the absolute fuck." He had a handful of his enchantments in his arms, looking like he was continuing to fortify the van.

"No clue." I looked out at the jets as they flew away, only to bank off to the left. "But I think we should get out of here."

"Can't you blow them out of the sky?" Maddie asked. "You know, just like spit lightning and stuff?"

"Don't think I want to. Any footage captured is going to get looked at by people we don't want to know about me. The less I do, the better. Come on." I made a portal inside Goldie's shelter.

Maddie shook her head. "Bigger. We need to bring the van through." She jumped in the driver's seat and turned the key.

But the engine didn't start.

"It's just having a little trouble." Maddie frowned at the steering wheel.

"Uh huh." Helena didn't sound convinced. "Get through the portal before they come back around. Your car is dead."

"Maddie. Let's go," Frank urged her.

"No. We spent so much on this damned van. We can't leave it behind!" Maddie jammed the key, turning it with enough force that the key bent between her fingers.

The van didn't even sputter.

"We'll get you a new one." Frank grabbed her shoulder.

"Helena, get the angel," I told her.

"I don't think he made it." Helena picked up a head that was cleanly severed from the body.

I grit my teeth. His head hadn't been removed by gunfire. And I wanted to know how the hell somebody got to him. "Portal. Move." We needed to go and regroup.

Someone or something had gotten in the van and removed the angel's head while we had been distracted.

Frank pushed Maddie through the portal, and Helena followed. I went last, with Goldie covering me and coming through with me. As I was stepping through, I was thrown forward by an explosion behind me. I just barely managed to close the portal before more than a puff of fire belched through and into my kitchen.

"Seems they didn't much care for us," Frank muttered, dusting himself off.

"I want to know who killed that angel." I rolled to my feet, feeling a little bruised by the explosion. Luckily, my body was pretty fortified.

"She was the one with sharp things." Maddie pointed at Helena.

"I did nothing of the sort." Helena twirled her spear, making it disappear. "He was already dead. Someone killed him in your van while you were supposed to be protecting him."

I could tell that the tension was rising. The fight was about to get heated if Maddie and Helena got going.

"Ice cream?" A nymph in the kitchen perked up to break the tension.

"Oh yes, please." Frank rushed forward. "We just had a hell of a morning."

"Oh no," the nymph said sympathetically.

"Frank, stop flirting with the nymphs," Maddie grumbled.

"I wasn't flirting. Fighter jets just blew up our van. It has been a rough day." Frank threw his hands in the air.

"Sorry." Maddie rubbed his back. "He'll take mint chip ice cream if you have it."

"Great, now that that is settled, how the fuck did someone get in there and cut your angel's head off?" I glared at the two of them.

Frank watched the nymph scoop ice cream, staring at her shapely ass as she bent over. "I honestly have no clue. I was busy refreshing blocks as all those bullets tore through my enchantments."

"This is why we should have just baked them into the car," Maddie replied.

"No. They would have overheated and warped several times over if they had been made from aluminum," Frank sighed. "By making them from wood and allowing them to slot in and be replaced, they are far more durable. Zach, you explain it."

I scratched the back of my head. "What he's saying makes sense. Especially if he's got dozens of replacements in the back. The fact that he can easily replace part of it quickly probably saved your lives."

"And you, vampire." Helena crossed her arms. "You saw no one get in the van and kill your prisoner? Were there no enchantments to stop something like this?"

"Like I said. I have no idea how this happened. I don't even have a knife on me." Maddie held her hands up. "How am I supposed to cut someone's head off with a gun?"

"She's got a point," I agreed.

Helena rubbed at her forehead. "We needed more information. Every piece we can get is vital."

"We got plenty of information, though," I pointed out and pulled out my phone. "Whoever silenced this angel pulled a fucking huge stunt to do it. Someone, somewhere is going to know something about jets flying around Philly and firing."

"Special Agent in Charge, Georgia's office," a woman whose voice was far too pleasant to be Georgia herself answered. "How can I help?"

"This is Agent Nashner." Helena made a face when she was forced to use her last name, but she spoke loudly enough that I held the phone out. "I need to speak to her immediately."

"One moment." There was a click and the new voice was Georgia's.

"Hello, Helena?"

"Hi. I was just with Zach. Two of his people were carting the angel for us. The angel is dead. The transport was driven off the side of the road and five jets showed up and did two passes," Helena reported.

"Just now?" Georgia suddenly was giving us her full attention.

"Yes, ma'am. Zach extracted his two safely, but the angel was killed during the commotion. We aren't sure what killed the angel."

There was a pause on the other end of the phone and a faint tapping of a keyboard. "I'm going to have to make a few calls. Would you all be willing to come to the field office and give formal statements?"

Helena glanced at me.

I shrugged. "We can give you the full details or just the 'normal' ones."

"I'll take the full details if you'll give them to me, and then if I need to involve anyone outside the new department, we'll redact them." Georgia sounded desperate for a compromise.

"Fair. I'll portal in a few minutes and walk in with Helena and my two mercenaries." Even as I spoke, I saw Pixie spot me and start marching down the hall. She looked very determined. "Can't promise I'm going to have tons of time. But we'll make it work."

Pixie tapped on her tablet. "So. Appointment with Georgia? Think I can get you squeezed in with a little golf with Rupert after that? He's been begging for it."

"Yeah. I can give him a few holes. Hopefully this doesn't take too long."

The nymph serving ice cream snickered. "The Dragon King loves holes."

Frank shoved a spoonful into his mouth to cover up his own laughter.

"Well, given how short his appointment with Helena went..." Pixie appraised Helena and her clothes, which weren't wrinkled and still contained all the buttons. "He is able to control himself."

I smiled and nodded at Pixie. She gave me a wink in return. She'd known I had hoped Helena would agree to a date.

Pixie started swiping on her tablet, and a few moments later, my phone chimed with a notification of a dinner reservation. I was starting to forget what life was like before my nymphs had come and helped organize my life.

"Well then. If you'll finish your ice cream, Frank, we'll portal to the field office." I pointedly looked at my friend, who was taking his time with the giant bowl.

"What? I have to keep up the calorie intake, or Maddie drains me dry." He shrugged and started to shovel more ice cream into his mouth.

Helena tapped on her phone for a moment, no doubt notifying her partner. The two of them told each other everything.

I sighed, taking a seat and waiting for Frank. It would likely take Georgia a few minutes to track down any helpful information anyway. Goldie jumped out of my bracer, taking the moment to start massaging my shoulders. I leaned back, enjoying the moment of peace.

CHAPTER 4

Rebecca Till joined us with her ever-present cup of coffee. The career agent was addicted to the liquid. It didn't help that the nymphs enabled her, happy to be of service.

"So you guys survived two passes by fighter jets?" she asked the question as we stepped through a portal into Georgia's waiting room. "Zach, can you take that large of ammunition?"

"Goldie can," I answered.

"My Zach doesn't need to." Goldie piped up from my bracer.

"Sometimes I forget she's always here." Maddie glanced at the bracer on my arm.

"Me too," I admitted and felt a little pinch on my arm. "But she's wonderful to have around. Especially when she can take that much gunfire, and I didn't even feel it."

"She did eat an entire section of Hell," Helena replied. "Would be a shame if a few bullets took her down."

"Few bullets?" Rebecca snort-coughed. "A fighter jet, if it was anything recent, has a rapid-fire *cannon* that fires 20mm rounds. Calling them 'bullets' is an insult. Besides, most of them are explosive, and technically, they are shells."

Helena glanced at me, and I shrugged. "I learned to clean and fire guns, that doesn't make me an expert. I'm going to trust her on this one."

"I'm right. And that's really all you need to know." Rebecca took another sip of her coffee and tossed her hair as she marched into Georgia's office.

"Agents. Dragon King and... entourage. Hi, Pixie." Georgia frowned at the number of people that followed me.

"This is Maddie and Frank. They were bringing the angel to you and in the van when they were attacked. You've met Pixie, Nyske, and Fiona before." I reintroduced my nymphs who quickly made for the chairs that lined the edge of the room and sat down, making it clear that they were only present to listen and take notes. The rest of us sat across from Georgia.

"Right. I just got off the phone with the pentagon. We are *well aware* of the rogue operation that just occurred today. All five planes are being grounded as we speak. Those pilots in them will lose everything and quite possibly be flayed alive during their court martial. I have informed them that said jets took out an informant of the FBI and injured two of my agents," Georgia told us.

"That was fast." I blinked, surprised at her efficiency.

"Five jets doing a fly-by just outside of a city? You bet there are calls going all the way up to the top concerning this one. There are more than a few videos being suppressed of them firing on American soil. Which is why I need to know that if I can get you a few of the pilots, if you can get me information. We all know this likely wasn't their bright idea."

"Given the angel's involvement, it is a safe bet that your pilots were heavily manipulated by angelic magic, which includes emotional manipulation. Said angels only get one emotion to play with, so if we know which one we are dealing with, then we could probably manipulate a different emotion and get them to squeal like a pig." I worked through the problem while I spoke.

A human wouldn't have the same resistances that our previous angel had been able to display. Though, they'd probably have less information too.

"Can part of this squealing be sharable with the military?" Georgia gave me an overly polite smile.

"I assume the military has no idea about the paranormal?" I asked. "Actually, who all knows now that the FBI does?"

"Access to the information and knowledge of the paranormal are two very different questions. No one outside of the FBI is aware at this point. Should a situation like this occur, I think there is a decent chance that the Director loops in a few people in the military on a need-to-know basis. Don't worry. Despite media bullshit, we are actually very good at keeping information secret."

I wrinkled my nose but leaned back in my chair. "Regardless, I think it would be a good idea if we could get our hands on those five pilots as quickly as possible given what happened to the other prisoner that we had." I waved my hand in the air, making a small portal. "We can get anywhere we need very quickly."

"Let me make a call." Georgia picked up her phone and stabbed at the numbers. "Hi, Fanny, can I get back on with Colonel Washington? Yes, this is regarding the previous matter and is very urgent. I can hold for a moment." She covered the receiver to talk to us. "What do you need for a portal?"

"A video of the space I need to put on the other end is best. A picture doesn't quite do it, and I'd prefer to have a live video if I'm going to open a portal without killing someone on the other end," I answered with a smile.

Georgia eyed me for a moment but then nodded, shifting her focus back to the phone. "Isaiah, I hope... Yeah. Two are already dead? I have agents enroute. I want a chance to talk to these pilots. Given that whoever is behind this just killed someone we had in custody, I don't think they are going to last long." She paused and was listening while glancing at me. "Yeah. Two agents and a contractor, don't worry."

I shrugged and made eye contact with Pixie, who bobbed her head in agreement. I waved my hand and a portal opened up back to the manor.

Nyske seemed resistant to leaving me, but she focused on getting Maddie and Frank moving to distract herself. In moments, the room was cleared save for me, Helena, Rebecca, and Georgia.

"Thank you, Isaiah. We'll be on our way and get there shortly." She hung up and then called someone with her cell phone. "Anthony, can you give us a video of the space? The Dragon King will make a portal."

I scowled at her.

"He's part of the new division. Actually, he's a werewolf. An omega. That isn't offensive to say, is it?" Georgia asked, covering the phone for the last part.

"No. They are omega if they are packless either from their alpha dying or being kicked out," Helena replied. "That's just a reality they face."

"Harsh, but not untrue." I agreed. "Also if he's a were, he can probably still hear you."

Georgia frowned and her phone switched to a video call showing a black SUV.

"Yeah, I could hear you, boss. Here's the video call. I'm outside the base."

"Pan the camera around. I would like to see where I'm going," I instructed.

Georgia scowled at me for giving an order, but she seemed to deal with it.

Anthony was doing a slow circle with the phone. When he got back around, I made a portal beside the SUV. Georgia got up quickly and marched right through the portal.

Rebecca shrugged and slugged back the rest of her coffee before moving forward. "She wants to show you that she trusts you."

"I'm also not a walking transport," I grumbled.

"I mean, you *are,* but you don't want to be used as one." Rebecca Till smirked before she went through the portal.

Helena gave me a 'don't look at me' expression as she followed Rebecca.

Goldie spread protectively out underneath my clothing as I walked through, closing the portal behind me. Luckily, there was no trouble on the other side.

"You look like you are walking into a fight." Georgia looked me up and down.

"Happens more often than I'd like lately." I smiled, but Goldie didn't retract herself to the bracer. "That and Goldie is very protective of me."

"Damn right," Goldie piped up.

"Okay, this way." Georgia led the way to the air force base ahead of us.

The area was all giant concrete structures. Clearly, they were focused on function, not form. Behind the building in front of us was an airfield that stretched out for miles. Brightly gleaming, and I hoped scrapped, fighter jets were staged in front of the building.

I snorted at the idea of using a hundred-million-dollar piece of equipment as decoration. That sort of spending might even put Jadelyn and her family to shame. There were three of the jets propped up on giant steel beams to look like they were flying.

Otherwise, the yard was sparse. The grass was cut within an inch of its life.

"This way," Georgia reminded me and went down a path that would take us to the side of the building.

Several men in uniform stood at attention. One opened the door for us, revealing a metal detector and several more men in uniforms on security.

"Name?" the man greeting us asked.

"Special Agent in Charge, Georgia Lopez. Two of my agents and a mercenary contracted to the FBI," she introduced us and handed the man her badge.

The man looked the badge over before his eyes rose to meet mine. "You're a big one."

"Have to be in my line of work." I smirked, thinking of being a dragon more than being a big human. "Georgia, I'm not going to pass a metal detector."

"Really?" she asked, blinking.

I held up the bracer on my left arm. The tungsten carbide would set off a metal detector. "It doesn't come off."

"Please put everything in the tray." The airmen gestured to shallow, gray bins and grabbed a metal detector wand. "Please keep your arm out to the side."

I threw my phone into the other bin and complied. Everything else I needed was in the bracer.

The man ran the wand over me several times, eyeing the bracer. "Does it really not come off?"

"No. It's welded on. Need to do anything else with it?" I asked.

He wrinkled his nose and grabbed some swabs and a light, pulling at the bracer that was connected to my bones. When Typhon had blessed me, the serpent had wound itself around the bracer, it had bit deep into my skin, connecting with my bone.

The airmen checked me over several ways before letting me go through and join the others.

"An ancient being melded it to my bones. But I like the bracer; it was a gift from my wives," I told Georgia as we walked through the base at a brisk pace.

An airmen in their service dress uniform caught up to us. "Please, this way. The colonel just sent me to watch for you. We weren't expecting you so soon."

"We were already on our way. This is very important. Let's hurry." She didn't give any other information as the airman picked up the pace.

He led us through several long halls and down three sets of stairs until we passed security heavy enough for this to be a prison, or a brig? I wasn't sure what the air force would call it.

We came to a stop in a rather bleak room with a few uncomfortable plastic waiting chairs. There were a few doors that came off of the room, but no windows. One of the doors was particularly heavy looking.

"Georgia?" A well-built man with his buzz-cut going gray noticed her. "Didn't expect you so soon." He glanced at the airman. "Dismissed."

The man didn't even salute before he hurried out, leaving us in the room with Isaiah.

"We were on our way," she explained.

But the man didn't seem interested in her answer, or her. He was sizing me up, clearly considering me a larger threat. To be fair, I was the largest threat in the room, but he didn't necessarily know that just based on my size.

"Who's this?" He glanced at my waist where the other three had badges.

Mine was noticeably missing said badge.

"Zach Pendragon." I held out my hand. "Contractor for... special situations."

He took my hand, but he did the briefest handshake possible. "Not sure what's so special here. But we got a guy coming up for interrogation now."

The heavy door in the room unlocked with a click and two airmen marched a man in. The man's clothing was torn, his eyes were hollow, and he was covered in shallow cuts.

Something didn't sit right with me. I desperately wanted to shift my eyes.

"Bring him into room one. Georgia, I know you want at him, but I'm going to talk to him first." Isaiah nodded to a room that was separate from the one the prisoner was going into. "You can watch, though."

"I want a go at him." Georgia stared down the colonel.

"Of course. But he's my man. I'm going in first," Isaiah replied.

"Where's my lawyer?" the man in question asked.

"You'll get one after, but it's only a formality. JAG took one look and proclaimed you well and truly fucked." Isaiah followed him into the room.

Georgia let out a soft whistle. "He's a stickler for the rules. He must be pissed."

"I would be too." Agent Till went with Georgia into the observation room.

The room that had Isaiah and the pilot was a small room with a table in the center and a pair of microphones to pick up everything that was said. The two escorting the pilot cuffed him to his side of the table and left before Isaiah sat down on the other side.

"Who?" His tone was steel.

I blinked and shifted my eyes to see if there was any lingering mana on the pilot that might explain what I was sensing. I did not like what I saw. "Oh... shit."

"Huh?" Georgia asked.

"He's possessed." I turned to her, showing her my shifted eyes.

With them, I could see the chains that bound him and the faint outline of something living inside of him. "He's not going to give Isaiah anything. The geist that is controlling that body doesn't give a shit about what happens to it. Probably thinks it'll just fly away after this is all done... or it could try to jump to someone else."

"I need a crash course on ghosts. Now," Georgia ordered.

I didn't take orders from her, but I understood that the lack of information probably made her uncomfortable.

"Immaterial beings created with strong emotion after a person or paranormal's death. It also requires a concentration of mana where they died, because they are basically really thin bubbles of mana keeping a consciousness alive. Using magic literally shaves away their life because they don't really recover mana. Instead, they use humans like hosts to recover any mana and preserve their own," I told her the basics. "When they have a host, they are like really poor sorcerers."

"What about the... host's memories?" Georgia asked.

"Depends. Normally, the host is basically drowned in the negative emotion until they lose consciousness. Other times, they weather it and are prisoners in their own bodies," I replied.

"How do you kill one?" Georgia asked.

"They are balloons of mana, you just need to pop them," Helena answered, her spear appearing in her hand as she started to twirl it.

Georgia eyed the weapon but said nothing.

I jumped back into the conversation. "She's not wrong, but with how close it is to this body, you are going to have to stab him pretty badly to pop it. And if you just puncture a single spot, they live on for a few moments and they know they'll never need that mana again."

"So, they use it all at the end. Is there a safer way to expel it?"

"There are some spells to eject them. Magi make really great hosts and have done a lot of research to get rid of them. Sadly, I'm not an expert there. I can coat it with summer fae magic and burn down the entire bubble in one go," I offered.

"Okay, besides the fact that I now need to figure out how to ward our division of the FBI from possessions, what is happening here? Is Isaiah in danger?" Georgia asked.

"Depends why this one is sticking around." I watched them both a little more carefully now that I knew about the possession. "You said that two already died? That probably means their geists killed them and ditched that body for another. Or they bailed entirely. I will say that it is strange for these geists to be working together. They are sentient, but I think trolls are better able to control themselves. Honestly, they aren't that different from a newly born wrath demon; the only difference is that they are on Earth and unable to feed on mana."

Helena snorted, leaning on her spear. "I could just throw this through the window and kill it."

Georgia shook her head. "I would rather you didn't. But if it attacks Isaiah, I'd allow it."

"I can try and surprise it with some of the summer fae magic. But I'm going to give the airman a nice sunburn." I watched the two. "We'll wait for them to finish talking."

Colonel Washington was leaning over the table. "Come on. Just give me something. You aren't going to see the light of day again as it is. But I can make it more comfortable, make it less painful for your family if you give me something."

The pilot showed the colonel his hands. "I can't do that. The person that I shot? They needed to die." The pilot smiled. "My only regret is that those holding him didn't die too."

The colonel sat back, not letting any reaction show on his face. "Pity. You had a promising career in front of you."

Georgia shook her head. "Knowing that man is possessed really gives a different perspective here."

"Welcome to my world," I grumbled. "Now. What can I get away with down here? Do you want me to do anything when the colonel leaves? Do we want to try and talk to the geist?"

"Can it harm you if you go in?" Georgia asked. "Am I putting you at risk by not just immediately killing it?"

It was touching that she somewhat cared. Although, she could be influenced by the fact that my wives would burn down the world if I were harmed.

"No. A geist can't do more than give me a few cuts that would heal instantly at worst," I spoke with confidence. The biggest problem was that I normally didn't want to kill the hosts. "What about the colonel?"

"I'll run interference. Helena, knock on the glass for him to know it is safe and tap twice when he has to get out," Georgia marched out.

The colonel didn't last much longer and got up to leave.

"I think this is the part where you portal in and get this done." Rebecca lifted her hand like there was a coffee in it, only to find it empty and frown down into the cup.

"We really need to get you to stop drinking so much coffee," Helena sighed.

The door clicked behind the colonel and a portal popped open between the interrogation room and the viewing room.

I stepped through. "Hello, geist."

CHAPTER 5

I watched as the geist became rigid at my appearance.

We knew nothing about this geist or his group's agenda. And I wasn't going to give him anything, even if I thought he already knew it. So, I decided to play off the reason I'd come into the room.

"What? Did you think flying jets near my city and home didn't get my attention? Well, the Dragon King is here now. What the fuck were you doing?" My expression shifted from ambivalent to angry in a second, my last sentence coming out clipped.

"Trying to kill you." The motherfucker's eyes actually glowed red with anger, and the entire room exploded as the geist threw far more magic around than he was supposed to be able to possess.

The table ripped out of the bolts holding it in place on the floor. The chains around the geist exploded into shrapnel and the concrete blocks all around me were pulverized.

Goldie rapidly expanded to protect me as I was thrown back and through the reinforced door. The tearing of the steel door deafened me, and I covered my head as I was blown out into the waiting room.

The shouting and the gunfire did little to help my ears as I worked to pick up what was happening.

Two guards were firing at me. Georgia was yelling at the top of her lungs, and Isaiah was holding his head as another soldier dragged him clear of the explosion.

I stood up, ignoring the two men who had shot me, giving all my attention to the crazy geist, trying to piece together the puzzle. A geist shouldn't have that level of power.

"Zack!" Georgia shouted at me.

"Hold on." I held up a hand that was covered in liquid gold. "It's coming out."

Rimmed in red light, I could see the geist coming through the dust.

The pilot's face had seen better days. Whatever type of explosion that was, the geist clearly hadn't been able to protect the human host. Metal shrapnel was embedded in the human face and neck, doing enough damage that the host wasn't going to survive this.

The geist shrieked and threw its hands forward.

This time, I wasn't caught unprepared. I braced myself. "Goldie, as much weight as you can."

This time, the blast only scooted me back a foot, which was still impressive given that I weighed more than most cars at the moment.

The geist stumbled, and I could see the glow in the pilot's eyes flickering. It was like he was clinging onto that body with pure spite.

I summoned a small ball of summer fae magic and blasted the geist backwards. The hit was like blowing out a candle; the red light around the pilot winked out in an instant.

I blew out a breath. "That was a surprise."

The dust was quite literally still settling as the airmen around me racked their guns and pointed the weapons towards me.

I didn't even bother putting my hands up. "Won't do anything to me, but you shouldn't fire. I'm concerned about the ricochet in here."

"Don't shoot." Isaiah pushed against the wall and grunted as the last airman helped him to his feet. "What was that? Georgia, this guy is with you?"

"He's... a specialist." Georgia hesitated. "I can't read you in here."

"Is he like a cyborg or something?" One of the guards kept his gun trained on me.

"Something. Put your damn guns down. You both just unloaded a magazine into his back and he went through a steel door. But as you can see, he's taken no damage. I don't think there's any point in trying to shoot him. Are the other pilots like this?"

"Probably." I faced the colonel. "What you are seeing is not really your pilots, though."

"Can you fix it?" The man scowled, and I had the feeling the gesture wasn't directed at me.

I glanced at Georgia. "Do I get to bill this?"

"Yeah. Yeah. Can you badge him into the cells? He'll take care of the rest." Georgia waved some of the dust out of her face.

Some of the rubble shifted, and Helena sheltered her partner as they cleared the viewing room. "That was some-thing. Do we need to get out of here before this place collapses?"

"Not a bad idea." Isaiah waved to the guards. "Get them upstairs. I'll take the specialist to the cells."

"No need. Besides, it might be dangerous," I told him.

The colonel deadpanned. "What part of me makes you think I'm concerned about danger?"

"Good point. But please stay back. I really don't need Georgia throwing a fit when she has to deal with a lot of paperwork after your death." I watched as he tapped his badge to the door, and I opened it, moving through at a brisk pace. The prison wasn't large at all. I quickly shifted my eyes to find the two I needed.

The whole place was just a single square with eight cells. Both of the possessed pilots were in my line of sight immediately. I knew the colonel would have to be read in anyway, so I ignored trying to hold back.

I blasted out summer fae light, torching the first pilot and giving the airman underneath the geist's control a decent burn. The second wasn't going to be so easy after watching what I did to the first. He jumped to attention and tried to break free.

But when he threw his hands forward, they fell into a portal that I made.

Both of his hands came out right next to me, and I broke them before grabbing and jerking the man through the portal. The brief disorientation and the close range was enough for me to simmer him with another blast of fae magic.

The smell of burnt hair filled the place.

"Easy enough." I grimaced, letting the man's hands drop as he curled in on himself groaning in pain.

"They are back to normal?" the colonel asked, kneeling next to the pilot on the floor next to me.

"Well, as normal as they are going to get. Being possessed really messes someone up," I told him.

"Possessed? Like ghosts? What does that make you?" he asked.

I grinned and raised an eyebrow. "Who you gonna call?"

"Ghos—"

"Geist Busters. Geist Busters. Damn, you almost got me sued. You can't say the other one." I clicked my tongue.

"This isn't a joke." The colonel straightened up on me.

"This is my daily life. Actually, this was rather easy." I knelt down next to one of the injured men and started to pluck death mana from them to heal them. "Hey. Do you remember anything?" I shook one of them.

The man's eyes snapped open and he choked on his tongue.

"Breathe. It's okay," I coaxed him.

He glanced over to see the colonel bearing down on him. "Sir. Sorry, sir! But where am I?"

"Listen up. What's the last thing you remember?" I asked him, grabbing his chin and forcing him to look at me.

"Her. She was so beautiful." There was a dazed look in his eyes. "Like an angel." He started coughing and rolled over as blood sprayed out of his mouth and he started convulsing.

The colonel barked at me. "Do something."

"Not a doctor." I shrugged and plucked more of the death magic from him, but it was building up so quickly that I knew his current issue wasn't natural. The man was dying. "He's dead."

Glancing over at the other pilot, I thought about waking him, but then I thought better of it. "Probably best to keep that guy asleep until his body can recover. Trying to wake him is going to end up brutal."

"I'm going to need some answers." The colonel stared me down.

"Not part of your command structure. Take it up with Georgia. I'm just the hired help." Sometimes being a contractor was sweet. I stood and dusted off my pants. "Actually, it's time for me to go check back in with my group."

He didn't stop me as I got up and headed back out of the prison.

My mind was whirling with possibilities. It seemed there was more than just a passing connection between the geists and the angels. Given the attacks and the FBI's current investigations, I doubted it was a coincidence.

"One is still alive. The other talked about an angel before dying," I spoke to Georgia as I came through the doors. They hadn't left. "We should go, and I think we should talk about your current investigation in a little more detail."

The colonel was out shortly behind me. "One prisoner needs medical attention. Keep them sedated until the doctor gives them a clean bill of health. Georgia, I'm going to file the paperwork. Then you will read me in on whatever this is."

"When you have the paperwork, I will gladly do so." She gave him a tight, but friendly smile. "Zach. I think we should exit quickly."

"Can do." I snapped my fingers and a portal opened up back to Georgia's office.

"I very much look forward to your explanations." Colonel Washington stared at the portal as the ladies filed through.

"Don't worry, this isn't at all common. I'm one of two." I smiled and stepped through the portal.

The portal closed behind me as we were back in Georgia's office.

"We need to talk." Georgia was already getting behind her desk.

"Angels and geists," I said, taking a seat. "A very odd combination." I glanced at Helena. "Anything you know about this?" I turned to Helena.

"No. Geists are considered kill on sight for the church... or at least... they were. I can't comment on their current policy," Helena replied.

"You said they were made from strong emotions." Rebecca crossed her arms and leaned back in her chair. "Could angels whammy someone and then kill them to make geists?"

There was a pause as Helena and I considered the question.

"No clue," I said. "Mind if we get a second opinion on that?"

"Please," Georgia answered.

I opened a portal to Morgana's garage. She was there, her belly slightly swollen and wearing a puffy black dress that didn't hide her growing belly at all.

"Morgana."

She put down the gun she was cleaning. "My love, how are you?" She zipped through the portal and was on me, necking me and licking at the spot she wanted to feed from.

"Good to s—ee you too." I stumbled as she bit into my neck. "We had a question."

She nodded, and I wasn't sure if the gesture was to tease open the holes a little more or to show she was listening.

"We encountered a few geists that had taken over air force pilots and did a run on an angel hostage we had. Then when we got to them, they tried to attack me. A few other details, but I wanted to get your take on geists working with angels."

Morgana slurped noisily from my neck.

Georgia looked queasy while Rebecca Till leaned in with fascination. "Does it hurt?"

"Not if she licks it before she bites. But I can feel the pressure," I told her.

"Are you high right now?" Georgia asked.

"A little. But it is just like a light buzz; I'm getting too resistant to it."

Morgana pulled her fangs out of me and lapped at the holes for a moment.

"Feeling better?" I asked my lovely wife.

"Much. So hungry." She licked the spot on my neck a few more times and kissed it, telling me I had healed over. "Okay. So, geists and angels. Odd combination. If they emotionally manipulated someone and then killed them, they'd probably go to Heaven." Morgana sat in my lap and tapped her chin. "Nothing is saying they *couldn't* make a geist, though. But it's just a geist."

"Do normal geists blow up cinder block rooms?" Rebecca asked.

"No. No, they do not. They might throw a coffee cup across a room or injure their host." Morgana paused in thought. "A geist's strength is based on how they die. The amount of mana concentrated in the area and how much emotion they have when they die. So, these angels could in theory be making these people unbelievably angry or fill them with such resentment, and then kill them amid a big pool of mana to make powerful geists, but I don't know how that fits Heaven's agenda at all."

"Because they would want them in Heaven?" Georgia asked.

"Yeah. Every soul provides more mana and potentially spawns a low-level angel," I answered. "A geist might have some usefulness, but honestly, most angels could just force a human to do anything they want rather than relying on a geist."

"I want geist detectors or something," Georgia demanded.

Helena glanced at me. "Can I ask Sabrina to make them?"

"Yeah, but please don't take advantage of her. She needs to be paid for her efforts."

Helena rolled her eyes. "Last I heard, you have billions."

"Most of which I stole from my mother and will one day need to be replaced. I'm just a poor Dragon King." I smiled.

"If she can make these, she'll be paid. I just don't want any of my agents suddenly doing what we just saw. The explosion was all of the geist's power, though, it looked like. It burnt itself out to attack you?" Georgia asked.

"Pretty much. I'll take this back to the paranormal council. Geists aren't well liked by anyone. The dead should move on," I told her.

Georgia's eyes moved over to Morgana.

"Vampires aren't dead." Morgana rolled her eyes. "I hate that myth. We have a magical virus that took over when our bodies got weak. It's just like any other illness ramping up on an injured person. Mine just happens to come with magical powers."

"You are getting crankier," I told her.

Morgana turned her red eyes to me slowly. "Careful. I am still hungry."

"What does this mean for our trip to Brazil?" I asked, ignoring the thirsty vampire.

"That we can't be late." Georgia set her jaw. "If they think attacking us is going to stop our investigation, then they have another thing coming. I'm going to pluck all of the angels if I have to."

Helena raised an eyebrow.

"You're a Nephilim, though, there's a difference." Georgia smiled. "But, point taken. This isn't a genocide or a war between races. But we know that whoever behind this seems to be leading a lot of angels. I'm sure there are plenty of good ones that aren't torturing people and killing them in magical pools to turn them into angry geists and sending them to kill us. But the ones that are will face justice."

Rebecca chomped the air, clicking her teeth while she looked at me. "How many angels do you think you're going to eat before this is over?"

"I hope not many. Don't exactly need it anymore. Are we done? I have a few things to wrap up before we head to Brazil and try to solve whatever this is."

"Yeah. I need to fill out some paperwork and figure out how to present the paranormal secret for when someone from the military gets read in after today." Georgia waved me away.

I snapped open a portal.

"Mind if I tag along?" Rebecca asked before I stepped through.

I jerked my head in answer, telling her to follow. She came through with Morgana and I while Helena stayed with Georgia.

My nymphs were already in my office waiting.

"Do I have time for a trip to The Dreamer?" I'd been putting the visit off, but with the trip to Brazil looming, I needed to get it done. "Also, can someone get Sabrina thinking about geist detectors for the FBI? Georgia wants them."

"I'll get Sabrina." Fiona stood up and marched out.

"I'm coming with you if you are meeting The Dreamer." Nyske gave a look that dared anybody to object. I knew she had history with The Dreamer, so I wasn't about to say no.

"Guess that leaves me rescheduling." Pixie seemed happy enough as she pulled out her phone and got to work. "You know, with the court sessions in the morning, it really does clear up your calendar a hell of a lot."

"Good. I'll have to keep them up. Morgana, are you coming?"

My vampire wife kissed my neck and nibbled, but she didn't break the skin. "No. I am not welcome that deep into Faerie. And with the pregnancy, I'd rather not have to use much energy."

I bit back any comment. Morgana taking it easy was both terrifying and a miracle.

"Alright then. Rebecca?" I'd begun using Agent Till's first name more lately.

"I would love to tag along. And I wouldn't mind some time to talk to you along the way." She smiled.

Another portal opened up beside me. "Ladies first." I gestured through the portal.

"Don't mind if I do." Nyske daintily stepped through, followed by Rebecca. I entered the portal last.

"So." I stepped through and closed the portal. "What did you want to talk about Rebecca?"

CHAPTER 6

I waited for Rebecca Till to answer as I scanned our surroundings. The Dreamer's giant flower loomed in the distance. We'd have to walk through the mist and nymph pools to reach the flower, but that wasn't our goal anyway. The Dreamer would make a path for us when she was ready.

Hopefully, this time, The Dreamer wouldn't have monsters made out of living thorns.

"I want to suck your dick," Rebecca blurted out.

Nyske stopped and turned with a raised eyebrow. "Not that I really can blame you, but maybe you should clarify?"

I stood there, more shocked than anything. I nodded dumbly, hooking a thumb at the nymph-dragon in agreement.

"Look. I joined team Dragon King. Jadelyn gave me a plushy and then I felt like... I don't know." She looked over Nyske, eyeing the nymph up and down.

The wild nymph with dragon magic was in a black pencil skirt that shined blue when it caught the light just right. It hugged her lithe figure, but she was still a nymph. The loose blouse pulled tight at her chest with a figure that people would die for.

I pulled my eyes up to Nyske's beautiful face, with dark hair falling loosely and glowing with an iridescent light when it moved.

Rebecca pointed an accusing finger at Nyske. "That. They are all so beautiful. It's like everyone but me is a runway model or belongs in some sort of fetish porn hall of fame."

Nyske raised an eyebrow.

"You're the runway model type," Rebecca clarified, making Nyske smile. "All I'm saying is these twenty-something stunners orbit you, and then here I am Mrs. Forty-five career woman."

"You look sharp," I told her.

Her blazer cut a mean figure, and honestly, it cut down on any visible curves. I had seen a nice ass that had been built more naturally than the women in my harem, but the blazer was long enough to keep her modest despite her pants being tight.

"Uh huh. You didn't say hot, beautiful, or can I please bend you over and pound it in. Just because I don't look like the nymphs doesn't mean I'm not horny. And damn, Zach, you are like a walking slab of beef. But we got off topic. I feel like I'm getting forgotten, and I want my shot. So, let me try this again." She paused and then met my eyes with a saucy wink. "Can I suck your dick?" She grinned. "Please."

"So you just want to initiate something? Sure, let's get a date set up," I told her.

"No." Rebecca held up a finger. "We'll go on a date after your mojo kicks in. I talked to Morgana. It could take months of regular exposure to your magic semen before I am date ready."

"What?" I frowned.

"Morgana and Jadelyn have said that dragon semen is incredibly magical. Apparently, I'll look a little younger after taking your load a few times. I'll probably become immortal, might even become a magi." Rebecca smiled a giant smile.

I stared at her. "A relationship though?"

"Zach. I don't want kids. I want someone to stuff their big cock in me after a romantic date every now and then. Maybe also in some non-romantic times where we just angrily fuck... god, I'm jealous of Helena's deal with you."

I blinked, unsure of how to respond.

"The correct answer is to just drop your pants right here," Rebecca grunted as she got down on her knees. "I can't even pull the 'experience card'. Ikta is like a bajillion years old."

Unsure of the correct answer, I did as asked and undid the top button for my jeans.

"Wow. That thing is like a little pocket dragon." Rebecca put both of her hands on me like she was trying to keep it warm before she pulled the head close to her lips and gave it a few sensual kisses.

I swelled under her affections, and she grinned up at me. She looked up, and I could see in her warm brown eyes just how much she wanted my seed inside of her. Despite her straight forward attempt here, she really did want something between us.

She leaned back with a little strand of precum clinging between us. "I've still got it. Just relax. I blew like half of the football team in high school."

Any questions I could have about her statement were cut off when she swallowed the head and folded her tongue around the base of the head, starting to rock back on her heels.

I blew out a breath, curling my toes as her tongue dragged along the underside and made me twitch between her lips.

She smiled, really getting into the motions. Her eyes closed, and it looked like she was savoring every moment of it.

"Damn. You're good." I held her head and adjusted the pace a little.

But apparently, she didn't want to give me any control. Instead, she swallowed me to the back of her throat and said, "I know I am."

Though the noise came out a muffled mess that I barely heard as I held onto her head to stay on my feet.

"Fuck. I'm cumming," I told her, surprised at how quickly she'd worked me.

Rebecca deepthroated me and purred until I emptied my balls down her throat. She had wanted my seed, and she had certainly gotten it.

"That was impressive. You popped him in record time." Nyske checked her phone.

"Thanks. Just like riding a bicycle." Rebecca dabbed at her lips and got to her feet before dusting off her knees.

"Just like that?" I asked.

"Just like that. Well, one of these times, I'm going to let you push me up against a wall and mark me, I suppose. But I think that'll require a little more commitment, don't you think?" she asked.

I was thoroughly off balance. "Yes. I do think that requires a little more time."

"Glad we agree. Now, let's go meet Mrs. Dreamer." Rebecca had a pep in her step and she turned and moved ahead of me.

I turned to Nyske. "You don't actually keep a record, do you?"

"Oh, we do. Morgana's going to be really upset that she lost the record. Then again, she liked to play with her food." Nyske smirked, clearly enjoying the thought of my pregnant, hormonal vampire love going off the deep end.

I was a little less enthused.

Rebecca screamed as she suddenly fell through the mist.

"Guess she's ready for us." I moved to where Rebecca had fallen into the deep hole and stepped forward, pulling my arms in and sliding down the slide made of slick roots.

Just like the last time, I was deposited in a large room with a small pool in the center. I looked around. The pool had the nymph practically swimming the last time I'd visited. But at the moment, the pool was running dangerously dry.

"Hello, Zach." The blind nymph lifted her head to greet us.

"I thought The Dreamer would be taller." Rebecca crawled to her feet after the fall.

"And I thought an FBI agent would resist giving someone a blow job in the middle of my jungle." The blind nymph turned to her.

Rebecca shrugged. "Girl's gotta do what she's gotta do. I hear you swung and missed on Zach's dad. Maybe if you had just been willing to get on your knees, things would have been different."

I braced for something to happen, but nothing did.

Instead, The Dreamer laughed. "Maybe. But it is hard for someone like myself to throw away propriety like that. I am very old and set in my ways." Her blind focus shifted to Nyske. "Daughter."

Nyske crossed her arms and grunted. "Ignore me. I'm just here because Zach is, and I want to make sure you don't pull anything."

"I'm dying," The Dreamer tried to garner sympathy.

"About time." Nyske refused to show any sympathy. "You make ancient seem like a new trend."

"Daughter. I did what I thought was best." The Dreamer looked saddened.

"For you? Sure. For me? No way. I told you what you asked me to do went against my morals, but you still pulled on that oath to force me." Nyske turned away, indicating that all attempts of communication were over.

I knew Nyske well enough to know she was well and truly done talking.

"I apologize for my daughter's attitude," The Dreamer addressed me.

"Huh? Nyske is being completely reasonable. I'm not your biggest fan either. First you tried to force someone to steal my egg. Which, by the way, killed my father. Then when you met me later, you made me drink your... nectar and made me weak to nymphs."

"My blessing did far more than that. But you already know that, or you wouldn't have been able to make your own small plane and take control of mine." The Dreamer smiled and leaned over the edge. "Figured it out yet?"

"You made me a titan. I think Typhon was trying the same thing with this." I held up where he'd fused my bracer with a serpent. For a long time, I'd wondered why Typhon had enabled me to eat Iapetus, and why The Dreamer had forced her nectar upon me.

"Yes. Though, that was for you to eat some of Iapetus. It might have worked, but it would take too long. I didn't have the time for that. I have been delaying my own death for quite some time." The Dreamer lay against the edge of a giant petal that held her pool as if she were physically exhausted by this conversation. "By keeping myself dormant and just using this nymph to communicate, I've been preserving my strength for millennia."

She looked away wistfully. "Titans were born with a finite amount of magic, and nowhere near the mana absorption rates of many paranormal today. We were forces of nature that would eventually wear ourselves out. Storms to change the landscape and give life a chance. My seclusion to this realm and my subsequent rationing of my mana is why I'm the last. I assume my brother is dead in Hell?"

I nodded. "The princes of Hell killed him, ate him."

"He was a dick anyway. We all were, really. Like giant toddlers who never learned to share." The Dreamer smiled.

"Not the most flattering comparison. But I can see it. Why make me a titan?" I asked.

"Dragons are unique in that their simple existence continues to produce mana. Other creatures might produce it too, but it requires another form of energy. They are just converting that energy to mana. A dragon titan won't have the same problem that we did. Instead, you'll grow stronger with age and be able to use your strength freely."

She smiled to herself. "We created many things. Three planes that hover around your own, as well as shaping

Earth in wondrous ways. Most of my brothers and sisters wouldn't admit it. But they want to see it all continue."

I stared at the blind nymph, trying to read her, to understand her. "Why try to take my egg?"

"Because you could have kept me alive had we started this process sooner, had I been able to bring the bounty of the Wilds to you at a young age. I'd hoped your father would have seen reason and joined me in raising you." The Dreamer pursed her lips.

"Good news. My father is in Tartarus, where you are headed. So you can let him know," I told her.

The Dreamer smiled. "I'm well aware. We've had our differences, but maybe I'll give your friend's method a try. Everything else hasn't worked."

I put my hands over my ears. "Please don't put that image in my head."

"I did nothing of the sort." The Dreamer cocked her head to the side.

"You did with your words. So, new subject. If you'd kept my egg, you would have made me a very fat dragon and then yoked me with Faerie?"

"That sounds crude, but not inaccurate." The Dreamer smiled. "You would have been a very happy dragon with a large territory. Unlike me, it wouldn't have been a burden for you. Even at your present size, you are large enough that Faerie and Hell are growing from being connected to you. Even your own little plane is growing."

I nodded along. "Because I'm a dragon and mana is pouring out with each heartbeat."

"Into your domain. Then out pouring from there into the others. You could attach Heaven without any difficulties too. I know you have an angel among your harem."

"Nephilim," I clarified.

The Dreamer made a face. "Nasty creatures. There is a reason that Hell doesn't let half-demons exist. That Heaven practices it, even sparingly, is abhorrent."

That had my attention. "Why is that?"

"Well, because of what they become," The Dreamer spoke, and I could tell, despite being blind, she was watching my reaction. "Ah. You don't know. It's been a while since I've seen one. But angels and demons are both born in areas with defined food groups. A set of emotions to feed upon and grow. Those born on Earth have no such limitations, and they can become quite odd as a result."

"Well. Helena is fine," I told her.

"Yes. If it hasn't affected her by now, then maybe it won't happen." The Dreamer gave me a smile that made it seem like she was only reassuring me. "Still, she would be a great vessel and could help you take over Heaven. By controlling all three planes and living on Earth, you could grow into the greatest titan to have ever lived. And in the process, keep life moving forward." The Dreamer smiled.

"This was all your plan from the start..." I shook my head. "Yet despite the attempts I've made to change it, I've ended up here anyway."

The Dreamer smiled. "Well. In time, you can become the one pulling the strings. That's your future. One day soon, you'll be the most powerful living entity." Her smile faded.

"What do I need to know? What's going on with Faerie and the other planes?"

"They need a titan. Mana is sapped from us to keep everything glued together. A very slow trickle, like a charge to keep a device running. By using your plane as a cornerstone, you are keeping everything moving."

"And Earth?"

"Tartarus," The Dreamer replied quickly. "The prison that keeps all the titans keeps Earth whole."

I rubbed at my forehead. This was a lot to take in. I had half-known all of this for a while, but hearing it laid out by The Dreamer was intense to say the least.

"How much longer do you have?" I asked, regretting the words as soon as they left my lips.

"If my daughter would be willing, I'd give the last of myself to her before you leave," The Dreamer said.

That statement caused Nyske to whip around. "What?"

The Dreamer smiled. "I didn't plan it. But you are my daughter, and now carry the heart of a dragon. You are everything I could never be. It would take years for you to blossom into a true titan. But I can think of no one better to carry my legacy."

"I don't want your legacy," Nyske snapped. "I won't be like you."

The Dreamer looked down at the petal, hiding her expression. "Then think of it as killing me. You'll take the last of my life, my energy, and my essence. As one of my creations, you have my spark in you already. As a dragon, the power won't burden you as it would every other nymph. Ikta, by just carrying the smallest fragment of my magic, has nearly been driven insane."

"No. You don't get off that easily." Nyske was clearly pissed. "Stick around and watch Zach rule a thousand times better than you."

"I won't last ten years as it is, even if I just go into hibernation. Nyske, I betrayed your innocence by shackling you with an oath. Then I forced you to betray your own morals and banished you from your home. Surely you want to kill me," The Dreamer egged her on. "It was all my selfish ambitions. You were right. I did what was best for me. Time and time again. I chose to elevate myself to chase after my own desires. Take my power, daughter, and do better than me."

"I know what you are doing." Nyske narrowed her eyes.

"Oh. Is that because you don't think you can do better? You think if you get this sort of power that you'll go down the same path? Maybe understand me?" The Dreamer taunted her.

I stood back as it all played out, grabbing Rebecca's hand to keep her quiet.

This battle was between Nyske and The Dreamer.

"I would be a thousand times better." Nyske stomped forward.

"No you wouldn't. You'd be just like me. Pursuing selfish ambitions with your near unlimited power. Yes, actually, I don't think you deserve this. You won't make good use of this power."

Nyske was at the edge of the pool, and she grabbed The Dreamer, lifting the blind nymph out. "I know what you are doing."

"Is it working?" The Dreamer smiled.

"Keep watch from Tartarus. Because I'll show you exactly how this sort of power should be used and not abused. I will take your powers." Nyske threw the nymph into the pool, splashing the magical nectar into the air.

Nyske didn't wait and stepped over the edge of the petals into the pool.

"I will be watching, daughter. You were always my favorite." The Dreamer's blind eyes rolled up into her head as the thin pool of nectar flew up into the air and into Nyske.

My girlfriend staggered back under the onslaught of the liquid and fell down as she tried and failed to stop it from pressing into her eyes, mouth and nose.

The nectar poured into her for a few more moments until the flower pool was completely empty, with Nyske laying at the bottom.

"You all right?" I asked, moving forward quickly.

Nyske held a thumbs up into the air. "Just peachy. If there aren't any pickles when we get home…"

"If there aren't, I'll make all of the nymphs go out and hunt down the city for your favorites," I promised her.

"I love you." Nyske rolled over.

"Love you too. Now, I have a very important question… I'm hoping you know how we get out of here?" I looked around at the giant room with no clear exit.

"Portals," Rebecca answered. "Or just singular portal will work, I think?"

"She's not wrong." Nyske pulled herself up, and I rushed to the edge of the pool to give her a hand to help her out. "Ugh. That gave me a huge headache."

"I doubt that's any more than just the beginning, Nyske." I tried not to smirk. Normally, I was the one getting pelted with some new, fate-changing power. I couldn't wait to have Nyske going through the same thing beside me.

CHAPTER 7

I stepped through the portal, carrying Nyske. Rebecca followed behind me.

"Need a portal somewhere?" I asked her.

"Nope. I am going to go find my nymph, get some extra coffee, and saddle up in Helena's room to go through some paperwork." Rebecca got on her tiptoes, then frowned before pulling my head down so that she could kiss me on the cheek. "Take care. Both of you."

I shifted my focus back to Nyske in my arms as Rebecca left my office. "You okay?"

"Sure." Nyske's voice sounded distant.

"I'm going to smash your pickles," I teased, testing her.

"And I'm going to smash your balls. Do not touch my pickles." Nyske looked up. "How are you?"

"I didn't just watch my mother die, nor did I get stuffed with her mojo. So, no better or worse than before, save for having a few interesting answers to things." I placed Nyske down on the couch in my office and knelt next to her.

"Don't forget how old I am," Nyske chided me.

"Don't forget you have more intense emotions than humans," I shot back and brushed her hair out of her face before running my hands through it, trying to calm her.

"She forced me." Nyske leaned into my hand, pressing it between her face and the couch. "She forced me to take you away from your parents. Don't you hate her?"

"To me, all of that is pretty distant. I hate her manipulations of you more. Seeing you hurt from the actions makes me want to punch her in the face. But ultimately? What's done is done. I'm not going back in time, and she's now dead."

"Being logical while your girl is being emotional is not helpful," Nyske pouted at me. "I guess I never really processed all of it. I just shoved it aside by never seeing her again."

"And now?" I asked.

"Now I have to deal with the emotional backlog." Nyske pulled my face closer and kissed me. "Or we could deal with it another way?" She bobbed her eyebrows.

"Uh huh. I don't think this is how we want to get back in that saddle." I kissed her again before moving up and kissing her forehead. "But I'll happily cuddle you on the couch while you talk."

Nyske rolled over and threw her hands above her head. "The one time he doesn't want to sleep with me."

"Hey. There was that time I found your vibrator." I nudged her. "Got kind of jealous of that thing. It had four speeds and did that weird twisting thing." Crawling over her, I put my back to the back of the couch and wrapped my arms around her.

There was no way I was going to be the little spoon.

"That doesn't count. You slept with me just before you found that." Nyske was pouting. Even if I couldn't see her face, I knew that tone.

"Sure it counts. We had sex constantly. Now that I know you are a nymph, it makes a lot of sense."

"Don't make it sound like it was all me. You were plenty eager." Nyske wiggled herself against me.

"Can you blame me? You even toned yourself down when we were dating. Still had that wild sexual magnetism that I'm learning is just a nymph thing."

"You like me better like this?" Nyske pulled my arm tighter around her and started playing with my hand.

I nuzzled her hair and kissed her neck. "I like you in every way."

She stretched out and exposed her neck to me. I kissed it tenderly several times before settling down. She wasn't going to lure me into sex so easily.

"So. How do you feel about your mother?" I brought her back to the topic she was trying to avoid.

"Darn. I would have gotten away with it too if it wasn't for my meddling boyfriend," Nyske sighed. "Really thought I could distract you."

I felt like I could back off, but it wasn't necessary. Nyske was just being playfully evasive.

"So. You see her for the first time in decades, and she gives you the last of her power."

"What a selfish bitch, right?" Nyske huffed. "Just had to go and steal the show. I was supposed to be angry with her, but then she goes and gives me everything. You try having a mother that is older than dirt and predicts/maneuvers everything the way she wants."

"Older than dirt part is true. But between you and me, Tia is just a loose cannon. I'm not entirely sure she's that bright."

Nyske chuckled. "Careful. Someone could use words like that against you."

"Well the last time you all invited my mother here, she helped you steal my hoard." I couldn't help the growl that entered my voice as I remembered them carting off my hoard.

Nyske burst into laughter and turned to see my expression, her laughter dying. "Right. It wasn't that funny, just a little situational humor. You know." She let out a nervous giggle. "Anyway... so, my mother is a little shit. I'm supposed to be angry, but in the end, I'm just sort of sad. She was a constant, you know? For thousands and thousands of years, she was there. I don't know how to describe the feeling. I just lost the thing that never really seemed possible to lose, and now I'll never find it again." Nyske settled back down on the couch, going limp.

"Wow. Deep." I nudged her. "Mother of the year award right there."

"Don't tease me. You asked. I can't believe I'm actually sad that she's gone. I can't hate her for what she did. Now I'm just upset that I don't get to hate her anymore."

"Wanna go to Tartarus and yell at her?" I asked.

Nyske blinked and turned to face me again. "That... that would be very cathartic one of these days. But not today. Today she's dead, and I'll let that be. But she made me a titan."

"Is that a bad thing?" I asked.

"No. I was a nymph, now I'm a dragon-nymph abominat—"

I slapped her on the ass. "Don't call yourself that."

"Fine. A dragon-nymph hybrid. Now I'm going to become a titan?" she asked.

"With a dragon heart. So you won't die like your mother."

"Nor will I live like her," Nyske spoke defiantly and started wiggling against me. "See? Emotions all talked over. Good job getting that one out of me."

I chuckled at her playful way of telling me that we were done talking about her mother. Instead, I just rested my weight against her and pressed my face into the crook of her neck. "I'm just going to take a little nap."

"You have a schedule," Nyske reminded me.

I yawned as an answer. "Sometimes I just need to take a nice nap with a lovely nymph who isn't at all being obtuse about showing emotion for her mother's death."

Nyske pulled out her phone and sent a quick message before putting it down on the floor. "You know that Pixie is going to be upset."

"Not about rescheduling," I answered confidently. "She's going to be upset that she missed a midday nap and cuddle session. Given how much she switches between being a boss-ass secretary and a sexy nymph, she really likes cuddles."

Nyske wiggled in closer. "I'll set an alarm so that you don't sleep too long."

I only grunted in reluctant agreement before keeping my eyes closed and focusing on wrapping up Nyske with as much love as I could muster.

***

"He's so adorable when he sleeps," Scarlett whispered.

I peeked open an eye to see my foxy lover, who was crouched by my face. "Hi."

She leaned in and gave me a peck on the cheek. "We wondered where you went." Her tails all swished playfully behind her.

Nyske was still in my arms, but she had woken up before me. "He needed a nap."

"I can see that." Scarlett played with my hair. "Unfortunately, my father has been trying to get in touch with you, and it's important."

I reached around Nyske, grabbed Scarlett, and pulled her onto the couch before pretending to snore.

"Maybe I could use a nap," Scarlett admitted.

"That couch is not big enough for me too, is it?" Jadelyn made herself known as she leaned over the back of the couch.

"Sneak up on me, why don't you?" I looked over at her.

"Love you too, Husband. But unless you can—"

I grabbed her and pulled her over onto me. Goldie helped so that I didn't injure anyone with the move. Now I had three lovely ladies in my arms as I laid on the couch, and I hoped that they would all remain quiet so we could cuddle and sleep more.

"Perfect. Now we can sleep." When I closed my eyes, fluffy tails started to bat me in the face. "Really?" I cracked one eye back open.

"Yes really," Scarlett answered, her tone mournful. "I haven't seen you take a midday nap before. Know that it pains me to ruin such a golden opportunity."

"Must be important," I groaned and pushed away her excited, yet fluffy tails. "What's this about?"

"Geists taking over fighter pilots." Scarlett's face was serious.

"You already know about that? Damn, the paranormal group has some pull." I shifted a little, considering how I was going to move out of the pile of women.

"Of course my love is at the center of the trouble." Jadelyn squeezed me once and extracted herself and held a hand out for Nyske. But Scarlett just pivoted so that she sat on my hips, letting her tails playfully pummel me.

"What do you know?" Scarlett interrogated me using her fluffy tails as delightful torture implements.

"We had an angel in custody. A bunch of other angels ran Maddie and Frank off the highway into a trap with a bunch of cherubs, then fighter jets came. When all was done, we found that even though we protected the van, someone had gotten in and sliced the angel's head clean off," I answered.

Scarlett let out a whistle. "That's not good."

"That would be an understatement. Since Georgia and the FBI were involved and are looking into the cults and their roots down in Brazil, she went to the Air Force base and got us a chance to talk to the remaining pilots. Only one is alive now, by the way. Two of them died before being detained. One went super-geist on me and blew up a cinderblock room. And the other two, I killed their geists, but one didn't make it." I tried to summarize the entire situation quickly.

"No way. Geists don't blow up rooms. They break a mirror or throw your food across the room in a tantrum." Scarlett frowned.

I shrugged. "By the way, does the Scalewright family do anything about them?"

Jadelyn held up a necklace. "Prevents a lot of mind-altering effects, including possession. But for our businesses? Nothing. A geist isn't common enough to really be a concern more than any other destructive issue that insurance would cover. Does this have anything to do with the FBI's angel investigation?"

"That's the thought," I replied, lifting the playful kitsune off of me and standing. "We might also want to increase security here if they are active in Philly."

"Level three?" Scarlett asked, immediately shifting from playful to serious as she switched into security mode.

"I was thinking four, or maybe even five," I told her honestly.

"No way." Scarlett crossed her arms. "That's overkill. It's just a few geists. How about we get Sabrina and Ikta in a room and see what sort of crazy thing they could cook up for us?" She grinned. "Besides, they probably blew their load at us and are done."

I frowned. "If they can come up with something that keeps a geist from getting close, then maybe."

Scarlett was all smiles. "They'll get something, and we'll stick to level three."

"I like level one." Jadelyn gave me a bright smile.

"You don't like any security." I eyed her, daring her to object.

"Not true. When it doesn't get in my way at all, I don't mind it one bit. That, and I love you, Scarlett." Jadelyn tried to pinch her cheeks, but Scarlett sidestepped her. "No fair. Let's go for a swim."

"Nope. I'd rather not get almost drowned as you try and prove that you can handle yourself. Which, to be fair, you can. But only in water." Scarlett sighed. "Husband, some help please with our wife?"

"Or. Now just consider it. What if you take me with you to Brazil? Where would I be safer than in the arms of my husband?" Jadelyn batted her eyelashes.

I grunted. "Probably going to be portaling back at night anyway. I'd rather sleep here than some stupid hotel."

"You wouldn't be in a 'stupid hotel'." Jadelyn puffed out her cheeks and waved a hand in the air as if dismissing the crazy thought. "My husband only stays in the best. I gave Helena carte blanche to use personal funds to up-grade you as much as you want."

I stared at her.

"What? You are not staying in some cheap FBI per diem level hotel. That's how you bring back bed bugs. Do you realize how hard bed bugs are to get out of a house? Not to mention this probably costs me less than that custom bed."

"That bed was pretty expensive. I saw that bill." Scarlett tapped her chin. "So, your claim is that by spending now you save in the long run?"

"Yep." Jadelyn nodded furiously. "Besides, it is already done." She smiled.

I sighed. I'd learned not to fight Jadelyn as she tried to spoil me. It was part of how she showed her love and care. "Thank you. Now, if you'll excuse me, I'll go talk to Detective Fox and make sure that we can settle down the concern in the paranormal community so that I don't come back to a fire that should have had us at level five." I glared at Scarlett.

She blew a raspberry at me. "Go. Say 'hi' to my dad. He does like you."

"Now he does. At first he was trying to figure out how to get away with putting me six feet under." I rolled my eyes. "Fine. Is he at the precinct?"

"No, he's at the manor," Jadelyn spoke up. "Now, shoo. Helena is coming over soon for a girl getting ready session."

"Wait a second." I pulled out my phone. "What happened to my afternoon?"

"You enjoyed it thoroughly napping with me. Which is for the best because you and Helena are going to stay up late." Nyske shook a finger at me.

"Yes, dear." I snapped my fingers and opened a portal to the portal room attached to the master bedroom.

Jadelyn's home was a magical fortress. Her family had sunk a considerable amount of money in protecting themselves. It was just easier to use the portal we had established and show up in the portal room than potentially surprise someone.

That and it was just common courtesy to come in through the door that they provided.

I stepped out of my own portal and into the Scalewright mansion.

"Dragon King." A siren standing guard saluted me.

"Hello. Looking for Detective Fox. Apparently a situation is developing." I kept it brief.

"Yes, sir. He's in his workroom with Mr. Scalewright."

"Thank you." I nodded to the guard and strode out alone, knowing exactly where the 'work room' that his wife often called his man cave was.

I had to go up two floors through a hall and then back down two more before alternating left, right, left, right.

When I finally reached the large oaken doors, I pushed them open.

"Ah. Detective Fox," I spoke loudly over the soft rock music.

The room was every man's dream man cave. Rich mahogany covered the walls, and there were a few twelve-point bucks on the wall along with just about any sports paraphernalia that could be dreamed up.

Rupert had quite the collection of framed balls and jerseys. Not to mention a few bent golf clubs that seemed to have their own story. Beyond that, the place had a theater with plush reclining seats for everyone. No couches or loveseats were present. Their wives didn't enter the work room.

"Ah! Son." Rupert came around the corner. "We have a situation."

The man was a walking sculpture of Poseidon, with a big, white beard yet looking like a 6'4" bodybuilder. He even liked to wear a pair of gold bracers that were heavily enchanted to protect him.

"Geists and airplanes. I'm aware. Sorry, Rupert, this is why I had to cancel on you. I went with Georgia to the air force base to gather more intel," I told him.

"Thank god. You never disappoint. I think this calls for a beer." Rupert wandered over to the fridge and opened it up. The inside held every beer I could name, carefully and cleanly organized.

"Hold on. Is the situation resolved?" Detective Fox asked. "What about the exposure to the air force?"

I sighed. "Want to give me the Double Head? I'm going to need it. Let's sit and I'll walk you two through all that's happened."

CHAPTER 8

Rupert leaned back in the oversized leather chair and massaged his temples. "This isn't good, Zach. Integration with humans never goes our way. The military finds out and then they make contingencies on how to 'deal with us' should we ever become a threat. Then people start getting drills and rumors trickle down."

"Fighter jets opened fire on American soil. A colonel was attacked in the prison," I countered, comfortable in my own giant chair.

"Traitors and bomb vests," Detective Fox answered. "Or at least, that's what someone would end up chalking it up to if someone wasn't making portals in front of them."

I didn't have quite as little faith in humanity as they apparently had built. If anything, werewolves and vampires would have a sexual awakening with the way romance treated them.

"Well, at least we are exerting some control rather than having it just thrust out there in the open. Since we picked up attention after the vampires tried to invade Faerie, the cat was already out of the bag." I sighed. "We aren't going to have this conversation again. What you need to know is that it appears the angels from South America sent some people up to attack the investigators."

"Think it'll stop when you guys head south?" Detective Fox asked.

"Chances are high that they only sent a limited number up here to stop or slow us down. But all it has done is make the FBI pull the flight up as much as they could," I worked through the information while I spoke.

"We'll still keep an eye out. Two of the five weren't confirmed dead. I still can't believe geists and angels are working together." Detective Fox shook his head. "Geists are horrid creatures. Most of the paranormals don't really consider them sentient. Putting them down is considered a mercy."

I shrugged. "My concern is just dealing with the present issue. We can figure out how geists and angels are working together later, after I've plucked a few for this. Keep an eye on the church too."

"They've still been very quiet since Morgana relocated their portal," Rupert replied. "But I'm glad that you are on this one. Not much is going to get past you."

"Thanks, Mr. Scalewright." I lifted my beer.

"I've told you a thousand times, call me Father. Or Pops, or something more familiar than just my last name works too." The large man shook his head, making his beard flop about.

"Well. At least you are right. Not much is going to get past me. I have a whole mansion full of ladies who can take care of themselves too."

"Everyone wants to be in your good graces," Detective Fox chuckled. "Things among the paranormals are calming down considerably for fear that the Dragon King will get involved in a dispute."

"Good." I gave them both a toothy smile. "At least my 'big bad' reputation is worth something. Cheers, you two." I held up my beer and clinked it with them. "I have a date that I can't be late for. Then tomorrow we are heading to Brazil."

"Good luck. Which lucky lady is it tonight?"

"Helena," I answered, causing Detective Fox to snort.

"Good luck. You'll need it." He broke out into a full laugh.

I gave him a big grin; he wasn't wrong. But I was determined to make something of the date.

Helena and I had always been in a very different place when it came to the relationship. To me, she was marked as my mate, and therefore, she was mine. But she was still trying to figure out what I meant to her. For the moment, all she could seem to handle was physical intimacy, and even then, pretty rough sex.

I wasn't truly sure she could love with all the trauma she'd been through, but I was willing to meet her where she was at that moment. I had to admit to myself, the longer we went on, the more I hoped it would build into something more.

Call me a greedy dragon, but I wanted love from her.

***

I stood in my nicest navy suit while Nyske ran her hands over my shoulders to smooth out any wrinkles. We were waiting in the front room of the mansion for Helena.

"She's just running late," Nyske comforted me.

"Or..." I started.

Nyske put a finger to my lips and gave me an amused expression. "Were you this nervous for our dates?"

"You showed up early," I grumbled. "She's late, and she's also strangely disinterested in a date."

"Poor Dragon King. A woman uninterested?" Nyske teased me.

"It's not that. I'm worried that she's going to reject me in an attempt to reject the intimacy that she's so afraid of." I straightened my tie-less collar. Ties always felt like nooses to me, and I never really appreciated them.

But just then the click of heels announced Helena, catching my full attention.

Helena came around the corner dressed to the nines, yet strangely still Helena. Her hair was the same as normal, but there seemed to be an extra shine to it. And she was wearing a touch of makeup she didn't normally wear that made her hair appear extra white.

A pair of elaborate silver feather earrings dangled from underneath her hair that matched a triple stranded necklace. The necklace hung down into the light blue dress she had on, which hugged her like a second skin. Banded layers squeezed her already impressive figure into a shapely hourglass.

My eyes found their way back up to her intelligent and beautiful eyes before realizing that for the first time she was displaying my mark openly.

"Enjoying it?" Helena lifted a toned leg and did a small twirl that made me step forward in case she fell.

But the angel was comfortable enough with her tall heels that it didn't seem to even unsteady her.

"You look incredible." I swallowed.

"Good. Now come on. We don't want to be late." Helena marched forward, hooking a finger at me.

Nyske chuckled. "Shoo shoo."

"Sending me off so easily," I pouted.

"I'm in love with a man who has over a dozen wives." Nyske rolled her eyes. "Let's hope I'm over jealousy."

Rather than rush to catch up to Helena, I opened a portal that I stepped out of and fell into step with her.

"It's a lovely night." I held out my arm, surprised as she wrapped her arm through mine.

"It is." She opened the front door for us. "But there's no car."

"No. It's just on the other side of the park," I explained, taking a nice trail that had been put in for my mansion to connect with the park next to it.

"Ah," Helena said. "Then we walk."

She leaned a little heavier on my arm as we stepped off the paved trail into the grass, but she refused to utter a peep about the uneven ground. She walked carefully, making sure her heels didn't sink into the ground with every step.

But I let her do as she wanted, supporting her as best as I could with my arm.

"So. Outside of wandering my mansion and working for the FBI, what do you do in your free time?" I asked.

"Why don't you come to my place after dinner tonight and you'll find out?" Helena's offer nearly made me miss a step.

"I have to admit, I'm curious. Don't regret it when I find you are obsessed with pink," I teased.

Helena snorted. "No. You won't find much pink. The Nashner lifestyle, even if I've abandoned it, came with a decent amount of money, and I have taste."

"Oh no," I gasped. "Is it all modern, black and white? Truthfully, this is one of the few times I've seen you out of black and white."

"That's because those colors work well with my hair, while being professional. With my figure, it is hard to keep people professional." She clicked her tongue. "Tonight isn't professional in the slightest."

"Uh huh," I hummed. "Because our relationship has been strictly professional." Sarcasm dripped from my tone.

She narrowed her eyes at me in warning.

"Helena. I like you, and you spend enough time around me that people think we are together. We've never really broached the topic. But, are we exclusive?" I tried to act casual, but she wore my mark. I would likely have to hunt down and rip the head off any man who had touched her.

A sly smile graced Helena's lips. "You know, I'm really tempted to throw out some guy who needs to disappear."

I put on my best innocent smile. "Me? Make someone disappear?"

"No. I haven't seen anyone else. No physical relationships, nor have I even gone on a date since…" She reached up and traced the mark on her shoulder from the outside to the inside until she brushed her necklace. "Not in a long time."

I stuffed away the smile that threatened to bloom down. It was unfair for me to have a dozen wives yet be so possessive. I blamed that fully on my dragon instincts. He was a very greedy dragon, but I wasn't going to apologize for who I was and what I wanted.

"So. What kind of restaurant are we going to?" Helena changed the subject.

"Fancy," I cryptically answered.

"No Karaoke. If another bozo tries to get me to sing, I'm going to gut them," she threatened.

"Because you're an angel?" I asked.

"Heaven's Choir. I can't tell you how many times when I worked for the church that people would try to get me to sing, thinking that it must sound heavenly." By Helena's expression, I assumed her voice either wasn't heavenly, or too pretty and embarrassing for her. I was fairly sure I may never find out.

I clicked my tongue and pulled out my phone. "Drat. Let me change the reservation..."

"You didn't actually?"

I chuckled. "No I didn't. Besides, I'm only a great singer when I've had too much to drink, and nothing here is going to get me drunk enough to sound halfway decent." I smirked. "We are going to a foodie place, but it's not so snobbish that they don't do live music. There's a jazz band playing. You can enjoy music, right?"

"I do. Though I'm not particularly into any type of music," Helena clarified. "Will there be dancing?"

"I don't think so. Unless you want there to be?" I hazarded. "We could find a place."

"The only dancing I'm good at is the kind with loud music and making out in the corner," Helena replied.

I raised an eyebrow at her. "Sometimes I wonder what I've signed up for."

"You signed yourself up. Don't look at me like that." Helena smiled. "So. Foodie place. Been there before?"

"Nope. Jadelyn recommends it, so it can't be bad." I shrugged.

Helena raised an eyebrow. "If Jadelyn recommended it, can I assume you are paying?"

"She's not that bad."

"The place is going to cost a fortune, and I only have an agent's salary." Helena rolled her eyes. "Some of us make do without giant chambers filled with gold."

"It's just a little gold." I smiled.

"A little gold," Helena snorted. "You swim in it."

"It is very swimmable."

She ran her hand down my arm. "Sure it is. I'm not going to ever swim in gold with you, though."

"Fly together?" I asked.

"Oh, I'll happily ride you like a giant pony." She gave me a giant smile.

"You've ridden me plenty of times." I gave her a sly grin.

"Of course. You have to break in those young ones."

I snorted. "You break a lot of things, but I'm not one of them."

She tsked and shook her head. "That was a horrible thing to say. Now I have something to prove."

"Do your worst." I grinned. "After the date, of course."

"Of course." She grinned right back, though there was more than a hint of predatory pride in the look.

I understood Helena. She liked to be rough and be treated rough. Yet it all needed an underlying level of respect if it was to work at all.

Helena sniffed the air as we got towards the end of this stretch of the park and back into the city.

I sniffed. "Pizza so greasy it is practically fried."

"Smells heavenly." Her cute little nose wiggled.

I stared at her.

"What? Surprised I like greasy food?" She smiled, knowing exactly what she did.

"Heavenly? Really?"

"You aren't allowed to make Heaven references about me, but I can make them." Helena smiled.

It was a beautiful and genuine smile.

"Okay. Well in that case, why don't we go get some greasy pizza and then just go have a few drinks and listen to the live music?"

"Can't," Helena said and shook her head. "I'd get grease all over this dress and that just won't do. Besides, you made the plans and we'll stick to them."

"Want to wear a napkin bib?"

"If you tell anyone *ever* that I was wearing a bib of any sorts, I will break your dick. Let's go get pizza." She shifted to veer off to the left.

I chuckled. "Wrong way. Trust me, what you are smelling is this way." I touched my nose. "Dragon senses are a lot better than angel senses."

Helena pulled me right. "I knew that. Congratulations, you passed the test."

We went down the street, past the fancy restaurants, to a little place that seemed to be delivery oriented. I opened the door, and the teenager manning the counter was busy making boxes.

"Can I... help you? We have an app if you want to order," he said, putting down the next box. When he saw Helena, his jaw hit the counter, and he stumbled while trying to reach for the next box.

The place smelled like deep fried pepperoni with a hint of dough yeast.

"Actually, we were just walking down and thought it smelled incredible." I was realizing that we'd probably have to wait. "Have any orders that aren't going out?"

"Uh. Yeah. We always have a canceled order or two."

"What are you feeling?"

Helena sniffed the air. "Got anything with lots of meat?"

The teenager was still staring at Helena. "Yeah. I have meat you can eat." He fumbled, his eyes widening as he realized he'd spoken out loud.

I stared down at the kid, but Helena burst into laughter.

"Kid. You don't know it, but you are walking the border between life and death." Helena leaned on me.

"You don't have to worry about me. She's the one who carries a weapon." I pointed at her, and the teenager sprinted into the back.

"Not carrying my gun right now. You probably have a dozen in your bracer."

I looked her over.

"Where would I hide it?" Helena crossed her arms under her chest.

"I don't know. Maybe you have one of Morgana's bras."

"She did make some for the rest of the harem." Helena's smile quirked. "But you'll never know what's in mine."

I narrowed my eyes, but I didn't say anything as the teenager came back with a small tower of pizzas.

"I wasn't sure which one you would prefer, so I grabbed a few canceled orders." He put the stack on the counter.

"Going to give me all of your meat?" Helena teased.

The boy's face turned bright red. "Th-this one." He held out the top box.

Helena flipped the cardboard lid open and took a big sniff. "This'll do. He's paying." She took the box.

I smiled at the teenager and took out a card from my bracer, pretending it was in my pocket.

"It's fine, sir. We were going to throw those away anyway." The boy stared dreamily at my date.

"Then thanks for making her night." I pulled out a twenty and gave it to him as a tip. "Can I get a big stack of napkins?"

A few minutes later, we were back at the edge of the park, and I was helping Helena make a several-napkin-thick bib so that she could eat her greasy pizza without damaging the dress. Sadly, the napkins were too flimsy to enchant or I'd have made a better bib.

Helena moaned as she folded and ate the pizza that was dripping with grease. "They don't have food like this at fancy foodie places."

"No, they do not." I leaned forward and ate my slice carefully.

"But foodie places are good for one thing." Helena smiled, cradling her slice away from her dress.

"What is that?"

"Nice bathrooms." She grinned.

I raised an eyebrow.

"We have to celebrate after you take me out on our first date. Just be sure to put a silence enchantment on the door." She took another bite of her pizza.

"Wait, what?" I nearly flung grease all over both of us with how fast my head whipped around.

"We should get the rough, angry sex out of the way before we head to my place. If you wreck anything, you're in trouble." Helena went back to daintily eating the pizza as if she hadn't just offered up nearby bathroom sex a moment earlier.

CHAPTER 9

I wiped water out of my face, but the broken sink continued to spray up into the air.

The toilet was missing its front half. The sink was completely obliterated to the point that it was now spraying cold water in a high arc above us. The handicap rail had dents where Helena had gripped it while I'd pounded into her from behind. Meanwhile, the hand driers and towel dispensers were crushed to the point they wouldn't be usable.

As we started to get dressed, another tile fell off the wall and shattered on the ground.

Helena wiped back her hair and attempted to straighten her dress. "That was lovely."

I chuckled. The only thing in the room that wasn't broken was the mirror. We'd finished with me behind her while we'd watched each other in the mirror.

"That was something." I blew out a breath. "We can't walk out of here like this. This place is trashed."

She stuck out her tongue. "Nyske is on call to fix it. I checked with her before tonight."

I raised an eyebrow and opened up a portal back to my office.

Pixie, Fiona, and Nyske immediately stepped through the portal with hardhats on. The hardhat looked particularly ridiculous covering Pixie's pink, voluminous curls that were springing out all over.

"Wow." Nyske glanced around. "I know we were expecting to fix a few things, but this is pretty intense. Did two angry rhinos have sex in here?" She turned to me with an amused smile.

Pixie opened up an umbrella and held it out to shield them from the currently spraying sink.

"Something like that." I scratched the back of my head. "Can you fix it?"

"Yup." Nyske's magic was unique. She had dragon magic, which could directly affect and shape the world in place of her fae magic illusions. She still crafted glamors, only hers were real. Her magic was practically miraculous, but it came at a high cost.

The broken sink fixed itself, the pieces jumping off the ground before air dried. The dents popped back out, and the toilet and tiles came back together.

After a moment, the room was whole again, but Helena and I were still dripping wet.

"Well, you two have a lovely night." The nymphs filed back through the portal.

"So. Your place?" I asked, pulling up my pants.

Helena rolled her eyes. "I don't think a taxi will take us. Portal to the roof, then we'll fly?" Her wings snapped into existence, and she gave them a good flap.

"Will wet wings be a problem?" I asked.

"I already defy gravity with my flight. Why should water stop me?" Helena smirked.

I rolled my eyes and popped open a portal into a deep part of the park. I had never seen the roof, so making a portal there wasn't safe.

Stepping out, Helena crouched before launching herself high into the air with a flap of her wings. I had to run to catch up after throwing my shirt and jacket into my bracer. I jumped and let my body shift mid-air, a pair of giant golden wings coming out of my bare back.

The air shimmered around both of us as I cast the spell for invisibility. It didn't work under great scrutiny, but up in the air, it worked just fine.

Helena chuckled and dipped around me, grabbing my hand and spinning me in the air. "Remember when you were a really bad flier?"

I tilted my wings on instinct now, allowing myself to maintain forward momentum and not worrying about being upside down for just a moment.

"Nope. I was always a consummate flier as far as I'm concerned, and you never wore any sort of napkin bib."

Her eyes flashed dangerously, and she spun us so that I was on top, but I noticed that she held my hands. "You play dangerous games."

"I thought you liked to live on the edge?" I had to pump my wings hard to keep both of us aloft in our current position. "Also where are we going?"

"By the river. I have a condo." She gave me a threatening look, but there was a shy smile beneath it. "You tell no one where I live."

"If half of them don't already know, I'd be downright shocked. Morgana probably investigated you the second you came near me, and Jadelyn probably paid someone for the information."

Helena stared at me for a moment.

"What? Just because I'm a big bad Dragon King doesn't mean I can't have protective mates. Very capable and very protective mates."

Helena clung to me as we flew. "You are a very lucky man. So many beautiful ladies, all interested in a pervert like you."

I rumbled. "Would a certain angel be interested in becoming one of them?"

She huffed and looked away. "Who says she already isn't?"

My heart skipped a beat at her answer. Helena wasn't typically so direct about feelings or desire to be with me. I kissed her mid-air, holding her shoulder and her hips to press her to me.

Her arms wound around my head and she bit my lips as much as she kissed them. I smiled. Helena would never love without just a little bit of fight. Giving up all control would be too much, but she was already giving much more of herself to me.

She pulled away with swollen lips. "Bank left. It's that building." She pointed over her head.

"Why don't you show me which balcony?" I saw the balconies and assumed that she had one of them given she'd want to be able to fly.

She smirked and shoved off of me, twirling in the air before flapping her wings out. Turning, she glided smoothly down to one of the balconies.

I dropped down with her, releasing my invisibility. "Nice place." The building was a newer high-rise by the river with a fantastic view of the city.

"Water is calming for me." She fished out a pair of keys from her bra and unlocked the balcony door as I dropped the invisibility.

I was more keen to poke around and get to know her by seeing her place, but it was dark.

"The light switch is terribly placed." She walked into the darkness, familiar with the layout.

A light flipped on deeper into her place, but Helena hadn't been the one to flip the switch. My brain changed gears at the same time as I took in the intruder.

An angel sat at Helena's kitchen island with a smug smile, and I desperately wanted to wipe it off her face, but that would give away my location. It was pitch-black outside, and the little kitchen light didn't reach far. Until Helena needed me, I would remain hidden.

"Helena," the angel spoke.

Helena stood a bit ahead of me, her glock out and raised with a firm stance, ready to put a bullet through the angel's forehead. "Give me a reason not to end you, Andie."

The light that the angel had flipped didn't do much besides illuminate her, and Helena stood at the edge of the light. They knew each other, and they certainly weren't friendly.

I shifted my eyes for better vision in the dark and crept around her apartment. The current situation was not how I'd intended to see Helena's place, but protecting my mate was most important. I tried to get myself into a position where I could grab the intruder.

"Your mother requests your presence in Brazil," the angel spoke calmly.

"My mother is in the Celestial Plane," Helena responded firmly.

"Not any more. Three of the archangels have come down to Earth through other means. What is happening in South America is important. It is quite literally why you were born. If you don't come, your mother will come here directly. I'm sure she can convince you." Andie gave a smug smile, like she believed she had already won.

But my muscles were like loaded springs as I got into position to capture the angel and my hands turned into powerful dragon claws.

"Andie. I never want to see my mother again. But I guess this time, luck is on your side. I already have a flight out tomorrow to head that direction. I'm going down to stop your stupid cults from coming to America, and hopefully put down as many angels as I can." Helena stepped closer, never dropping the gun.

"We are working to restore our home. A nephilim is the key," Andie objected.

"Too bad. Find another."

Andie gave her a bored look. "There aren't any others. They are taboo for... reasons. You were carefully cultivated to assist us with this task. Your brief vacation from serving your mother is over. It's time to come back."

Helena chuckled darkly. "Is that why you sent the geists?"

Andie frowned deep enough, and I was grateful for the extra piece of knowledge Helena had extracted. Andie didn't know about the geists.

"Seems that my mother doesn't have that tight of a leash on everyone. Angels attacked my group this week, and then geists serving angels attacked." Helena watched Andie's response.

"You don't understand," Andie scowled. "That means you need to come to your mother for your own safety then." She got up, her bright white angel wings sprouting from her back in preparation.

I sprang from the darkness, one claw wrapping around the angel's neck, and the other grabbing the base of both wings as I pressed her to the counter. "She doesn't need anyone's protection," I growled.

Someone threatening my mate was making my dragon instincts flare and I couldn't keep the growl from my voice.

Helena put down the gun. "Andie, I'd like you to meet my mate, Zach Pendragon, the Dragon King."

Andie chuckled with her face pressed to the counter. "Some upstart Dragon King? Helena, we angels are well versed in the warfare against dragons. He cannot protect you."

Helena stepped forward and slapped the angel. Hard. "He's not some upstart. But you'll learn that soon enough if you keep fucking around. It seems that, while most of you have been stuck in your own plane, you haven't been aware of the changes on Earth and the other planes."

Andie's eyes flashed with anger, then she looked over at me. "What have you done to her?"

"Mostly fucked her if I'm honest." I shrugged. "Oh, and treat her right. You should pass that along to her mother. Clearly, the woman doesn't actually understand love, which is pretty sad given it's her power."

Andie struggled, but I had her in a vice-like grip. My hands didn't even move as she threw her strength around.

"You are well and truly stuck," Helena spoke as she leaned forward into the angel's face. "You are going to go back to my mother because you are her little worker bee.

Tell her that I'm coming for her. When I get a chance, I'm going to shove the spear she gave me right through her heart." She turned to me. "Let her go. She's not important."

I glared at the angel, wanting to pluck her wings instead of releasing her. But Helena had history with this angel, and it was up to her to make the next move with her mother.

I pushed Andie far enough away that she couldn't lash out in retaliation.

Andie ruffled her feathers and shook out her wings to get them back into place, all while glaring at Helena. "When I see you at your mother's side again, I'll smile."

She turned, shooting out of Helena's open balcony door.

"I'm sorry." I stepped over and grabbed Helena as she leaned against the counter.

"Do me a favor and lock the door." Helena put her head in her hands as her body shook.

I wasn't sure if she was shaking with rage, fear, or something else. But her mother coming back was clearly affecting her in a big way.

I closed the door and clicked the lock closed. "Maybe you shouldn't go tomorrow?" I had a feeling I already knew the answer, but I still hoped she'd take the offer. I didn't want her mother messing with her brain any more than she already had.

"Fuck that. I wasn't joking when I said I would shove my mother's own spear through her heart." Helena looked up, and I could see the anger in her eyes. "That bitch."

"Anything I can do to help?" I asked.

"Hold her down while I shove the spear in?" Helena grinned.

"Can do. After what I saw she did to you... I'd shove it in myself."

Helena shook her head. "Don't you dare. That's my job."

"Then what can I do for you now?" I asked.

"Get out of your clothes and come to bed." She slipped her dress off and walked through her place in nothing but a pair of high heels.

"Really? After that?" I asked, feeling like the romance had been sucked out of the evening.

"Yes, really. I knew she was going to come back into my life eventually. It is just earlier than expected." She blew out a breath. "When I made the decision to help you back in Switzerland, I knew it would eventually end in me having to stand up against my mother."

"So right now, you want a distraction?" I asked.

"Yes. And since I'm not going to let you wreck my condo, you are in for a treat."

"A treat?" I took my pants back off, and kicked my shoes to the side, my mind starting to get back into the mood as she walked across the room swaying her ass back and forth.

I moved towards the bed. Her room was immaculately decorated, and her sheets looked like they had been pressed.

"Yes. Come cuddle. Who expects a dragon to want to cuddle?" She smiled over her shoulder at me.

"Uh. I like rough, but sometimes it is the variety that makes moments enjoyable." I crawled under the covers and turned as Helena sat on the side of the bed, kicking off her heels.

Then Helena slipped under the covers with me. "Well then. Enjoy this. And yes, you can touch my mark." She gave an exaggerated sigh, but I could tell that she was pleased by my obsession with the mark.

"I don't know what you are talking about." Pulling her waist against me, I nibbled at her shoulder where my mark resided. Her soft, warm body against me felt incredible. It was just so right in the moment.

"Uh huh. Gonna bite it?" She looked over her shoulder at me.

My jaw crackled as I held back the urge to shift.

"I consent. Mark me up. I'm pretty sure I'm never going to get rid of you. But it turns out that you aren't half bad. And I might as well let you satisfy me."

"So romantic." My jaw shifted and I bit over my mark. There was no magic in the bite, but it was so satisfying to have her let me mark her.

She wiggled up against me. "Sorry. Romance isn't my thing."

My jaw returned to normal, and I held her tightly against my body. Despite her tough exterior, I could tell the news of her mother's return was bothering her. Otherwise, I doubted I'd get cuddles.

My breathing slowed, taking in the scent of my mate and holding her close. It was oddly more romantic to curl up together with her than to have sex. I loved this woman, and this was something she was doing for me, letting me satisfy my desires rather than hers.

Honestly, this was her showing her love. Not that she'd ever say it.

My tough angel was a nut I didn't need to crack, just cuddle up and hold.

***

I woke up to bright light streaming in through the window and the other half of the bed not only empty, but cold.

"Early riser," I mumbled.

Getting out of bed, I pulled out a pair of pants from my bracer and headed out into her apartment. We'd crashed as we'd cuddled, so I hadn't had a chance to get to explore the space yet.

"Morning," I called. "Hope you had time to hide away your most exciting things."

"Morning." Helena was sitting at the kitchen island, eating eggs and toast while reading emails on her laptop. "Anyone ever tell you that you are a super heavy sleeper? I was able to move my whole sex dungeon without you waking."

"Ha." I let out a mock laugh, looking around the space.

Everything was put away, her shoes were all tucked away in little cubbies by the door. And the kitchen was neat. No dirty dishes, no clothing hanging over chairs.

There was even a cute little planter by her kitchen window that had neatly organized home-grown herbs.

"I honestly thought you'd be messier," I told her.

"That's the back. Come on." Helena got up and put a napkin down by the bowl before waving for me to follow her. Here at home, she had her wings out and was wearing stockings, but no shoes.

We reached the back of her condo, and she opened a barn door to a big open space.

Her painting studio.

"You paint?" I asked, taking a step in and giving her a questioning look to ask if I could snoop.

"Go ahead." She waved me in but waited by the entrance.

The piece still on the easel was of a bird taking flight from her balcony.

I stepped around that piece to where a number of canvases were stacked against the wall with a tarp covering them. Reaching forward, I pulled the tarp off.

Dozens of finished paintings. Many of them depicted birds taking flight.

"Got a thing for birds?" I asked.

"I like birds." She frowned at me, her wings twitching.

But when I looked at the paintings, I didn't see just birds. I felt a woman's desire to be free. Or rather, the joy of taking flight and finally being free.

I was curious what Jadelyn would think. She was the art connoisseur in our family. "You ever think about putting this up in a gallery or something? Jadelyn knows people."

Helena looked like I'd just shot a puppy. "Absolutely not! You don't even get to tell your harem about them. I had to swear my nymph to secrecy."

"Think we could quietly smuggle one into the mansion?" I asked. "It would be nice to hang one up. We could use your nymph to bring it in."

Helena narrowed her eyes as she considered my question. "Maybe."

"The other problem is that you'll need a place to paint if you are going to stay at my place," I argued.

"I'm keeping the condo. I like having my own space if I need it." Helena crossed her arms.

I raised an eyebrow, curious if there was more to her statement. Yet there was the agreement to move in.

"Why do you think Morgana gave me a spatial enchantment? I asked to move in," Helena told me, and I tried to hide my smile as she continued. "But I'm still keeping my paintings here, and I'll need to come back to water my plants. So a nice private portal in my room would be perfect."

I realized she was trying to negotiate for a portal. But it was unnecessary. If Helena wanted to keep the space but mostly use mine, I could handle it.

"Deal," I told her, enjoying the slight surprise that crossed her face at not needing to negotiate harder.

But before she could respond, her phone rang. She took one glance at the number before she had the phone against her ear. "Yes? What?! Hold on. Slow down. We'll be there in a minute." Helena's eyes locked onto mine, and all playfulness was gone from her face. "Zach, we have to go."

CHAPTER 10

W e were out in the suburbs to pick up Rebecca. She had a small but nice one-story home in the middle of an otherwise upscale neighborhood.

Rebecca Till's twenty-something daughter opened the door looking frantic and wearing a baggy t-shirt.

"Wait. Rebecca has a daughter?" I blurted, staring at the young woman in front of me. Rebecca had never mentioned a daughter, and honestly, I was a little surprised given how married she was to her job.

"I don't have a fucking daughter. LOOK AT ME! How am I supposed to go on this flight? I bet my fucking passport will get rejected. No one is going to believe I'm forty-fucking-five." The woman, who it was now clear was actually Rebecca Till herself, threw her hands in the air and stormed back into her house at the edge of Philly proper.

"It's not that bad," I tried, walking in behind her.

Helena made a noise. "It's pretty bad. She looks like she's just graduated college, much less the FBI academy."

"How am I supposed to go through TSA?!"

"We'll get you a fake ID," I answered calmly.

Agent Till glared at me. "Are you telling an agent of the FBI that you are privy to counterfeit passports and government ID?"

"No. Just a random suggestion that you get one. How do you think vampires like Morgana manage the anti-aging thing?"

Rebecca rubbed her face. "This is all your fault."

"How is this... oooh." Helena chuckled. "How does dragon cock compare to coffee?"

"That isn't even a question. Nothing is better than coffee." Rebecca waved away the comment. "How am I supposed to explain all of this?" She gestured up and down her body. "Passports, IDs... then there is my whole career at FBI. Oh don't mind me, I just suddenly lost twenty years of age. Don't worry—it's botox and really great surgery. This was supposed to move far more gradually."

"Zach doesn't do much gradually." Helena leaned on me.

Rebecca looked at us again, her eyes squinting. "I take it that the date went well?"

"She cuddled me," I proudly stated.

Rebecca gasped. "Does your cock turn women into docile ladies too?" She enjoyed teasing Helena.

"Laugh it up. I can't wait to show you to the nymphs."

"You wouldn't."

"Get dressed in something professional. We'll speak to Georgia and figure this out," Helena replied.

"Can't. Clothes don't fit anymore. I have never been fat, but something about all of this gave me a waist like I have an eating disorder." Rebecca pinched her clothes to show just how tiny her waist had become.

"It probably takes a lot of calories to completely reverse twenty years overnight," I answered, only to receive a glare. "What? That is sound logic."

Helena ignored my comment. "Someone at the mansion has to have something you can fit into."

"Also, I can just portal you past security," I offered.

Rebecca covered her face. "Stop suggesting illegal activities."

"I mean, I suppose it's likely illegal technically. But it is in good faith." I shrugged. "Let's get Georgia on the phone. Get your stuff and we'll head to the mansion and find you something to wear."

I opened a portal in her house that led to my bedroom.

"One second." She grabbed a suitcase and then glared at it. "It isn't going to have anything that fits me either."

"We can always portal some clothing to us. Just take what you have." I stepped through to find Kelly turning back and forth in front of the mirror while holding her stomach.

"Hi, Alpha-alpha." Taylor swayed her foot back and forth from where she sat in the corner.

"Alpha!" Kelly spun around and bounced over to me on the balls of her feet before jumping into my arms.

"How are you?" I asked, struggling to hold the woman close whose stomach was now extended.

Kelly didn't answer my question, her attention turned to the woman over my shoulder. "Rebecca?!"

"Hi."

Kelly narrowed her eyes. "Something is different..."

"I'm looking twenty years younger." Rebecca sighed. "I'm so fucked."

"Ah! You did the thing? Just got down on your knees?" Kelly looked proud.

"Tada!" Rebecca twirled. "Now none of my clothes fit."

"Girl." Kelly bounced out of my arms to grab Rebecca's hands. "We can go shopping in The Closet."

I raised an eyebrow at my mate.

"Don't worry. A lot of us share clothes. Just come with me. I might be a little shorter than you, but Tyrande's stuff might fit. And Tyrande and Jade swap clothes all the time."

Agent Till was dragged away a moment later by an excited Kelly. She looked over her shoulder, her eyes pleading with me to help, but honestly, Kelly was probably her best bet for clothing at the moment.

"Think she'll be all right?" Helena asked.

"Probably for the best if we just let it happen." I shrugged and turned back to Taylor. "How's the pack?"

"Golden." Taylor was tall and had legs for days. She was dressed in bright blue cowboy boots to go with her torn up jeans. "But, Alpha-alpha. You are going on another trip after being out for a few weeks. I'm afraid that the pack is going to run out of potions before you get back." She stepped into my personal space.

Helena snorted. "I'm going to go call Georgia. You two stay dressed. We'll probably need a portal to the airport given my partner's situation."

"Why would she think that we wouldn't stay dressed?" Taylor asked, pressing herself up against me.

"You know exactly what you are doing." I gave her a knowing look.

"Yeah. I'm head bitch. My Alpha is busy being pregnant, and I want to step in to make sure my Alpha-alpha stays happy." She gave me a grin.

"I'm very happy. There are plenty of women here to help ensure that." I glanced down at her.

"Yeah, but we want you to keep close ties with the pack, ya know?"

"I think having kids with Kelly takes care of that."

Taylor puffed her cheeks out. "How hard are you gonna make me chase you?"

"You'd do better if you got Kelly to help you," I answered.

She sighed. "The good ones are always taken a dozen times over. I'll let you go this time." Taylor pushed off me as my nymphs came into the room.

"Struck out again?" Pixie clicked her tongue.

"He's a tough nut to crack." Taylor put her hands on her hips and swaggered them as she left.

Pixie cleared her throat. "You missed court today. Thankfully, we were prepared for that and things are running smoothly." She gave a look as if warning me that I couldn't miss regularly or she'd find me and not in a pleasant way.

My lovely summer nymph was an immaculate assistant, which meant pushing me into meetings that I needed to keep.

"That said, Nyske is going with you to Brazil, mostly because she's the only one of us with a passport. We'll correct that for future trips."

Nyske gave me a brilliant smile. "You'll be in good hands."

"Yes I will be." I gave Nyske another look over. "There's no way we don't attract a ton of attention walking around with you."

"Time to stop sweet talking her and get moving. We have your things ready in the office, and you can just stuff them in your bracer. It sounds like Rebecca is having some trouble with clothes, but the harem is convening to help her out," Pixie replied.

I raised a brow. "How do you know that already?"

"Because it's my job to know everything happening in your life. That, and Goldie can be bribed."

"Goldie?" I asked the bracer on my arm.

She made a yawning noise. "Hmm?"

"You don't even sleep. How are you giving Pixie information?"

"Hmm? Oh. There's a cellphone in my mass now. I can text her. We text a lot lately. Lots of it is Golden Plushie Society business, so I can't tell you about it."

I narrowed my eyes at my nymphs and the elemental before shrugging. "This is what I get for outnumbering myself so heavily."

"You like it," Goldie chimed in. "Pixie said so."

"Don't teach Goldie bad things," I scolded Pixie.

"She's not a child. She ate thousands of demons and drained their minds. Goldie has the emotional maturity and mental experience to know herself and what she wants," Pixie spoke out for the elemental. "Besides, she's really helpful."

"That is all very true," I answered, glancing down at the bracer. "But you shouldn't spy on me."

"Just because you forget I'm here half the time doesn't mean I'm 'spying'," Goldie huffed.

"She's got a point," Nyske smiled. "Now. Let's gather everyone and see if we can't sneak into the airport. You suck at going through metal detectors with your bracer fused to you anyway."

***

"Please review the safety card in the seat pocket in front of you. It contains all of the safety information specific to this aircraft. On behalf of everyone at Hot Air, we thank you for choosing to fly with us." The flight attendant continued on. "We'll be coming around with offers for Hot Air credit cards, bonus miles, and more."

I groaned and Nyske patted my arm.

"You have it so bad." Maddie rolled her eyes at me from the seat in front of me.

"I'm spoiled from Jadelyn's private jets and then my own means of travel." I shrugged. "Sue me."

"I am. You made me abandon my van." Maddie crossed her arms.

"But this is a very high-paying job. You'll be able to get another one that's even better."

"She wants a hummer." Frank joined the conversation, leaning forward from the chair next to Maddie. "But then we'll gut everything but the front two seats and enchant it into a fortress."

"You said 'no' to a tank. So hummer is the next best thing." Maddie shrugged as if that answer were obvious.

I shook my head. "Well, you can probably afford it after they pay us for this one. So, let's focus on getting the job done."

Maddie looked forward towards the crowd of bureaucrats that were accompanying us on the trip. "Yeah. How

about you just let me loose and I go play whack-an-angel."
She flashed her fangs.

"Honestly, not the worst idea you've had. But we need
to be more subtle. This isn't our home turf," I reminded
her.

"Yeah. That's why we go at night to play whack-an-angel." Maddie rolled her eyes.

Frank nudged her. "Take this seriously. Please."

Agent Till sat down into the seat behind me with a
baseball cap pulled low over her face.

"How's it going, Rebecca?" Nyske asked.

"I feel like a fraud. We didn't even go through TSA. My
own team didn't even recognize me."

"Georgia said she would loop them in once we got on
the ground. Then it is off to the races."

Rebecca rubbed at her face. "Fucking dragon semen."

I choked on a laugh.

"You would think this is funny," Rebecca scowled at me.

"At least you don't just look your age, but you actually reversed your aging," Nyske pointed out. "Pretty sure
there are billionaires throwing more money at that problem than we can imagine. And they're failing."

She blinked. "So I take a drink from the fountain every
twenty years and I'll be immortal?"

"Dragons are greedy creatures. They don't like to lose
anything that's theirs, including their harems." Nyske leveled a stare. "A 'drink' every twenty years doesn't cut it."

I went to speak, but Nyske held up a finger to stop me
before turning back to Rebecca.

"I let you go down on him to see what happens. But
so far, you've blamed him and treated him like a fountain
to take a drink from. I mean this in no uncertain terms:

the Plushies will eat you alive if they see you treat him like that."

Rebecca swallowed. "Understood. I love the sisterhood in the Plushies, and Zach's not bad."

"Zach's fucking fantastic." Nyske made it clear with her tone that her reply was a correction. "Now, what is the plan besides go and kill angels?"

Rebecca looked at me.

I shrugged. "She's not wrong. I love having you around, and you are always welcome. But me and the rest of my harem, we are emotionally close. You are welcome to join that or stay on the outside."

She made a face. "It's not that I'm not interested. I just haven't really done much in a long time. Sort of closed that door a while ago."

"Congratulations. The door is back open." Nyske gave her a smile. "You got a twenty-year rewind. After being a bossass FBI agent and making a great career for yourself, you get to go back and try the option of having a family too."

Rebecca nodded. "Thank you."

"No problem. Plushies stick together and let each other know when they fuck up. Anyway, you were about to tell us about the plan," Nyske urged her forward and squeezed my hand before flashing me a smile. "Sorry, that was Plushie business."

"That was badass," Frank whispered from his seat. "I want a harem that fights for me like that. Ouch. Ouch ouch. It was a joke, Maddie, come on."

"You were saying?" Maddie urged Rebecca on.

"Right. We'll go over this again. There are three organizations we believe to be behind the cults bleeding into

America. One is a church, another a corporation, and finally, there's a cult that's been spreading."

"Religion tends to do that. If it doesn't spread, it dies," Maddie added.

Rebecca gave her a sour expression. "Religion gives people hope. It's not all bad, but yes, it seems to create zealots and those who would take it to the extreme from time to time."

She sighed and continued on. "We have a meeting set up with the corporation for three days from now. Until then, our job is to snoop around the other two and the corporation if we have time."

"I can snoop." Maddie smiled. "A lot better than this guy." She hooked a thumb at me.

"So. We do reconnaissance. If we find anything, what are we going to do about it?"

"We have to find the money. And then either show that it is being funneled out of the US, or into the US through this organization. That's how we do it legally and bring them to justice. Georgia knows that paranormals handle things their own way. So after we prove they are guilty, I'm going to ignore it if you ever burp up feathers."

"Am I a cartoon now?" I asked.

"Sometimes." Nyske patted my hand like she was about to break the bad news to me. "You eat people."

"I don't burp feathers. Okay. So, Georgia is going to be upset if I start putting angels down before we have proof," I checked.

"Yes. Thank you. We are trying to adapt to this whole paranormal justice system." Rebecca looked uncomfortable.

"Execution," Maddie clarified.

"Yeah. That."

"So. We need to infiltrate these locations and see what we can learn. We should probably split up if we only have three days," I worked through the plan.

Rebecca nodded. "Given your resistance to mental attacks now, we'd like you to go into the cult. Meanwhile, the others are going to go after the church and dig around the corporation."

Nyske held onto my arm. "I can pretend to be your wife."

"Not much pretending necessary." I smirked. "But that all makes sense. When we land, we'll hit the ground running."

Rebecca nodded and leaned back into her chair.

But Frank leaned forward. "So, if I suck your cock, would I become immortal too?" He nearly choked on a laugh, knowing how uncomfortable that question made me.

"Frank. I'm going to punch you when we get off the plane for that. And no, you'll be dead," I answered.

"Why will I die? Is it a dragon thing? Are you like deadly..."

"Frank, because I do not consent."

"Man. I'll say no homo. Just between bros, you'd be making me immortal." Frank gave me puppy dog eyes.

"We'll ask Hestia if she can make something for you when we get back." I held out my hand, and Nyske gave me a pair of earbuds that I promptly put in my ears, working hard to pretend that that conversation never happened.

CHAPTER 11

I was in the hotel room, alone.

"What are you doing?" Goldie asked, reminding me that I was never really alone.

"Stocking the fridge for Nyske." I reached through the portal back to the mansion and pulled some of her pickles from our fridge.

"You care for her."

"Greatly," I answered without hesitation.

"Then... why aren't you two... you know." Goldie hesitated, which meant she was talking about one thing only.

"Breaking beds?" I asked. Despite her new knowledge, she still hesitated around topics that involved my romance.

"That. Why aren't the two of you breaking beds? Instead, you are getting her pickles and having the nymphs fill the closet for her." Goldie pooled off my arm and sat in the kitchen chair, leaning forward.

The elemental took a humanoid form with a gold dress that looked like it had been painted on, and braids going down her open back on a strapless dress. Yeah, it was painted on.

Goldie was feeling a little sexual. It was time to see what she really understood.

"You have the experience now, why don't you tell me?" I asked her before closing the fridge. Nyske would be staying in my hotel room, and I wanted her to feel at home.

Goldie leaned on her elbow. But something in the position came off oddly. She didn't need to actually lean, she was simply mimicking a pose she knew. "Because you already have? Are you bored of sex with Nyske?"

I snorted. "No. She's a wild nymph who has been suppressing her urges in polite human society. When she wants to have sex, it would be any man's pleasure to accept her."

Goldie pondered a little longer. "Is it somehow special for you to not have sex?"

"I want to connect with her again before making it physical," I answered.

The gold elemental nodded. "Because your relationship before was very physical, so by focusing on the emotions now, you want to make it special?"

"Yes. That, and despite being a nymph, Nyske hasn't asked me to bed."

Goldie blinked, another motion she didn't actually have to do. She'd been working harder to be able to simulate life. "But she's a nymph. She should be dragging you to bed."

"Exactly. But she isn't. Instead, she's doing little things for me, and I'm doing little things for her. Showing each other that we still know each other, that what we learned about each other never went away and neither did our affections." I shrugged. "She's setting the pace. Nyske quite literally makes my schedule."

Goldie perked up. "So, if I want sex, I can just drag you to bed?"

I tried not to fumble as I put another jar of pickles into the fridge. "We are different. Each lady in the harem is different."

"Of course I'm different." Goldie molded around me, wrapping my shoulders in heavy liquid gold as she started to give me a massage. "No one can do what I can."

I groaned. She was getting really good at backrubs. "And why do you even want sex? You can feel pressure but no pleasure as far as I know."

"I don't care. I want to make my Zach feel good."

"We need a little more than that." I frowned at her.

"I'm *obsessed* with you. If you told me to go wipe out all humans in Brazil, I would flow over this land like a biblical flood and kill them all. As long as you smiled at me when I got back, I would be happy." Goldie's eyes rippled with color as she tried to make them as human as she could and lean forward around my shoulder to meet my eyes.

I had to suppress a shiver. Sometimes Goldie's level of obsession was intense.

"Maybe that's a little too much."

"Too bad. If you ever banished me, I'd just ground all of my magic and turn into an inert lump of gold rather than be away from you." Her massage squeezed me enough to hurt just a little as she found a knot and made her point.

"And what of me?" I asked. "You aren't giving me much of an option."

Goldie let up on her massage, resuming a more soothing massage as her head wound around to face me. "I am living gold. You are a dragon. I should be the perfect woman for you."

"Goldie. Stop worrying about that part so much and just let us develop naturally," I told her.

"NO! If I just remain as your bracer, you forget about me. I'll fade into the background, and it won't work. Rebecca just got down on her knees." Goldie pooled a humanoid form in front of me while a huge chunk of gold still rested on my shoulders and back, massaging me.

Her form rippled a few times as she got all of the details right.

Goldie had an immaculate hourglass shape and wore a thin gold dress over slightly paler gold skin. Her lips were plump, and I knew if I kissed them they could be as firm or as giving as she wanted. Her face was slightly alien, a little overdone, like a smut artist rendition of a face.

"Goldie, stop." I actually didn't know if I could physically stop her if she tried something. In this position, she'd be able to pin me in an instant. But Goldie was also mine, created from my mana. She would still listen to me despite her power.

She let out a frustrated groan and spun in a whirling dervish of gold, tendrils spinning out from her and threatening to rip the room apart. But she destroyed nothing.

A moment later, Goldie collapsed into the size of a dime before exploding back out, covering every surface in the room and filling the room with enough gold that I was worried that she was going to collapse the building with her weight.

Finally, she reformed her human shape. "Give me a next step. Something I can *do*."

I knew that she was hitting a limit that no one needed her to hit. "Well, if I'm honest, you've made it all about me, and that makes me uncomfortable. I enjoy stocking pickles because I know it will make Nyske happy. What can I do for you?"

Goldie looked down at her feet for a moment. "I want to do things for you."

"Tough. I need this to go both ways. Can I polish you?" I threw out an idea.

"That wouldn't happen to be a euphemism?" she hedged.

"Nope. I want to do something for you besides the basics of feeding you mana. That's how this works; that's how I show my affection."

Goldie turned into a grumbling puddle for a moment and swirled herself around. "Can I take some time to figure this out?"

"As much time as you need, Goldie. We have to get moving, though." I straightened my shirt.

She shot back onto my wrist, swirling and becoming nothing but a golden bracer again. "Of course. I'll be here when you need me."

She sounded surly.

I knew there was more that we needed to address for the issue to be resolved, but I didn't have the time at the moment. We needed to head down to the conference room and go over details with Georgia.

I left the room and got in the elevator.

"Maybe you could let me massage you," Goldie suggested.

"That's still about me." I replied.

"But I like giving them. You seem so happy," Goldie grumbled. "I want to make you happy." Before I could open my mouth, she sighed. "I know. I know. Think, Goldie. What do you want that isn't about making your Zach happy."

The elevator stopped, and the doors opened to let in a couple who looked around strangely, having heard Goldie, and they looked around but were unable to find anyone else in the elevator.

We all rode down the elevator in awkward silence, and when we hit the ground floor, I smiled and waved them out before hissing to Goldie. "Careful."

She squeezed my wrist in acknowledgement, and we kept on moving to the conference center. I glanced at my phone and then back up at the names in Portuguese, making sure I had the right one before stepping in.

"Good of you to join us." Georgia smiled at me.

Nyske raised an eyebrow as if asking what I had been up to, but I waved her off and took my seat.

"Frank, could you lock the door and put up a silence rune? Magic is quite handy like that sometimes." Georgia clicked and moved to the first slide. "Our targets are here, here, and here." A broad map of the country appeared on the screen. "Given Zach's resistance to influence and his ability to fly, we'd like you to take the cult. They are all the way out here. Agent Till will go with you." Georgia paused when Nyske pointedly stared at her.

"And so will Nyske," she added. "Agent Albright will bring my team into the church along with Frank and Maddie."

Those two nodded along.

"Do you have any resistance to angels' emotional manipulation?" Georgia asked.

"Yeah. They just make me hungry." Maddie flashed her fangs. "Frank is a wizard. He has some resistance, but not as much as Helena."

Georgia nodded along. "Then we all need to be aware of the potential for emotional manipulation. Remember to question your thoughts constantly while in the presence of a potential paranormal while we are here."

The door to the conference room exploded, sending wood chips everywhere.

I made myself as big as I could to cover the people on my side of the conference table. But without knowing who was entering and if they were aware of the paranormal, I didn't want to risk calling on Goldie or using my magic. The last thing I needed to do was inform Brazil's people of the paranormal.

Thankfully, when an angel walked through the dust with their wings up, my handicap was gone.

"Goldie." I held out my hand, and a gold sword pooled into it.

One after another, angels poured into the room through the debris that was still settling.

"You didn't hear my knock." An angel with six wings fanning out behind her pouted as she stepped in with a white dress and white heels that looked like that had never seen a speck of dust, despite what she had just walked through.

Her face was a lovely heart shape, and I instantly recognized her for who she was. The angel in front of me was the Archangel of Love, Helena's mother.

There was a flash of silver and white as Helena shot forward.

Four angels all converged on Helena, restraining the pissed off nephilim as the spear shook inches from her mother's chest. Helena was struggling with all her might, even her wings were twitching as she tried to get that last inch and shove her spear through her mother's heart.

Her mother put a finger on the spear and pushed it gently aside. "Daughter." Her mother didn't even pay me any attention, which was annoying. But more than insulting, it was a mistake.

I moved, channeling magic in my hand and hurling a web of lightning at her mother while swinging my sword to attack the angels holding Helena. The angels were forced off Helena, and after they dodged away, I extended my sword and took the arm of a second angel.

The angel screamed, and Helena used the chance to curl back in on herself, throwing her weight into the other two angels and smashing them against the wall.

Helena's mother was completely unperturbed by my magic, waving her hands and warping the space between me and her for my lightning to hit the wall harmlessly. "Now now. You shouldn't try and strike a lady. The rumors said you weren't Bart, but it's good to see it for myself."

"You know my father?" Her statement caught my attention.

"Know him? Of course. When they organized that little fun gang to hang out on a mountain and give the Greeks gifts, who do you think would be a more fitting figure for Aphrodite?" Helena's mother held her chin aloft and ran her nails along her neck, posing with a breathless look that would make the cover of any fashion magazine.

Something about the movement made my skin prickle and blood start to rush south.

She grinned at me like a predator. "I kept the name. You can call me Aphrodite. I see exactly what you are.

Those two finally couldn't resist each other, huh? And you released Ikta. Unfortunately, despite what gifts you may have, I have need of my daughter."

Helena recovered from fighting the angels and lunged at her mother again. Space fluctuated and her spear went past Aphrodite without touching her.

"Daughter." The archangel scolded as Helena swung again, but the spear shrank to the size of a knife and missed again. "You will not strike me."

Gunfire went off as Maddie pulled a submachine gun out of somewhere. The bullets all went wide, spraying a semicircle into the wall behind Aphrodite.

Aphrodite clicked her tongue. "Vampires." With a wave of her hand, the distance between her and Maddie shrank such that she could grab her by the throat and hoist her into the air. "I hate vampires."

"Morgana Silverwing almost got you, I bet," I tried to irritate the incredibly powerful angel.

She snorted, throwing Maddie against the wall with enough force to break bones. "She ate a baby archangel. Like the one you fought in Switzerland. We haven't sent any of the original three down in ages. Not since the paranormal were free to play gods."

The fight was at a stalemate. So far, our attacks had proven useless.

"I'm not your enemy, whelp." Aphrodite gave me a smile that threatened to melt my heart and turn me into a puddle. "Heaven is dying, and there is an opportunity. We have a dragon that is breaking the great patterns and reshaping the patterns for the future, mucking about with magic greater than he understands. I need Helena to fix Heaven."

"My mate isn't going anywhere." I stepped around to put myself between Helena and Aphrodite. The FBI agents all had guns out, and Frank had a wand out as he hovered over Maddie, but no one was firing.

Her mother's eyes flashed. "Mate? I thought that was a joke."

Helena wrapped her arms around my back. "I'm his mate, mother. He's marked me and you'll never get me away from him."

"Daughter. You do not understand. There is an opportunity, and if we don't take it... someone else will." Aphrodite took a step towards me, her white heels clicking on the floor.

I could feel the mana pouring off of Aphrodite and into her daughter. Realization of what she was doing made me growl and grab onto Helena and force her behind me.

But I'd waited a few moments too long.

Helena thrashed against me. "Let me go."

"Damn you. Don't torture her like this! Goldie, bind Helena." Liquid gold shot out of my bracer, binding Helena's arms and wings, pulling them both back painfully. "This isn't love. It's control."

Aphrodite's eyes were glowing a soft white as she turned her powers on me.

I put up every mental barrier I could, calling on my powers from Hell and Faerie to stop her.

She chuckled. "Ah. So you went and took a piece of Hell. Were you coming for Heaven? How naive. Heaven is united, and you can't even harm me."

"I won't let you keep doing this to her. Stop forcing her to love you."

Aphrodite's lips curled up in a small smile. "I didn't do it to control her. I did it to make sure she turned into a nephilim of love. This world is so full of putrid hate. Even the angels that wander from time to time end up feeding on hate-tainted emotions. They become abominations. I couldn't have that for my daughter."

"Well, you failed. I'm certain she's full of hate for you."

"No. She's still well aligned with love." There was a distant look in Aphrodite's eyes. "She will work, and we'll get this done to save Heaven."

I threw myself at Aphrodite, swinging with every ounce of strength I had. But when space warped around me and I found myself punching the air with concussive force behind her, I spun again, swinging with Goldie's sword.

My hit missed, but Goldie stretched herself. Spikes shot off of her as she tried to reach for the archangel.

A small thorn of gold nicked Aphrodite's cheek. Fury filled her face.

Suddenly, she was in my face, grabbing my head. Her softly glowing eyes filled my entire vision. I couldn't move as she tried to completely drown me in love. She wanted me to bend to her, throw my entire harem aside and endlessly worship her.

Goldie screamed, and a storm of golden blades pushed Aphrodite back, scoring a number of small red cuts on the beautiful angel.

I was caught up in a moment of indecision, my emotions swirling. And unfortunately, that opening was all that Aphrodite needed. Aphrodite grabbed Helena, and with a flap of her wings, was gone.

I felt endless loss at the beautiful angel leaving, like my heart was ripped out of my chest and crushed.

"Zach." Goldie took on her human form and grabbed my face in a firm grip, holding me still as she pressed her lips to mine. "Come back, my Zach. That woman does not deserve your love."

I staggered and shook my head several times. "Sorry, she really juiced that one."

Glancing over the rest of the agents and Georgia, I frowned. "Think any prison in the world can hold something like that?"

Georgia shook some of the dust off her jacket. "No. At least not one we've built yet." She too took in her agents that were currently reeling from seeing what the power at the top of the paranormal food chain looked like. "If anyone gets a chance, put a bullet in the bad angel's head, I'll help you with the paperwork."

Chapter 12

I frowned, sensing for Helena's mark... but... I couldn't find it. A growl built in my throat as I pushed on my senses. I had been able to sense my mates amid the fae Wilds and across planes. How could Aphrodite hide Helena from me?

"Is he okay?" Georgia asked.

"I will be. Give me a second. It feels like I just went through the worst breakup of my life." I groaned and let Goldie's obsessive love come through with how she held me. Feeling the loss of the connection of one of my mates hit me hard in the gut.

Part of me didn't want to take advantage of her, but after what Aphrodite just put me through and the sudden loss of Helena, it helped.

"We'll need to change the plan." Georgia moved into strategy mode.

"No. We are scrapping the plan. Well, I am. Please feel free to continue to snoop around for financial crime," I answered. "A woman like that doesn't wander around here for nothing. She wants something, and there is no way that the paranormal in this country don't have at least a small idea of what's happening."

"What are you suggesting?" Georgia asked. I'd expected her to toe the line, but it looked like Aphrodite's display had brought her to her senses.

"We are heading to El Dorado. It is the paranormal city in South America; well actually, there are seven cities of gold. El Dorado is just the most famous one." I rubbed my forehead against Goldie for a moment before pulling away. "We need to find it."

I was rapidly thinking through how to get Helena back. That was my top priority.

Nyske was tapping away on her phone. "Morgana will come show you."

"She's going to drain me dry," I chuckled.

Nyske shrugged.

"That's fine. Tell me where I'm making a portal." I glanced over at the FBI team. "What are your plans?"

"Going for the financial angle still. It's my only option." Georgia frowned. "But get my damned agent back."

Rebecca looked torn as she bit her lip. "SAC, my partner just got taken."

"Go. We'll focus on the church and see what we can't dig up. The cult will almost certainly have a few angels, and we are suddenly without the help needed to deal with that." Georgia wasn't happy, but she also wasn't stopping me.

I flashed her a smile.

"Morgana is ready in your office," Nyske told me, putting her phone away.

I waved my hand and a portal opened.

My blue and now showing vampire wife stepped through. "Dragons aren't welcome in El Dorado, for obvious reasons."

"Don't care. I'm going. Helena's mother just showed up and ripped her out of my hands. I need to know what's happening here and how to stop it." I set my jaw.

Morgana nodded, apparently anticipating that answer. "Then what are we waiting for?"

I didn't need to wait. Goldie snapped back to my arm without another word while I marched out of the hotel with Nyske, Morgana, and Rebecca trailing behind me.

"Helena is going to hate being a damsel. She's going to yell at you for freeing her and insist that she can do it herself." Rebecca laughed.

"Oh god. She's going to be the worst damsel in the history of damsels. How much do you want to bet she's beating some angel's face in right now?" Morgana chuckled darkly as she mimed holding someone down and punching them.

I looked over, smiling at my mate who was now wearing silk shirts instead of her typical corsets. But she'd kept her leather pants, now with an elastic band at the top stretching around her growing bump.

I groaned as the last time I'd tried to save Helena came back into my mind. "She's a terrible damsel. But we need to get moving. Nyske, can you cover us while we take off?"

"Sure. As long as I get to watch you undress." Nyske waved her hands, and a glamor settled around us in the field next to the parking lot.

I shucked my clothes and threw them in my bracer, ignoring the leering gazes from my ladies. At this point, I was comfortable in my skin. Trusting Nyske's glamor, I went straight into my dragon form, packing on thousands of pounds and letting my wings fan out.

"Really?" Nyske grumbled as she worked to keep the glamor active.

"I like to spread my wings," my voice rumbled. "Hop on."

Goldie poured over my back, making little bucket seats for each of the ladies.

Once they were on, I was able to cast the invisibility spell over all of us and take off.

I beat my wings hard, pressing my face into the wind and enjoying the feeling of it rushing between my scales. Flying myself felt so much better than that damn tiny metal tin they'd put me in to bring me to this country.

"Head north. It's along the Amazon river," Morgana explained.

I leaned into the wind and climbed higher to see if I couldn't rise above the wind. With Helena now missing, I felt an urgency as I pushed myself harder.

"Zach. You might not make the whole flight if you push this hard." I could hear the frown in Nyske's voice. "I know you aren't happy."

"Damn right I'm not happy. Aphrodite just took my mate."

"Yes. But you have all of us with you, and you need to be careful. And dragons are not welcome in the cities of gold." Nyske reminded me.

"But I'm not an asshole dragon," I answered confidently.

"Good luck proving that as you drool all over their gold," Morgana chuckled.

"Then why are you leading me there?" I shot back, more than a little upset about Helena.

"Because you asked, and even if she's a grumpy angel, she's one of the Plushies. Plushies don't abandon each other," Morgana answered.

"She's right. Plushies are family," Goldie chimed in. "We are all stronger together."

I rumbled, happy that my mates were all getting along just fine.

"Who's a good dragon?" Rebecca rubbed my back. "Now, slow down so that you get there rested. It sounds like you are going to have some trouble. If you need to blow off some steam though, I'm down. We just need to shrink you a little."

"Just a little?" Nyske snorted.

"I like 'em big, and he did not disappoint." Rebecca howled with laughter.

***

I used my face to part the clouds.

"See it?" Morgana asked after two hours of flying.

"No. I don't see the shining golden city."

I could almost hear Morgana's eyes rolling in her head. "It's heavily warded, so you might not."

"My dragon eyes are up to the task of seeing through that," I reassured her. "The place is huge. Any advice on how to approach it?"

"I'd just fly in, perch on the tallest structure, and let out a nice loud roar to get things started," Morgana sighed. "You aren't much for subtlety, so we might as well fly in and get the hostilities over."

"She's not entirely wrong. And the move would get you talking to the important people pretty quickly," Nyske agreed with Morgana's plan.

I smiled, pleased that for once I could play to my strengths.

"Great. Let's make a stink." I curled down from the clouds, flying over the rich green rain forest with a giant winding river that tore through it.

The city rested on the river banks like a jewel atop a crown. It was big, probably a few hundred thousand people, all hidden from the world. The difference between it and Philly was stark. Where the paranormal community there had integrated and hid among society, these people had hidden themselves entirely.

It came as no surprise to me that as soon as I crossed the threshold for their wards, alarms blared in the city and paranormals shot up into the sky.

Three of them were different types of birds that I had never seen before, and another three were strange serpentine angels, the basilisks. They were heading my way, but they were also spread out, not quite sure where I was.

I let my invisibility drop, my gold scales glittering in the sky before I shifted half of my scales to red. The look on their faces when they realized what exactly they were up against was priceless.

"Halt! Dragons are not welcome here!" One of the Basilisks flew towards my head.

I got to pretend to be a cantankerous dragon and blow smoke over them. "I mean you no harm. However, I am searching for one of my mates. Do not bar me." I had to flap hard to hover my giant ass body.

"Leave." The basilisk in front was a big man who's only clothing was a cloth tied to hide the transition from his chest to the serpent tail that was the bottom half of his body. "Or I will turn you to stone."

The three different birds swirled around us while the other two basilisks hung back. They apparently didn't wear much clothing even for the ladies.

"I'll kill them for threatening you." Goldie appeared between my horns. "Crush them and their city, and then we can go to the second one and ask them. Maybe they'll be more polite."

The basilisk's eyes shot to her. "Is that a gold elemental?"

"I'm Zach's," Goldie announced.

Her answer seemed to incense the basilisk. "Kill them. Aim for his wings. Even a dragon won't survive a fall this far."

One of the birds became a bolt of lightning as it shot into my wing. The animal tore through my relatively weak membrane.

I roared and spun midair, trying to bite the bird, but it was fast and slipped away in a field of static. Golden Faerie fire erupted from my mouth, chasing the bird through the sky as I dove to pick up some speed.

"Your wing." Goldie sounded murderous.

"Don't worry about it. This is my fight." I dove, spotting the blue bird below me, my claws outstretched.

Seeing me, it folded its wings and went straight down into a nosedive. I knew I was being baited. The bird being far smaller and lighter, I assumed it could pull out of a dive a lot faster.

But I wasn't without my own tricks.

My weight made my dive faster, and I rocketed down on top of the bird, grabbing it in my claws.

"ZACH!" Rebecca was screaming as she held onto her seat.

A portal popped open in front of me as I shot into it, reappearing above the clouds where I could easily pull myself out of the dive with the bird in my clutches.

"Who are you?" The bird tried to freeze my claws, but they only shifted to silver and white.

"Ice won't work on him either," Goldie proudly announced.

The bird shifted into an old woman, and I had to be careful not to crush her as she shrank and I tried to maintain my grip.

"The rumors are true?" she asked.

"I can't confirm when you don't tell me which rumors." At that point, I'd heard a bit of everything.

"You took control of part of Faerie? The Wilds?" the old woman asked.

I laughed, and as a dragon, it made a satisfying rumble. "No. I took over *all* of Faerie. The Winter, Summer and Wild queens are now my mates."

"And you've set your sights on the cities of gold." If she could, she would have tried to kill me with her glare alone.

"I have not." I glided around, high over the clouds watching for them to come for me in more force. "One of my mates is a nephilim, daughter of Aphrodite. Aphrodite recently attacked her and brought her here to Brazil. I want to know where."

"There are plenty of angels here. I will not sell them out." The old woman tried to freeze me again and failed.

"Goldie, contain her. I don't need to start killing people if I want a friendly reception." While I wanted Helena back quickly, I also recognized that I had an opportunity to change the way the golden cities saw dragons. Killing them all would not win over their hearts.

A small army of figures shot up above the clouds. There were the two remaining birds and the basilisks, but this time, a choir of angels had joined them.

I let fire spill out of my jaws as Goldie took the old woman, and I flew down above the sky, blanketing it with lightning. If someone were down below, it would look like a terrifying storm had rolled in.

Angels twisted and turned, trying to avoid the lightning. More than a few were struck and their bodies locked up, falling back below the clouds.

I took the chance to swoop in, and my jaws crushed an angel before I pulled away from the group. They threw spells at me, but Goldie covered my back.

The sky above the clouds descended into chaos as the fierce battle raged on. The fliers from El Dorado huddled closer together and continued to try and knock me out of the sky. More than a few of their attacks were focused on my wings.

Only by staying at a distance could I dodge them. I wasn't entirely on the defensive, pouring lightning out of my mouth and raking it through the group. But just as the distance helped me, it allowed them to protect themselves.

One of the basilisks with shimmering emerald scales lunged from the group. Her eyes bore into mine and her hypnotic eyes threatened to lock up my muscles. But the mental effects of a basilisk was far from the toughest thing I'd dealt with lately.

I swooped down. Now that she'd broken from her pack, all I had to do was get close enough for Goldie to shoot a hook off my back and reel her in. "Good work."

One of the angels suddenly sparkled bright red, his wings changing color as he surged through the crowd for me. As soon as he charged me, the others followed suit.

I felt a different emotion slam into me.

The feeling was different from the wrath I'd felt in Hell. Wrath was about violence. This was stronger; they were hitting me with hate. The feeling wasn't just destructive, but self-destructive as well. It was suffering for both parties.

Drawing on Hell, I pushed the emotional magic away. As the emotion cleared, I suddenly spotted an angry, destructive burst of magic fly from the lead angel.

I wasn't able to get out of the way in time, but I was able to take the hit on my side rather than my wing.

The magic burned and cracked my scales as I shifted my flight to careen away from the charging mass. I dipped into the clouds to hide myself as two more jags of red magic surged through the clouds.

I let out a small groan.

"Zach?" Goldie asked.

"Fuck that hurt," I answered.

"It's hate," the basilisk replied, still trapped by Goldie.

"I know… that's… what happens to angels when they stay on Earth too long, isn't it?" I played back what I was told.

"Yes. We are supposed to kill angels of hate on sight." The new basilisk was apparently chattier than the first.

I got far enough away to be safe and started to climb back above the clouds. "But they aren't getting killed now?"

"No... people have been angry. First one wasn't killed; instead, people argued over whether it was right. The delay caused more and more to appear." The basilisk bit her lip. "There are too many now. Some factions among the city rely on their support and continue to encourage this spread."

"So. How badly am I going to piss someone off if I kill them all?" I asked.

"You'll have chosen—"

"Princess," the old bird cut her off.

"Oh. Didn't realize I was carrying a princess around. Better make sure we keep you safe. Goldie, Nyske, please join me in taking out these angels. You don't have to hold back."

"What about me?" Morgana scoffed. "Just because I'm pregnant—"

"I thought you weren't using your magic," I answered.

There was a loud clack as Morgana racked a large rifle on my back. "I'm not. Goldie, make me a tripod."

"I feel like a battleship," I grumbled.

"You're a very good battleship," Morgana cooed like she was talking to a baby before bursting into laughter.

I rose above the clouds, and as her gun began to go off, I decided I should reclassify it as a cannon. "How long have you been holding onto this?" I shouted over the wind and the rapid-fire booms of her gun.

"For like six months. Ah, it feels so good to finally use it! Wahoo!" Morgana shouted into the wind as she fired over my shoulder with a cannon that felt like it belonged more on a battleship. Every time it fired, I could feel the recoil through the tripod.

The rattle of her cannon drowned out any other noise. I hated the racket, but the gun was very effective at picking angels out of the sky.

Not to be outdone, lightning poured from my mouth into the crowd of fliers once again, giving Morgana more than a few easy targets. It didn't take long for the angels group to break and flee back down towards the city.

"If I come down with you, do you think I can avoid getting shot long enough to talk to someone important?" I asked the princess.

The basilisk huffed. "I am someone important. But yes. Let's talk."

CHAPTER 13

Ryley, which I'd learned was the name of the basilisk princess, pointed down at a large temple amid the city. "You can land there. Umm... but don't break everything."

The temple below was entirely made of gold with little in additional decorations, but the detail of the carvings on everything blew the mind. No two were the same, and it had all been clearly done by hand.

"Don't worry. He comes with landing gear," Rebecca chuckled.

"Goldie, can you peel them off me as I shift?"

"Yes, Zach!" Goldie chirped, excited to be asked to help me.

I was understanding more and more what she needed.

Backwinging above the temple, I slowed myself down as Goldie pulled the people off of me as I started to shrink. She gently put my riders down.

Goldie even shot several pillars of gold down to support me as I shrank and stood naked among dozens of wide-eyed basilisk guards who watched me like I was holding a deadman switch and screaming at the top of my lungs.

"I got it." Goldie wrapped herself around me, giving me a golden robe that flowed with my movement.

"That actually fits in better than your shirts and jeans." Morgana smirked.

I looked out over the rest of the city and felt my greedy dragon heart clench. I wanted it all. Yet, it wasn't mine to take, and I forcefully pushed it from my mind.

"This way." Ryley slithered forward on her emerald-green scales.

The old woman who had been a large, blue bird hurried after her, fussing over the princess.

Now that I had a chance to really look at the basilisk, I took her in. She had bright red hair that contrasted with her emerald scales. Her body was lithe and athletic. There was barely a hint of fat on her as a long row of abs stuck out. Though, that didn't make her very curvy. Instead she had a fluid grace that fit more in tune with her serpent half.

"We are going to see my mother. She leads the city." Ryley looked Goldie over. "Can I ask, is that an elemental?"

Goldie spoke, "Yes, I am. When Zach was young, before he knew he was a dragon, he panned for gold and slept with said panned gold under his bed for years and years. I am *his* elemental. His mana is the only mana for me."

Ryley's eyes flickered to my face before she kept on moving.

"Don't worry. She won't ruin your city either, as long as no harm comes to me. I know that given her element and what your city is made out of that she might be a bigger threat than me," I answered.

Goldie grumbled, "If they hurt you, I'll rip it all up."

"It isn't that." Ryley hesitated. "We'll talk to my mother when we see her."

The hallways of the temple were worn smooth, with a few clear tracks, no doubt from all the basilisks. It seemed the temple was a haven for them as our group ran into many of them in the halls. I knew the city at large housed a large number of different paranormals, but all I saw were basilisks in the temple.

Thankfully, Ryley's presence stopped them from doing more than staring at us with hostility.

"This way. I'll ask that you wait here until you are called to enter." Ryley stopped in a small room that must have just been a waiting room.

I glanced around. Strategically, the area was a very unsafe place to wait. Yet I was trying to convey that I wasn't a threat, so putting up a fuss and showing distrust likely wouldn't help discussions.

"Sure. We'll make ourselves comfortable." I squeezed a smile onto my face.

Ryley ducked her head and slipped out with the older woman giving me the stink eye before following after the princess.

"They could just blow up this room and take us out," Rebecca muttered. "Goldie, can you give me a suit of armor?"

"No, they won't do that." Morgana had a vicious grin. "If they did, they might hurt my baby. And if that happened, I'd bathe in their blood."

"Would you like to go back to the manor?" I asked her, but I left the question open for all of them.

"Nope." Morgana waved away my concern. "Just because I'm a little pregnant doesn't mean that I get benched. Besides, now you are more bite size, and it appears we have a moment before all the fun kicks off." Morgana swayed her leather ass towards me, putting her belly to the side so that she could get close and pull my head down with her hands, nuzzling into my neck and starting to lick and kiss her favorite spot.

"That's oddly hot." Rebecca watched.

"Want to get a ticket and take a seat?" I teased her.

Rebecca wrinkled her nose. "I'm fine with being human. Especially if I can learn some magic." She wiggled her fingers.

Morgana didn't take to being ignored and bit down hard on my neck before teasing the holes open wide and slurped like a fat kid trying to get the last out of his juice box.

"Shit. Are you that thirsty?" I groaned, feeling light headed for a moment before my healing kicked in.

Morgana didn't respond as she kept drinking while wrapping her arms around me gently. Finally, she pulled away with a sigh like somebody savoring their drink.

"It's not so bad. But the kid is taking a lot." She licked at my neck. "That, and I think I've crossed the border into being a bloodlord. I don't have the reserves yet to go long."

"Congratulations." Rebecca beamed.

Morgana pulled away from my neck as it healed. "We knew I was close, or else I couldn't have gotten pregnant. I wasn't sure how much of that was him, but my base needs have gone down as this little parasite continues to leech from me."

"Don't call my kid a parasite," I grumbled.

Morgana smirked. "He/she kind of is. Oh, can you wait until we get the gender? Maybe we'll do one of those big gender reveals."

I dead panned, sure she must be kidding, but still cringing. "No."

"But those are all the rage. We can make national news if we turn it into a forest fire." Morgana had a grin that told me she didn't really want one as much as she wanted to tease me about one.

"Imagine if every nymph wanted a gender reveal," I prompted.

Morgana's eyes went wide in horror.

"Thank you." I gestured at her and chuckled. "Now you understand my fear. I'm standing firm on a hard no gender reveal policy."

"At least we are doing a giant joint baby shower," Nyske answered, pulling me over to a seat, planting me down and then sitting in my lap.

"So all of you are buying gifts for each other?"

"With your gold," Nyske clarified.

I growled at her.

She booped me on the nose. "No growling. You growl too much."

I wiggled my nose playfully. "I'm a dragon."

"You can still overdo the growling," Rebecca chimed in, and Morgana nodded in agreement.

"You can growl all you want for me." Goldie chimed as she poured off my bracer, making Nyske roll her eyes. "I saw that."

"Yes. I know. You are a very nosy elemental," Nyske chided her.

"I can make my nose smaller." Goldie's nose shrank down until it was gone.

I ran my hand over my face. "That's not what she meant."

Goldie blew a raspberry at me. "I know." Her nose popped back into place. "How long do you think this is going to take?"

"As long as it has to. I'd like to repair a little bit of dragons' reputation here as well as figure out what the heck is going on with the angels. That angel of hate was far stronger than the ones I'd fought before." I remembered the dark red blast from the angel and shivered. "Where did these angels of hate even come from?"

Morgana shrugged. "It sounds like it's angels that have been out of the celestial plane for too long."

I had a realization and ground my palm into my forehead. "We did this. By moving the portal, we probably stopped a lot of angels and cherubs from going back. At the very least, we made this worse."

"They've been turning to hate to survive." Morgana's brows pinched down. "Don't feel sorry for them, though. If anything, it proves just how disgusting some of those birdbrains are. They could have pushed for so much better, but instead, they took an easy path."

"They attacked my Zach." Goldie literally bristled, creating spikes all over her skin. "They die."

"Now that we've once again confirmed that Goldie will wipe out a small city for you, what's next? Because the way I see it, the angels of hate might actually be our best allies." Rebecca quickly got everybody's attention with that statement.

I raised an eyebrow. "How so?"

"Think about it. Unless they can revert, they aren't going back to Heaven. So, whatever plan Aphrodite has, it might not be in their best interests." Rebecca's answer made sense, and I was mad I hadn't considered the possibility.

I rubbed at my chin. "That's very possible. Let's see what the basilisks have to say before we set a course."

As if summoning them, there was a knock on the door before the old woman poked her head through, still glaring at me. "She'll see you now."

"Time to face the music." Morgana pushed through the door first and every protective instinct that I had clawed at me to stop her. I even reached forward, but I stopped myself from scooping her behind me. I had no doubt I'd pay for it later if I did.

Rebecca moved through next as Nyske put her hands on my chest and went up on her tiptoes for a kiss.

"What was that for?" I grinned like a fool.

"For being you." She settled her heels back on the floor. "And for not pushing Morgana down so that you could go through first."

"Shh," I teased. "She has really good ears. But, yes, I'm trying. The dragon instincts do not help with all the pregnant ladies around."

Nyske winked at me, pulling me through the door a moment later. "Well. I hope I was a good distraction there for a moment." She grinned and the kiss suddenly made sense.

"Thank you."

"I'm here for you." Nyske grew serious as she stepped into the room.

I followed after her.

The room was a giant chamber with ornate gold pillars all around. A few pillars had what looked like large emeralds set into them, and with the basilisks around, I wondered how often those were changed.

"Welcome." A large female basilisk rose from the top of the dais. Her expression was unreadable, but she looked like Ryley's spitting image. Only, she was several times longer and much heavier in the chest. Her tail coiled back and forth, and I would be impressed if she could still take flight.

"Thank you for having us." I bowed slightly at my waist. "I know my ancestors and yours did not always get along."

"They never got along," she corrected me. "Dragons have always let their greed rule them."

I flashed her a bitter smile. "Hopefully, I can be better. I was actually raised as a human, and I'm more than just a dragon."

Her eyes flickered to Goldie before returning to me. "The new Dragon King, I presume?"

"Apologies. Zach Pendragon, Dragon King, Emperor of Faerie, and King of Hell." I smiled.

"Quite the conqueror." Her expression turned downright chilly.

Goldie squirmed next to me like she wanted to say something, but she held herself back. I was proud. She really was learning to control her impulses.

"I don't think of myself that way, but I can see it. No, I married into the Emperor of Faerie title, and I retaliated against Hell for coming to Earth and stirring up so much attention that the FBI cracked down hard on the paranormal."

"Yet you still conquered among your vengeance," she answered.

I nodded. She had a point.

"I did much of the conquering." Goldie lifted her chin. "Mammon tried to attack him, and I crushed the Prince of Hell."

The basilisk queen's brows rose higher with each word. "You are a powerful gold elemental to be able to pull off that feat."

Goldie stuck to me like glue. "I'm his elemental. His mana is the best and most powerful."

"I see."

They wanted something with Goldie; that much was clear.

"Yes, well. I also killed Asmodia, who attacked while we were working to take down Beelzebub. He was behind the attacks in our city." I painted the whole picture. "Asmodia and Mammon just got in the way, unfortunately."

"Is my city in your way now?" She raised a single eyebrow.

"I don't think so, and I certainly don't hope so. My mate was taken by angels." I wasn't sure how much of what I said earlier had been relayed to her.

She leaned back on her coils. "Yes. Angels are certainly the topic of the day. I would thank you for ridding the city of some of the more hateful ones." She steepled her fingers. "I'm not able to speak for any of the angels, so I'm not sure what I can give you."

I resisted narrowing my eyes. She wanted something, but she wanted me to give up my strategy first.

"A lay of the land would be nice. I'm a long way away from Philadelphia, and even further from Hell and Faerie."

She nodded. "In South America, the seven golden cities each control part of the continent, much like Philadelphia is the hub for half of the United States."

"Only you get to let your freak flags fly." Morgana grinned.

"Yes, Mrs. Silverwing. We enjoy being out in the open, which means we have rules. And infighting is one thing we strive to control. Many different manners of paranormals call the cities home. The angels have been particularly active lately."

"Three archangels are here in South America." I waited to see her reaction.

The queen's eyes narrowed at that for a brief second. "I had not known that. Three." She tasted the word. "Are they here to deal with their fallen brethren?"

"The angels of hate?" I asked to clarify.

"Yes. They are... problematic at present."

I almost felt a little bad knowing that Morgana and I likely had a hand in exacerbating the issue. "Again, that's where my information is lacking and preventing me from taking action. Are they all working together or against each other?"

"With the archangels present, I expect change to come. They have no tolerance for such angels of hate. But in the last years, more and more angels were going down the path for power and survival." The queen pursed her lips. "This increase was organized. There was one behind it all."

"You are sure?" Nyske blurted out.

"Positive." The queen's gaze turned distant. "They were recruiting and have taken over one of the seven cities. As you can imagine, their presence in the other six has grown... concerning. Even here, we've felt the pain."

"They pack a punch." I touched my side.

"Yes, well most of us cannot survive such a blast as my daughter described that you took." The queen looked over her shoulder.

Ryley was lurking in the back, watching quietly. But when her mother glanced her way, she nodded again in confirmation.

"Thank you for not harming her. Given our two people's history, that goes a long way to relieve me. But despite my willingness to help you, my hands are tied. The protector of our city was severely injured when they went to assist the other city that was attacked."

"And who protects a golden city full of paranormals?" My eyes slid to Goldie. I was starting to piece together what they were going to ask me about.

"You are correct. Each city has an elemental. Enough gold, infused with our blood and mana for centuries, has created elementals of gold. To hear that your Goldie was born in the short span of your life is a miracle to my ears."

I nodded. "You want help with your elemental?"

"It would go a long way towards building trust, and it would enable me and my people to assist you should the worst come to pass." She smiled as the conversation stalled.

It would shock me if she didn't know more, but I also knew she was not going to offer everything up until she got the help she was seeking.

"Is there any more you can tell me?" I probed for more.

"I'll reach out to the other queens; no doubt, they know more. But until our elemental is restored, it would be very dangerous for us to pick a side in this conflict." Her smile was tense for just a moment.

Her answer and what it would take to win her assistance was clear. Thankfully, the ask seemed fair. The help of a queen never came cheap.

"If you'd be willing to help me understand more of your elemental's situation, then I'll see what my harem and I can do to help."

"Wonderful. Ryley, please guide the Dragon King to the lower levels. Unless, of course, you need to rest from your journey?" The queen added the last part as an afterthought.

"No. Let's go now. But I may require rest before I'm able to truly start helping." I didn't make promises, but her urgency told me she knew more than she was telling me, and it likely was time sensitive. I trusted her motivations enough to know it was in my best interest to keep moving.

CHAPTER 14

"Why do you not just pin her down and force it out of her?" Goldie asked as we walked down the golden hall behind Ryley.

I noticed Ryley's steps falter a little at Goldie's words.

"That isn't how we are doing things, Goldie," I spoke a little extra loudly on purpose, smiling to myself as Ryley seemed to relax.

"But you, or I, could just smoosh the whole city." Goldie winked at me. "You know. Splat!" At least I now understood that she was playing this up to get a reaction from the basilisk princess.

"Not going to happen. Even if I could, I genuinely don't want to. I've spent my time trying to protect paranormals." I laid the protector card on thick for Ryley to hear. "Besides, they need help with a gold elemental. Isn't that like a relative to you?"

"No." Goldie crossed her arms. "I'm related to you."

Rebecca snorted.

"Not like that! More in a m..." Goldie grumbled and muttered under her breath, too soft for me to hear. Though, I could guess what she was saying.

"Down this way." Ryley took us down a set of stairs that had wide, shallow steps that allowed her and anyone else without legs to smoothly glide down.

But the nature of the stairs made them twice as long for anybody stepping. We slowly started winding our way down the temple.

"This is going to be a lot of stairs, isn't it? At least my back feels great," Rebecca commented while stretching her back.

Morgana glanced at her.

"What? I'm feeling particularly youthful. Being my age was no cake walk on the physical demands of this job." Rebecca shook her body back and forth.

Ryley glanced over her shoulder. "I took you for a human?" It came out as a question.

"Oh, I'm human. But I'm forty-five. I recently sucked some Dragon King cock and bounced back to my twenties." Rebecca grinned at the basilisk.

One of Ryley's eyebrows rose slowly but steadily.

"Don't mind her," I reassured Ryley.

"Your harem is quite lively. I expected you to have a firmer grasp on them." Ryley slowed down to walk closer to our group. She hesitated when I didn't respond immediately.

Truthfully, I didn't know exactly how to take that.

Morgana burst into laughter while Goldie shot her a dirty look, and Nyske shook her head slowly.

"No. He does not have a 'firm grasp' on us. His harem, and harem hopefuls, are part of a group called the Golden Plushie Society. We work together. Besides, Zach is a very friendly dragon," Rebecca clarified.

"Dragons aren't friendly," Ryley stated emphatically.

160

"Eh. I wouldn't say I'm a giant teddy bear, but I'm fair."

"He's really a softy," Morgana interjected. "As long as his mates are fine, he just wants to cuddle in a giant pile of gold."

"Yes. That is the problem," Ryley grumbled. "Dragons can never control their greed. Mr. Pendragon, while we will tolerate you for now, I do not believe my mother will allow you to stay long term."

"What about at least establishing a relationship that, should issues cross our borders, we can cooperate?" I asked.

"That... would be feasible." Ryley cast a wary glance at me. It seemed the fear between basilisks and dragons was still very much alive in the princess.

"Then that will have to do." I gave her my most charming smile.

We wound our way down the long stairs into the bowels of the temple.

"What happened to the elemental?" Goldie asked.

"Like you saw before, the angels of hate are quite potent. They attacked one of the other golden cities. Our elemental had a pact with them and left to defend it. The city was lost, and our elemental returned and immediately retreated to recover." She shook her head. "Truthfully, we know little. The elementals here in South America are ancient. It retreated down here and merely warned my mother that she would be unable to call upon it for some time."

"It's down here?" Goldie clarified.

"Yes."

Goldie frowned down the stairs. "I can barely feel anything."

"Not all elementals are you," I teased her. "You are a walking giant magical battery that constantly absorbs my mana."

Goldie puffed out her cheeks. "Did you just call me fat?"

All of the ladies turned to stare at me.

"Of course I didn't call you fat. You aren't fat."

"Called me giant," Goldie grumbled.

"You are, uh... an excellent battery, and you do drink my mana constantly," I answered.

Goldie sighed. "Is that all I am?" she pouted, and I held back a deep sigh. This was not getting better.

Trying a new tactic, I pinched her cheek. "You know that you aren't fat, and I don't think you are fat."

She beamed at me. "I know, but watching you squirm a little is fun. The other wives do it."

I noted that she was counting herself among my wives. And I also noted that apparently she could learn from their bad behaviors.

Ryley watched us out of the corner of her eye as we reached the bottom of the stairs. In front of us were a huge pair of golden doors. "Through here. But the doors are hea—"

I had to put a little strength behind the pull, but I managed to open the doors.

"Don't underestimate him," Rebecca chirped from behind me.

Beyond the door was a cavernous room, dominated by a pool sunk into the ground and filled with swirling gold liquid. There were red streaks cracked through the liquid, sending off small black plumes.

A deep voice rumbled through the room, "Who dares enter my chambers unannounced?"

"Shut up, you weak ass puddle. That's no way to talk to my Zach." Goldie stepped forward and splashed the golden liquid with a swift kick of her foot.

There was another rumble, then the elemental pulled itself up into a humanoid form amid the pool. He was tall and broad chested, with red veins crackling through him. Yet he either wasn't as skilled or just wasn't trying to emulate humanity like Goldie. There wasn't enough detail on his face for an expression.

"Who are you?" he rumbled, the room once again shaking when he spoke.

Goldie stomped her foot, and the room stopped rumbling. "Cut the shit. You don't need to vibrate all the gold here to talk. Make a mouth and project it out of there, even if it sort of sounds a little brassy." Goldie crossed her arms and tapped her foot, waiting for him.

His mouth sort of ripped open, gold dripping from his low detail lips and his voice came out in a whiny high pitch, like someone over playing a note on the trumpet. "Who are you?"

"Goldie. Nice to meet you. This is Zach Pendragon. I'm his." Goldie gestured to me. "He came here, and the basilisks have information he wants, but would like me to assist you in return."

The elemental focused on me for a second. "Dragon. I will not be captured like your elemental."

I rolled my eyes. "That's fine. She's a hell of a lot prettier than you. What happened? It looks like you got a little messed up by the angels of hate." The red magic was a match for what I'd seen before in the attack.

"They attacked Cibola, and I went to their defense as promised, but I was too late. The elemental there was destroyed. I... I absorbed him in an attempt to strengthen myself for the fight."

I glanced over the crackling energy in the elemental. "Guessing that didn't go as planned. What can we do to help, and what more can you tell us about the attack? Any idea of their forces?"

The elemental swirled in his pool. "There were many angels." His head didn't move, but I could almost feel his attention shift back to Goldie.

"Any of them normal angels?" Goldie asked.

"No. Only the hateful." The elemental's humanoid form rode on a wave towards Goldie until he was only a few inches away. "You are very powerful."

"I'm a gold elemental that serves the Dragon King. I take much of his excess mana and have conquered Mammon's territory in Hell. He had lots of gold. I'm a lot bigger than you."

I glanced at her, scowling that I'd just had to backtrack from making a very similar statement about her size.

Goldie noticed and blew a raspberry at me. "Yes, I can say it."

The elemental stared at Goldie as she bantered with me. "You are young, but so full of power. Help me." He held out a hand for Goldie.

Goldie hesitated, glancing back at me for agreement.

"How about you explain how she can help you?" I pushed the elemental. Something was nagging at my gut. "We can't help you if we don't know what you need."

The elemental ignored me, continuing to focus on Goldie. Something about him made me uneasy, and that was all I needed to know.

"Ryley, we are leaving," I told our host.

"What?" The basilisk princess turned to me. "You can't."

"Goldie, come. Yes, we can. Your elemental is acting all sorts of weird."

Goldie shot back to my side.

"I did not say you could leave!" The elemental tried to make the room rumble, but Goldie stopped the vibrations.

"You can't keep me here." Goldie stomped her foot. "You either tell me what you need, or I leave."

"I am weak from my fight with the hateful. You must give me some of yourself." The elemental flowed around the room, blocking the door.

"Ryley, you understand what is happening here, correct?" I growled at her. "He wants to harm Goldie."

"Maybe he just wants a small portion of her. She could spare it, right?" Ryley turned to her city's elemental for him to confirm.

"No. To excise this magic, I will need a substantial amount of her power. That, and I have the experience to use the power better when the hateful eventually come to this city." The elemental rose up, its body continuing to pour out of the pool and solidify around the walls to keep us in the space.

"Yeah. You do that and I squash you like a bug." I stepped between Goldie and the elemental. "If you need a small amount of power for you to recover, we can help, but you aren't taking a bite out of my Goldie."

"Dragon." The elemental didn't seem to like me very much. "Do you think your kind can stop me? I have protected this city from your kind in the past." Its brassy voice echoed even without vibrating the whole chamber for the effect. A suffocating pressure began to build from the elemental as it pulled away and its mass rose from the pool, building on the humanoid form it already possessed.

The elemental was gathering itself into something far larger than the room could hold.

I lifted my hand, activating winter fae magic and creating a silver and blue barrier between the elemental and the rest of us. "You won't touch a hair on any of their heads." Despite my bravado, I wasn't thrilled to be trapped underground with the gold elemental surrounding me.

This entire structure was gold, and though Goldie had stopped him before, I knew that this elemental was far older than her and likely had his own tricks.

Goldie pressed up against me. "I can fight him." She wasn't going to back down, yet I wasn't sure I wanted the two elementals to tangle still. We weren't here to kill the city's elemental.

I looked over. Ryley was caught up in a whirlpool of emotions, fretting as her allegiance towards the city and its protector was challenged by the present situation. Either the elemental had thrown away its once noble bearings, or she never really knew it.

"What's happening? You are supposed to protect the city, not threaten a guest that I brought to help you." Ryley found the courage to speak up.

The elemental's head snapped into her direction. "I must do what it takes to survive and protect this city. If that means this young elemental must be consumed, then so be it. I do not fear dragons." Red energy of the angel's magic crackled over the surface of the elemental, causing its form to waver.

"I have brought them down as guests. They will return to my mother unharmed." Ryley puffed herself up behind my barrier, extending her wings and rising on her tail.

The elemental's form rippled as he stared Ryley down, its empty gold face expressionless. "Such words are useless in the face of death. I have lived this long protecting your people. This once, I ask for you to look away."

I could practically smell the fear wafting off the elemental. The elemental's judgment was clouded by its desire for self-preservation.

Glancing at Ryley out of the corner of my eyes, I tried to convey the gravity of the current situation. "You have a choice, princess. Are you going to allow your elemental to attack us, or are you going to stand up against it?"

Turmoil clouded her face as she turned back to the elemental. "You are the pillar of security and safety in this city. As long as you have lived, we have survived countless terrors." Her voice gained strength as she spoke. "But I will not tolerate you attacking a guest that came with good intentions."

The elemental roiled in the pool. Its liquid gold form bubbled with the invasive red magic before it pulled a step back. "I understand. I am sorry for my actions."

Letting out a breath, I relaxed slightly.

But then the elemental threw not just its humanoid form, but its entire golden mass, against my shield.

"I will apologize to your mother when I have recovered!" it yelled.

An entire pool of gold ground against the barrier I had erected, trying to wear it down. My barrier held for the moment, straining as many tons of liquid gold pumped against it, squeezing all of us into a narrow space.

I had both hands out and could feel the precipitous drop in my mana as the elemental tried to crush me. I could feel jets of gold slam repeatedly against my barrier.

"So. How about a portal?" Rebecca asked from behind me.

I bared my teeth at her. "Not a good time." My concentration was entirely on keeping the barrier up around us.

Nyske put her hand on my back and pushed with her magic to help me reinforce the barrier.

"No. Stop this!" Ryley shouted at the elemental.

"Princess, I do not think that it is going to listen to you." Rebecca clicked her tongue.

Morgana was the calmest out of everybody present. She had shifted into a fighting mentality. "Goldie, can you take it?"

Her question brought my attention to the elemental still at my side.

Goldie's face pinched down in a frown. "I am unsure. Zach?"

"Unless you are confident you can take it, I wouldn't risk it." I pushed with my magic, feeling my connection to the manor and the planes beyond swell as I drew mana from outside myself. I was barely holding back the elemental.

Goldie nodded sharply and turned to the barrier with determination on her face. "I can draw its attention away from you long enough for you to get out. That, I'm confident in." She pulled herself completely off my wrist and readied herself, pulling her shoulders back and standing up straight.

I suddenly found her missing from my wrist, which was highly concerning. Goldie never left me. "Don't take unnecessary risks."

"Open me a space there." She pointed at my barrier and started running straight for the barrier.

Her steps started to shake the room, and I opened the barrier in front of her. Like a bomb went off, Goldie exploded in a single direction, pouring out through the hole without sign that she was stopping.

The gold elemental pulled away from my barrier as the room shook. The two distinct streams of gold began to fight, folding over each other while twisting and thrashing against the room.

Goldie had a cooler, bluish hue, while the elemental of El Dorado not only crackled with red mana, but had taken on a warmer, darker color.

"Time to get out of here," I ordered, making Ryley jump as she had been staring at the two elementals that started twisting and thrashing in the large underground room.

While Goldie was distracting the other elemental, we were given our chance to get everyone out.

"Is she going to kill our elemental?" Ryley was frozen in place.

The doors burst open as basilisk guards rushed into the room, spears in hand radiating mana. The two elementals slammed into the ground, and the guards used their spears to steady themselves.

Morgana reached forward, grabbing Rebecca and zipping out of the room.

"What is going on?!" a guard screamed at Ryley.

"Get out. We need to get out of here," Ryley shouted back.

I had Nyske's hand in mine, and I pulled her with me.

The guards blocked our path with their spears. "Not until we get answers."

Both elementals shot up like twisting geysers before hitting the ceiling together. Liquid gold exploded everywhere.

I wasn't going to let my mates' lives be at risk any longer. I roughly pushed through the guards. Despite the magic on their spears, they were no threat to me.

Ryley slithered out with me, and the guards had no choice but to let us pass.

"Will someone tell me what is going on?" Ryley's mother came down the steps, her tail trailing long behind her. The queen glared at me, clearly thinking I was responsible for the current turmoil.

I glared right back. My mates had been attacked, and my dragon instincts were yelling at me to smash something.

Her face seemed like a nice target right about now.

CHAPTER 15

Goldie had no choice but to fight the other gold elemental in front of her. Her Zach had been trapped, but that might have been his plan all along. He always got out of sticky situations usually through his opponent, but this was her turn.

Goldie threw her body up as she flowed out of his shield, the other elemental following her perfectly for her to entwine them both. Then she slammed them back down to the ground, only for their liquid forms to explode everywhere.

The other elemental used that moment to collect some of her golden body that had been separated. He gobbled up her gold and the magic within. As he grew stronger, he threw all his mass against her in another attack.

Goldie might have been stronger than the other elemental, but she had already made one major mistake. She wasn't experienced in fighting another elemental, and he was.

They slammed into the floors, ceiling, and the walls.

Each time, a bit of them would splash away from their main bodies, and each time, they would wrestle over the loose pieces of themselves. Unfortunately, he was faster, used angles in this sort of fight better to have an advantage in picking up their splatter from each attack.

Time after time, he gained ground while Goldie found herself weaker. It was a battle of attrition, one that Goldie was losing ground against. She couldn't handle the more experienced opponent.

Every time the two elementals clashed, Goldie found herself scrambling to gather herself back. Instead of worrying for herself, Goldie was more concerned about her Zach and the potential consequences of the other elemental winning.

The distraction was not helping. Nor were her experiences on how to fight derived from demons that fought far more carefully than two elementals.

Once again, the other elemental slammed into her. She resisted fiercely, trying to rip the other elemental apart and feast on his golden form. Despite gaining some ground, her adversary was noticeably more experienced, skillfully maneuvering around her and severing a large portion of her golden substance before absorbing it.

All they had done was an even trade.

"Have you had enough? This would be far easier if you just surrendered," the other elemental taunted her smugly. It was apparent to both of them that, at the current pace, he would emerge victorious.

But Goldie wasn't ready to concede; her faith in Zach remained unshaken. She believed that he would come through for her, just like he always had, regardless of the circumstances. Summoning her remaining strength, she transformed into a massive wave, crashing into her foe and pushing him away from the doors to buy Zach some more time for his plan.

Their battle escalated, with both transforming into titanic, swirling waves that violently shook the temple and even the surrounding city. Despite the relentless battering from her adversary, Goldie persevered, and her spirit soared when Zach finally reappeared, overpowering the basilisk guards who had tried to restrain him.

With a triumphant smirk, Goldie taunted, "Now you'll see why crossing the Dragon King is a mistake." Transforming her face into a humanoid form, she flashed a smug smile at her opponent before launching herself at him, intending to sever another substantial part of his being.

But before she could fully take action, a colossal wave of furious, tyrannical mana engulfed both elementals. The raw energy tore at the opposing elemental, but to Goldie, it felt like a gentle shower of sunshine and rainbows.

They were being hit with the tastiest treat of them all, Zach's mana. Taking advantage of the other elemental's weakened state, Goldie regained her offensive stance, severing another piece of him and assimilating it into herself.

Zach maintained his intense aura, overpowering the room and forcing the adversary further back. Goldie seized the moment to dive straight into the core of her enemy, voraciously consuming his golden essence, tearing out massive chunks and integrating them into her own fluid form.

With Zach's support, Goldie managed to turn the tide of the battle quickly. She absorbed more of the other elemental than he had gotten in all their earlier hits, successfully regaining her lost mass and then some.

Determined to protect Zach at all costs, Goldie pressed her advantage, continually harrying the enemy and assimilating more of his entity.

***

I watched Goldie as she expanded, aware that the adjustments I had implemented had shifted the dynamics of the battle. It hadn't taken long outside the chamber to notice that the El Dorado elemental had a home-field advantage. Not only in that room, but the entire city of El Dorado was suffused with familiar mana, enhancing his power in the duel with Goldie.

I could tell she was losing, and I could not bear the thought of any harm befalling Goldie. For the first time, the absence of her usual presence on my arm felt like a persistent, painful reminder, akin to a phantom limb sensation.

My draconic aura washed over the room, driving off the home-field advantage of the other elemental and washing Goldie in her own source of power.

Fragments of wild fae magic floated before me and shot into the other elemental like a grater, tearing large strips of gold off of him as Goldie pummeled him into the back side of the room. A puddle came from her to greedily devour the strength she had lost.

"Don't kill it," pleaded the basilisk queen from behind me, her voice tinged with desperation. "It has protected our city for millennia. Please, show mercy."

I thought over her request, seriously contemplating allowing Goldie to obliterate the elemental that had attacked us. It had attacked us when we had come to it with open arms and offers of help.

But I also wanted to foster an alliance with El Dorado. Given Goldie's newfound dominance in the battle, I believed she could withdraw safely and put an end to the conflict.

"Goldie!" I called out, desperate to catch her attention. "If you can retreat without danger, come back to me."

As if a tether had snapped back into place, Goldie hurled the battered elemental against a distant wall before rushing back to me. For a split second, I braced myself for the impact of a tidal wave of molten gold. But the moment she made contact, she seamlessly reverted to her usual form, encircling my wrist as a bracer.

A tidal wave of gold stopped just short of crushing us all and continued to pour into the bracer.

I tenderly touched the bracer, eager to reconnect with Goldie. A smile spread across my face as I felt her familiar warmth enveloping my arm once again. "Good job."

The other elemental rose back up, posturing and threatening to attack me again.

I turned to the basilisk queen. "I pulled back my elemental, now it is your turn to do the same. If it comes at me again, I make no promises to its survival. You have already asked a lot of me."

The basilisk queen set her jaw before turning to the elemental. "Cease this at once."

"I am weakened." The elemental roiled and twisted in on itself in the center of the pool.

"You were weakened when we found you," I clarified. "The state you are in now is your own fault."

"I will not be able to protect this city." His brassy tone echoed around the room.

"Don't see how that's my fault." I nodded to the basilisk queen. "We'll see ourselves out."

"Ryley," she shouted for her daughter. "Please show them the guest rooms. I would like to discuss recent events with them in the morning after everything has settled down."

I raised an eyebrow at Morgana, asking her opinion. She gave me a subtle nod. Apparently, they were trustworthy enough to give them a chance.

"Please, follow me." Ryley slithered in front of our group.

It was then that I noticed that Rebecca was leaning heavily on Morgana.

"Is everything okay with you?" I asked her.

"That aura did a number on her." Morgana flashed her fangs as she smiled. "And more than a few of the guards."

I shrugged. "Goldie needed my help."

After the debacle with the elemental, Ryley led us away just as the basilisk queen began to scold the guardian of El Dorado. The atmosphere was tense as we maneuvered silently through the temple, Ryley guiding us up and through its corridors to a series of guest suites.

Eventually, Ryley broke the silence, her voice tinged with remorse as she held the door open for us. "I had no idea that was going to happen. If I had known, I would have never allowed you to go down there." She avoided my gaze, and it was evident that she was grappling with a sense of guilt.

I tried to ease her burden somewhat. It was fairly clear she hadn't anticipated that the other elemental would attack.

"That's water under the bridge," I spoke firmly. "I came to Brazil to find my mate who was taken from me. I came to El Dorado to gather information. My objectives remain unchanged, and they are my utmost priority." I sent a stern glance towards the basilisk princess. "To be honest, I'd prefer to leave as soon as possible."

Ryley finally met my eyes, her emerald-green irises reflecting a mixture of surprise and respect. "You're not as terrible as I assumed a dragon would be."

I couldn't help but smirk at her comment. "Oh, dragons can indeed be tremendously greedy creatures. I would be willing to wreak havoc across your city, perhaps even the rest of Brazil, if it meant finding my mate. But rest assured, I have no interest in your gold; I have more than enough of my own." As I spoke, I trailed a finger gently over Goldie on my wrist, feeling her resonate with my touch. I nodded at Ryley and closed the door behind me as the rest of my companions entered the suite.

As soon as I closed the door, Morgana swiftly pulled a knife from her bra, carving an enchantment into the back of the gold door before imbuing it with her magic.

"Fuck. That was a mess," Morgana said once she'd finished, shaking her head. "Are we sure we even want to spend the night here?"

"We could fuck off back to the mansion?" Rebecca asked.

"No. I think there's a decent chance we will meet with the basilisk queen again tonight. Otherwise, she wouldn't have asked us to stay." I rubbed at my chin. Nyske gently set Rebecca down on the bed, responding, "I don't think we have much of a choice at the moment. However, it would be prudent to ensure we're protected."

I had to agree with her, which was why I transformed one of my fingers into a dragon claw to carve additional enchantments into the door as well. The last thing I wanted was an unwelcome surprise in the middle of the night.

"Let me handle that," Goldie answered, separating from my arm. She circulated around the room, securing the perimeter and sealing the door with her body. "No one is getting in here, at least not without a fight," she declared, her humanoid chin jutting out proudly as she melted up from the floor.

While most of her mass was used in sealing the room, she still retained enough to form a humanoid body. I reached out, pulling her into an embrace and squeezing Goldie with a force that would have broken a normal person's back.

But Goldie's body could easily withstand the pressure. Her elemental body was far more resilient than that, and the way she squeezed me back indicated that she enjoyed the pressure.

"You did wonderfully," I praised her.

Goldie nestled her head against mine, finding comfort in our close contact. "It got a little scary there for a moment," she admitted.

Nyske settled down on the couch after ensuring Rebecca was comfortable in bed. "Now, we need to discuss our next steps." She crossed her legs and rhythmically tapped her foot in the air.

"She's right," Morgana chimed in, taking a seat on the couch as well. She patted the space between them, inviting me to sit. "Even if Goldie won, there's a significant issue: their inability to control that elemental."

I took the offered seat between them, still holding onto Goldie. She happily settled into my lap, causing me to sink further into the plush couch cushion. "Well, the simple answer is to get out as quickly as we can."

"Ask the queen if we can get the information and fuck off? In case you didn't realize it, she's in a tough spot. One of the other seven cities was destroyed," Morgana pointed out.

I leaned back, letting Goldie push me into the seat and mulled over everything for a moment before speaking out. "So, she likely knew more than what she was letting on. But she didn't tell us. Why?"

"Because that'll weaken her own situation?" Rebecca's tone came out as a question from the bed.

I motioned for her to keep going.

"If her enemy is the angry angels, and she doesn't want us to go for Helena, then that means that Helena's mother and the angry angels are in conflict. Enemy of my enemy is my friend sort of thing," Rebecca worked through the situation aloud.

"Right. So, she's in a corner, scared the angels of hate could come knocking on El Dorado's door with her elemental weakened. Us going for Aphrodite doesn't help her. It's only more likely to stir up the action at a time when she cannot handle more. So she bargained for us to help her elemental in order to strengthen her position." I glanced at Goldie. "Could that elemental take a bunch of angels?"

"Out in the jungle? No way. But here in the city, surrounded by the city's mana? Probably. You saw it before I stopped it. The elemental has superb control of all the gold in the temple. Much of the city would likely be the same. On its turf, it is likely extremely powerful," Goldie explained.

"And we just weakened it further." I rubbed at my temples. After being attacked, I wanted to help El Dorado less, yet it was the right thing to do.

"Okay. So, what if we make ourselves the enemy of both sets of angels? I don't know what they are up to here, but if they are both fighting over these cities, we probably want neither of them getting their grubby hands on it."

Morgana made a face and waffled her head. "True. But we need to prove that you are on the side of people who are suspicious of you for what you are."

"Let me take care of that tomorrow," I answered, my body starting to feel the intensity of the day.

"Banging a princess isn't the solution either," Rebecca spoke up, making Nyske chuckle. "If you are in need, I think one of us can help, though."

"Is that an offer?" I teased.

"I'd need help. Don't think I can wreck all the furniture and still walk tomorrow even if I'm feeling a whole hell of a lot younger." Rebecca smiled.

Goldie pooled between my shirt and my pants, pushing some of herself down under my shirt as she searched my face.

I gave her a slight nod. I'd gotten so worried about Goldie in the earlier battle; it felt nice to have her close to me. And I didn't want to push her away when I knew she was already feeling vulnerable.

Sometimes I worried about Goldie and how experienced and mature she really was, but the day's events had shown that Goldie had my back and was willing to do whatever it took for our family. She cared for me, and for those brief moments she'd left my side, I had to admit that I'd felt lost.

"Don't do that yet, Goldie." Nyske swatted her. "We still need to talk through our plan."

"I'm just checking his body for injuries." Goldie blushed. It was odd to see the expression on an elemental, and it was even weirder because I knew she had to do the change on purpose.

"Right. No banging the princess," I repeated. "I think the easiest solution is to ask for where the hateful angels are and take them out." I got us back on topic.

"Easier said than done, most likely. The other side has three archangels on the ground and still hasn't wiped the floor with them." Morgana leaned on my shoulder and played with Goldie's side as the elemental was slowly encasing me in gold.

"We could offer to help them. Given that Zach's now a fae, he's got to hold his oaths. He can make one to come to the city's aid should they be attacked, or give them some conditional vows of peace," Nyske offered.

I paused and raised my eyebrow at her. "That's actually a pretty good solution. If they bite, I'll need a solid oath that isn't going to cause problems for me."

"We can have one drafted up for you." Nyske watched as Goldie melted over me like a giant golden puddle.

My arms were now caught up, and I was pinned to the couch. "Can you get someone on that? Not sure that I'm going to have a chance to do much else tonight." I smirked at Goldie.

"About time for you two." Nyske got up and pulled out her phone. "I'll be in the other room. You two take this bedroom."

Goldie poured off the couch, dragging me with her. "This way. Rebecca, want to join?"

"I have so many questions," Rebecca answered. "But yes."

CHAPTER 16

Goldie deposited Rebecca and me on the bed, pulling her mass all over it and smothering both of us with her gold. "Mmm. I just want to touch you," Goldie purred as she poured over both of us and into our clothes.

She felt cool and smooth. I expected her to be harder, but she flowed like the finest silk over me, giving with my movements.

"Can you even orgasm?" Rebecca asked. "Sorry, was that insensitive?"

"We'll have to try," Goldie answered as her liquid flowed over Rebecca, quickly stripping the now twenty-something FBI agent as a dozen tendrils undid her buttons at the same time. "But I'm just excited to get you ready for him."

Goldie bit her lip and flowed over me, easily peeling off my clothes. Then I felt her amorphous form flow over every sensitive region of my body, slowing and gently caressing everything. It was like having cool water running over everything, washing every inch of me clean.

"Wow. That's a lot at once," I spoke, grabbing onto Goldie's main body. "That, and we are going to have to figure you out."

Goldie kissed me, her lips remaining firm before her tongue snaked into my mouth and circled around my own before sucking on it. "I'm going to experiment with you too."

Her hips stuck to mine, enveloping everything as her body rippled and pulled at my cock, exciting it and firming it into a rigid spear.

"Wow. I can see that." Rebecca leaned on her hand. "Is it like being trapped in a whirlpool?"

"Something like that," I grunted. "Goldie, this is a bit much. Focus on Rebecca for a moment."

Goldie pouted but flowed off of me and onto Rebecca.

Rebecca let out a little gasp as she was quickly lifted off the bed, her eyes going wide as she was surrounded by Goldie. "Whoa. Fuck. Fuck." She jerked in Goldie's cocoon before going slack. "Warn a woman."

Goldie pulled away with a smile. "That was just the opening salvo. Be prepared for far more. You've been warned."

I raised an eyebrow at the two of them.

"She just completely filled me and turned the vibration up to a thousand in both my g-spot and my ass." Rebecca touched herself. "Though, I'm pretty wet now. Wanna have a round, big guy?"

I pressed myself forward. Goldie parted around me but pressed around me, running her smooth liquid gold over every inch of exposed skin like she just couldn't stop rubbing herself against me.

It was endearing. Goldie really did just want a lot of attention and love.

But my focus was on Rebecca for the moment. I grabbed her hips, making sure to be more careful than how I handled my other mates. She might have become younger, but she was still human and more fragile. "Let me know if this hurts at all."

"Oh I will." Rebecca hooked her ankles behind my hips and pulled me closer. "But you are going to have to do a little more for us to find out. Besides, I have my twenties' libido back."

I pressed into her slick folds and lifted her shoulders to kiss her as I pushed deeper.

She groaned into my mouth and pulled back. "Goldie, I think we need a bumper."

"Bumper?" I asked, feeling myself hit the end of the road with a few inches still out in the cold.

"Yeah. So you don't crush my cervix. Goldie, just make a few rings around the base of his massive cock," Rebecca instructed my elemental.

Goldie complied, coiling a band of gold around what wasn't all the way in.

"Much better. Now you can go wild." Rebecca kissed me back and ran her nails over my back, but they barely even made my skin pink.

I thrust into her sex, feeling Goldie stop me from going too deep as Rebecca continued to scratch me as I held her close.

"Fuck." I was enjoying her slick, tight sex. My fingers sank into her thigh as I let myself go wild on her.

Rebecca arched her back, shoving her chest into me. "That's it. Go wild. Fuck my tight pussy."

I growled and nipped at her neck as she gasped from another thrust. "Careful what you ask for."

She grabbed my head and thrust it down onto her shoulder, holding onto my head as she started to sway her own hips, adding to my own motions. "Come on, big boy. I dare you."

My jaw crackled with magic, and I knew exactly what was happening. While I slid into her, I leaned down and marked her, pushing her against the bed as I hammered into her sex.

Rebecca spasmed under me as she came from penetration. "Fuck. Fuck. Hold on." She pushed me off as I continued to sink myself into her, her body shaking from the previous release.

I grinned. "You know, I'm not done with you yet." I slid out of her.

"Goldie, I'm tagging you in." Rebecca touched her shoulder and tried to look at the new magical scar.

"My turn." Goldie was a force of nature as her liquid gold form consumed me and cupped my erection, suckling on it. Yet she settled into her humanoid form with me balls deep in her. "Fuck me. Please, my Zach."

"We'll see what feels good for you." I started to find a rhythm. Goldie was surprisingly solid at the moment, but she hugged my cock like a second skin.

Goldie bit her lip, and I felt a little magic somewhere in her body. With the next thrust, Goldie gasped and vibrated as I felt magic at her hips.

"What have you done?" I asked, pushing myself into her and feeding mana to an enchantment inside of her.

Goldie gasped, and her whole body shook before melting over my cock in a wholly unique sensation. The constant dripping and running of her body over me felt like someone had wrapped me in a cold silk sheet and was running it all over my cock and balls.

"Whoa." Rebecca propped herself up. "I thought you didn't have that much sensation?"

"I am lustful for my Zach. Why shouldn't I enjoy him inside of me." Her sex rippled constantly, flowing like little ripples of liquid pulling at me in a continual motion.

I had to hold onto her hips as it drove me wild. "Goldie. What did you do?"

She groaned. "Made an enchantment with Sabrina." Her legs locked around me, and her sex went into overdrive, something wrapped tight around me and continued to squeeze and massage the head. "Cum for me, Zach. Feed me your seed. Give it to me," Goldie begged with gasping breaths.

My resistance was already low after being inside of Rebecca, and what was happening inside of Goldie wasn't helping. I gripped her golden form and pushed deep as I came inside of her.

Goldie wrapped herself around me and squealed with delight as an enchantment flared to life inside of her. I was suddenly hit with the same feelings she was getting, and I was nearly drowning in pleasure as my cock twitched as if it was cumming again, but it was still squeezing out the last of my previous round.

I let my jaws crackle as I bit her shoulder, marking the elemental as she continued to extract every single drop from me. She was worse than a succubus.

"Yes. You're my Zach and I'm your Goldie. Give it to me!"

"Careful what you ask for." I grabbed both of my women and squeezed them to me while I recovered. I was already anxious to try some more.

***

Getting up off the bed where Rebecca was passed out, I felt my mind free in post-nut clarity. Everything that had happened recently came into perspective.

"Oh fuck." I threw on a pair of pants.

Goldie groaned and snapped back to my bracer. "Where are we going?"

"To the basilisks. I have a few urgent questions for them."

Somehow, the moment away from the problem had brought more of the pieces together. Something wasn't adding up. Somehow, these hateful angels were holding off three archangels, and Aphrodite had some need of Helena.

I needed to talk to the queen to confirm my guesses. It wouldn't answer what they were after, but it would tell me the players.

Storming out of the room, Goldie pulled back her protections for a moment and hesitated. "I don't want to leave you. But we also shouldn't leave them alone."

I opened a portal to where the dragonettes were supposed to be stationed. Larisa and Sarisha popped out of the portal with hard faces.

"Guard the doors. Morgana, Nyske, and Rebecca are sleeping still. I need to go have a conversation with some basilisks. Oh, and no stealing gold."

"Yes, mate." Larisa snapped a salute. "No harm will come to them." She picked at the wall, and Sarisha slapped her hand before she could start carving away gold.

I nodded and continued to rush off as I rubbed Goldie with my other hand. "You're staying with me."

"Yes, mate," Goldie echoed Larisa, making me smirk.

I went through the temple. My dragon instincts were actually very good at navigating tunnels, and I remembered the way back to the throne room. Even at the late hour, the throne room was busy with people coming and going.

Ryley was motioning some people into the room when she saw me. "How did you know?"

"Know what?" My face dropped.

"Come in." She motioned me into the room and closed the door behind me, rushing me into the throne room. "There's a situation. But my mother will explain."

"Thank you everyone for the last minute..." Her gaze shifted to me as she paused, but then she continued. "We've received reports that there is a large group of angels headed this way."

I closed my eyes briefly and shook my head making a decision in the moment. "Which faction of angels?"

Many basilisks in the room turned towards me.

"We aren't sure..." She hesitated.

"Look. I know I came here to find more information about the group of angels led by Aphrodite, but I don't much care for the hateful either. Both of them are fighting over something that can only go poorly. As the Dragon King, I have resources. I can call upon the aid of Faerie Queens and titans." That last part of that statement was a bit of an exaggeration. If I called Nyske into battle, it wouldn't be what they were expecting.

The room was quiet except for a subtle murmur rippling around the room.

Finally, the basilisk queen bowed her head in my direction. "We would appreciate your help."

I opened a portal to my manor and grabbed the first nymph I saw. She happened to be wandering around the kitchen with a bowl of ice cream, dancing. "Please wake my wives. I will summon them shortly from here to fight."

The nymph nodded rapidly and glanced at her ice cream for a moment before putting it down and rushing from the portal.

There was a collective sigh of relief from the people present in the room. Me bringing my people to bear was more firepower than they could have hoped to scrounge through their entire city.

"Thank you," the basilisk queen acknowledged again.

"You're welcome. Now, I have questions about what we are up against. I believe I've pieced together a few parts. I've been working to figure out how the hateful could stand up against Aphrodite, but then I realized, they have a nephilim, don't they? How else would they stand up to multiple archangels?"

The queen looked around the room, checking who was present. "That is our understanding. An old nephilim leads them."

"What are they after?" I asked. When the queen seemed hesitant to answer, I told her what I knew. "My wife is a nephilim, daughter of Aphrodite. The archangel captured her because she needs a nephilim to complete some part of the task. Now I realize that both sides have a nephilim, and they are going to use them for something. I think it's relatively clear it won't be for our or Earth's benefit."

The basilisk queen coiled around herself. "The Tupinamba were largely destroyed, but there are several sacred sites still around. I believe they intend to use one of those, because they took the city on the coast that is central to several of the historical sites."

"There's a lot of belief in the Tupinamba people?" I asked.

"Yes. They were the native people. Once great friends to the paranormal." The basilisk queen rose from her throne. "We don't have much time. Please follow me to the walls." She slithered down the throne, and I fell into step with her.

"You have more to say?" I asked.

"This is not the first time in our history that the angels have come and made their presence known. Many generations ago, they did something similar." She glanced around to make sure we weren't heard. "It was then that the hateful began. The records of such time are poorly kept, but it seems they failed last time and created these angels of hate."

"Or created the nephilim that now leads them. I can only guess that, without that nephilim, they wouldn't survive as well as they have." I started feeling more comfortable with my assessment. Likely, Helena's mother's actions were similarly driven.

"Yes. Well, I have never met this nephilim, and I dread to do so now." The queen quickly guided us out of the temple where her feathered wings flapped idly for a moment. "Can you keep up in the air?"

Wings sprang from my back, one red and one gold. "Lead on."

The queen used her tail like a spring, coiling up and throwing herself high into the air for her feathered wings to expand to their full length and carry her up into the sky.

I crouched low before launching myself up to her height and kept up. "Your wings are a lot larger than your daughter's," I observed.

"Serpents do not stop growing their entire life. In multiple ways." She looked down to where her silk caged her chest.

I coughed into my hand. "Is now the time for such things?"

"You've seen my daughter. Is she pretty?" the queen asked me.

"Now is not the time, and my harem is quite full," I answered, gliding with her over to the walls where all manner of paranormals were gathering.

"Maybe not. But I will join this battle head on. If something happens to me, I would be more comfortable if a man of your stature were to help my daughter should she need it." The basilisk queen landed on the wall. "You seem intent on helping, and after this battle, I should give you the benefit of the doubt in the future."

I nodded my head graciously to her as we landed. "Thank you. Let me bring my people through."

I opened a portal down to the room that Larisa had been guarding. "Larisa, gather everyone. You are coming through the portal."

"Yes, mate." Larisa went straight through the gold door behind her, and I heard Nyske squeak in surprise shortly after.

While Larisa worked to grab the group that had traveled with me, I opened another portal to my kitchen in the mansion. Immediately, they marched out in full force. The three queens of Faerie let their mana explode over the wall and ripple through the city.

The basilisk queen gasped and recoiled. "All three? How?"

"My mate keeps Faerie together. He's replaced The Dreamer." Summer scanned the horizon with her chin aloft. "We have angels to kill?"

"Angels of hatred, likely led by an old Nephilim," I clarified.

Summer glanced over her shoulder at the others coming through. A small troop of my dragon mates, along with Sabrina and Leviathan exited. Kelly came out next, with her pack in tow. They took over the nearby section of the wall.

"Werewolves?" The queen almost seemed disappointed.

Kelly pointed a finger at her. "The biggest, baddest pack in North America." Her pack had truly swelled in multiple ways. Not only was it closing in on a thousand wolves, but many of her bitches were pregnant.

"Is it wise to bring them?" I raised an eyebrow.

"Hell yeah. Don't look down on them just because they have baby bumps. Plus, the betas will fight like crazy with their girls behind them." Kelly smiled with pride as she hunched over, swelling like the alpha wolves I'd seen in the past and continuing to grow to epic proportions for a werewolf.

"This is so exciting." Jadelyn clapped with a big grin.

Scarlett was next to Jadelyn and was currently dragging a hand down her face. "Don't worry, I'll keep her out of trouble."

"What do you mean?" Jadelyn pointed to the raging Amazon River next to the city. "I'm in my element." She then took off for the river and Scarlett didn't stop her.

"She'll be safe in the water." Scarlett moved in the same direction, with a large rifle case over her shoulder. "I'll make sure of it."

"Thank you." I kissed my first mate. "You make sure to take care of yourself too."

She nodded sharply, making the fox ears on top of her head flop.

Reinforcements continued exiting, but I didn't have time to give them all attention as a line of red appeared in the sky, falling from the clouds. I crouched low and shot off the wall with a boom. I pumped my wings, launching myself towards them to meet head on. I wanted to know the face of who I was dealing with.

Scales replaced my skin as I grew to eight feet tall and entered my dragon knight form. Goldie flowed over my hand and made a terrifying sword while she also seeped between my scales to offer me even more protection.

As I flew up to meet the angels, they slowed down and one hovered in front. Many of the angels had red wings, but the woman in front stunned me.

"Helena?" I blurted out.

CHAPTER 17

The nephilim looked exactly like Helena, only her wings were a bright, angry red, and her hair had turned the same red and fell down to spill over her shoulders.

The woman grimaced. "Is that my mother's latest new toy?" Her wings pumped to keep her aloft. "I am not this Helena. I am Odima, the once daughter of Aphrodite."

I shook my head, stunned by how similar she appeared to Helena. But I felt comfortable this woman was not Helena. The way she spoke and her body language was clearly different.

If Helena was a sharp weapon pointed at your face, this woman was a blade so caked in blood it had rusted, only to make itself more deadly.

"Why have you stopped me? You are not from El Dorado. Allies come to protect the city of wretches?" Odima crossed her arms and judged me.

"No. Actually, I'm here because Aphrodite kidnapped my mate, Helena. Helena is, I'm guessing, your sister." I watched the older nephilim carefully.

Even with my eyes shifted, her mana was so in tune with the world that I could barely see it. Rather, it was like all of the world's mana was her own.

Odima sneered. "Then I'll put her out of her misery soon."

A deep rumble reverberated in my chest as she threatened Helena. "You will do no such thing."

Odima's sneer softened to a malicious smile. "Oh. Do you hate me already? It comes so easily, doesn't it?" Her voice had a dark, poisonous allure to it that curled around my head. "You're a dragon. I'm sure you feel it. The gossamer of love has probably already been punctured by the temptation of lust. I'm sure you have no shortage of mates. But you've felt it, right? Hate?"

She continued on, watching me. "The strength, the vicious power lying beneath everything. From every corner of this world and every other plane, it beckons. It is a gift that everyone tries to deny, it rips away the weakness that festers in all of us, gives us glorious, brightly burning power." Her eyes glittered, sparkling as if they were two bright rubies.

"Take it. Take the hate and burn down this world so that it may start anew. It is simply nature taking its course, like a wildfire that will scour this world only to bring forth a new future. A brighter, better world, without all of today's pain." Her voice echoed through my mind and made my heart clench.

I shook my head and backed away a few feet as I wrestled free of the emotional manipulation she had tried on me.

"Why resist? Do you deny the sublime ecstasy that is the dark embrace of raw, untamed power that courses through every fiber of your being? It's intoxicating, is it not? It urges you to dominate, destroy, and rip asunder everything to let it be born anew in relentless, beautiful cycles of chaos."

Even though I'd already shaken off her abilities, her eyes continued to glow brighter with renewed fervor.

"You are insane," I answered.

She barked a laugh. "Of course I am. I will destroy everything, myself included, and I will do so with a smile on my face." Something twisted in her hand as she thrust forward. The weapon warped into a spear, rushing at me, but it was similar to Helena's weapon. I was ready for the attack.

I pulled in my wings and let myself fall out of the way.

We were clearly done talking. The worst part for me was that I could see Helena in her. Not just physically, but I could tell the path between them and where they deviated.

I plummeted down towards the wall and snapped open my wings, ready to join the others, but Odima apparently wasn't interested in me providing assistance.

She came flying down like an angry meteor, joined by the other hateful angels, who threw themselves down with mana crackling over their bodies.

But those below me on the wall weren't idle. Magical attacks erupted from the wall to clash with the falling angels. There were so many spells being thrown around that I was struggling to find all my mates.

Odima came up behind me. Her spear had become a wicked sword as she slashed out, trying to hit me.

I blocked with Goldie, feeling the nephilim's strength through the exchange, and let her push me away. She was far stronger than Helena.

A strong cluster of ice, fire, and lightning told me where my mates were clustered on the wall.

Fragments of wild fae magic rained up on Odima, forcing her to cover her face and giving me a moment to escape.

I had seen Ikta's magic rip into powerful creatures before, but to Odima, the hits only left shallow cuts that were healing immediately.

A blast of golden fire from Summer hit Odima next, and I lost track of the nephilim. Even with my eyes, I couldn't find her mana amidst the night sky. Considering how well she had blended in with the world before, that didn't make me feel any better.

But their attacks gave me a moment to turn my attention to the other angels crashing down on the city.

"Goldie, I'm going to be a big distraction. Kill as many as you can." I let my dragon half out of the cage.

My body swelled as muscle and bones competed for space and my body expanded. I was more than a rival for the previous Dragon King, Brom, though I wasn't as big as my mother yet.

My wings felt like they stretched out forever as they caught enough wind for me to career over the city as the shifting continued.

An angel, thinking they had the upper hand, flew into me with their fist crackling with red mana. Goldie handled them, lashing out with a razor-thin wire of gold that circled their waist before tearing right through them.

"Terrifying," I mumbled as my throat fixed itself and my shift finished. Pumping my wings, I pulled myself up and away from the city.

The angels hadn't been keen on fighting fair. Rather than fight on the walls, many had thrown themselves amongst the city, making the defenders more careful about where their attacks landed.

Kelly and her pack were already pouring in between the buildings. Fighting in close quarters would benefit the werewolves more than the angels. Not to mention they fought with enough numbers to pin down and rip the angels to shreds.

I kept myself aloft, heading for where basilisks met the angels in the air. I was doing a great job as a distraction. My giant fucking dragon body made me big target, and more than a few angels peeled away from fighting the basilisks to come after me.

That decision led to their death.

Goldie lashed out from me, tearing into any angel that got close enough to pose any risk. In the dark, they couldn't even see the razor-thin gold wire before it was tearing through wings and severing body parts.

I soared over the angels as they dropped from the sky in pieces. With the chaos of the current fight, there wasn't an easy way to use my breath or bulk without hurting foes and allies alike.

So I continued to sweep through the angels, letting Goldie tear them out of the sky. All the while, I was watching for Odima to reappear. I knew she was only biding her time, trying to find the right opportunity.

I saw her a moment before she attacked. A red beam of light slammed into my side, only slightly pushed aside by Goldie. The hit sent me rolling, and I had to strain my wings to pull myself out of the dive.

"Oh no." Odima pulled hard on my horns as I came out of the dive.

"Get off him!" Goldie tried to cut Odima to pieces, but the Nephilim of Hate just looked like she'd walked through golden spider webs as Goldie's strands strained and eventually broke against her body.

Odima laughed. "I've been bathed in hate since the Romans. One little gold elemental and whelp king aren't a match for me." She jerked my horns to the side and pulled me away from the fight.

I knew she was trying to keep us out of the fight. My protective nature wanted me to run back to give my mates even more protection, but my brain knew that I'd married strong, scary powerful women who could hold their own. The only threat I was worried about was the nephilim currently riding my head, and I was helping keep her from the fight.

"What do you want?" I growled and pulled myself higher into the air as she continued to jerk my head around and disrupt my flying.

"Maybe I want a new mount to go kill my mother with." She threw her hand to the side, and her weapon twisted into a giant whip that wrapped around my throat, searing my scales.

"Bullshit. But that gives me helpful information. You and your mother have fought, and you haven't won." I tried to buck her, knowing that it would be useless. I wanted her to keep talking.

"My mother is an ancient being of untold power. Thankfully, she won't recover nearly as well as I will on Earth. I can throw myself at her, foil her plans, and wait. Even if we don't activate it this time, I will get it eventually," Odima cackled.

I ducked into a roll and tried to throw her. "What are you two fighting over?"

"Wouldn't you like to know?" Odima gripped my horn tight and twisted.

More pain than I realized my dragon form was capable of feeling shot through me. Done with her riding me, I shrank and twisted out of her grip as Goldie hammered her hard to give me a moment to shift.

Back to my winged dragon knight form, I swung around, keeping an eye on Odima.

The nephilim hovered in the air, her blood-red wings fanned out behind her as she watched me. "What? Don't like people pulling on your horns? Noted."

"You are going to die." Goldie was more angry than I was as she shrieked across the sky. "No one harms my mate." Golden spikes exploded from her, trying to take down the nephilim.

Odima fanned out her wings and sprayed red, dagger-like feathers over me. Each one cut through my scales as she laughed and rolled midair to escape Goldie's wrath.

"You are such a cute little whelp with your pet gold elemental." Odima lashed out with her weapon again as it branched into nine leather cords, embedded with glass and nails.

Goldie blocked her hit as I focused on maneuvering in the air. I threw a ball of fire from my hand, but she warped space and dodged out of the way. Angels, especially old ones, were so damn agile. Odima swam through the air like a fish in water.

"So. You and Aphrodite are fighting over something. Why attack the seven cities?" Goldie transformed into a sword as I clashed with Odima.

Odima's own weapon returned to a crackling red sword, and we locked blades. Her eyes were red with a wild craze as she stared at me through the blades. "Interesting. They haven't been honest with you. They know exactly what we are after, and they are holding onto something we need." She grinned like a madwoman before she pushed hard against me.

I let us break apart before flapping my wings hard to slam back into her, using my heavier weight to drive her down from the sky. The cycle of us throwing ourselves at each other continued as I pushed us both closer to the ground.

"Even then you could just— you already have someone in the city," I realized.

She smiled. "It's probably already gone. But these people need to learn not to say no to us." Odima spun and flared her wings to come right back at me.

I caught her blade and rolled with it. "You just want to destroy everything."

"Now you're getting it." Her eyes glowed, and she threw an angry ball of mana at the wall.

I didn't have time to pay attention to where the hit landed as one of her wings came down on my arm, each feather like a serrated dagger trying to find purchase in my scales. Freeing one of my hands, I swung a right hook into her face and launched her down to the ground.

She made a lovely crater, sending dust up into the air. "If you become my mount, I'll get you your mate back," she offered from amid the dust.

"No deal. I'll get her back on my own and then crush you and your mother both."

An oddly erotic moan came from amid the dust. "I'd love to see you crush my mother."

Shooting out of the dust, she came at me with her spear in front. It grazed my cheek as I twisted. Odima's smile was wild as her arms strained to bring the spear back around and take my head.

A pillar of gold shot out from my chest, separating the two of us enough that Odima missed.

"Thanks, Goldie." I felt sweat bead on the back of my neck. That attack had been a far closer call than I would have liked.

Odima's spear shortened in her hand so that she could bring the blade to her tongue as she savored a drop of my blood like it was pure ecstasy.

"I know you like crazy..." Goldie hesitated.

"There is such a thing as too crazy," I answered confidently.

"Good. I was worried all she was doing was arousing you," Goldie admitted.

Odima heard us and chuckled as she rolled her tongue around her mouth. "There's no such thing as too crazy. Only not crazy enough. Trust me, I could break you until you want nothing but all the hate I could give you."

"Pass." I spun the sword in my hand and pointed it at her as the cut on my cheek healed over.

"You don't get a choice." She moved fast, her spear stretching through space as she tried to stab me.

No matter how I moved, the attack always remained poised to pierce my chest. The crackling red spear grew closer and closer no matter how I tried to dodge, and I started to panic.

I had thought that getting her on the ground would let me leverage my strength and remove her better flying abilities from the equation. Yet it seemed she was going to show me just how great she was at angelic magic despite not having any of the angelic emotional proficiencies.

Throwing up a portal did nothing as her spear somehow avoided it and kept coming for me.

I was running out of options, and her spear continued to close in.

Rather than let it hit me, I dropped Goldie and reached for the shaft of the spear to stop the hit. Odima manipulated space, and I cut both of my hands on the head of her spear, stopping it with just the tip piercing my chest.

I panted heavily, holding onto the spear with all of my might as she leaned forward, trying to skewer me.

CHAPTER 18

O dima pushed, and her smile cracked into the depth of depravity. "Come on. Just let me put a saddle on you."

I saw the flicker of something behind her and tried to school my face, but she noticed the shift in my attention. She tried to move, but I held her spear tight as Morgana appeared out of the darkness, her twin blades coming down with supernatural speed and the ripple of spatial magic on their edges.

Odima let go of her spear, blocking one blade with her wing. But the block still sprayed blood into the air as Morgana wounded the wing and spun low under it to cut with both blades. She left deep cuts in the nephilim's thigh and hip before the angel was able to throw herself away from my badass vampire mate.

"I thought I trained you better than this." Morgana clicked her tongue and rose back to her feet.

"She's a tough one," I answered.

The spear disappeared from my hand and reappeared in Odima's. I glanced down at my empty hand and frowned at the cuts that were struggling to heal as leftover mana from her spear resisted my regeneration.

"Oh. One of his breeders?" Odima smirked.

"What did you call me, bitch?" Morgana cocked her head. "Oh, I'm going to enjoy putting your head on a platter."

"Don't let her get under your skin," I warned Morgana.

"Too late. I hope there's enough meat under those feathers that I can make some mean chicken wings." Morgana spun both of her blades, waiting for the angel's next move.

Odima had healed almost instantly, but my cuts were still struggling. Every second Morgana bought me was time I could use to recover.

"Oh. That's cute. You think you can hurt me? The surprise attack might have gotten me, but you won't get a second one of those."

Morgana blurred forward, her blades trying to cut Odima in two. But every time she struck, even at full vampire speed, the hits gravitated towards Odima's spear and were blocked.

My wife pulled back panting, her face a bit paler than normal. With the baby taking up much of her strength, she was faltering quickly, and a protective instinct inside of me was surging.

Odima's head jerked to the side. Clearly, she'd heard something we had yet to register. She snarled before launching herself into the sky.

Morgana took another swing at the nephilim and missed before pulling out a rifle from her bra and taking shots at the fleeing figure.

"Stop." I put a hand on her shoulder. "You are severely depleted, aren't you?" I pulled her close and offered my neck.

Morgana was quick to latch on and start angrily sucking my blood. "Stupid chicken."

"I know." I held Morgana. "It is oddly frustrating how much she looks like Helena, isn't it?"

Morgana nodded, teasing open the two puncture wounds and continuing to slurp my blood.

"Alright, we are heading back. I'm going to carry you so that you can continue to feed as much as you need. Our baby comes first." I picked up Morgana as she continued to drink my blood.

I knew my priorities. Something had pulled Odima away, and I'd use that chance to make sure my harem was all intact and healed. Odima had been tough, which meant there was far more to come.

I'd learned that, in a head-to-head fight, I wouldn't have the advantage. She had no care for the city or the people inside, and that would continue to limit some of my actions.

But a plan was forming in my head for the next time we fought. Tonight we had been surprised, and my primary goal in fighting Odima had been to keep someone that powerful away from the city.

I surveyed the damage around the area the battle had been contained to. The walls still stood, and the city, despite the destruction, seemed to have repelled the angels.

I walked to the river to check on Jadelyn while Morgana continued to lick at my neck. The giant Amazon River rushed past, and I noted several red-winged angels washed up on the side of the river.

A quiet humming that resonated down to my soul made me glance up river to find Jadelyn combing her wet hair with a brush.

"Oh. Husband." Jadelyn kicked her mermaid tail in the water. "Nice of you to show up. Morgana, you've had your fill. Let him take a break."

Morgana pulled her teeth out of my neck and licked at the wounds. "He offered himself up. Plus, I saved him."

"I don't know if you..." I stopped talking as Morgana's eyes turned to meet mine. I decided to let her win that battle.

"Well. I'm glad you were able to look out for our husband." Jadelyn beamed at both of us before turning to Morgana. "Do me a favor and go check in on everyone. Get Pixie to do a roll call."

"I should help her."

"No, you shouldn't." Jadelyn slipped into the river and shot over to me, holding out a hand. Her white shirt was completely see-through as she leaned out onto the bank. "You are going to come here and let me distract you. Besides, Morgana can do it faster without you."

Morgana zipped off, taking the opportunity.

"Really?" I wanted to go find and count all of my mates and make sure they were untouched.

"What? I'm feeling bossy right now. I just drowned half a dozen angels. It isn't often that I get to come out in the field with you." Jadelyn jabbed the air playfully as I got closer.

"Well, you are pretty awesome." I glanced at the dead angels.

"You bet I am." Jadelyn was all smiles. Sometimes, with her running her family's massive shipping company, it was easy to forget that she could be a badass when she wanted. And when there was water around.

She hooked a finger at me as she swam a foot away from the bank.

"Come on out." I stepped up to the bank and held out a hand.

The beautiful siren came up and grabbed my hand, instead slowly swimming back into the water while giving me a half-lidded gaze and slowly shook her head. "No, husband. Let Morgana and Pixie do the roll call. You just had a hard battle and need to relax, not tramp around the golden city making our recently made allies nervous as an anxious dragon searches for his mates."

"I'm not that bad," I said, realizing that she had tugged me so that I was up to my knees in the water.

In a flash, she jerked me off my feet and into the water. There was an ache in me to go find and count my mates after the battle.

"It's not often that I get you in the water, and your siren wife is just too excited after seeing you let loose. You are a terrifying, powerful dragon." Jadelyn kissed me and ran her hands up my chest before she flipped us over.

I made a wild splash, and she wrapped me up in her arms, singing her song into my ear for a moment. It was like I short-circuited as her song wrapped around my mind, drowning everything else out. A giant ball of tension in my back unclenched.

She held me tightly as she swam through the river for a minute, singing her song and making me painfully hard despite my earlier activities tonight.

"Husband." Her voice cut through the water before she kissed me and breathed for the both of us. "I love you. You need to relax. Let me take care of you for a minute. The fighting is over for now."

***

I pulled myself to the shore a half an hour later, turning around to watch as a naked Jadelyn strolled out of the water behind me.

"Oh. This is where you are?" Kelly was holding her stomach swollen more than the others with her twins. Someone had given her a loose dress to wear.

"Alpha-alpha. Were you out here having fun with the fish?" Taylor cocked her hips. She was still nude except for a pair of bright blue cowboy boots. The werewolves were comfortable in nudity.

"My husband was very stressed after the battle and needed to relax. Honestly, if I hadn't helped calm him, he'd probably have torn through half of El Dorado to make sure all his mates were safe." Jadelyn combed her hair as Scarlett sauntered over, likely having watched us together from the wall.

"She's not wrong." Kelly shrugged but held onto her smile. "Probably would have scared all of those basilisks into kicking us out. They are already pretty nervous around Poly."

A portal opened up a moment later, and Ikta started to lead my wives through.

"We are all accounted for." Morgana smiled at me as she walked out.

I let out a huge breath that I hadn't known I was holding as soon as the portal opened up.

"Need some clothes?" Morgana pulled some from her bra and held them out to Taylor.

The werewolf wrinkled her nose. "Do I have to?"

"Yes," Kelly answered. "You had your chance to show him your body, now cover up."

My wives continued to come out of the portal, and I wanted to shift before wrapping myself around each and every one of them protectively.

"Look at him. Go give him hugs." Pixie shook her head and stepped up to me before falling down and wrapping herself around me. "We are okay. And I killed two angels!"

"She glamored one of them when they were dropping from the sky so that it ran face first into the wall. It was brutal. Like a bird flying full speed into a sliding glass door," Ikta chuckled, clapping her hands.

I pulled the nymph closer against me, glad she was able to stay safe. A moment later, Pixie was replaced by Sabrina who made my blood boil with her soft, supple form. Yev followed after. One by one, they all comforted me, reassuring me that they were fine.

"Okay. Now, what's next?" Scarlett brought the group back around to focus on the challenges before us.

Everybody present made up my harem. And it looked like the Demon Prince Leviathan had joined us. And somehow, Ryley had slithered her way into the meeting. A few helpers and nymphs moved through the group, making sure everyone was comfortable.

"Well, I had a few realizations before the fighting even started. Before I'd met Helena's sister. First off, Aphrodite said she needed a nephilim. Yet I realized that, if they were fighting this other side for something, then they had to have a nephilim too."

My wives waited for me to continue. "The stronger balance of power would make sense too, because somehow these angels have been holding off three archangels. So I started to wonder just who was on their side. And now we know.

"Her name is Odima. From what I gathered, Aphrodite tried to do whatever she's doing now back in the days of the Roman Empire. Odima was that first attempt, but she's become an angel of hate," I started out with what I knew.

"Wait." Sabrina spoke out. "Did Helena's mother do those horrible things to her to force her to still be an angel of love?"

The whole group went quiet.

"That's sick." Scarlett shuddered. "But it makes sense. So, she needed Helena to stay on the emotional paths of the angels while still being a nephilim. If three archangels came down to work on this, then we can assume it has to do with helping the celestial realm?"

"She could be triggering the rapture for all we know." Kelly threw her hands in the air. "I don't trust these angels at all."

"On that, I think we can all agree." I nodded along with many of my wives.

"It doesn't change that we are going to go fuck up Aphrodite and get Helena back. No one messes with the Plushies." Jadelyn stood, now in a pair of jeans and a silk top. Her hair was somehow perfectly in place, despite the mess we'd made of it in the water.

"Plushies!" Multiple voices shouted while other wives gave me a smug smile.

"Of course not. Helena is still the first priority, but I also don't want Odima to trigger the rapture or whatever they have planned." My eyes shifted over to Ryley, who shrank under my gaze. "Everyone, meet the princess of El Dorado, Ryley." I gestured at the basilisk. "Odima was attacking to steal something from your city, which leads me to believe that you might know more than your mother led me to believe."

Ryley's tail curled around her as my wives turned their gazes to her. Ryley shrank a little more under all the intimidating stares.

"I can check with my mother as to what they stole, and we might have more answers." Ryley cowered as Ikta leaned over her.

"Ikta, dear, please stop." I glared at the Fae Queen.

"Okay." She popped up, bouncing on the balls of her feet. "I thought we were doing the stare down thing until she was a shattered wreck of her former self and told us everything through blubbering tears. It's a specialty of mine."

Ryley looked at Ikta with horror.

"Not today." I shook my head. "Ryley, I'd appreciate if you could get us answers by the time I wake up. I think I need some sleep."

Ryley glanced around at all of my wives. "Are all of you staying?"

"No. We were in the middle of something and would probably like to get back to it," Jadelyn answered. "Actually, you can come with us."

I raised an eyebrow at Jadelyn.

"Oh, don't worry." She waved me off. "I won't let Ikta turn her into a shell of her former self."

"There's a lot of space between where she is now and there," Ikta added with a far too cheery tone.

Ryley's eyes were large as she looked to me for help.

"They taunt and tease, but you should be safe. If anything, you'll be better off than you are now," Leviathan answered, hand on her hips as her sapphire hair cascaded down her back. Her dress was torn up, revealing unblemished, porcelain white skin. The Demon Prince held the power of invincibility and a second form of a giant sea creature. Though her actual prowess in battle was lacking.

Ryley nodded rapidly as Jadelyn smiled and pushed her along. "Come on. Let's go talk to your mother first."

I realized I was oddly relaxed for still being so soon after the battle. But fighting was in my dragon blood, as was mating with my beautiful wives. Without Jadelyn's intervention, I wouldn't be nearly as calm as I was right now.

And I felt better knowing that the mysteries that had plagued me were starting to all become clearer.

The angels of hate were the ones who had sent the geists. It made sense that they were capable of making such creatures. It also would make sense to try to keep us away from the fight. Odima apparently won and got what she wanted if she could get control of whatever they were fighting over, or if she was able to stall until she was able to use whatever it was.

If nephilims were required, that also meant that it had something to do with the planar connection nephilim had both to Earth and Heaven. I could think of plenty of terrible things that they could use a connection like that for.

But if they needed the nephilim that badly, Helena was at least safe for the time being. Until Aphrodite could get her hands on whatever they were battling to gain, Helena was a necessary tool. And until then, she'd give her mother hell. I had no doubt that Helena was not being the perfect, doting daughter or considerate houseguest wherever they were keeping her.

I took a few deep breaths, realizing I was working myself up thinking about Helena's capture. I really wanted to punch something.

Pixie squeezed herself to my side. "You know. Some of the nymphs are starting to get pouty that you've been ignoring them."

"We just got done fighting," I argued.

Pixie tilted her head and raised an eyebrow. "Sounds to me like you probably have some energy to burn off so that you can settle back down." She pulled my head down to claim my lips and whispered, "Come with me. Let your Plushies handle the basilisks. They want to help. Jadelyn is yours and is going to put that queen in her place for you."

She ran her fingers through my hair and started to pull me backwards with her. "Portal to the manor. I'll make sure you get nice and tired so that you can sleep."

CHAPTER 19

J adelyn walked down the golden hall, unimpressed by all the gold. But she could respect the decorative touch they used when working so monochromatic in their decor.

"Does it really take basilisk blood to turn stone to gold?" Jadelyn asked Ryley to make conversation.

The Plushies were making a bit of a show as they headed back into the temple, wanting to back Zach and show the force behind them. From what little Nyske had told them, they'd already gotten the picture that the basilisks were less than welcoming. So they were here to show off.

Sure enough, everybody they passed had stopped to stare at the procession.

"No, but blood is the fastest. Our dead skin cells and other materials from our body do the same thing. At a certain point, you just have to accept it is going to all be gold," the basilisk explained.

"Is there a way to stop it?" Jadelyn asked.

The basilisk blinked.

Scarlett burst into laughter. "Jade, you are the only person that would ask her to not make gold."

"What? I appreciate gold as much as the next person... maybe not as much as our husband, but quite a bit. Unfortunately, I do like wood tones, beautiful marble works and contrast more." Jadelyn was thinking long term.

"Umm..." Ryley hesitated. "You could probably replace anything that turned into gold fairly easily. I mean, the gold itself would pay for the change."

"Then you don't know the cost of the best Italian marble," Jadelyn sighed. "It's not just about cost but availability too. It's fine. You'd be surprised how talented we Plushies are in our passions. Sabrina or someone might be able to cook up an enchantment so that you don't ruin the bathroom." Not to mention the whole place just smelled metallic. It would take a lot to cover it up.

Scarlett continued to snort.

Jadelyn just rolled her eyes.

"Can I ask why that's a concern?" Ryley hesitated.

"We are planning to invite you back for some wine after we talk to your mother. The Plushies are a very prestigious organization; we could probably take over the world if our husband wanted us to." Jadelyn set the hook.

"Oh." Ryley didn't know what to say.

"So, I didn't see you making big, dreamy eyes at my husband?" Jadelyn asked.

"It wasn't what you thought!" Ryley insisted. "I would never think of your husband. I— I—" she stuttered as the Plushies started laughing around her.

Jadelyn had a big grin on her face. "Yes. Well. Given how large his harem is, we aren't particularly concerned about other ladies eyeing him."

"Speak for yourself," Tyrande butted in. "His time is scarce enough as it is." She glared at Leviathan, who was still walking with the group.

Ryley drew back onto herself, but Jadelyn stepped in.

"Don't worry about them. You just need to focus on what you want." Jadelyn walked with Ryley to what was clearly a throne room.

Jadelyn would have decorated it a little differently, but the gems set in the walls were a nice touch. Putting them that high must keep them free of most of the transmuting effects of basilisks.

Jadelyn started to consider how the cleaning crew kept them safe and so shiny.

"We put an oil over the gems." Ryley had followed her gaze.

"Ah. See? There are some ways to solve these things." Jadelyn smiled. "Think outside the box."

"I thought the Dragon King's harem would be more... docile?" Ryley regretted the word as soon as it exited her mouth.

Jadelyn reached over, patting the basilisk's head. "Don't worry. We love our husband very much, and he does everything he can to show that he loves us too. But he's actually a big softie underneath those hard scales. Sometimes we have to be the bad guys for him." She winked as the previous person in the throne room left and it was their turn.

Ryley's mother, the basilisk queen, cleared her throat. "Thank you all for coming to our aid." Her eyes shifted through the crowd, probably looking for Zach.

"Hello. Zach is with a few of his mates who needed his attention." Jadelyn squeezed a smile onto her face, letting the woman make assumptions.

"Ah."

"Yes. You'd be best served to let him spend some time with them." Scarlett's tails flit back and forth in a tell that Jadelyn knew well. Scarlett's tails moved that way when she wasn't being entirely truthful. It was the same motions she made when doing illusions.

"And you are?" The queen was getting her bearings.

"I'm Jadelyn Scalewright, second mate. This is Scarlett Fox, first mate of the Dragon King." Jadelyn's smile grew as their titles made the queen straighten up.

Somehow Scalewright didn't get her to budge, but being the first two mates of the Dragon King did. Then again, she just saw him and his harem fight outside her city.

"Yes, and what can I do for you two?" The queen's eyes traveled behind them to the other women present.

The Fae Queens were well known, along with people like Morgana and multiple dragons. Yet the two of them were the ones up front doing the talking. It said quite a bit about Jadelyn and Scarlett.

The queen's coils rippled as she tried to shift back into a relaxed pose.

"Ah. During my husband's fight with Odima, the nephilim leading the angels, it seemed her true goal was to steal something rather than to destroy the city." Jadelyn laced her fingers and put her hands down, smiling at the queen.

She thought she'd start with simple discussion before she pushed too hard into negotiations. Trade into Brazil through portals would be a big boon to the expansions she'd been working on with Scalewright shipping. In order to make that route work, Morgana would need two or three relays.

Jadelyn looked around, reconsidering. She might need four. And then she'd space them so one was redundant and the lane would stay should something happen to one. It seemed like the area was frequently experiencing conflict.

She was already mapping where the four would go in her head and where there might be cheap real estate to drop a small bunker into when the queen replied.

"Yes. We are aware that things have been stolen. Apparently, there is an angel among her group that specializes in stealth. My people have only become aware of that after the fact. Unfortunately, we don't have cameras and some of the other technological improvements you take for granted."

Jadelyn beamed at her. "If you'd like them, I'd be happy to set up a trade route."

"Unfortunately, they don't last long." The queen's dour smile told Jadelyn all she needed to know.

Sabrina would be working on an enchantment to keep the transmutation at bay by the end of the week. They might think they'd tried everything, but Jadelyn was sure there had to be another way.

"We'll see what we can do. But can you tell us what we are dealing with based on what was stolen?" Jadelyn asked.

"Unfortunately that is a private matter for the city. While we accept your—" The basilisk queen gave her a faux polite smile.

"Ah, I see. Well in that case, Zach and all of us will pull away from your city and publicly fly on the other side of Brazil. Do you think your city will stand another night if he does that?" Jadelyn mirrored the queen's smile but it didn't reach her eyes. No, Jadelyn's eyes said under no uncertain terms that she was going to give up something for their help tonight.

Ikta took out a fold-out chair and stepped forward, placing a chair for Jadelyn.

Jadelyn gave a nod of thanks as she casually sat down, spreading out the folds of fabric over her lap as she tilted her legs to the side. She made sure she was perfectly poised before she looked back up and gave the queen a sweet smile.

The queen watched her carefully. "Your husband wouldn't do that."

"No. No, he wouldn't. That's why you are negotiating with me." Jadelyn put as much politeness as she could into her voice. "If we need to go to another of the golden cities because you've been a poor host, he will come to protect us."

"She's right, mother," Ryley supported Jadelyn, making the siren have to keep the smirk off her face.

"The power of the Golden Plushie Society shouldn't be taken lightly either." Summer stepped forward and put her hands on Jadelyn's shoulders. "This is the leader of the Golden Plushie Society. While the Dragon King controls Hell, Faerie, and exerts a large amount of control on Earth, who do you think are his eyes, ears, and when it is necessary, his fists? He can't do everything himself, and his wives are here to support him every step of the way. That includes negotiating when he's otherwise busy."

It wasn't quite a lie, but Jadelyn noticed the gaps that Summer was leaving, letting the queen make her own assumptions. Their husband really was too caring at times.

The queen tightened her coils and seemed to relent. "They took part of a Mouros artifact that was used by the Tupi to sacrifice powerful warriors."

"What's it called?" Jadelyn insisted, suddenly more interested. She loved a good antique.

"Serpentis Víbora Boca," the basilisk queen answered begrudgingly. "It is a giant golden serpent's maw that was said to grant the power of the warriors sacrificed onto it into the tribe's blood. Not that it actually worked. It was once made by the various basilisk tribes that are now the seven cities."

Jadelyn pursed her lips. "I think our biggest concern is that even if it doesn't work, they are going to sacrifice Helena. So, please let us worry about it. Was there any specific place where the sacrifices were held? Anything you can tell us that will help us prevent what they will attempt? I can promise you, what you felt from Zach before will be nothing compared to his wrath if one of his mates dies. Especially if you kept vital information from him that could have avoided that death." Jadelyn let her voice grow slightly more forceful, her own feelings of protectiveness over one of her Plushies rising up.

"My daughter would be a great candidate for this... society, don't you think?" The queen moved the negotiation in the exact direction Jadelyn had predicted. It was why Jadelyn had already discussed the concept with Ryley. She wanted Ryley to know she'd come of her own choice, and not because of her mother.

Jadelyn looked at Ryley hiding a wink from the queen. "I think we can do that. Now, the information."

"The artifact was broken up into many pieces... Manoa held the base, and it should still be there at the top of their temple." The queen sounded like giving up the information was painful.

Jadelyn looked over her shoulder and Morgana shook her head. "I'm going to need directions there. Then we are going to need a way to communicate so that Zach can come back here if the angels return. We'll coordinate with your daughter for that part."

The queen nodded and motioned for one of her people, who pulled out a large rolled up map. Jadelyn avoided letting out a sigh. They really needed to enter the digital age.

"The seven cities," Ryley spoke up, pointing at spots on the map but being careful to avoid directly touching the parcel. "We are here." She was pretty accurate as she indicated the spot on the Amazon river. "Manoa is over here, on the coast."

"Looks like a very nice bay for shipping." Jadelyn studied the geography around the area.

"Ah." The basilisk princess sounded awkward. "It's heavily warded to keep people away and appears to be incredibly rocky. As things have advanced, there are even wards to make people think it would take too much effort to clear out."

Jadelyn chuckled, already imagining Scalewright ships cruising into the docks that likely already existed on the coastal city. "But they have a bay and ships? Right?"

The queen laughed. "Gold doesn't float. Basilisks don't sail."

Jadelyn hid her horror. "That's fine. Luckily for you, sirens do. Thank you for your information. Is there anything you can tell us?"

The queen shook her head gently. "Not that I'm aware of now. But I will share with you anything that comes to my attention."

"Wonderful." Jadelyn glanced at Ikta. "Let's head back now."

The fae queen's spider limb cut a circle in the air that became a glowing portal.

"Come with us." Jadelyn grabbed Ryley's hand.

"What if they come back tonight?" Ryley asked.

"Someone will tell Zach." Jadelyn led the basilisk princess through the portal, noting that she carefully avoided the edges of the portal by rather awkwardly flexing her tail. Jadelyn could imagine trying to cross the portal with her fins.

They stepped into a room with several tall party tables, many of them had half-drunk glasses of wine, and silk robes littered the floor and hung off the tables haphazardly. Lavender candles made the whole place come together.

"What's this?" Ryley asked.

"We had been interrupted." Jadelyn pulled off her shirt and pants, returning to just wearing her bra and panties amid the Plushie Society meeting before looking the basilisk up and down. Ryley already wasn't wearing much. "You can wear that. We'll get you a robe for future meetings. They are twice a month right now."

"They are?" Ryley's eyes were wide as many of Zach's other mates stripped around her. More than a few of them had started to show their pregnancy.

"What happened to all the nymphs?" Kelly asked.

"I think Pixie took them." Scarlett found her wine glass and downed the remainder before pouring herself another.

"Good for them." Summer smirked and glanced at Maeve. "Did Evelyn run off with them?"

"Who do you think was suggesting it to Pixie?" Maeve mimed. "Given that it is for Zach, I can't really complain."

"How many nymphs?" Ryley asked.

"Dozens." Kelly stared angrily at Scarlett as the Kitsune had no issue pouring herself a third glass of wine.

"What? I'm still on birth control. I can drink." Scarlett did a little cheers motion and took a swig.

"Really wish I could," Kelly grumbled. "Worst part of all of this." She rubbed her stomach protectively.

"Then I'll just have a glass for you." Scarlett had a wicked grin as she threw back another.

"I'll get you back for this." Kelly narrowed her eyes.

Jadelyn patted Ryley on the shoulder. "They are just joking. It's all in good fun."

Ikta twirled past them with a glass of wine in her hands. "This is why you need to be me. Already got pregnant. Made the egg sacs, and now I get to drink."

Several of the dragons looked about to speak up but Kelly held up a hand. "Save it. These two are going to be the best children ever. No drinking for me." She cupped her swollen stomach.

"So." Jadelyn grabbed Ryley a glass of wine and handed it to her. "What do you think of the Golden Plushies?"

Ryley looked her up and down. "Revealing."

Jadelyn sputtered into her own glass as she went to take a sip. "Fair. I hope we can show you a lot more as the meeting goes on. I was really hoping to strike up a deal with you or one of the other seven cities. You see, my business is shipping."

"Must be a big business if you get to be in charge of Fae Queens." Ryley's eyes kept gravitating to Summer, who stood out like a sore thumb. She was practically glowing.

"It isn't small. That's for sure. Come, let me bring you around and introduce you to everyone." Jadelyn flashed a disarming smile and brought the awkward basilisk princess around to introduce all the women. Meanwhile, the women shared stories from the fight, laughing and drinking together.

CHAPTER 20

I blinked away my grogginess to see Pixie sliding her skirt back on. "Time?"

She put her finger to her lips and pointed at the oversized bed currently covered in nymphs, half of which were on top of me.

Peeling limbs away, I climbed out to find Pixie with a set of clothes ready for me. She winked and motioned for me to follow her.

I stepped outside the bedroom, and she waved her magic over me to clean me and started handing me my clothes.

"So. I should be back out there finding Helena."

"Well, the good news is that Jadelyn negotiated with the basilisk queen. We know what is likely the last target for both angel groups. And we know where it is located," Pixie answered.

"Really?" I pulled my head through my shirt. "That's fantastic."

"Yes. The angels are gathering pieces of some old artifact so that they can sacrifice Helena." Pixie paused. "Or Odima, I guess? Maybe we should let her do that."

"If she's willing to sacrifice herself, she would only do it for something that's going to burn down the world." I had never seen so much hate in someone's eyes before. "Any choice she makes is going to be bad for us."

"The basilisks don't think the artifact does anything. But the artifact relates to the origins of basilisks, so each of the seven golden cities have a piece of it. One city has the base still mounted on their temple," Pixie continued, reading off something on her tablet.

"It does something if they are all after it. Aphrodite is older than dirt. She would know. Most likely, the basilisks were probably using it wrong. Given that the last time the angels made a play for this artifact was over two thousand years ago, I'm going to bet that whatever she wants it for can't be done on any given weekend. Aphrodite had Helena under her control before; she would have made a move earlier if she could."

My heart clenched at the idea of the torture I knew Helena was enduring every moment that she was away from me. I hated the feeling of failure flooding my body; I wanted to rip someone's throat out.

"It's okay. We'll get her back," Pixie reassured me.

I took a deep breath to steady myself. "I'm going to fly to this final city and survey it to make sure they don't stab me on sight when I open portals. Then maybe I can see the other five cities so that I can react if any of them come under attack," I thought through my options.

Pixie nodded.

My stomach growled like a caged bear, reminding its zookeeper that it hadn't been fed.

"After breakfast?" Pixie asked, an eyebrow raising.

"After breakfast," I agreed. "Whoever needs to be in the loop on this one can join me for breakfast, and I can run through my ideas and what to do next."

Pixie tapped on her tablet as she walked down the steps. "Done. Now, there is just one problem."

"What's that?" I asked.

"You took all of the nymphs out of commission, so someone is going to have to cook." Pixie smiled. "And it won't be me."

I rolled my eyes and went to wash my hands. "Can you get things to make pancakes and bacon out of the fridge?"

***

"I think that's a sound plan." Morgana lounged at the breakfast table where I had piled plate after plate of pancakes and plenty of sausage and bacon.

"It's by the coast too!" Jadelyn perked up with stars in her eyes. "I can be helpful."

I glanced at Scarlett who shrugged in agreement. "She's pretty safe in the water."

Jadelyn bobbed her head. "Yeah. What she said. I can join you on this adventure."

"Fine," I relented, knowing that we'd end up bringing everyone anyway. This would be a huge battle, and we were a family. We defended each other.

"You should eat more bacon." Jadelyn pushed the plate in front of me.

I chuckled, feeling oddly lighthearted despite everything that had happened. Reaching out with my senses again, as I had a number of times, I suddenly felt a connection I'd been unable to tap into growing stronger.

The table toppled over with how quickly I got up, causing Scarlett to jump up, her tails whipping out. Morgana was fast enough to get out of the way while Jadelyn just sat still, eggs plastered across her typically immaculate face.

"What?" Jadelyn asked.

I ripped open a portal back to Brazil and threw myself through it.

"Helena," I breathed, feeling her mark. I held onto the sense as my clothes ripped off. I exited the portal in the middle of El Dorado.

Scarlett, Morgana, and Jadelyn were on my back already as I shifted and threw myself into the air, beating my wings as hard as I could to push myself into the sky and towards my mate.

"Zach. We'll get her." Scarlett held onto my horns, her fluffy tails comforting me as they continued to bat the crown of my head.

"Of course we will," I growled, propelling myself forward with each stroke of my wings. "Then we are going to put her in a nice safe box until this is all done."

Morgana snorted. "Good luck with that."

"Really, husband. You should know better than trying to do something like that." Jadelyn patted my back. "Goldie, if need be, just tell us where he locks the poor angel up. We'll free her and you'll have to protect him from her wrath."

I grumbled as they all started laughing.

I knew they were trying to lighten the mood, sensing that my dragon instincts were on fire. But no amount of laughter was going to keep me from zeroing in on my mate.

The feeling of Helena grew closer and closer until I found myself straining my neck and squinting out into the sky, searching for her. As I grew close, I found she wasn't in the sky, but down in a forest below.

Homing in on where she was, I crashed down into the forest, fire in my throat ready to burn down a legion of angels to get to her. Trees snapped all around me, and I reared up, ready to crush my enemies.

"There you are." Helena's clothes had seen better days, tattered all around her. She was currently clearly exhausted, leaning on her spear. "Come to pick me up?" She pulled her spear out of a dead angel on the ground.

I huffed over to her, sniffing her with my nose and sensing my mark on her in a way that made me salivate. I wanted to nibble the nephilim.

"If you want to bite me that bad, you are going to have to get smaller. I'm not down for rough sex with someone your size."

I sputtered, an odd sound from a dragon. "How?"

"Maybe save that for later when I'm not looking over my shoulder?" Helena offered.

"Right. Everyone off. We are heading home." I popped open a portal with a flick of my claw. "Then you are going to tell us what happened." I glared at Helena.

The portal opened to my kitchen and I shooed them all through, keeping watch around us. I wasn't going to let us get lured into any trap.

As soon as I got my mates all through, I closed the portal behind me and grabbed Helena, prodding my mark to make sure it was her. "I am very happy to have you back, but I'm calling Sabrina and Ikta to come check you over."

"Prudent." Helena took a seat.

The table I had flipped over was gone, which meant the nymphs had clearly gotten up. I looked over, noting that the ice cream freezer had been raided and there was fresh food on the counters.

I got up to pile a plate brimming with food and deliver it to my angel while Scarlett wandered off to find a few magical experts to come look Helena over.

"I don't know if me getting free is really good news, though." Helena scooped some eggs off her plate. "A bunch of red-winged assholes crashed my mother's little space bubble at dawn today."

"Odima?" I asked.

Helena was still chewing and shook her head as if she had no idea who Odima could be.

"Your sister, or half-sister, I guess. Sounds like your mother has done what she did to you in the past. You are her attempt number two," I said the words kindly, not sure how Helena would take the news. I studied her face for any reaction, but she simply chewed her food slowly.

When I'd paused longer than she'd expected, Helena prodded me. "Go on. What else do we know about her? If she can kick my mother's ass, I kind of like her."

"Red-winged angels feed off of hate rather than one of the other celestial emotions," I explained.

Helena wrinkled her nose. "In case you are worried, that's not a risk for me."

"How do you know?" Scarlett leaned forward. I was thankful she'd saved me from having to ask the question.

"Because if I was going to feed off of hate, I would have already done it, given how much I hate my mother. And to be clear, I hate her a metric ton, but I have no inclination towards eating hate." Helena took the situation in stride and continued eating.

"That's... great." I squeezed a smile onto my face. The idea of her shifting into hatred had been a heavy concern on my shoulders. "But why would it be a bad thing that you are free?"

"Well, from what I gather. My mother and this Odima are competing for this thing—"

"Serpentis Víbora Boca," Jadelyn added.

"That sounds right." Helena chewed on a sausage. "So, basically, I use it and it turns ambient mana into emotional mana of love. My mother wants to pump that mana into the celestial plane to balloon it back up."

"Not a terrible thing." Jadelyn nodded with her.

"It would drain a decent amount of mana from Earth," Helena pointed out. "Not that it bothers us too much with the walking mana generator here, but it could disrupt a lot of other paranormals. But the real problem is, if I don't do it, this Odima probably will. If she's an angel of hate, then she'll flood the world with hate. That unfortunately feels even more problematic."

I rubbed at my forehead. "Yeah, it would be like a world-wide emotional manipulation?"

"Yep," Helena said and made an explosion with her hands. "If no one throws a nuke, we'd be lucky."

"That bad?" Jadelyn asked.

"I've felt the pure hatred from them. People would probably start shooting each other in the streets. It would be like that horror movie where everyone goes on a murder spree for a day, but that stage would last a lot longer." I stole one of Helena's pieces of bacon and nearly lost a finger for it as she tried to stab me. "We can get you more," I offered.

Helena glared at me while I ate the piece of bacon, but she returned to the conversation. "Yeah. What he said. That means that even if we escaped my mother, we still have to go stop these other angels. I think my mother knew that already."

"You could sit this one out." I smiled at Helena.

She slowly shook her head. "No. I need to be there. This is my family. I'm going to put an end to this."

"You being there raises the risk substantially." Scarlett shifted into her security planning mode, assessing risks and options.

But the nephilim didn't back down. "I'm going." She turned to me. "If you have a concern with my ability to fight, then you'll have to have my back."

"This is bringing exactly what your mother wants right to where it needs to be," I groaned. "Helena, sit this one out."

We both stared at each other for a long minute before I finally relented. "You stay back. We'll have Ikta with you at all times."

"Really? Who am I babysitting?" Ikta wandered back over with Morgana and Sabrina.

"Helena. She wants to join us for the fight against her mother, likely at the city where the artifact is going to be put together. The artifact they want to sacrifice her to use." I sighed.

"That sounds like a terrible idea." Ikta grinned like a mad woman. Her violet eyes could barely contain her crazy. "Let's do it."

"Thank you, Ikta." Helena nodded.

"The wise thing to do would be to sit this one out." Sabrina pointedly glared at Helena, clearly not willing to give up the fight.

The angel couldn't meet the succubus' gaze. "Would you miss a fight against your past tormentors?"

"No. Probably not. But most of the time in a fight, you are just risking yourself. With this, you are risking a whole hell of a lot more," Sabrina rebuked.

I cleared my throat to change the topic. "Can you two make sure she's herself, and isn't under any influences?"

Ikta started to walk around the table, glancing at the nephilim.

"Question." Scarlett's tails curled with curiosity. "What happened to your asshole of a brother?"

"Half-brother." Helena's lips quirked up in a slight smile. "When I defected and Zach stole his sword, he went crawling back to the church. Last I heard, they dumped him in some back-ass posting because he lost a templar sword, and I was at least half the reason he had gotten it in the first place."

"How bad of a posting?" I asked.

"Northern Greenland. There is only running water for a few months a year. It's a nice place for isolated projects, though." Helena snickered. "Poor Jared. But it's best for him. Otherwise, I'd kill him with how he always looked at me."

A growl slipped out of me before Scarlett's tails started batting me. "We are glad to have you back," Scarlett added. "Bonus points for not having to be a damsel for him."

"Did he call me a damsel?" Helena shifted her gaze slowly in a way that made the hairs on the back of my neck stand up.

"No. Damsel? You? Never," I adamantly refused.

"She passes," Ikta declared and pulled back magic that was in her hands.

"I have to concur." Sabrina had taken out a few small enchantments. "Nothing I can find. But if Aphrodite had been able to hide her mark from you, I'm a little wary to be confident in my abilities."

"Na. It's fine." Ikta slapped Sabrina on the shoulder. "Aphro wouldn't sit still this long and be polite. She's kind of a raging bitch."

"Thank you." Helena smiled. "How does she like that nickname?"

"No idea. Just made it up."

"Well I love it, because I think she'd hate it." Helena was all smiles. "Question is, what do we do now?"

"Before I had to go rescue you—" A spear flashed before my nose. "I mean... pick you up, I was going to survey the other golden cities so that I could portal to them. Maybe I could get my hands on one of these artifacts and bury it in the backwoods of Faerie. But I was planning on showing up at the altar that's still in one of the cities when something eventually goes down."

"My mother already has three of the pieces, and you said one was stuck where it was? I think that puts us at low odds of finding one of the remaining pieces," Helena pointed out.

"Odima said she had two. So that leaves one still in play." I rubbed at my forehead. "Who wants to go to the altar and turn the place into a magical fortress?" I raised my hand.

Jadelyn had a big grin on her face as she raised her hand too.

"Can I blow something up?" Ikta asked cheerfully.

"Pretty sure that's the idea." Sabrina calmly raised her own hand. "But first, we have to get there and then we have to convince a bunch of dragon-hating basilisks to let us play with their wards."

I patted my knees. "That would be my job."

CHAPTER 21

"Maybe I should get to be a damsel one of these times," Goldie spoke from my wrist as we closed in on the city.

"You? A damsel? How is anyone going to cart you off?" I asked as she literally clung to my body.

"Are you calling me fat?" Goldie accused me.

"No," I was very quick to answer. "Not at all."

"Well, us five-hundred-thousand-pound girls want to be damsels too," Goldie grumbled.

"Wait, is that how much you really weigh?" I was suddenly incredibly curious.

"No. And do not ask for my actual weight because I don't know, and it is rude to ask. Seriously, how did you get so many girls?" she teased me.

I chuckled. "Because I'm charming, and mostly because I'm a dragon."

"Fair. I still want to be a damsel. There are some odd memories I have of... role-play that I would like to work with."

My draconic brow rose up to my horns. "Sure." I wasn't sure what to say.

Goldie let out an unamused. "Uh huh."

"You can't drop something like that on me and expect me to be quick on my feet," I replied, watching the jungle below us for movement as we approached the golden city.

"Good thing you aren't on your feet," Goldie responded.

"It is an expression, Goldie," I sighed, a heavy affair for a giant dragon.

"By the way, I know what I want from you," Goldie spoke softly.

I recalled our prior conversation and nodded. "Anything."

"Can you dig up other precious metals besides gold and give me a lump of them?" Goldie asked.

"Sure? Can I know what they are for?" I asked.

"Well... I can't have kids, but I could put another type of metal in my mass, and, you know... saturate it with your and my mana. It would kind of be like making a kid together, but it would take a really, really long time," she finished and there was a long pause. "Zach?"

I hadn't really ever thought about the issue. For Goldie to bring it up, it must have been on her mind. "Of course," I answered quickly after her prompting. "Was just thinking about the logistics, but we can always figure that out later."

"Thank you!" Goldie squealed, excited at the prospect. "I'll keep them from eating all of Jadelyn's stuff, I swear."

Chuckling, I didn't think that would be the biggest problem. I could only imagine what trouble a few young silver or platinum elementals could get up to.

"Now, get ready. The upcoming city might send some people up to bother us as we fly in." I hit the wards, which started flashing.

Once again, blaring alarms sounded. But this time, I didn't stay in the air. I immediately shrank down to my human form and landed on the steps to the largest building before dropping my invisibility.

Basilisks rushed out with spears drawn as I opened a portal back to the mansion and started to put on pants.

"Oh, don't mind me." I gave my most charming smile. Unable to help myself, I took a deep breath, and the metallic tang of gold tickled my dragon instincts telling them to take it all. It only took a brief moment to suppress those feelings.

"Dragon," one of them hissed.

Ryley and Jadelyn stepped out of the portal. "I am Ryley Esmer and wish to speak with the queen."

I noticed that the basilisks in this city had serpent tails that were all hues of red. I wondered if their differences were really that simple between the cities.

"You come with this dragon?" the one that had hissed at me spoke up.

"I have joined the Golden Plushie Society." She lifted her chin. "We fall under the protection of the dragon."

Jadelyn earned a glare from me when I heard about Ryley joining the Plushies. My second wife looked behind her and then pointed at herself, playfully mystified at what I could be upset about.

"Ryley, I know your mother well. To let a basilisk get involved with a dragon... it never ends well," one of the guards tried to offer advice.

"I'm sorry for my ancestors, but I have made some strides with El Dorado. Unfortunately, right now the danger to the seven cities is large enough that I am trying to help." I bowed my head, trying to lower their perception of the threat I posed.

"Ah. A dragon comes to offer his aid. And how many temples of gold do you want for it? Or maybe you'd like to trade in basilisk blood?" A red-tailed basilisk slithered her way out of the temple, her head tilted back so that she could stare down her nose at me.

"None." I met her eyes. "The cities—"

"I am aware of the attack on one of our dear cities. I have increased our fortifications and doubled our guard," she cut me off.

"Then you must also be aware that those angels of hate attacked El Dorado last night? That they called on me to defend them?" I took several steps up the temple so that she couldn't look down on me.

In response, she rose herself up among her coiled tail, trying to stay above me.

I reached the same steps as her. The basilisk guards tense as I grabbed her hand and kissed the back of it. "The angels are fighting over the Serpentis Víbora Boca pieces. One of the pieces was stolen from El Dorado during the attack. I have it on good authority that the other group of angels has stolen at least three more pieces."

The Queen of Manoa stared at me for a long moment. "Since we have the base, you believe these angels are going to come here at the end."

I nodded.

"Then let them. I'll open the front gates and let them sacrifice whatever they want on the stupid thing. It doesn't do anything." The queen rolled her eyes.

"Yeah. I understand that you think that. But Aphrodite, an ancient angel, is going to all this effort. I suspect she knows more than you or me on how it works."

The queen snorted. "Doubtful. This is a basilisk artifact. The Celestial Plane is struggling, and she is grasping at myths that will not aid her."

"She tried and failed to do this about two thousand years ago too," I added.

The queen continued to shake her head. "Say I believed you. Then what? I'm supposed to let a dragon come nest in my city to protect me?" Her face fell as she spoke, her feelings on that proposition clear.

"I was hoping that I could bring my mates, and we could help fortify your city."

"You wish for my city to undertake a siege on your word? The word of a dragon?" The queen snorted.

Ryley slithered forward. "Minthra, they come with good intentions. The Dragon King and his mates defended El Dorado."

"It sounds like you still lost the artifact," Minthra shot back.

"We were not accommodating of the Dragon King and worked to conceal what we knew, instead asking him to help our elemental before helping him," Ryley admitted.

Minthra's eyes narrowed. "Your elemental?"

"It is greatly weakened after going to assist one of its fellows. How is yours?" Ryley asked.

"Gone. It never returned to us." Minthra's frown deepened.

They were greatly weakened. All of the seven cities likely were. Minthra was scared that she was letting in an enemy when her defenses were gone. She was so concerned with protecting herself that she'd let the angels have their way with her city to pretend to be strong.

I raised my hand. "I, Zach Pendragon, Dragon King, Fae Emperor and King of Hell, do swear to Minthra of Manoa that I will not covet her city or its gold. Nor will my people. Instead, if she will allow it, I will aid the defense of her city against angels." I repeated the statement three times while the basilisk grew more and more concerned.

Finally, a link snapped to life between Minthra and I.

She recoiled. "What manner of magic have you done to me? Fae oaths are not a dragon's magic. Are you some fae in disguise?"

"No. I'm the new Fae Emperor. Winter, Summer and Wild Queen are my wives." I smiled. "I also have a fraction of The Dreamer's power and my own plane. Really, we could say I'm a titan rather than a dragon. Creating new planes is their domain."

Minthra blinked several times and glanced to Ryley.

The other basilisk nodded. "I've gone with his harem to see it all. What he says is true. Though, the talk of titans is above me."

"As it should be," Minthra muttered. "You made the oath conditional. If I allow you to defend the city, you'll fight the angels?"

"That's the goal." I did my best to give her a friendly smile.

"How?" She wanted details, but started moving. We both knew the angels wouldn't just use her temple for the sacrifices if she let them. They would fight over it and, in turn, destroy her city.

I fell into stride with her slithering. "My harem is quite large, with more than a few ladies very capable of making enchantments. We would adapt and upgrade your city wards as well as create more protections and some offensive enchantments around the base for the artifact as well."

Minthra nodded. "And during?"

"My harem and I would be here fighting of course. One of my mates is the leader of a large werewolf pack. Another is good friends with a powerful lich. I would bring all that I could to assist you."

She was quiet for a moment as we finished ascending the steps to the top of the temple. The area was ringed with tall golden pillars and a roof over top. In the center sat her throne, in an open-air throne room. The throne was shaped like the hood of a cobra with its mouth open.

"I accept your aid," she spoke at last. "My request is that you prioritize the safety of my people. While this is all happening, I ask that you reinforce their homes so that they can shelter this storm safely."

"Thank you." I bowed low. "We will get started right away." I summoned a portal to the side of the throne.

Sabrina swaggered out, her succubus form on full display and her lips curling up seductively as her tail curled playfully behind her. "I assume I am getting a large enchanting project?"

"Yes. Bring the nymphs and do some reinforcements of all the buildings to start. Then we can work on the big guns and protect this." I pointed at the throne, which clearly sat on an older, more ornate dais that had two large spaces that were filled with decorations. "This is the base, correct?"

"Yes." Minthra nodded, her eyes opening wide as she watched woman after woman file out of the portal. "You are married to an army."

"He's a very greedy dragon." Jadelyn came around my side and clung to my arm for a moment before stepping towards Minthra. "I'm Jadelyn Scalewright, and I noticed that you have a lovely bay."

The queen blinked at the sudden change of subject.

I stepped away to let Jadelyn do her thing, moving over to Ryley. "Thank you for your trust. I think, without you, we wouldn't be able to help."

"It is my pleasure to help when it is for a good cause." Ryley bowed low. "Do you not covet the gold of these cities at all? I don't see the greed in your eyes that is mentioned so often in our history."

"No." I glanced at the nymphs and my wives. "I am a very greedy dragon, but some things are worth far more than gold."

Ryley nodded slowly. "I think I understand." The basilisk was cute, clearly a little sheltered, but opening up to what she was seeing.

"Good. Now, do you have any experience with enchantments?" I asked.

Ryley shook her head. "Not enough for what you are doing."

"Go join the nymphs then. Sabrina is going to give them some easy ones. The succubus is the expert here."

"The succubus..."—Ryley frowned—"is your enchanting expert?" She struggled to keep the doubt from her tone.

"Oh yeah. She sealed her succubus nature for a long while and learned from one of the best magi in the world. Then I went to Hell and killed a few Demon Princes to stuff her full of power. Don't underestimate her. She loves studying magic more than she likes fucking, which means a lot considering that she's a succubus."

Ryley blinked at me. "Okay." She watched Sabrina "I'll just go learn magic from a succubus." It sounded like she couldn't believe she was actually saying that aloud.

She slithered off and I was left scratching the back of my head. Sabrina wasn't that odd, was she? Either way, we had work to do, and I didn't mind the odd ones.

I opened a portal to a familiar room in a nursing home.

"Oh. Finally come to see this old man?" The tall and ancient elf turned lich rolled his eyes from his rocking chair where he was watching soap operas.

"Really? Weeks of our lives?" I looked at the TV.

"No, this is Hospital," T answered, still not looking away from the screen.

The once feared lich who had held off the church during an all-out war was enjoying his 'retirement' in the nursing home. Though, since going and visiting his family tree, it looked like he had taken his one foot out of the grave. Now he just looked geriatric as fuck and not a walking corpse.

"Well. I came for something."

The old elf shook his head. "It is always something. Can't you just stop in to say 'hi' now and then? Come. Sit. I've been watching barber videos." He pulled out a bag from the drawer next to him and opened up a small grooming kit. "While we are at it, I can clip your nails and maybe nick your skin hard enough to get a few drops of blood."

I glared at him. He was also famous for his knowledge in potions, and dragon ingredients were a rare treat that he always tried to weasel out of me.

"I meant there are some first aid things in here too, if that were to ever happen." The old elf smiled up at me through his overly bushy eyebrows.

"Well, I guess we could do that, but we might be late to kill angels invading Earth."

The entire room turned into a gloomy maelstrom of power.

"Angels?" the lich asked.

"Yeah. Just came to tell you that Aphrodite herself and two more archangels came down and are cooking up something. Some sacrifice and rip a bunch of mana from Earth, change it and siphon it up to Heaven is my best guess." I shrugged. "But if you'd rather play barber, I understand."

Turning back to my portal, I was blocked by a wall of bones that grew over the front.

"Now, now." T patted the air. "Why don't you sit down and tell me more about these angels?"

The friendly old grandpa was completely gone. His eyes burned with an eerie green fire. Once upon a time, the church had destroyed his entire tribe of elves and forced T to relocate their family tree down to the gates of Tartarus.

If there was one thing that would get T off his rocker, it would be angels.

"Well... it all started..." I explained everything to T from the start to the current affairs.

Along the way, he asked a number of clarifying questions.

Finally finishing, T leaned back and steepled his hands. "Interesting."

The door to his room opened up and a nurse stepped in. "Time for your medicine." She had a plastic cup with a few pills in it. The bags under her eyes were so deep and she was so tired that she didn't even notice the glowing bone bound portal or the green flames in T's eyes.

T frowned deeply at the woman and took the pills before waving her out with a hint of mana to stop her from asking any questions.

"Trouble with the nurses?" I teased.

T shrugged. "They cut the staffing down to bare bones. Pretty sure she's given me last night's pills and this mornings. Not sure she's slept in the last day. What? They'll wear themselves to bare bones at this rate. Not to mention the service is going downhill."

"Or you could just move out. I know Hestia would absolutely love to take care of you."

T gave me a look of absolute horror. "That would ruin her dating life."

"That she doesn't have," I added, fairly certain that Morgana would be gossiping about it if her best friend was dating.

He shrugged. "Her problem. I will stay out of the way. But back to the matter of Aphrodite." He clearly didn't want to hear about his daughter's dating life. "She's old, vicious and knowledgeable."

"If she's going after this artifact—"

"Then it does exactly what she thinks it does. Or worse. For all we know, she could have been there when it was made and stripped the basilisks of the real way to use it." T shook his head.

"What about Odima?" I leaned forward, my hand clasped. "If she gets the artifact put together and sacrifices herself, do you think it'll work?"

T grimaced. "That, I am unsure of. Aphrodite plots very deeply. It would not surprise me if she somehow sabotages it all just for Odima to finally kill herself. The Archangel of Love is a web of lies so deep that those she ensnares rarely ever free themselves."

"What does that make Helena?" I asked, feeling a pit of dread in my gut.

"Someone she has known and been able to plot against since she was born. Either she knew her daughter wouldn't stay out of it, so she allowed her to escape or somehow that's all part of her grand plan. You said she insisted on coming?" T confirmed.

"Yes. She hates her mother more than I think is healthy. Helena wants to be the one to end her." I did not like her coming to the fight, but knew it would be impossible to keep her away. By allowing her to fight with Ikta, I could keep her safer than trying to push her out of it.

"Then you've done what you can. I'll join you and add some more wings to my collection." T sat back with a grin that I knew too many people had seen right before they died. "Fucking angels should stay in their plane. Or better yet, you should take over their plane and then lock them all up."

I sighed. The idea had honestly been in the back of my mind, but I wasn't sure exactly how to execute it. During the fight, there should be several archangels. It certainly was an opportunity if I could grasp it.

CHAPTER 22

I stood atop the temple and watched everyone working. Sabrina had outdone herself. She had neatly divided tasks into various levels of difficulty and put people to work accordingly.

Frank was having the time of his life. He was moving about among a gaggle of nymphs who had a basic understanding of enchanting and was making a rather large, if simple, net of enchantments all around the city walls while Maddie menacingly followed behind.

Those who had little to no experience in enchantments were down carving very basic shapes into the homes of the basilisks that were being checked by Pixie's eye for detail.

Meanwhile, those of us that had enough experience to be helpful were working on more complex enchantments on the temple itself.

"Here, like this." Sabrina touched my hand and used my claw to finish the stroke of that part of the enchantment. "It needs the tail because we are going to link this one to that one." She lifted up a piece of paper that she had scribbled some notes on. No one but her could understand the plan.

"What is this one for?" I carefully lifted my claw from the soft gold.

"Well, most of these buildings already have some enchantments on them." She rolled her eyes. "Gold is not a great building material. So after getting a peek at them, I realized we would have to amplify and work with the existing enchantments rather than just make our own because half of their enchantments are actually built into the structure. Most of these are supplementary for the defense. Then we'll get to work on the offensive ones."

She pulled a pen from where it was resting between her horn and her hair and made a few more scribbles on the piece of paper before looking up at me.

I flashed her a smile. "Supplementary, I can do."

Then I stepped behind her and ran my hands over her shoulders. Even in the heat, she was wearing a baggy sweater because too many people had been staring. Still, I loved the feeling of touching her. "Thank you for all the work you are putting in."

"I like this sort of thing." She melted into my touch.

"Yes. But this is more work on your shoulders. That, and I just want an excuse to thank you." I moved my arms down from her shoulders and around her waist, pulling her close and smothering her against my chest.

"After this, we should take some time off." Sabrina leaned into me.

"I'd like that very much." Dodging her horns, I kissed the side of her head. "Maybe we can go have some intensive enchanting study sessions?"

She ran her fingers over my arms. "Don't tempt me here. These basilisks are scared enough. They don't need to see you bend me over that throne and feed me."

She pulled my hands off of her and sauntered away, swaying her hips and checking over her shoulder to make sure I was watching. She knew exactly what she was doing to me.

"Damn," I muttered and rubbed my cheeks to get back in a mental state where I could focus on enchantments.

But I couldn't get the image of her bent over the throne out of my head, so I stepped away from my pillar, putting a sticky note on where I had left off.

We had been working for most of the day by that point, and I knew I needed to give myself a mental breather. Opening a portal back to the mansion, I figured food was the best thing to keep my mind off sex.

The kitchen was empty except for Nyske, who was making a sandwich that was one part bread, one part ham, and four parts pickles. It was hard to see if there was anything else among the pickles.

"You know, they always joke about pickles being a pregnant thing. You aren't pregnant, right?" I leaned against the island.

Nyske fished a pickle out of the jar and waggled it at me, splashing the marble top. "When I'm pregnant, I expect to lay on the couch and have you feed me pickles twenty-four seven." She was wearing a basic t-shirt with a jar of pickles labeled 'pickle slut' over a pair of leggings.

"Fun shirt," I adroitly avoided her declaration.

"Thanks. Pixie got it for me. Also, someone went through so many of my pickles!" She opened the fridge door to show me as she put away her current jar. When she turned back around, she had a new pickle in her hand and took a bite.

I chuckled. "That was me. I put a bunch in our hotel fridge. But we haven't been back there to retrieve them."

The anger on her face smoothed over. "Oh. That's so sweet."

I came around the island. "Just trying to do little things." My arms found her waist and pulled her close as she quickly finished the pickle. "I'm going to bring the pickles back."

"The little things." Nyske wrapped my arms tightly around her. "We seem to be doing a lot of little things... but not the big thing."

"I can wait however long you need," I reassured her.

Nyske squeezed my arms. "I feel like we've been set up by my mother," she admitted.

That statement had not been what I was expecting. "Huh?"

She giggled. "You are cute when you are surprised." She patted my cheek and turned around in my arms, pressing herself to me and tilting her head back for a kiss.

I lifted her slightly off the ground and pressed my lips to hers. There was a wonderful familiarity in them. It was just a kiss, but we mashed our lips together like we wanted to become one. We stayed there for a long moment before I put her down.

"You are going to have to explain that one. Eat your sandwich and I'll make my own." I put her down and opened the fridge, also opening a portal to the hotel. I got situated to move all the pickles back.

"Well, first she wanted me to steal your egg. She could have chosen any nymph," Nyske began.

"You are her first nymph. Probably her most capable," I argued. "There was no way she would have known my father would catch you and make that deal."

"The ruler of Faerie would ride a dragon never before seen. That was part of the false prophecy that you guys found, right?" Nyske smiled at me. "That's me. I'm the brand-new type of dragon. Maybe my mother knew all of this." Nyske ran a hand through her hair, making it shimmer in a dozen colors.

"No way. Your mother wasn't a prophet or anything, was she?"

"No. That was always her creations and unintended side effects. But she knew everything that happened in Faerie, so she could easily collect all of the prophecies." Nyske took a loud bite of her sandwich.

I finished up replacing the pickles and started tossing my ingredients on the counter. "Okay. So then it was fate, not your mother."

"I don't like having my choices taken away from me," Nyske grumbled. "First she had me steal the egg, then she gave you the nectar and made you weak to nymphs. Finally, she makes me a titan. Even if she didn't plan it from the beginning, by the end, she was trying to push us together."

"Okay. So she might have a hand in our coming together. But how does that mean we need to stay apart?" I asked.

Nyske pouted and put her sandwich that seemed more like an excuse for more pickles down. "What if it's to make us both titans and have titan babies that she can slip back into or something? What if this is some giant plan to revive herself or... I don't know. These really old beings are too crafty."

"Maybe we ask another equally old creature to help?" I suggested.

Nyske gave me a bland expression. "Your mother is not a schemer, and I'm not sure even her power is enough to break through all of this."

I snorted and squirted far too much mustard on my sandwich. "No. I meant go down to Tartarus and talk to my father. I had already been thinking about going to ask about Aphrodite."

"Oh. OH." Nyske's eyes went wide. "My mother is down there too."

I put the second slice of bread on top of my ham and Swiss sandwich, squeezing mustard out over the edge and picked up the mostly meat sandwich. "Yep. You can curse her out if you want too."

Nyske narrowed her eyes and took another bite of her sandwich while she thought. After a moment of us just eating in silence, or as quiet as a pickle sandwich could be, Nyske spoke up.

"Okay. Let's go. But aren't you supposed to be enchanting a golden city?" she asked.

"I'm on my lunch break," I mumbled around my food. "Even dragons get lunch breaks, right?"

"Oh yeah. Just a jaunt to Tartarus and back on a lunch break. You make it sound so casual." Yet she quickened the pace on her sandwich, and I followed suit.

Quickly, we both devoured our lunch, and I opened a portal to Spain. "We'll be back before anyone misses us."

Nyske glanced down at her shirt and hesitated for a moment before shrugging. "My mother is going to hate this." But her smile told me she was excited to piss her mother off.

I held out my hand, and once she took it, I led us both through the portal.

The way to Tartarus was just a hole in the ground, concealed with magic. There was a small city built around a port that gave access to the Mediterranean Sea.

But no one was around the cliff, and I shifted my eyes, spotting the hole. I got down on my knees before starting the climb down. "If you have any issue with the climb, just let me know and I'll take you the rest of the way down."

"I am a dragon too, you know," Nyske huffed.

"You never really show me your dragon form," I answered, starting down and glancing up to see Nyske coming in above me and giving me a wonderful view with those tight leggings.

She didn't even look down. "Stop staring and keep moving."

"It's a good view," I chuckled, but then looked down to continue my progress. The descending time was the longest leg of the trip, and I didn't dare make a portal directly to Tartarus. While I could cross planes, this one was different. It was filled with dead titans and beings of great power.

I would rather not accidentally let anything out.

The climb was long enough that my questions bubbled up out of me. "So. If she gloats about how she pushed us together, what happens?"

Nyske paused above me. "I don't know, Zach. My feelings are genuine. I truly care about you, but the thought that us being together is part of my mother's plan really grinds my gears."

"Well, either way. I think a lot of people have influenced and shaped us in our lives, purposefully and not. As your mother, she had a hand in a lot of who you are, just like those who raised me shaped me into the man-dragon I've become. I love you, Nyske; her involvement or lack of has no impact on that for me." A very real fear that I'd lose her because of what her mother said crept into me.

Nyske sighed and pressed her forehead to the wall. "I love you too. Even if you were an idiot and broke up with me."

"Hey now. You were keeping secrets. You decided not to tell me that you are a smoking hot nymph that knew I was hatched rather than born." I frowned up at her.

She leaned over her shoulder and gave me a smoldering smile. "I really thought the sex would have been enough to keep you around."

"It was painful. I pretty much went through withdrawal. You never glamored me in our time together, did you?" I asked.

"WHAT?!" Nyske slid down the face of the cliff, her hands shifting into two pearlescent claws and digging in to find purchase. "I can't believe you'd even ask me that."

"Nyske, I fell for you really hard. After learning about everything, I had always wondered. When you were hesitant to start things back up, it was bothering me that maybe it wasn't real in the first place."

"Zach." She climbed as close as she could to me in the small passage, making sure that we could see each other's eyes. "I would never. If you asked me to glamor you, we could make it a fun thing, but it would be with rules first and of course your consent. What we had— have is genuine."

I clung to the cliff face with a single hand and ripped Nyske off of the cliff with the other and slammed her lips to mine, kissing her with every ounce of passion I had in me. "Then when we are done with the angels and can play around, I want to remind you how incredible we were together."

She blushed and her eyes danced over my face. "Deal." She paused. "Did you do that on purpose?"

"Do what?" I feigned innocence.

"Oh, you tricky dragon. Making parallels between the two relationships and getting me to admit that what we had was genuine." Nyske clung to me. "As punishment, you are going to have to carry me the rest of the way down."

"Whatever you wish, my Pickle Slut." I bobbed my head. We both knew that her weight didn't make a difference with my draconic strength.

She flicked the side of my head. "I think I liked it better when you had a little trepidation."

"Too late. You've sealed the deal. Now I just get to be happy that you'll join me in my bed again." I gave her a big grin as we continued down the cliff.

"You are a big goof. Has it been worrying you that much?" she asked.

"Not at all," I lied.

"He's lying," Goldie pipped up, breaking the moment. "Sorry. I know you were having a thing, but he confided in me that he was worried that he'd done something." Goldie wing-manned me like a professional.

"Thank you, Goldie. At least one of you two is honest with Zach's feelings." Nyske hung onto me. "How was your first night with him, Goldie? Did the enchantment work?"

"It worked wonderfully!" Goldie nearly shouted. "That and I'm going to get pregnant!"

Nyske sputtered. "What?"

"She's going to put a mass of another precious metal in her mass and then... well, take my mana and hers during sex and inject it into the metal. It'll take years."

"But it should eventually make another elemental," Nyske finished. "That's brilliant, Goldie! When it is close, you can even make a bump for yourself. Zach doesn't like to admit it, but he's been paying Kelly a lot more attention now that she has a bump."

"Really?" Goldie sounded excited. "I could do that right now."

"I do not get excited over the bump," I grumbled.

"Do too." Nyske stuck her tongue out. "Pixie noticed too."

I rolled my eyes. "It is the pheromones. The pregnant ladies just set me off."

"Uh huh." Nyske was unconvinced. "Just imagine me with a nice, rounded tummy, holding your child." She rubbed at her stomach while pushing her chest against me.

"That's not fair."

"His pulse is increasing," Goldie reported.

"Because she's... oh look. We are almost there." I slid down the last section of the cliff and landed with a big thud.

Nyske held onto me the whole time. "Well, I guess we should get to the reason we came down here in the first place." She pulled her hair back, preparing for what was to come.

"Aww. Teasing my Zach is fun," Goldie pouted.

"Don't worry, we'll team up on him in more ways than one later. I am very interested in the bedroom uses of your abilities, Goldie." Nyske flashed me a smile that promised a wild time. "But first I have to piss off my mother like the rebellious daughter that I am."

CHAPTER 23

I walked with Nyske up to the River Styx. The black water lapped at the bank of this side of the underworld in a slow rhythm that made me wonder what was even causing the motion to occur.

The whole place felt like it was in grayscale. The pale light that shone seemingly from nowhere didn't reflect much color, and the river's black water seemed to swallow all of the light, making it seem like there was a fog not far off the shore.

After a while, a single lantern bobbed in the distance. The ferryman was coming.

"So, we ask your father for a trip to the titans and then we poke my mother?" Nyske asked.

"Pretty much how I see it going down. But who knows?" I shrugged.

The lantern continued to grow ever bigger as it bobbed with the boat it was attached to.

I held my breath, a tension in my body as my father grew closer. Despite everything I tried to tell myself, he was my father. I wanted him to be proud. Shaking my head, I chuckled at the thought.

"What?" Nyske asked.

"Even as the Dragon King, I still want my father's approval," I told her honestly. "How did you get past that feeling with your mother?"

"Who says I have? A rebellious daughter still cares what their mother thinks. The determination to still do what I want is what makes me rebellious." Nyske flashed me a smile and then leaned against me. "If your father isn't proud of you, then he's an absolute idiot. And I'll sink his little dinghy."

As the ferry came closer, not one, but two figures emerged into the light.

"I heard the end of that, daughter." A fae woman who looked startlingly like Nyske, only with kaleidoscope eyes, spoke up.

Our positions were mirrored. The Dreamer leaned against my father much like Nyske leaned against me. But I would never compare Nyske to her mother out loud. That was a sure-fire way to get clobbered.

"Mother," Nyske nearly hissed.

The Dreamer glanced at Nyske's shirt, her smile fading. "Pickle Slut."

"Is that a euphemism?" my father asked me.

"Nope. I just love pickles," Nyske answered for me. "Like a lot."

My father stared at me, as if I might have a different answer, but I could only shrug. She was a nymph, but it wasn't meant that way.

"Well. This is Nyske," I tried to cut the tension.

"I'm aware of who she is. I entrusted your egg to her." My father tilted his head. "She lost it."

"You know, I'm more interested in what The Dreamer is doing riding on your ferry," I changed the subject before Nyske took any more questions from my father.

"Oh. That's simple. She's riding with me now." Bart made it sound like he had decided on a burger instead of pizza.

"I don't get along with the other titans. Never did. That's why I ran off and made Faerie." The Dreamer leaned heavily on my father's shoulder, but he didn't seem to mind the familiarity.

"Ah, so you finally snagged your white whale?" Nyske asked.

"We are both stuck down here. Why not make the best of it?" My father kissed The Dreamer, with tongue.

"Eww. I'll make sure to tell Tia next time I see her." My brain did not need to have the image of those two kissing.

Bart pulled away, clearing his throat. "Son! How are you? I love your mate's shirt, and it's interesting that your other mate is pretending to be a bracelet." He quickly changed his tune. "As lovely as it is to see both of them, is there a reason you came down here?"

Nyske grinned at me.

"In fact, there is. Back in the days you played around as Zeus, you spent some time with Aphrodite?" I asked.

Bart held up his hands. "Not in that sort of way. Your mother would have killed me. I only went and slept with a few hundred mortals. Never Aphrodite. Besides, Aphrodite would have twisted anyone up into knots and had them dancing to her tune. She is... a badly broken woman. Crazy can be fun, but there is such a thing as too crazy."

I blinked at his statement. "Well. She's down on Earth now, trying to do something. I fought her once, and she kidnapped one of my mates. Honestly, I couldn't touch her when we fought. She manipulated space so well that anything I tried never reached her."

My father was nodding along with me. "What do you know about her past?"

"Not much besides that she's actually Aphrodite," I answered.

The Dreamer shared a look with my father, and he nodded with a heavy sigh before starting into a story. "So. The Greeks were declining. We worked to mold the Roman religion to hold our pantheon. It worked, at least for a while."

I could feel that he was settling in for a story, and went to sit, Goldie making a love seat for Nyske and me. "I'm guessing that wasn't perfect for long."

"No, it wasn't. A second religion started to work its way into the culture. This one had a singular god. It pulled on an existing religion and built upon it. We tried to squash it, turning our followers against them and issuing direct decrees to counter it." Bart shook his head. "If only we knew."

I could take a guess. "Aphrodite spread Christianity?"

"More like she adopted and molded it. I don't think she started the whole thing. But she had us chasing our own tails. Meanwhile, she twisted her husband up in knots, always cheating on him and coming back to him and wrapping him around her finger once again. He's the one who killed that round of my reincarnation." Bart sighed. "After I was out of the picture, my understanding is that she pushed hard and flipped the religious culture of the

Romans. They then spread it far and wide with little resistance. Even started a few purges through all the human worshipers she cobbled together. Nasty woman."

"She's a schemer; we know that much. But what can we do against her?" I asked, feeling a sense of urgency to push him to an answer.

My father made a face. "Truthfully, she's extraordinary. Her control over spatial magic is the best there has ever been. You could catch her unaware—she can't stop what she doesn't see coming. But otherwise..."

The Dreamer gave my father a look that caused him to pause. "If you don't mind. I am well aware of Aphrodite. She's tried to steal mana from Faerie in the past. That, and she found nymphs to be an affront to her own powers. We've collided in the past."

Nyske bristled against me.

"The truth is, both of you already have what you need to fight Aphrodite. While she might have the power of space well under her control, you two are titans. The powers of creation can work against her easily. There is a reason that the titans were feared." The Dreamer's soft features became a brutal smile. "Aphrodite learned that in the past as well."

Nyske couldn't stay quiet. "You planned this, didn't you? You are a worse schemer than Aphrodite."

The Dreamer's smile lost its heat and she stared at her daughter. "What do you want me to say? If I say 'no', then you'll call me a liar. If I say 'yes', then you'll throw a fit because you want control over your life."

"Of course I want control over my own damned life. Who doesn't?!" Nyske stomped her foot, shaking the rocky shore. "You've always pushed and pulled. I'm done with it."

The Dreamer narrowed her eyes as the ferry rocked after Nyske's outburst. "Look at where you are. Are you content with your present situation?"

"No. Not if it is the result of your manipulations," Nyske growled. It was utterly adorable to watch her take on her mother, but once again saying that wouldn't get me anywhere.

"So. What would you have me say?" The Dreamer asked.

"The truth." Nyske demanded.

"When my two options both lead to a bad solution?"

"Don't care. Just give me an answer."

The Dreamer didn't move, didn't change in any way. But somehow, it felt like she was filling the room when she spoke next. "I am your mother. It is my right to guide you."

"I'm old enough that my mother doesn't need to have a hand in my life!" Nyske was panting with how forcefully she'd spoken the words.

"You know, you've always been my favorite. Not because you were among the first. But because you've reminded me of me. Back when the titans and the paranormals who called themselves gods gathered, I was always on the outside. Doing my own thing, like you. Unlike your sisters who went on to build, to war and feud. You just were happy with the arts and remaining a wild nymph." The Dreamer's face softened and her aura retracted. "So yes. Because I had always planned on giving you the last of my essence, I had to remain in your life, watching you and making sure my choice would be the right one when the time came."

Nyske's frown wavered. "You could have told me."

"I found that, in my long life, promising someone power tends to backfire." The Dreamer shrugged. "Look on the bright side. From henceforth, you get to prove to me that you can do better. Without my guidance."

"It's less fun when you allow me to rebel, and when I don't get to rub it in your face." The corner of Nyske's lips curled up. "For the record, I am coming down here in the future and rubbing it in your face. Don't go hiding in some corner of Tartarus when time comes for me to gloat."

"I won't. For what it is worth, I am sorry for the pain I caused." The Dreamer looked at her daughter with a plea in her eyes.

"But not for the outcome?" Nyske asked.

The Dreamer gestured at how she was leaning on me. "I don't think either of us should regret that outcome." Then she leaned on my father again.

Nyske suddenly saw the similarity and pulled away from me, scowling at me like I had done something wrong.

I wasn't going to let her pull away and grabbed her before fiercely hugging her back to my chest. "Mother in law, I hope we don't see you again. So, use titan powers to overcome Aphrodite?"

"An understatement, but yes. Just channeling the titan aspect of your mana will cut through her attempts to distort space. You should bring my grandchildren to see me sometime." She beamed.

Nyske huffed and I knew the answer. "Yeah. It might be a while, and you should apologize to Nyske if you want that to happen."

"I am not sorry for what I've done. Any apology would be hollow." The Dreamer gave me a quirky smile.

"Save it, mother." Nyske stopped resisting me. "I never expected an apology. We are going to make the cutest babies that have ever existed, and I'm not going to bring them down here. In fact, I don't think I'm going to tell them about their grandmother except in passing for a very long time."

The Dreamer's smile faded. "Don't make me come up there."

Nyske just huffed. "We are done here."

I shared a look with my father, and he slowly shook his head, warning me not to get between the two. In this, I agreed with him. "Have a good one, Dad. I'll bring Mom next time."

"Please don't." Bart shook his head. "But do come back. You don't need a reason. Also, you need to work on protections before you bring a kid down here."

I looked over my shoulder. Nyske was already starting her climb back up. "Catch you next time." I hurried after Nyske.

She climbed a few paces up and then waited for me. "Can I ride back up?"

"Sure, as long as you tell me what that was?" I let her hold onto me as I continued up the cliff face.

"Oh. Just me and my mother having a spat."

"Are we good?" I asked.

"Yeah. I love you, you love me. And my mother's a cunt." Nyske had a big smile on her face. Somehow, arguing with her mother had cheered her up considerably.

"Are we never going to let our kids see her?" I asked.

"Of course we'll bring the kids down or make a portal enchantment thingy so that she can see them and they can see her. I'm not a monster."

"But you—"

"We were bickering. I wouldn't actually withhold her grandchildren from her. Even if I hated my mother, that would be cruel to them too. I can show her to my children and use her as an example of what they should strive not to become." Nyske was all smiles.

I wasn't quite sure if it was just remnants of their bickering or if she was being truthful. "So then. Time to come back from our lunch break?"

"Yes. We should probably get back to warding up the golden city. It would be a shame to see it smashed, and we have to figure out how to get you to use your titan mojo," Nyske replied.

I nodded. "Yes. I think that's the only way we'll defeat Aphrodite. Chances are slim that we'll be able to find her and ambush her."

"Only way we get this all wrapped up, and I get to fulfill my oath and let you fill me. It's been too long since I had sex. I'm a nymph. We need it like air." Nyske pawed at me playfully. "I need it."

I chuckled. "Well then, *we* have to figure out this titan thing."

Nyske made a face. "Fighting isn't really my thing. Even when I go full dragon, my scales aren't nearly as hard as yours. They are kinda flimsy."

"Then you, the ancient nymph, can help me figure out the magic part of it."

"You just called me old," Nyske accused me. "I can't believe you just called me old."

I got to the top of the passage and opened a portal. "I did not call you old." My voice rang out across the kitchen that was brimming with nymphs. My harem turned towards me as I stepped in.

"Actually, you called her ancient," Goldie piped up from my arm.

Her words made more than a few of the nymphs purse their lips.

"Not helping," I hissed at Goldie before looking back up at the room. "I needed help with magic. Ancient in that context is a compliment."

"Ancient is never a compliment." Ikta skipped up to the counter and held out a plate for the nymphs to fill. "You really shouldn't call a lady 'ancient', no matter what her age is." She pointedly looked in my eyes. "Right?"

Feeling stubborn, I snorted. "I can if it's true."

The nymphs handing out food gasped.

"How old is 'ancient'?" Petal asked. "Because from what we understand, you are quite young. I doubt any of the nymphs are younger than you."

I glanced around at the room of paranormals. "What is age, but a number? At this point, most of us are immortal anyway."

"Good save." Nyske patted my shoulder with a chuckle and passed me in line. "Can I have some pickles?"

Petal hesitated. "We are out."

"Out? I just saw a bunch of jars in there." Nyske waved her hand at the fridge.

The closest nymph opened the fridge to show Nyske that the row we had deemed 'the pickle row' in the side door was empty.

"How?" Nyske frowned.

"There are a lot of us, and pickles are getting more popular." Petal flinched back.

I opened a portal to the hotel fridge, having saved one in case we returned. "Tada."

Nyske happily grabbed the jar and went up on her tiptoes to kiss my cheek. "I knew I loved you. No machinations of my mother could ensure I got a man that respects my pickles." She threw a glare at the nymphs. "I'm officially getting a pickle fridge to go next to the ice cream freezer."

I was about to argue, but then I thought better of saying anything. There were a few dozen pregnant women in the house; we could have a pickle fridge next to the ice cream freezer.

Even thinking about how many pickles Nyske would eat if she ever got pregnant made my skin crawl.

CHAPTER 24

My claw carefully finished the last curve of the enchantment that Sabrina had tasked me with completing.

Glancing down at my cheatsheet, I double checked all of the elements. The golden roof had been heavily carved up by me, Sabrina, and a few others who knew enough about enchantments to get this one right. It was critical.

Thankfully, the city was made of gold. Gold was a wonderful conductor for mana and would allow the new enchantments to really shine. The gold roof warmed as the sun sank on the horizon.

"Think they'll come tonight?" Sabrina appeared at my shoulder, pulling herself up to give me a kiss on the cheek. But I also caught the way she carefully scanned my enchantment to make sure it was all correct.

"Maybe. Do me a favor and check over this?" I offered dryly, knowing she had already looked.

She made a bigger gesture of scanning before she told me that it was perfect.

"Did you expect any less than that?" I asked.

"Given that Goldie can help us reset, and that after all this work people have been getting sloppy enough for us to actually need that option, yes." She glanced up at me, the golden grains in her eyes caught my attention every time I looked at them. "Do you need to relax?" Her lips curled up.

"Tempting, but I need to stay on my game. My bigger question is do you need a boost?"

She licked her plump pink lips. "I'll never say no. Besides, maybe taking the edge off of you will help should Aphrodite try anything."

I grabbed my succubus by the hips, her tail curling possessively around my arm as we kissed.

Her lust hit me like a truck.

Instantly, my awareness was consumed by the soft, wet sensations of her lips, only to flow down to the satin touch of her skin. I couldn't help but sink my fingers into her hips a little, reveling in just how comfortable she felt against me.

A moment later came the warmth that radiated off of her and into me like a relaxing spa. Only one part of me didn't relax. It jutted out, begging to be stuck inside of her.

I wanted to devour her, throw her down on the roof and touch every inch of her. I wanted to savor the good parts and shove myself into her paradise. That, or grab her by the horns and have my way.

As the tempting lust drained out between our lips, Sabrina pulled away from the feeding.

"You are a little pent up," she teased, her eyes practically glowing.

"Question, do I taste different?" I asked.

She tilted her head curiously. "Yes. The flavor of your mana has continued to grow stronger, but that is expected because you've been growing stronger."

"No, but The Dreamer and Typhon have both tried to make me a titan. Do I really have that magic in me? Because I can't find it." Doubt around whether I could draw on my titan power when it came to fighting Aphrodite had been weighing me down.

"Of course you have it." Sabrina kissed me again, drawing on my lust and siphoning off a bit of my mana. "There's a little bit of an old, earthy taste."

"That doesn't sound pleasant." I joked.

She kissed my neck and I gave it to her, just enjoying her touch too much to stop her. "It's more like tea or mushrooms," she replied. "Yet my succubus nature very much wants to greedily gobble it up like it is pure sugar."

I lifted her chin so that I could claim her lips again and savored a long kiss that wasn't flooded with lust, but my affection for Sabrina. "Thank you."

"No problem. If nothing else, you could try and drain your magic dry. Maybe when nothing else is left, you could find it." Sabrina lingered in my arms for a moment before flashing me a seductive smile.

"Well, there are other ways to drain me dry." I wiggled my eyebrows.

Her laughter did things to me. Sabrina wasn't holding back her nature, and I loved seeing her finally comfortable in her own skin. It was up to me to keep my head on and focus on the fight to come.

"Too bad you need to be ready for this upcoming battle. We are going to have you pouring a lot of mana into these enchantments." Sabrina pulled away, her hands sliding slowly off of me. It wasn't necessarily an attempt to seduce me, just who she was. "So, I'll stop tempting you."

I wiped my brow and blew out a breath. "Phew. That was a close one. You are just so tempting."

"Maybe we can slow down, and you don't have to resist as much?" She quirked an eyebrow.

I nodded. "Not saying I'm retiring or anything. But maybe we'll keep me in reserve for only the big things. Frank and Maddie are doing a wonderful job lately. And the FBI is actually gearing up nicely. They've taken a decent number of troublemakers off the board before I had to deal with them."

Sabrina nodded thoughtfully and walked away, her hips swaying and her tail swishing behind her.

Damn, that wasn't helping me clear my head. I blew out a breath and smacked my cheeks, trying to get my head back on right.

We had mostly finished the enchantments. Now most of the work had shifted to helping refine and reinforce the enchantments on the homes of the city to protect them from the fallout of the battle.

Polydora appeared on the horizon, and I could see the shift when she spotted me and bee-lined towards me. Yev was with her, dwarfed by the larger bronze dragon. Despite Yev taking the role of Dragon Matriarch, she wasn't the biggest one. In fact, she was one of the smaller of my dragon mates.

They entered a dive with their wings half out to pick up speed and swept low over the city walls. As they drew closer, their wings snapped out and they glided quickly to me.

Polydora's shift was seamless as she went from a dragon to walking like it didn't take years of practice to manage that feat. Yev, on the other hand, hovered for a second before dropping down next to me.

Both of them were naked after their transformations, and after how Sabrina had left me, I was a little uncomfortable.

Poly spotted my rigidness in an instant and smirked. "Mate, we've checked the cult that the FBI had marked. It's empty now."

I clicked my tongue. "So, they are on the move."

"That's the thought," Yev agreed. "The FBI informed us that they were pulling up roots at the church too. I suspect they'll tell us that the central figures are gone tomorrow morning."

"If they are done there, then it means they are coming tonight." I gazed out at the setting sun. "Thankfully, we've been taking turns resting this afternoon. Otherwise, we'd be caught unprepared."

"You should rest. I'll wake you when we get news of the angels approaching," Poly urged me.

"Do we have people on the city gates making sure we turn away any angels that appear?" I asked, already knowing that we had set it up, but I hadn't checked on it recently.

"They were there when we just flew in," Yev reassured me. "Take a rest, husband. Scarlett and Jadelyn are ensuring everything is going as smoothly as it can."

I wrinkled my nose at giving up control, but I knew I needed to be at my best for what was coming. "Okay. Tell Ikta as soon as we know that she can come pounce on me."

"That should ensure she does it quickly," Yev chuckled. "Go sleep." She shooed me off until I made a portal and disappeared into the mansion.

The place was rather empty, and I made my way to the bedroom without even a nymph trying to drag me off.

***

"Wakey wakey!" Ikta landed on me.

"Ugh. It's time?" I rolled out of the bed, seeing the deep dark of night through the window. There was a brief moment where I wondered if since this was my plane, I could change the time of day.

But I put that thought aside and focused on Ikta as she gave me the rundown.

"The Hateful have been spotted taking to the skies about an hour out. Still no sign of Aphrodite and her angels." Ikta's spider limbs clung to me and she looked up at my face. "We have an hour, so you know, we could..." She pushed her tongue against her cheek.

"While I am flattered, I should get there early and make sure everything is ready. And I also need to activate the enchantments." I had slept in my clothes and twirled my wrist as a portal opened up in front of me.

"No fun." Ikta had her cracked smile on her face as she followed me through. "I have to babysit an angel."

"First sign that her mother is going to use her for something, you throw her into one of your people's spires in the depth of the Wilds," I instructed Ikta.

"She's going to be really weak there," Ikta reminded me.

"Oh well. I'd rather she was weak than dead. We can pull her back after everything settles." I was walking on the top of the temple already.

My dragon mates had gathered and were in the nude, ready to shift. "We are ready."

"Get down to the main gate and make sure no one gets in or out of the city. None of you are to fight with Odima; she's too dangerous. But eat as many angels as you can get your hands on," I told them.

Larisa chuckled darkly. "We'll stuff ourselves full of holy chicken." She jumped off the temple, shifting into her dragon knight form and unfolding wings to fly to the city gate.

The others met my eyes as they one by one launched themselves off to prepare for the battle ahead. I glanced around and found Scarlett purposefully striding in my direction with Jadelyn hovering behind her.

"Husband." Scarlett gave me a brief hug. "We are as ready as we can be. Kelly and her pack are down among the city, and they've been given notice. In forty minutes, they start activating every enchantment they can in twenty minutes, then they'll use the remainder to get ready."

"Won't that be a risk for Kelly? At the center of the pack, if they take that much from her..." I trailed off as Jadelyn scowled at me.

"Trust in her. She said she could handle the pull." Jadelyn put her hands on her hips.

"Fine. I do trust her, but I can also worry for her at the same time."

Scarlett nodded along with my words. "Don't worry. She's got a lot of her preggo bitches doing that while the betas gear up to fight. And Taylor is on full Kelly management duties. Beyond that, we have a wing of dragons ready to take to the air, and the fae are preparing to fight on top of the temple."

"Where's Helena going to be?" I asked, most worried about her.

"She's going to fight at the gates with Ikta. We are keeping her clear of the artifact until her mother shows up. After that..."

"Helena will rush her mother." I knew Helena's anger towards her mother would drive her forward. "That's in my expectations. Morgana?"

Scarlett looked around. "She had a really big gun and was chasing Regina last I saw her. But I don't see her now. Maybe she found another place to mount her weapon."

Jadelyn spoke up, "Leviathan is going to be with me, at the docks in case they want to come in that direction. I really hope they come that direction."

"Stay out of trouble." I poked Jadelyn in the nose.

She squeezed her eyes shut and flashed a gigantic smile. "I'll try."

"No, she won't. Something comes near the water and she's going for it." Scarlett rolled her eyes. "A lot of the locals that are taking up arms are arraying themselves around the temple. Morgana and Ikta stole a bunch of guns for them. Don't ask me where those weapons came from."

I tapped my chin, trying to think about who else I was missing.

"Sabrina and Tyrande are here," Scarlett informed me. "They'll be on the temple too. Leviathan is with Jadelyn, and if Aphrodite shows up, Levi is just going to go toe to toe with the biggest, baddest angel she can find and stall them."

"She's still invulnerable here on Earth?" I asked. "Will spatial magic hurt her?"

Scarlett shook her head, making her fox ears flop in a way that made me want to gather her up and hug her. "Not according to her."

"She has to have some weakness." I frowned. "But if she's willing to go up against Aphrodite or Odima, then I'll let her. Does she want in? I haven't really wanted to approach the prince of jealousy on joining a harem. Seems like a bad fit."

"She's participating. Let's leave it at that for now. That, and she's good in the water." Jadelyn was at least excited.

"With all of that in place, we should get ready. I'm going to activate the wards on the walls. Help Sabrina activate the ones up here." I let wings burst out of my back and jumped into the air.

"Stay safe, Husband!" Jadelyn shouted after me.

I could tell that I needed a moment alone to settle my mind before this started. This battle was going to be intense, and it was filled with people I cared about. I needed to get my head in the fight, or I'd be more of a liability than an asset.

Aphrodite was going to come for this fight. Which meant that even if the Hateful were the first to show themselves, Aphrodite wouldn't be far behind.

Odima and Aphrodite were mine. They were too strong for anyone but the Faerie queens to take on. And I would keep those two from getting close to my mates; the enchantments would help with that as well.

With my dragon eyes, I could see a wide web of enchantments carved along the golden walls. Each one of them was another link connected to six other enchantments. It would take a lot of them going down before the whole thing collapsed.

I pressed my hand to one of the enchantments and let my mana pour out from my hand. Enchantments just needed a magical boost to get started before they drew from the world. Their end came when mana running through the enchantment warped the material it was placed on. There was always some secondary energy produced in the form of light and heat.

But activating this massive wall enchantment was more than a little 'boost'. I had to brace myself and dig deep as mana flooded through not just the singular enchantment, but along all of the connecting ones that ringed the entire city. It all needed to be filled with mana for the enchantment to be active.

Powering up the enchantments in front of me would normally take a group working together. But with each beat of my heart, more mana poured out, filling the enchantments one by one, blossoming from where I stood.

Rather than push, I let my heart do the work, each pump thrumming through the city walls, lighting up more of the enchantments. I didn't want to rush the process and deplete my reserves. We had a fight ahead of us, and I'd need my strength.

I stood there for minutes, until the whole thing flashed on completion. The draw of mana lessened, and I could see the enchantments starting to pull from the world around us.

Luckily, I'd finished in time. I watched as a stream of figures with red wings came from the clouds above, diving down towards the city.

CHAPTER 25

I didn't wait to shift into a dragon and pumped my wings, starting to build up momentum. I crouched low, ready to throw myself up into the sky to meet the oncoming angel horde as a voice sounded behind me.

"Not without me." Morgana flipped herself onto my back as I took off. "Goldie, I need another tripod."

"I was wondering when you'd show up. There's no way for you to mount that thing on Regina," I answered.

"There is a way. She was just too big of a wuss to let me put bolts into her scales. Can you believe that? They would have grown out eventually." Morgana cackled as she adjusted the weapon on my back with several clacks. "Besides, you still need someone to watch your back. Remember what happened last time?"

I chuffed and shook my head. "Hold on." I threw myself into the air, pumping my wings and gaining altitude over the city.

Gathered in the night sky, the angels pulsed with an angry red energy that glowed against the clouds above. There had to be at least ten thousand angels in the sky. So many, gathered over the years. They'd been collected, put aside, and now they were being used.

I scanned the horizon, looking for my main target, but it appeared that Odima wasn't with this main body. She should have been leading them, but instead, there was another angel with bright red wings at the front.

Focusing back on the current threats, I drew fire into my throat and held it, continuing to build up the magic as the angels closed in on the city.

Basilisks were joining me in the sky, and my dragon mates were starting to spiral up from the gates. My heart was pounding in my ears like war drums as both sides prepared to clash, and I felt the tension in my throat reach a climax.

A ball of fire exploded from my throat and expanded as the angels broke their line and started to fan out over the city like a swarm of locusts. I didn't stop or slow down. Instead, I flew right into my own fire.

"Protect my wings," I told Goldie, half tucking them as the fire dispersed and I crashed straight into the mass of angels.

My wings were frozen, wrapped in heavy gold. Goldie lashed out in every direction, tearing through the angels.

The bulk of my body smashed into angels while my maw was wide open, catching a handful and chomping down as I fell through the mass of angels and plummeted down below. Many angels were wiped out from the impact.

"Fly." Goldie pulled back from my wings, her form crushing a few angels that had clung onto my wings in the vain hope of stopping me.

Morgana moved quickly, her blades cutting through two angels which were trying to hold onto my horns. "Stragglers all clear. Ready for another pass." Morgana got behind her mounted cannon and swung it up above us, peppering into the angels with a gleeful shout.

Some of the angels had broken off to chase me, while others were quickly occupied by the rest of our aerial forces coming up from the city gates.

My back shook as Morgana's cannon rattled away and angels fell out of the sky. I was pumping my wings to circle back up to the fight.

"That thing is obnoxiously loud." My voice thrummed with the effort to speak over it.

"I think you mean it's obnoxiously amazing." Morgana's face was lit by the muzzle flashes as I peered back at my badass mate. "Fall, little birdies!"

Morgana was in her element and more than happy to assist here. I doubt it would be often that she'd be able to use a weapon like this.

"Careful of my wings." I pulled myself up back where the angels were locked in combat with some of my harem and the forces of the city.

Odima was still nowhere to be seen.

I streaked into the fray. With the forces so intermingled, blasting out more dragon fire would do just as much harm as good. Instead, I had to be more careful, picking off angels in the back and letting Goldie and Morgana pick out individual targets.

The bulk of angels threw their angry blast of magic at me which seared my sides, but the hits weren't enough to stop me from ripping more of them to shreds.

A bright flash of white and red caught my eyes just inside the city, and I turned, zeroing in on the fight below. Helena and Odima broke apart, the two appearing like squabbling siblings as they clashed again.

"Odima spotted. Time to put the plan into action." I pivoted my body into a dive.

***

Helena had her arms crossed as she leaned down against the city gates. "Can't believe I have a babysitter." She glared at the Spider Queen, who was sitting on the side wall for the steps going up into the gate house.

They were waiting for Zach to come start the enchantments. He had just flown out over the wall, and the glow of his mana was breaking along the golden defenses.

"In fairness, you are like, what, twenty-eight? I'm... a lot older. So you are kind of like a baby from my perspective." Ikta had a wild smile that only became scarier because it reached her eyes.

Sometimes, Helena thought that the woman was far too unhinged. But now Helena wondered if Ikta was actually saner than this apparent sister Odima.

"What? Is there something in my teeth?" Ikta spread her lips as if to have it pointed out.

"No. I'm just wondering who's more crazy, you or this Odima." Helena knew the question wouldn't really offend the woman.

"Huh." Ikta paused and tapped at her chin while her foot swayed back and forth. "That's a very interesting proposal. Zach does like those of us that come with a little baggage, but is there such a thing as too much baggage? I would throw a question back your way. What if Zach were to try and fix your mother?"

Helena flipped her spear out, calling on it from the void, and pointed it at Ikta. "We are going to kill her before he even has a chance."

Ikta didn't even look at the spear, laughing a little gleefully. "That would work. But your mother is powerful. She's got something to do with what's happening here too."

"Why don't you know more, since you are so old?" Helena asked.

Ikta frowned at her. "I have been trapped for a hundred thousand years. Don't give me shit. I've missed a lot of things. Including your mother."

Helena tilted her head. "My mother? She's pretty hard to miss."

"Yeah. She wasn't around, or at least she wasn't prominent, before I was sealed." Ikta swayed her feet as a smile bloomed on her face. "I think I'm more wild than Odima. Really, she's straight forward, if in a direction we don't understand. I'm more unpredictable."

Helena shook her head. The woman had jumped back to the prior topic on a dime.

Lights started to flare up on the gate and continue down the wall, catching both of their attention.

"Damn that's a fuck ton of mana." Ikta let out a whistle.

Helena had to agree. "Zach is still growing stronger."

"Given how strong Odima is, I bet you will too." Ikta turned away from the wall. "Just give it time and take our husband's seed often."

Helena sighed and rolled her eyes. She wasn't interested in talking about sex. Everyone wanted to know about her sex life. Maybe it was because she didn't share that people wanted information. It always seemed that people wanted precisely what they didn't have.

A streak in the sky like a red ribbon came out of the clouds, starting to wind its way down. And they weren't the only ones to notice the new arrivals.

Zach took to the sky in his dragon form. His wings thumped in the air loud enough to make some of the more sensitive paranormals wince. He wasn't holding back either.

Just his presence crawled over her for a brief moment before it touched her mark, and like recognizing her, left her completely alone. As a dragon's mate, she felt completely comfortable in his otherwise overwhelming presence.

"Just think about how big his dick must be in that state." Ikta shattered the moment. "Think we could get a few girls, hold hands around it like a big tree and... you know..."

Helena was sorely tempted to egg Ikta on, but Helena knew that the Wild Queen would absolutely start going into detail as to what she meant. If anything, Ikta would go into immense detail just to watch Helena squirm.

Trying to shake the thought, Helena focused back above. Zach was leading the charge, but he wasn't alone. The dragonettes took to the air, followed by other paranormals of the city.

Helena cast a questioning glance to Ikta. "Do you fly?"

"Sort of." She made a portal in front of her and another that she fell into, sort of falling through the air only to go into another portal.

"That isn't flying." Helena sighed.

"No. It isn't, but I can capture an angel and tie them up with enough webbing that I can ride them like a little horsey."

Helena rubbed at her face. "Never mind. Forget I asked. Let's—" She was interrupted when a group of hooded figures walked up towards the gate; the lead one rushed her.

"We come from El Dorado and want to aid you!" Their voices sounded cheery, but they were keeping their hoods down.

Every instinct Helena had was screaming that they weren't in the city to help. Helena flipped her spear back out and pointed it at the front figure. "Hood off."

The woman lifted her face, and Helena felt like she was looking in a mirror for a moment.

"You must be my little sister." Odima's face turned full of rage as she exploded forward, a red cat o' nine tails lashing out from under her cloak.

Helena brought her spear up to block, yet her opponent's weapon wrapped around the shaft.

"Hurry in and set up. I'll take care of this one." Odima jerked Helena forward, snapping a kick into her midsection.

Helena grunted with the blow and was pissed off that she was being jerked around. Yet, something bothered her. It was like Odima hadn't even noticed Ikta.

Glancing around, Helena realized that the Spider Queen was nowhere to be found.

Odima's eyes were a wild red like flickering flames. "What are you looking for? Reinforcements? I think they all flew off."

Helena didn't bother with banter, whipping the shaft of her spear into her sister's face.

Odima took the hit without flinching, a cracked lip spilled blood for just a moment before healing over. "You've got some spunk. Even if you are all love." Odima headbutted Helena and pulled her weapon away, making Helena stumble back.

By the time Helena had reoriented herself, Odima's weapon had become a spear, but it was a twisted, barbed replica of her own. The two clashed several times. Helena's white magic flaring against Odima's red.

A moment later, a portal opened above them, and Helena used her wings to shoot back for whatever crazy scheme Ikta had cooked up.

Odima had noticed the portal too and dove backwards to keep herself clear.

Sure enough, a deluge of broken and bloody angel parts came out of the portal before a blood-splattered Ikta lowered herself with her spider limbs, wiping herself off with a woefully inadequate washcloth. She'd need something bigger for how bloody she had gotten.

"Hey. I found the ones you sent ahead." She waved like she was greeting a friend.

Odima's sneer fell. "No," she breathed. "Who are you?"

"I'm just your friendly neighborhood Spider Queen. Don't mind me. Also, the angel with the x shaved into the side of his head was a real dick. You should get better subordinates." Ikta stepped down onto the top of the pile of corpses, her heels cracking one of the skulls as her spider limbs fanned out behind her and the portal closed.

Odima's eyes shook with anger. "Die!"

Her spear stabbed forward, aided by spatial magic to stab into Ikta. But a portal opened at the last second, and Odima's spear stabbed into the portal and then through her own thigh.

"You shouldn't do that." Ikta shook her head playfully.

Odima wasn't dissuaded, stabbing rapidly at Ikta. Each thrust twisted and stretched, making it hard for Ikta to make portals for all of them.

But Ikta was a seasoned fighter. She caught or blocked every one of the hits, sending Odima's spear back at her. Odima's healing continued to save her. She'd remove the spear and her body would heal almost instantly.

Helena healed quickly too, but watching the speed with which Odima's body healed was almost scary. Odima must have seen her idle because she switched targets and tried to catch Helena unaware.

Helena stumbled to react, but Ikta got there first. Ikta covered Helena with a portal to stop the hit, and Helena dove below the portal, slashing her spear into Odima with the other angel's weapon occupied.

"You can't win," Odima called out, tilting her chin up at Ikta and Helena as she healed instantly.

The Spider Queen blinked. "Who said I was trying to win? My job was just to stall you and make enough flashes for him to come." She pointed up.

Sure enough, Zach had seen them. The giant red and gold dragon was bearing down on them.

"Yeah. He wants a piece of you," Ikta laughed.

Odima screamed in frustration and pulled out a giant golden fang from underneath her cloak. "You'll die."

***

I watched their fight as I dove, my eyes widening when I saw what Odima pulled out at the end. "Morgana, fire."

Dozens of muzzle flashes threatened to ruin my night vision as Morgana peppered Odima from over my shoulder. Blood went everywhere as she held her fire on the Nephilim of Hate and her cannon chewed Odima up.

Even as we got too close and Morgana had to hold her fire, I could see the red, blade-covered wings snap back into place. Luckily, forcing her to heal from the hits had stalled Odima's attack long enough.

My full mass slammed down on Odima as I grabbed her with a claw and crashed into the city. There was getting hit by a bus, but my full dragon form landing on something was more akin to someone dropping an oil tanker on you.

I skidded around a block, driving a large rent in the golden street and using Odima like a plow. "Don't touch my mates," I growled and held up the dazed nephilim before smashing her back into the city streets several times.

Truth be told, it was impressive that she wasn't splattered all over. But it wasn't much better.

The fight was over. She was strong, but this time, I wasn't going to fight with weapons, dealing small damage to each other. I had my claws around her, and I was not about to let go. Using my full draconic bulk was the answer to a swift end to this fight and keeping her injured was how I would end it.

"Damn. Smash her again." Ikta jumped up and down next to me clapping excitedly.

Helena had her hip cocked to the side, glaring at the nephilim in my clutches and leaning on her spear. "What are you going to do with her?"

"What I should have done from the beginning." I opened a portal.

"No!" Odima screamed. She must have felt what was on the other side before I threw Odima through; my bones crackled as I shifted down to my dragon knight form.

In the moment before I was small enough to go through, Helena got to the front of the portal and stabbed Odima to keep her inside.

"The mansion?" Helena asked, surprised.

Goldie formed a spear, and Morgana held her cannon as carefully as she'd hold a baby and went about checking it over.

I charged into the portal and fought Odima back away from the portal long enough for Helena to follow me though. Then I closed the portal behind us.

"She's a nephilim, just like you, drawing on Earth's mana so easily. Here, she's just an angel out of her element."

We were in the basement of the mansion which Morgana used for training.

"And you are in your plane," Helena answered.

I snorted at her answer. "So are you. Whether you like it or not, you've been reacting well to my own dimension. It might be fairest to say that, like me, my dimension has accepted you."

Helena shot me a look but spun her spear in her hand. "So, I'll regenerate here and she won't?"

Odima was covered in blood, and her body was repairing itself from being thrown around by my dragon form.

"Her regeneration will slow down. Yours won't," I clarified. I knew Helena needed to work off some of her feelings.

Helena grinned and shot forward to attack Odima, who defended herself. Their spears slid off of each other as they blocked and slashed at each other in a reckless duel.

"Envokus." I threw a thin but powerful bolt of lightning at Odima, catching her wing, and in a burst of fire, torching a swath of her feathers.

"Fight me fairly, you cowards." She jumped back, right into a web and got stuck before six spider limbs came out from behind her and spun her quickly.

The web ripped away from the wall, and wrapped around her as Ikta sang a lullaby. "Go to sleep. Go to sleep, my sweet angry angel. Go to sleep—"

"Shut up." Odima thrashed, but with every movement, Helena was stabbing into the cocoon. The silver threads of the web were soon painted red.

"Hey. She is trapped as it is." Ikta rolled her eyes.

"Maybe we should stab her a few more times to make sure she's drained of mana." Helena held her spear hard enough to make her knuckles white.

"Let me go!" Odima screamed, and Ikta spun her around, spreading spider silk over her mouth.

"There, there, dear. Go to sleep," Ikta murmured.

"Did you grab the artifact?" I asked Ikta.

"This thing?" Ikta held up a diamond-tipped, golden fang that looked like it belonged to a giant viper. "Looks kind of fun, doesn't it?" She waved it like she might accidentally stab Odima. It got so close that it tore the threads keeping her gagged.

The nephilim threw her whole body to the side to try and escape being stabbed.

"Oh. What? You don't like it? It's your own item." Ikta waved the fang carelessly.

"Stop!" Odima was actually scared of the fang. "Until you put it in the artifact, you shouldn't stab anyone with it."

"Why's that?" I asked, pushing Ikta's hand down and away from the nephilim.

"Because it will drain whomever it stabs. Unless you want my hate mana all in you, I wouldn't stab me with it." Odima grinned. "Actually, why don't you stab me sister?"

"Pass." Helena sounded bored.

There was a soft clap behind us. "Oh, there you are." An angel with a jawline cut from marble and swept back black hair appeared.

"Uriel." Helena tensed and readied herself.

"Hello, little Helena." He beamed back at her. "Hello, little Dragon King. I see you've found something of mine." His eyes lit up as he saw the fang in my hand.

"How did you get in here?" Helena snapped.

"My dear, as the angel of inspiration, I know how to get anywhere I want to be. And I know how to get anything I want. Hand it over now. It would be far easier than the alternative." He held out his hand like he owned the place, which was pissing me off.

"No thanks." I rolled my eyes.

"Have it your way. But if you waste your time here, Aphrodite will already have several of your wives by the time you return. She's in the city already after all." Uriel grinned.

CHAPTER 26

J adelyn spotted Zach up high above, following the trail of fire that was devouring the entire sky. She played with the necklaces resting against her chest. She'd decked herself out fully in her various enchantments. She'd accumulated them over the years, but Sabrina had recently added a few more.

Two chunky gold bracers like the ones her father often wore adorned her wrists.

"Awe inspiring." Leviathan stood nearby on the shore.

"Indeed. I'm proud to be his wife, and support him with everything I have. To think that the little lost one who got in a fight with Chad would end up here." Jadelyn couldn't keep her eyes off the red and gold dragon streaking through the air.

"Lost one?" Leviathan asked.

Jadelyn pulled her eyes away from Zach to look at the demoness. Leviathan had a set of giant horns coming out of the side of her waterfall of blue hair.

"You don't see them often anymore. But they are usually people cut off from the paranormal world by their parents or grandparents dying early. So they sort of wander around human society lost with the differences they feel but cannot explain."

Leviathan glanced back up at the show that Zach was putting on. "He seems to know he's a dragon now."

"That he does." Jadelyn beamed. "A terrifying dragon at that." Her eyes swept over the surface of the ocean but didn't see any signs of threat.

Really, guarding the water wasn't much of a job.

Jadelyn didn't think a bunch of angels would attempt to swim in to attack. But in order to properly defend, they needed to be prepared for every possibility.

"Question for you, Levi." Jadelyn shortened the other woman's name. "How does the whole Envy and harems concept work?"

The demon could certainly invite quite a bit of envy with her figure. She was tall and lean like a supermodel, maybe even slightly taller than many men would be comfortable around. Yet she somehow had curves where it mattered.

Even just looking at the mounds compared to the rest of the woman's lean frame, Jadelyn was a little envious.

Leviathan smirked. "I can taste that, you know."

"Does it taste bad?" Jadelyn asked.

"No. You are quite sweet. Obviously nothing compared to the Dragon King though. To answer your question, I am envious of all of you in the harem. I'm also envious of the Dragon King himself. His power and prestige are at an entirely unobtainable level," Leviathan answered smoothly.

"If you could taste that, how much are you eating when you spend time around the harem? Are there problems that I need to smooth out?" Jadelyn asked.

Leviathan's beautiful lips curled up in a knowing smile. "Why, there is something you could do. Let me in and let me sip on the small currents of envy to help remove the emotion from the harem. There will always be a small amount of friction. I can offer my services to make sure everything continues running smoothly."

Jadelyn narrowed her eyes. "Convenient. Or, you could worm your way in and make it all worse. I mean, if you upset Zach by doing it, what could he do to you?"

"I imagine he could do a many number of things to me." There was a wicked smile on Leviathan's lips now. "But to answer your question, while I am invulnerable and quite strong, I could still be sealed by someone like the Dragon King, I imagine."

Jadelyn nodded along with her words; they made sense. "I'll think about it."

"My understanding is that I will have your permission if I get a dragon toy?"

"Plushie," Jadelyn corrected her. "It's a Golden Plushie, for the Golden Plushie Society, a group we formed out of the harem and harem hopefuls."

Leviathan's eyes flicked out to the ocean. "Something is coming."

Jadelyn didn't hesitate, throwing herself into the water and feeling the water embrace her and everything she was as a siren.

Power filled her as scales dotted her skin and her legs stuck together, filled in with muscles she didn't otherwise have, and a large mermaid tail flicked her forward a dozen yards.

A large vessel moved through the ocean ahead of her.

"A submarine." She blinked, excitement building. It was her turn to act. "Levi." She turned to find the demoness in the water with her and beginning to swell.

Jadelyn had forgotten for a moment that Levi could shift and become quite large.

Jadelyn shot away as Leviathan continued to grow. Soon Levi was a massive serpent creature with an enormous maw and barbs coming out in every direction. She looked like a mix of a dragon and a dolphin with several large fins on the underside and plated scales covering every inch of the giant body. The oddest part to her were the tentacles. Four large squid tentacles that ended in bulbous, barbed pads came out from the neck.

But all in, Leviathan had to be several hundred yards from tip to tip.

"I'm going to stop it." Leviathan shot forward with a flick of her tail.

Jadelyn hurried to keep up. When it came to stopping the submarines, Leviathan was going to be much more useful. But when the angels emerged, Jadelyn was determined to be worth something.

As Leviathan attacked the first submarine, her tentacles slapped against the side, and pulled it closer. As the first submarine moved out of the way, Jadelyn noticed that the first submarine wasn't alone.

Four much larger submarines were coming up behind it, keeping a safe distance from each other.

"Crush it and we'll move to the next one," Jadelyn called out.

Levi didn't speak. Instead, her massive maw opened up and crunched into the submarine. Somehow, the move reminded Jadelyn of the first time Scarlett had had sunflower seeds and tried to eat the shells.

Once Levi had damaged the hull, the whole thing crumbled like a spent soda can, spilling out humans and angels into the sea.

Now was Jadelyn's turn. She shot forward, spotting a four-winged angel and tackling it in the water. The angel tried to pull away, but in the water, Jadelyn was stronger and far faster than the angel could react.

Before he knew it, the angel was smashed against the seafloor, and Jadelyn was calling on her magic to pull water into his lungs.

The angel thrashed. Like too many people, instincts overruled logic when water got in the lungs. He panicked. Even if he had magic that might save himself, he wasn't going to act fast enough.

Jadelyn swam away, looking for other priority targets as Leviathan pushed through the wreckage and many of the angels tried to attack her. Fortunately, they didn't even scratch the demoness' scales.

Jadelyn wondered what such a power would be like. If she were invulnerable, Zach would never leave her behind again. After a moment, Jadelyn shook her head feeling sheepish that she'd envied the demoness again.

Something told Jadelyn those feelings were probably a common occurrence for the demoness. Jadelyn didn't want to make it a common thing for her.

Instead, she went to take out another angel.

A metallic ping rang out through the water, and Jadelyn froze. She knew what that sound meant. Sonar was about to hit.

Jadelyn turned and swam as quickly as she could, not that it would make much of a difference, but sirens had long learned the dangers of sonar. She pushed out any remaining air in her normal lungs and tried to breathe down water. With her gills, she'd be fine until she went to the surface and she'd have to use magic to clear her lungs.

Those angels and humans in the water closest to the sonar pulse that came next spewed blood from their mouths as their lungs burst from the pressure of the sonar wave.

It wasn't just the pressure, but the difference between air and water as the vibrations switched between the two mediums. Or at least, that was what Jadelyn remembered from the old warnings when she was a child.

Jadelyn clutched at her ears as unbearable metallic shrieking hit her, and she rode the wave away from the submarine. Multiple enchantments lit up on her necklaces and bracers to help protect her. One of her necklaces popped and she swam upside down, stunned for a moment.

But she was still alive.

Sonar was no joke. Even if she had been trained on how best to survive it and had enchantments to protect her, it was a rough ride. Jadelyn groaned and twisted herself in the water to see the outcome.

Hundreds of red clouds bloomed from the bodies in the water as they sank. It was a beautiful, yet gruesome sight.

Past the scene of death, Leviathan, in her colossal form, was still fighting several of the ships. A tentacle broke through the clouds of blood and one of the submarines shot through, heading full speed towards the shore.

Jadelyn scrambled to get out of the way, unable to stop it. She wouldn't be very useful if she got sucked up in the pump jets. Before she could reach it, the submarine breached the surface and rammed itself ashore.

Leviathan shot up above the surface of the water, spraying seafoam everywhere as another of the submarines was wrenched in half and the angels and humans inside spilled into the sea with abandon.

The beached submarine opened its hatch, and templar knights spilled out of it, rushing into the city while several angels were more relaxed and walked behind, bringing up the rear.

Jadelyn looked to the skies for her husband. He needed to come stop the new angels that had infiltrated the city. Jadelyn's eyes scanned and searched, but she couldn't find him among the skies. And that meant that this fight was left to her.

Jadelyn sang her song for her dear husband as the water listened to her magic and swirled around her before waves crashed onto the submarine and the shore, trying to grab and reclaim the Church's forces.

Several succumbed to the sea, but a templar raised a bow and fired an arrow.

Ducking under the waves didn't stop the arrow as it chased her down and activated several of her enchantments when it hit her. Jadelyn huffed a sigh of relief, but knew she needed Leviathan to help.

A swish of her tail had her shooting around the clouds of blood to see the giant sea creature crushing the remains of the submarines and smashing survivors while her tentacles rose out of the water and tried to swat down angels who tried to escape to the sky.

She wasn't doing a perfect job of it all, but she was able to do far more than Jadelyn.

A wave of envy passed over her, and Jadelyn had to shake her head to snap out of it. Those feelings were just the demon prince's power. Jadelyn had to remind herself that she lived an absolutely fantastic life, and her one flaw of not being as helpful in wartime situations like these was minor in the grand scale of everything.

"Levi!" Jadelyn shouted under water. "One submarine got to the shore and I need your help." She swam past the colossal creature's head.

One eye tracked Jadelyn as she swam past, and the giant head nodded before twisting and turning back towards the shore.

Rather than swim herself, Jadelyn grabbed onto one of the spikes on Levi's face and let the sea beast carry her to the shore and explode out of the water.

Templars and angels were better able to fight on the land, and beams of light and white fire exploded against Levi without even harming the demon prince.

Levi's tentacles crashed down, smashing several of the templars attacking her before she froze. There was the flutter of wings and a click of heels against Leviathan's hard scales.

Jadelyn was filled with dread as she turned to regard the angel that had joined her atop Levi. And the angel wasn't alone.

"Hello. This one is Jadelyn, correct?" Aphrodite asked who Jadelyn recognized as Jared Nashner. He was wearing a brand-new gleaming sword across his back.

"Yes. That's the one. He's terribly in love with her." Jared glared.

"Levi." Jadelyn hissed only to see the demoness' eyes were completely focused on Aphrodite like a giant puppy seeing its master. "Fuck."

One of Jadelyn's necklaces grew hot as Aphrodite stared at her, but the enchantment held. But Jadelyn realized that meant the previous envy was her own, and not the demoness' manipulation.

"Don't bother." Aphrodite's voice was like honey in Jadelyn's ears. "She might be invincible, physically at least, but the Prince of Envy has always had a few chinks in her armor. No doubt while spending time around this new Dragon King that she's craving love. Isn't that right?" She rubbed the brow of Levi's head and the giant sea beast rumbled like a purring cat.

Jadelyn didn't even bother with the angel, instead turning to Helena's brother. "What are you doing, Jared? You know this woman is going to kill Helena."

"As a devout member of the Church, I am assisting in the restoration of Heaven." Jared crossed over his heart. "Besides, who says we are here for Helena?"

Aphrodite tilted her head. "Going to put up a fight, or will you come with me?"

"You want my husband," Jadelyn gasped.

"Precisely. My daughter fought me quite a bit because of this Dragon King, so I found an expert on him. This young templar has been brooding on ways to kill your husband and has even sent letter after letter to the Church outlining plans they could use to kill him."

"I wish to free Helena from his clutches," Jared tried to justify himself.

Jadelyn's anger rose. She wished she had more power to kill the man right then and there.

"See. Now that I understand that he's connected to Faerie and Hell, I had an idea. Why use Helena to drain mana from Earth to Heaven when I can just collapse Faerie and Hell and kill the Dragon King." Aphrodite smiled. "Several birds with one stone."

Jadelyn tried to throw herself off of Levi and back into the ocean, but Jared moved faster and snagged her arm, holding her by her bracer and roughly tossing her against Levi's scales. Soon her arms were bound behind her back.

"Zach will kill you," Jadelyn seethed.

"I'm hoping he comes and tries. My second says he fought Odima and is now being reluctant to give up the second fang." Aphrodite pulled out a large, curved piece of gold that ended in a wicked, barbed point. The whole thing looked like it could be broken down into pieces.

Jadelyn could not believe that that stupid hunk of gold was causing all the current chaos.

"It doesn't look like much?" Aphrodite turned it slowly in her hand. "The entire thing was built in fifteen layers of gold, layering many enchantments into the two fangs."

Jadelyn stayed quiet and glared at the angel.

"Leviathan, dear, please come set us down and revert to your more mobile form. I'd love to see you in the flesh." Aphrodite's eyes glowed white as she looked at the sea beast.

Levi lowered them to the shore where Jared roughly pulled Jadelyn from the sea beast and onto the sand while Aphrodite floated off. Levi shifted back to her humanoid form. She was beautiful enough to make Jadelyn a little envious, and Jadelyn was more than a little jealous that the demon would survive the entire situation.

No one had to worry about her.

It was Jadelyn that everyone had to worry about, and that would bring Zach right to where Aphrodite wanted him. The thought of preventing Aphrodite from using her by dying even crossed Jadelyn's mind, but she put it out the second she thought of the pain it would put her husband through.

Instead, she steeled herself and remembered all of the times that Zach had come through in the past.

He would do so again.

"What does this whole thing do?" Jadelyn asked.

"They were from a war in the past." Aphrodite held the fang, appreciating the artifact. "You see, dragons were an inspiration. They can eat other paranormals and grow quickly. The rest of us don't have such methods. Instead, these two fangs were made to siphon off power, and the base to distribute it. While your husband's mana isn't entirely compatible with Heaven, it should be enough to stabilize the plane. We can sort the rest out later, especially with Hell and Faerie collapsed. At that point, we can use Earth to provide mana for eons to come."

"So, if I stabbed you with that, I'd become the new Queen Bitch of Heaven?" Jadelyn asked.

"No. You'd become paste on the ground because you couldn't handle the mana." Aphrodite's lips curled up. "You are weak and frail, which is what makes you the perfect hostage."

Jadelyn stared at the artifact for a moment and licked her lips, not even bothering to hide the idea of stabbing Aphrodite with the fang.

"Leviathan, go take the temple. I'm sure they have lots of traps for us." Aphrodite ignored Jadelyn.

CHAPTER 27

I couldn't help myself and let out a low growl at Uriel. "That doesn't sound like a reason for me to give this up. It sounds like this is the best bargaining chip that I have." I held the golden fang in my hand. "Goldie, keep it safe."

"Yes, Zach." Goldie flowed over my hand and around the fang before pulling it into her mass and returning to my bracer.

Uriel only smiled. "It is amusing to see you try and struggle. It would have been far wiser to leave here and save your wives."

"Here I thought you'd be going for Helena," I replied.

"She's the old plan. We have a new one, and it is going splendidly." Uriel pulled out a bow and kept it low. "You are going to hand over the fang or I'll stall you until Aphrodite rounds up your mates." He ducked into a roll as one of Ikta's limbs appeared through a portal behind him.

The fight had begun.

Odima started screaming. "Free me and I'll kill them all!"

Helena shouted back, cutting her sister, who was still healing quickly. "You should eat her."

"No thank you. I don't want her mana." I was rushing Uriel while his bow was pointed away from me, packing on mass and entering my dragon knight form. I had every advantage if I got him down on the ground and wrestling.

Uriel came out of his roll, pointing his bow at Ikta and firing before twitching to the side and firing a second arrow right into a portal that Ikta had planned to use to divert his first shot.

The second arrow punched right through Ikta and sent the Spider Queen stumbling back as she glared angrily at the angel.

"Cheap tricks won't work on me," he proclaimed with a big grin as he positioned himself between the open portal and me.

Ikta closed the portal a second later.

Uriel pumped his wings to pull himself backwards, plucking his bow like a harp and raining arrows down on me.

The arrows cracked and scraped my scales, frustrating me until I breathed fire up at him and dodged to the side with one powerful step. Unfortunately, I twisted my ankle as I landed and threw myself at where he should have been.

But as I passed through the fire, I hit nothing but air and fanned out my wings to change my course.

Arrows punched through the fire and my wings as Uriel made himself known, back down on the ground with his bow and a smug grin on his face. "See? You can't even touch me. I know what inspires you, what makes you create new ideas. I see right through every move you make before you do it."

"That's why you are the second strongest angel?" I mocked him as my wings knit themselves back together.

"Yes, while Aphrodite has a unique love of herself and her magic, you could say she's obsessed with her magic to the point where she's gone past perfection with her control." Uriel made a face.

If trying to hit the angel was going to be so hard, then it was best to just hit the whole room. I breathed deep and called upon summer fae magic before turning half the room into a golden inferno, the stone catching on fire and its surface melting under the continuous stream.

The only part of the room that was safe was around Ikta, Helena and Odima. They had stayed out of the brief, chaotic battle.

When the fire died down, Uriel was coughing. His wings were singed and his clothing burnt. Space warped around him as he tried to create space between him and the fires. But Summer's heat was nothing to scoff at, even compared to dragon fire.

Uriel staggered and started firing at my women.

It was Helena that stepped forward, fanning out her wings and taking the arrows without batting an eyelash. "Going to have to do better than that, Uriel."

"We aren't on Earth. I'd like to see you keep it up." The angel thought he'd won as he fired again.

Helena stood tall, a smile on her face. I could feel her bathing in the mana of my plane, soaking it in as if she were a nephilim born in my plane.

Uriel's arrows stopped punching through her wings and started to thud against them before the arrows were pushed out instantly, the wounds healing over.

My scales shifted to white and silver as I watched Uriel's brows furrow into a deep frown. Hoping to catch him unaware, I filled the room with freezing fog that cracked the stone with the sudden change in temperature and left Uriel shivering as ice crept along his body.

I kept it up, filling the room with freezing fog as Helena beat her wings to keep it away. Portals opened up behind Ikta to blow hot air over the three of them and keep them safe.

Uriel's hand on the bow froze first, the cold metal conducting the chill quite well. His finger broke off and the arrogant archangel stopped moving.

I didn't hesitate, holding my hand out as Goldie pushed the fang back into my hand, and stabbed it into the angel.

If the fang was supposed to drain his power, and Aphrodite was currently taking on my mates, I wanted his power. It might make me strong enough to take down Aphrodite.

The fang pierced his chest, and the angel's wings shriveled as power pulsed into me. Uriel's skin went gray and wrinkled before he became nothing but dust.

A few more portals opened around the room as Ikta shivered and rubbed her shoulders. "That was intense."

"Yeah. I don't want to be anywhere near that thing." Helena stared at the artifact in my hand.

Angelic power flowed through me, and I struggled to make sense of the power for a moment as the new power continued into my heart and swirled around my body, working to settle in. It wasn't comfortable feeling the new power pulse through me, but soon enough, it had blended itself into my body.

"It is dangerous," I agreed. "Part of me wants to just destroy this." My eyes shifted back up to Odima.

"Sure, come stab me and become a paragon of hate." She held her chin up defiantly.

"Ikta, kill her and let her body rot in some hole in Faerie." I didn't want her mana in my mansion or around any of my harem.

"Wait!" Odima shouted, but Ikta had already sucked her into a portal.

"What now?" Helena's eyes didn't leave the fang.

"If your mother really has one of my mates..." I tilted the fang back and forth, working to run through my options and Aphrodite's next move. I held out the fang for Goldie to take again. "I need to get back to the battle." I opened up a portal and Helena hesitated.

"You're with me," Ikta reminded her. "Come on, we'll deal with your sister."

I stepped back through the portal, knowing Ikta and Helena could take care of the situation. My other mates needed me.

I scanned around as soon as I stepped through the portal. The first mates I spotted were my dragon mates, circling high in the air. The battle with the hateful angels was over.

Instead, all their focus was on the main temple whose top was partially melted. The enchantments on it had gone all out and failed.

My wings fanned out, and I rose into the sky, seeing more of my mates on the backs of the dragons. Quickly, I counted them. My heart lifted as I continued to count, but then it fell at the end. One was missing.

And it didn't take me long to spot her.

Jadelyn was standing behind Aphrodite, Jared, another archangel with blond hair, and... of all people, Leviathan.

A pang of betrayal and anger coursed through me, before I noticed the look on Levi's face. The pure adoration wasn't the look the demoness would have if she were in her right mind. Aphrodite had gotten to her.

"So glad of you to join us," Aphrodite called out across the space.

The entire temple and the surrounding area was covered in angels and agents of the church. Down on the street level, citizens of the city and the werewolves were held back.

"I see you've made ground while I was killing Uriel." I smiled towards her.

Aphrodite's face twitched. "So be it. Some sacrifices must be made."

"Cold. How does that archangel next to you feel about that? Hmm?" I stalled while I thought through the situation.

"Gabriel is fine where he is," Aphrodite insisted as the other archangel didn't even flinch.

"I expected Michael. Isn't he the big one?" I teased.

Aphrodite's smile was sly. "He was always a bit of a stickler for the rules. Justice never lasted long. Are you going to keep stalling, or are we going to talk about your lovely mate here." She gestured to Jadelyn behind her, but she didn't even turn to look at her.

"Odima and Helena are gone," I told her. "You want this?" Goldie pushed the artifact out of her bracer form and into my hand. "It won't do anything with them gone."

When I had used it on Uriel, it had only drained his personal mana, and let me tap slightly into his territory in Heaven and mana filled with inspiration. I tried to work out Aphrodite's next move. Both nephilim were unavailable to her, but she didn't seem unhappy. Who would Aphrodite even use?

"I have my reasons." Aphrodite held her hand out. "I think it is a fair trade. Your mate for the artifact, no?"

Jadelyn was shaking her head behind the archangel, and I wish I could ask her what she knew.

I stared at the golden fang for a long hard moment before glancing back at Jadelyn and Aphrodite. "Why don't you have Leviathan make the trade? Sorry, but I'd rather not get close to you."

"No. I don't think so." Aphrodite handed back an artifact that could be the twin of the one in my hand to Jared. "Hold onto this and snap Jadelyn's neck if he so much as tries to hit me."

"With pleasure." Jared sneered at me. "This is what you get, Dragon King." My title rolled off his lips like spittle.

I met his eyes and promised death if he touched Jadelyn. Although, if I was honest, I wanted his death either way.

We were both so focused on each other that Jared failed to notice when Jadelyn made her move. In one motion, Jadelyn jerked the artifact from Jared's hand, holding it tightly in her own.

The man spun and slashed out at Jadelyn who hobbled back, blocking his blade that must have hit her hard because the fang swung until it was parallel with the ground and stabbed right into Leviathan who had been so focused on Aphrodite that she didn't even register the scuffle.

Thankfully, Levi was invincible.

I waited for the next move, but my eyes were drawn back as the tip of the fang touched the naked Leviathan and her hair lost its luster. Her skin faded to black and she turned to dust as Jadelyn's thrust carried through the dust.

It all happened in just a moment, ending with Jadelyn's screaming as she flung the golden fang as far away from her as she could.

Gabriel and Jared jumped into action, racing for the artifact.

But a blur in the air reached the fang first. Scarlett had dropped off the dragons, grabbing the fang. Her tails waved behind her as she landed into a roll and then jumped up into the air away from Jared.

Gabriel slashed forward to hit Scarlett, who puffed into nothing. She'd used one of her illusions.

"She's a kitsune! Must I—" Aphrodite was halfway to me, but that just made it easier for me to dive at her and let my wives move to save Jadelyn.

Summer came down like a golden meteor and clashed her golden sword against Gabriel's burning silver sword. The two exploded in brief combat as Summer kept pushing him back.

Sabrina and Maeve landed next to Jared.

I didn't have time to worry about them as Aphrodite chopped at my arm, a spatial blade on her hand. The world seemed to press around me as I tried to shift, locking me in place despite my wings pumping hard. Even while I threw my weight to the side, Aphrodite wasn't weak.

Her hand kept coming down on my arm no matter what I tried. So rather than try to dodge, I was forced to block. Covering my arm with winter fae mana, I let ice form all over and jut out to protect me.

Aphrodite's hand cut clean through the ice, but stopped after slicing into my arm, space stopped compressing and I was able to pull back. In the same motion, I threw a punch as hard as I could at her with my other arm.

"Space, like many things, does not like to be compressed." She smiled as a shockwave ripped out from in between us, throwing me backwards. Then she used her wings to soar towards the action on the temple.

Maeve was quick on her feet, throwing up a giant wall of silver ice to cover the entire open side of the temple.

Before she had closed it off, I scanned the area and spotted Jared's bloody body on the ground beneath Sabrina while the succubus was hauling Jadelyn off with Scarlett. Summer was holding her own against Gabriel. The older Faerie Queen was reluctantly quite skilled in combat.

"Goldie, hold the fang for me." I looked down at my hand only to see the artifact was gone.

Aphrodite glanced over her shoulder at me and had the gall to wink as she flew after Scarlett with my artifact in her hand.

I threw up a portal in front of her, but space bent around and moved the portal out of the way. Growling, I charged after her.

The Archangel of Love tackled the open air, and my first mate came fumbling out as they wrestled over the second artifact, ultimately tossing it onto the ground of the temple.

Morgana appeared, her two swords forcing Aphrodite off of Scarlett as she drew a rapier and blocked both of them before exchanging a rapid series of blows with my vampire mate.

It bought me the time I needed. I hurtled down on top of the angel.

Aphrodite glanced up, and there was a moment of wide-eyed fear in her eyes before my progress towards her stalled and she slipped around Morgana, passed Scarlett and snatched the second fang.

She stood before the base, slotting both fangs into it quickly.

I landed next to Morgana and Scarlett. "How's Jadelyn?"

"Breathing," Scarlett answered, her tails lashing behind her. "We'll check her out more carefully when this is over. I'm sorry I failed to protect her. The beach was supposed to be low risk, and Levi was meant to protect her."

"We'll talk through all of that later." I glanced at Aphrodite's smug smile as she stood next to the two fangs slotted before the throne. With its big hood, the whole thing looked like the maw of a serpent.

But Aphrodite wasn't moving to grab her sacrifice. Instead, the archangel was standing by the fangs, waiting for me to come to her.

It had become clear that the two artifacts posed very real dangers. After seeing them kill an archangel and then in Jadelyn's hand kill Leviathan, they were quite possibly the most dangerous weapons around.

Gabriel broke off his fight with Summer to land next to Aphrodite, looking worse for wear.

My dragon mates landed around the edge of the temple, waiting for the signal. I didn't have to say anything. Instead, taking a deep breath, I poured out the hottest damned fire I could breathe right on top of the two archangels.

CHAPTER 28

"Look. You don't really want to do this." Odima struggled, only opening her many wounds that had long since stopped closing.

Helena shuddered, having seen the dark side of Ikta by that point. The woman was dangerous. She was glad Ikta was on their side.

"Pretty sure we do. Zach said to let you rot out here." Ikta lowered the bound woman into the hole, alive.

"I'll tell you something." Odima struggled.

"At most, I'm just willing to kill you swiftly." Ikta crossed her arms and let go of the woman in the hole. "You'll not make it out of this alive, but maybe it'll end."

"The artifact. It's part of the throne. Two fangs to pierce the sacrifice and drain them along with anything they are bound to. The one sitting in the throne can then either take on the power themselves, or if it is someone like my mother, then she can direct it to her domain in the celestial plane," Odima pleaded.

Ikta crouched by the hole. "More. I need more than that. Why now?"

"Because a titan just died, right?" Odima looked around. "That was what triggered her last time. Something about the titan's mana when it died, even on another plane, was necessary."

Helena shared a look with Ikta before focusing back on her sister. "Yes. The Dreamer just passed away."

Odima nodded. "That's the last titan, right? Aphrodite needs someone. She probably lost a huge chunk of the celestial plane to just come down with Gabriel and Uriel. This is her last chance. So, if she can't have me or Helena, she'll take the next best thing."

Ikta was faster than Helena at realizing what the next best thing was. "The Dragon King, who currently holds all of Faerie, Hell, and his own plane as well."

"It isn't Earth, but it is certainly enough to restore Heaven. And with that power, she'd crush Hell and be able to siphon more off Earth in the future." Odima nodded rapidly. "Is that good enough?"

Blood shot out of her mouth as Ikta pierced her chest. "Enjoy your death." Ikta's limbs worked quickly to ensure that Odima was well and truly dead before Ikta stood up from the hole and opened another portal to rain earth down over Odima, burying the nephilim of hate for good.

"We should head back." Helena found herself eager to rejoin the fight. With the news that had just been shared, it would be better if they went back and helped.

"Why?" Ikta tilted her head at an unnatural angle. "He asked for you to be pulled away."

Helena wasn't afraid of the Spider Queen, at least not as long as she had Zach's mark on her. "Because he needs us. More importantly, he needs you. You are a special kind of terrifying."

Ikta blushed and held her cheeks like a young woman. "You really think so? Aww. Well aren't you sweet. I did tell him I wouldn't."

"But you will?" Helena asked, keeping the eagerness from her voice.

"Mmm, I suppose. But the second your mother looks like she's going to throw you on the stupid fangs, we portal you out." Ikta leveled a glare at her. "Understood?"

"Perfectly." Helena flicked her wrist and spun her spear into her hands.

***

The combined fire of eight dragons cut off, leaving a crater in the middle of the temple except for one small block of gold around the throne.

Aphrodite stood with her arms out, the air warping around her as Gabriel knelt next to her holding the unconscious Jared. Aphrodite's hair whipped behind her and her white sleeves were just barely singed.

Fury was painted on her face as she glared at me. "I will not be stopped. Not when the very plane which I rule is at stake. I came here to restore my home. Since you have decided to take away my daughter, we'll use you."

As if on cue, the angels on the temple began to fight as more poured down from the skies above. Aphrodite had been holding back, and now she was making her move.

I hadn't thrown in all my chips yet either. T had been in reserve for when Heaven came knocking.

Green fire erupted around the city and the dead from the battle thus far rose back to their feet. They rushed the temple or flew to meet those coming to join the battle from above.

Aphrodite reached towards me. I grabbed her hand as she jerked me across the surface of the temple when she reset the space. Yet my hand was still around her wrist when it ended. I squeezed with every ounce of strength that I had.

Her eyes opened wide as she tried to move me, but I turned out to be far heavier than she realized, and Goldie was helping me. She was spilling out, using her mass to brace me to the floor and keep me from the artifact.

"You wanted to throw me on those, didn't you? Doesn't take a genius. If you need someone powerful, I'm your next best option. You might be able to make and remove space, but I'm still fairly sure you can't lift an entire temple." I grinned and squeezed her arm tighter, lifting her off the ground before throwing her at the fangs myself.

Space rippled, and it felt like I had been swinging her for over ten seconds before her wrist slipped out of my hand and she fluttered over the fangs with a light smile on her face.

"What a tight grip you have." She rubbed at her wrist that was an angry red.

Fighting surrounded us at that point. Powerful angels had come down from the clouds, and most of my wives at the top of the temple were busy fending them off. Kelly and her pack were on the ground, pushing their way up the temple.

The battles left an odd pocket for me and Aphrodite to fight, although the fight wasn't very impressive.

Goldie was keeping me rooted to the temple, which drastically slowed my movements. She moved her anchors with me, but I definitely had lost some of my nimbleness, which wasn't my strong suit in general.

Meanwhile, Aphrodite could flutter around on her six wings and manipulate space as she tried to sever Goldie's strands.

I called on my magic, but my lightning and fire went everywhere. Faerie portals shattered in purple explosions, and Aphrodite made my golden fire and silver ice fall short of reaching its mark.

The fight had effectively reached a stalemate, which was fine by me.

In a contest of magical endurance, I had no doubt that I could win. Each heartbeat flooded me with my own mana. Aphrodite was singed and favoring her left arm, but otherwise, she was perfectly healthy. Her control over spatial magic was truly something to behold.

A silver flash caught us both off guard as Helena reappeared in the fight. She swept forward before her mother could react and cut her brow as she dodged away.

"Daughter. I wondered when you'd join," Aphrodite sneered. "Never could keep yourself out of trouble."

Helena tossed her hair and stayed back. "Still talking? How's Heaven, mother?"

Aphrodite's brows pinched down.

I paused, realizing just how many angels were present in the battle. "Is the Celestial Plane even still standing?"

"Yes, and it will be restored once I've finished here." Aphrodite held her chin high.

"Why? Was it worth it?" I asked.

The archangel glared at me. "You have no idea. Our plane was on borrowed time. With the loss of the Silver Slave, it has been continually shrinking. If we didn't do anything, it would be gone in five years. This isn't about some greed; this is about survival."

I shook my head. "Through force."

"What goodwill have I garnered for help? I am aware of my own flaws. Despite being the embodiment of love, I have transformed angels into some of the most hated beings in the world. So, when my world is crumbling, I have no other option than to take. The Dreamer just died. I can feel the change in the air. This is my last shot." Aphrodite was so set in her ways that I knew there was no option to change her mind.

"So be it." I snapped my fingers and threw a fireball at her that she waved aside, sending it out into the fight outside the temple. "You won't survive this."

"All I have to do is get one of you two on the fangs." Aphrodite jerked and closed the space between her and Helena in a flash, grabbing her daughter's throat as her eyes glowing white.

***

Scarlett had escaped with Jadelyn and was checking on her sister not in blood, but in life and marriage. "Wake up."

"Ugh," Jadelyn groaned. "Did you get the license plate of the car?"

"You killed Leviathan," Scarlett answered, trying to put as much calming energy as she could into her words.

Still, Jade's eyes shot wide open. "I what?!" Her eyes were distant for a moment. "Shit. I don't think I can fix that."

Scarlett chuckled. "Yeah. Pretty hard to undo dead. Get on your feet though; there's a lot of trouble. The battle is still going." Scarlett's tails were whipping back and forth, keeping up an illusion around both of them. So far, they were staying out of the fight, but there was no guarantee it would last.

The Honor Guard was in the air, in full dragon form, fighting off an army of angels in the sky. Nymphs rode on their backs, casting magic and protecting the dragons' wings.

"The nymphs aren't half bad," Scarlett observed.

"Yeah. But they also were guzzling our husband several times in the last week." Jadelyn tracked her eyes to the nymphs. "They can be really greedy at times." Jadelyn rubbed her face with a strange look.

"There you two are." Nyske moved towards them in what must have been her half-shifted form. Rather than a completely scale-covered warrior or a werewolf-shaped dragon, she was just Nyske, with patches of loose scales covering her and a pair of black dragon horns that shifted colors as she moved. "We need to get you two out of here. Jadelyn, can you move?"

The nymph seemed completely unperturbed by the battle around her. Scarlett had seen some seasoned vets apply for the bodyguard detail and knew the tells. Nyske had seen some shit and this wasn't even registering on her scale of shit. Sometimes, Scarlett wondered how she could compare to these ancient Fae.

A blast of fire went awry, and Nyske held out a hand. A thin wall of ice just appeared between them and the fire, blocking the hit.

"Right. We need to go." Jadelyn gathered herself and stood, checking herself over. "I'm fine, just a shock to the system."

A half-melted sword fell down from the battle above, and Jadelyn reflexively shielded her face as the blade hit her. Molten metal fell over her shoulders.

"Jade!" Scarlett jumped to help her and then scowled at Nyske who was watching with a strange expression.

"I'm fine. Barely hit me." Jade showed her arms to Scarlett.

"No. That was a direct hit. Your dress is on fire from the molten metal on your shoulder." Nyske watched.

Jadelyn jumped like someone had told her there was a spider on her and smacked the molten metal off, along with the scraps of her shoulder strap. Underneath was completely unblemished skin.

"Shit," Jadelyn drew out the word. "I think I did more than just kill Levi."

"I'll say." Nyske nodded. "Why don't you help Scarlett join up with Kelly?"

An angel streaked down at them. The sword had broken Scarlett's illusions. His spear was rushing down at Scarlett, who whipped up her pistol and put three shots center mass in record time.

Unfortunately, bullets didn't stop gravity. The angel and his spear were still coming straight for Scarlett. Jadelyn reacted instinctively. She threw herself in the way, taking the spear straight to the chest and collapsing on top of Scarlett.

Reflexively, Scarlett scrambled to check on Jadelyn who was just laughing up a storm as she rolled to her feet and checked her chest where her dress was torn, but she was completely unharmed underneath.

"Look, Scar! Guess what?" Jadelyn let out another loud laugh, a little slap happy as her brain registered the change in her body.

Scarlett was trying to get her heart to settle down. "What?"

"I get to protect you now!" Jadelyn was all smiles. "Now you are the fragile one."

Scarlett sighed and rolled her eyes. "Don't push it. We don't know anything about your true limits yet. But come on; we need to get back into the battle and help." She glanced over her shoulder at Nyske. "What are you going to do?"

Just up the temple, Zach was fighting doggedly with Aphrodite, and Nyske was watching that fight. The dragon and angel continued to clash in a weird dance as Aphrodite made them slide past each other and warped space such that Zach couldn't get a hit.

"I need to help him," Nyske answered.

Scarlett had no doubt she could. "Do it. Then maybe we can settle this for good. Plushies stand strong."

"Plushies together," Jadelyn chirped in reflex. "Go get 'em, Nyske. Just avoid those fangs, they are nasty business."

Nyske held out her hand and made a sword out of thin air.

Scarlett couldn't help but wonder how Nyske's reserves of magic were doing. Unlike the rest of them, she wasn't getting boosts from Zach. But that would be a conversation for later.

She had confided her issues with her mother with the Plushies, and they all knew better than to push her too quickly.

**

Scarlett and Jadelyn ran off as Nyske walked calmly towards the fight at the center.

Helena had joined the fight, and it made Nyske grumpy. The stupid nephilim was putting her man in danger just by being in the area. Normally, she was durable enough that her presence couldn't be a hindrance, but today he was compensating to make sure Helena ended up nowhere near the fangs. And Goldie was hampering his movements as well.

Nyske slashed through a nearby angel as she continued forward.

Battle was just another passing hobby to Nyske. She was as old as the Faerie plane. Dueling, games of war, and mock battles had come and gone in Fae fashion many, many times. And she'd fought in a real war or two over her lifetime.

If nymphs weren't physically and magically so low on the hierarchy of the world, she'd probably have some terrifying name attached to her. While she had the skills necessary in spades, it was only recently that she had the strength to use it.

An angel tried to take her by surprise, but she sidestepped at the last second, her sword passing clean through the angel's bicep. Then she twirled, taking both wings and their head in a single stroke.

Fighting was disgusting.

Yet, at present, it was a necessity. Part of her always worried that some buried anger would ignite in her if she fought again since becoming a dragon. After all, mixing fae's emotional strength with a dragon's tendencies that were chaotic at best was a recipe for disaster.

But she was wrong. Only her normal calm remained.

Well, and one more thing.

Her utter obsession over Zach. If she wasn't so good at schooling her emotions from years of practice as a nymph, that obsession would have been given away.

Nyske had learned to perfect various masks as she'd pretended to be different humans that surrounded Zach's upbringing. When an egg hatched, they were supposed to imprint on someone, yet it seemed to have worked the other way around for Nyske.

Nyske moved forward quickly, wanting to help him in any way she could. As she watched the battle, she noticed that Aphrodite was trying to manipulate Helena again and Zach pushed on her mark, helping protect her from her mother.

Nyske smiled and entered the fray with her sword up.

Feeling her failure at controlling her daughter, Aphrodite tried to manipulate Nyske. Nyske smiled, using her obsession for Zach to shatter Aphrodite's power, grind it to dust, and spit it to the wind. Her fear that her feelings were something planted by her mother was gone and instead she had embraced it.

She wanted Zach.

Nyske flowed forward with a simple chop of her sword, gathering her will and struck. Zach needed a certain kind of inspiration.

CHAPTER 29

Nyske joining changed the tide of battle, but not in the way that I had expected.

Her sword passed through Aphrodite's spatial magic and scored a clean cut on the angel's hip, only for Aphrodite to explode with mana, throwing Nyske into the collapsed ceiling and then hurling her down onto the floor.

"I will kill every last woman who loves you," Aphrodite spat.

A cold calm came over me at her words, and my spine tingled as I struck with a new confidence that I would end her here and now. A new part of my mana flowed through me. It was slow and sticky, but the heat of my anger had loosened it up.

Aphrodite was too confident in her abilities, and though she turned my hand slightly as I reached forward, it wasn't enough. My claws grasped onto one of her wings.

We both knew at that moment that it was over for her. She couldn't win in a grapple with me.

I jerked hard, holding onto the mana flooding my system as I ripped off one of her wings. Then I threw the disoriented archangel back at Helena, knowing she would want to take down her mother.

Like a batter up for bat, Helena swung for the fences, and her spear removed another wing, sending Aphrodite sprawling back to me. Nyske was back on her feet and grabbed the woman by the throat before punching her in the gut and tossing her back to Helena.

The nephilim struck the archangel in several rapid blows before I grabbed her mother's shoulders and held her still.

Helena's grin couldn't have been wider as she rushed forward and buried her spear into her mother's heart. There was a white pulse a moment later as Helena absorbed something from her mother and staggered backwards.

"You all right?" Nyske asked as Gabriel's body hit the temple above us.

Aphrodite's death had signaled the end.

Helena hunched over. "I'm all right. I just know this is going to hurt."

I almost asked what she was talking about, but then two additional sets of wings burst from her back and shredded what remained of her shirt. Both sets of wings were smaller than the first, and the bottom set curled around her thighs while the top set fluttered above her original.

"Oh." I wasn't sure what to say.

"Husband," Ikta shouted as she and Summer landed next to Gabriel. "We got you a present." She lifted the larger angel and started dragging him to me.

"You know, this feels oddly like when a cat brings you dead birds because it likes you," I observed.

Nyske snorted as she tried to cover up a laugh.

"It really is, but you'd make such a cute catgirl." Summer poked Ikta.

"It's not funny, Summy. I would make a fan-fucking-tastic catgirl. Going to get myself a pair of cat ears." Ikta turned to regard me. "Meow. Meow." She dropped the angel at my feet and looked up, waiting for praise.

In the middle of all of this, I understood how ridiculous the scene must seem to others, but it was a normal day with Ikta.

"Good kitty." I rubbed Ikta's head as she pushed it into my hand and tried to mimic purring.

"You'll need to work on the purring," Nyske added dryly.

"At least I'm a good kitty, what are you? I mean— Meow meow meow," Ikta shot back.

I really had no idea what to do with the angel or Ikta at the moment.

Around us, it was as if the angels had felt Aphrodite's death. They all landed and hid themselves under their wings.

Ikta was still meowing as Summer interpreted for me. "She wants you to use this almost dead but still alive angel. Slam him on the fangs and take over Heaven."

"Oh. Right. Totally got that." I nodded at Ikta as she came in for more pets.

"I thought I heard a cat." Kelly lumbered over the top lip of the temple and shifted back to her human form. Several of my wives were following her, and the thud of the dragons landing announced the rest.

"Meow." Ikta tilted her head, looking at Kelly.

Kelly just paused. "A sex thing, already? Can't we like catch our breaths from the big ass battle before we start a new sex thing?"

Ikta just tilted her head cutely and gave off a soft. "Meow."

Nyske turned to Ikta and agreed, "Meow."

Kelly just rubbed at her face. "What now?"

"I think I'm going to take over Heaven." Picking up Gabriel, I made up my mind. Taking on Heaven would help me balance Hell. It was all a system, one that I was hesitant to break. Even if the leaders were unredeemable, that didn't mean the whole plane needed to die.

"Sit in the chair. I'll shove him on the spikes." Nyske stepped up and took the dying angel from me. "He should be the strongest one left, so just focus on draining his everything into your mansion. That should connect them."

I sat in the chair and closed my eyes, focusing on the connection I could feel blossom between Gabriel and me as he was impaled. It opened up high in the sky, and in my mind's eye, I saw the celestial plane for the first time. It was nothing like I expected.

Once grand marble and silver structures were cracked and toppled onto the floor of clouds. But the area held a grandness, even in its collapse. Great rents along the cloud floor showed that not just the buildings, but the entire plane was crumbling.

To make matters worse, the space was practically abandoned. Four weak archangels sat in the cardinal directions, using all of their strength to attempt to keep the plane from completely collapsing.

Then I touched upon the magic of Gabriel's territory and started siphoning his magic away.

The four angels looked around for me and settled on a single spot. "They lost?"

"Yes." My voice rumbled through the plane as I continued to drain the area and make it part of my own.

All four of the angels sighed in defeat.

Finally, I had taken enough of the mana, and the celestial plane stuck to my plane like a rug to the vacuum. At that point, I was able to push and pull, stitching the two together.

"What'll become of us?" the angels asked.

"Not sure yet. I'm going to send the other angels back, and I'd prefer that I don't have to go up there and start knocking heads. Until then, live and maybe focus on promoting some actual good in the world rather than using that to hide your self-serving asses." I cut the connection and opened my eyes.

Nyske was up in my face, like she was trying to remember every single pore. "There you are. Was wondering how long that would take."

"Not long at all, it seems. Heaven is attached to my plane now. I devoured Gabriel and Uriel's territory. Helena, are you going to do anything with your mother's?"

"TBD," Helena shrugged. "Maybe I'll go up there and cull them, or maybe I'll just let them be. I haven't decided."

"Spare us." One of the cowering angels had crawled to the top of the temple.

"Leave," I barked, opening up a large portal to Heaven.

The angels in front didn't even hesitate. They expanded their wings and shot into the portal. Soon they looked like a flock of birds as all of the angels left just as quickly as they had come.

"Too bad." Regina was still a dragon, hanging onto the top of the temple. "They tasted like chicken."

The dragons all started rumbling with laughter that made more than a few of the basilisks present shy away.

I scanned around, but the battle was done. Now, we just needed to clean everything up.

"Goldie, remove the two artifacts please and put them in your mass. I think I'm going to bury them in my hoard or shoot them off into space." I rose from the throne, a brief sense of longing filling me, wanting me to remain in the city and turn it into my hoard.

I worked to banish the thought as quickly as it came.

"I was just borrowing the throne for the artifacts," I explained to the basilisks, understanding why they were looking at me so carefully.

Goldie finished up removing the artifacts and swallowing them into her mass.

"Sorry for the damage." I glanced up at the collapsed roof and out into the city to know that this wasn't the only damage. Much of the city had melted or been crushed. And the area was littered with corpses.

Minthra, the queen of this city, slithered forward. "Damage can be fixed. Lives cannot. Thanks to you, we have preserved many lives."

I saw Regina scratching away some gold off the edge of the temple behind the basilisk's back and inwardly cringed while I smiled at Minthra. "No, thank you for trusting us and allowing us to stop this from happening. As the Dragon King, I have taken it upon myself to protect not just those paranormals around me, but the world over."

Glancing away from her, I found an excuse to get Regina moving. "Dragons, please help clean up the angel corpses, and if you can, remove the rubble from the city."

I looked to Minthra, who nodded her head in agreement.

"Thank you." By giving the dragons the ability to remove the rubble, they would absolutely steal said gold, but it would keep them busy. "We'll have them replace the rubble with stone? Or how best would you like us to help rebuild?"

Minthra blinked. "You'll help us rebuild?"

"I think you'll find the dragons very eager to help rebuild, but we'll have to watch them to make sure they don't steal entire buildings." I chuckled.

"Stone is enough. We can set them into the gold structures, and as they turn to gold, the stone holds up in the center. For purely exterior corrections, we can use wood," she explained.

Pixie came strutting over, fixing her hair that had gotten tangled in flying on one of the dragon's backs. "We can help arrange that." She pulled a tablet out of her bust. "Though, it honestly might be easiest to rely on the Scalewrights to deliver all the materials."

"We'll do it for free," Jadelyn called out quickly, catching up on the conversation. My beautiful heiress had come out of the battle unscathed.

I moved forward, quickly gathering her up and pulled her into my arms.

"Oh you. Don't worry—I'm invincible now." Jadelyn was all giggles and smiles.

I raised an eyebrow and lifted my gaze to Scarlett for a more detailed explanation.

"She has unfortunately proven that she's very durable after killing Levi." Scarlett sounded like she was struggling with the new reality and reluctant to admit just how durable Jadelyn had become.

I wanted to be more concerned about Leviathan, but honestly, I had never really gotten to know her.

"Yeah. I got shot." Jadelyn beamed. "And stabbed! Then there was this molten sword that fell down on me."

I clutched her tighter as she spoke.

"You aren't helping." Nyske had stepped up next to Pixie. She was back in a white blouse and a black pencil skirt ready to assist me, looking nothing like the expert swordswoman who had been fighting next to me a few moments earlier.

"Still want to put you in so much jewelry that you can't get out of my hoard," I grumbled as I held Jadelyn. "Besides Levi, did anyone else get hurt?"

"Trina is treating a few of the nymphs, and the wolves are licking their wounds," Pixie reported. "Otherwise, the Golden Plushie Society is an army that could roll over multiple countries. A few angels aren't a problem." She tossed her hair.

Minthra was watching our entire exchange, doing her best and failing to keep her face passive.

"Well." I looked down at Jadelyn in my arms. "Can we portal a few workers in to take measurements and get some stone cut, or concrete poured for the repairs?"

Jadelyn nodded enthusiastically. "Not a problem. I'll have it set up for tomorrow. We'll need some debris cleared before then, and the bodies moved, to make it easy to let them come in and do an inspection."

"Between the dragons and the lich, I think the bodies will be taken care of." Minthra glanced out into her city. "They can also take care of the debris."

DRAGON'S JUSTICE 9 333

"We'll get T on it." Pixie nodded, tapping her tablet. "The elf got a little excited amongst the ground forces and took on an army of angels." She frowned. "Though he seemed to be collecting wings?"

"He hates them. I have no idea what he does with the wings though." Morgana shrugged, joining the conversation. "When do we get to have a big celebration?"

"After cleanup," I scowled at her. "We'll take care of the mess we made first."

Morgana grinned wide, showing off her fangs.

"We'll take care of it." Pixie nodded at me. "Georgia has left us more than a few messages today."

"Shit. In all of this, we completely blew that meeting off." I scratched the back of my head.

"The audit was delayed a few days, and the cult completely disappeared, along with a big chunk of the church's leadership." Helena frowned. "Why is she contacting you and not me?"

"I think she wanted some Dragon King support." Pixie was looking at the messages. "They aren't making good progress with the business."

Helena flared her six wings. "Zach, make me a portal there."

"Haven't been in that building before. But I'm sure Georgia can take a video call for us." I raised a brow at Pixie who was tapping along.

"Five minutes," she answered.

I looked around at everyone getting to work and very much wanted to join in on the efforts, but Nyske put a hand on my shoulder. "You've already led by example. Let's deal with Georgia's issues first. Then we'll continue to help."

Kelly let out a big yawn. "I wouldn't mind taking a small break."

I opened a portal for my pregnant mate. "There is no problem with anyone taking a break. No sense in wearing ourselves completely to the bone to fix the city in a day. Please, those of you that need it, get some rest."

***

Georgia was in a conference room with a few of her agents and a dozen men in suits that looked ready to stonewall her every step. The two large rooms of files that the other agents were working on had shown us what was happening.

We had just portaled in down the hall. Helena looked pissed and charged into the room, glaring at each of the men before coming to a pause.

Her six wings flared out and she stared them down. "Give Georgia the records you are withholding. We will nominally cut off part of the problem, but you should be aware that those behind you are now gone. Completely."

Several of them fell out of their chairs, bowing to her.

"New wings." Georgia eyed the appendages. "New powers?"

"No. Just new authority," I answered, taking a chair and giving Helena a once over. "You knew that would work?"

"Not until I stepped in here and felt how much the angels had been feeding on a few of them." Helena glared down her nose at the businessmen. "They obviously had met at least a few."

One pulled a folder from his briefcase and slid it across the table. "The vulnerabilities we were hiding."

"Mr. Souza!" Another that hadn't bowed to Helena shouted, "You've betrayed our client."

"The same client that hasn't answered the phone the last two days?" The man crossed his arms as several of the other lawyers got up in arms. "I'd like a deal from the American Government," he addressed Georgia.

"We will see what we can do with the cooperation from your government here in Brazil." Georgia made no promises, but collected the folder. "We'll be in touch." She held it close to her chest as she stood. "I guess there's no need to be discreet. Can we get a portal out of here?"

I smirked and flicked my wrist, opening one back to my mansion. "Happily."

Georgia walked through, folder in hand. We followed after her. "You know, this is beyond convenient." The Special Agent in Charge stared longingly at the portal before I closed it.

"Not going to recall the people looking through the files?" I asked.

"Never know when there's something we missed. Sometimes, an admission can be too convenient." She waved the folder. "But I'm guessing a lot more than Helena growing new wings happened?"

"Long story short, Heaven was in shambles. There were two factions of angels: one current Heaven leadership, the other those that had abandoned Heaven. They were fighting over a way to injure Earth and restore Heaven," I answered, oversimplifying the situation. "The leadership for both sides now is dead. One side was entirely wiped out, and the other sent back to Heaven to wait for Helena or me to figure out what we want to do with them."

Georgia let out a long whistle. "Yeah. Just another day for you, huh?"

"No, this was a big one for me too. I brought the big guns and showed the entire paranormal world that you don't mess with me or my mates." My eyes flicked over to Helena and Rebecca.

"Noted," Georgia muttered, taking a seat at a table in the kitchen. "Then I'm going to review this folder, pin this all on a few guilty people, and let the rest of the organization quietly sink into the background after we've taken a few 'leaders'."

"That would be nice," I agreed. "Given that their real backers are completely gone. Doubt you'd want to try and jail an angel, anyway—would cause more than a few questions."

She snorted. "It would cause a riot. By the way, Isaiah was denied clearance for knowledge on paranormals."

"Really? After what happened at his base, I figured it would happen."

"Nope. The AD locked that shit down and told a few generals to take a hike. It isn't their problem, and the current mess has been taken care of," Georgia said. "So, score one for keeping the paranormal under the radar."

I let out a sigh of relief I hadn't known I was holding. "Good. I don't think we are ready for larger exposure. Staying quiet has worked for us so far."

CHAPTER 30

I was anchored to the ground with Goldie, having made herself into a crane around me. "A little to the left."

She gently set a concrete slab in place of the collapsed wall while also bracing the building itself.

"I'm going to start pushing gold into the slab," Goldie announced.

She straightened up the single-story gold house and used her control over the gold to inject it into the concrete slab better than any bolt anchor would be able to accomplish. She smoothed out the damages and retracted back to me.

"Please. Check your new home." I smiled at a family of basilisks.

The younger daughter batted her eyelashes at me before her father cuffed the back of her neck and hauled her inside.

"Is there a reason we didn't have Goldie fix everything from the start?" Pixie asked.

"Yeah. Because by the time it occurred to me, my mates were hauling off all the 'ruined' gold buildings."

"Your hoard is quite full of gold," Pixie snickered. "I think Regina was going to try and melt it down to coins today."

"Good. Coins are better," I agreed. Gold coins were much more swimmable, and swimming in gold was the best feeling in the world.

"Also, your mother is coming to the mansion tonight after dinner," Pixie told me as Goldie shifted her focus and started to work on the building next to the one we just repaired.

I froze. "Tia is coming?"

"Yes." Pixie grinned.

"Has she realized that she's free of The Dreamer's oath?" I asked, getting a little more anxious.

Pixie nodded. "Pretty sure. She specifically requested a meeting with all of the women carrying her grand whelps. Yev has asked for reinforcements."

"As she should," Goldie murmured. "I'm going to fight with her if she takes issue with me."

"Just don't wreck the mansion." Pixie didn't seem bothered by the idea of Goldie and Tia fighting. "In other news, we have a nymph taking the flight back under your name with a glamor so that we keep records clean. Isaiah Washington has reached out for a meeting. Oh, and Nyske is trying to claim a night with you. I thought I'd ask you which night you preferred?"

I swallowed hearing the last question, but I tackled them in order. "Good on the nymph. Isaiah... I don't think I should meet with him. If the Associate Director blocked him for me, then I shouldn't go around her. Hold the present line as far as paranormal knowledge is concerned. Finally, I feel like tonight. Is that too last minute?"

Pixie gave me a sharp look. "Tomorrow it is. I think you could have pulled off tonight, but that is a valid excuse."

"I'm not trying to make excuses." I sighed. "The delay has made me second guess a lot of things."

"If it helps, she's blocking off your whole night. Even Goldie is supposed to leave." Pixie tapped her tablet. "Though, she might call on me or Sabrina in the morning."

"Morning?" I frowned.

"Yes. She has you booked from dinner until five am the next morning. Only then are you slotted for sleep." Pixie giggled. "Damn, the girl is pent up. And I don't blame her."

"I'm supposed to leave?" Goldie asked as she moved four slabs into place to make new walls, then went to work fusing them with gold.

"Nyske wants the time to be private," I answered, having some recollections of our previous time dating. "She can get a little wild."

"Coming from a man who devoured two dozen nymphs in a single night, I'm honestly intrigued." Pixie was giving me a hungry look over the rim of her gold-framed glasses.

"How are Maddie and Frank?" I asked, changing the subject.

"Frank has been to a dozen gold exchanges in the last day." Pixie grinned. "I think he got away from this just fine. Morgana has been with Maddie; they are car shopping. They'll replace their van with something fancy. Morgana has been looking at getting her goblins in Sentarshaden to work on it for them. After all, with Jadelyn's portal lane, it is a very easy drive."

"What about the angels?" I asked.

"Not a peep. Helena 'casually' mentioned going to check on them with you later, but she didn't formally schedule anything."

I shot Pixie a look.

"I'll have it scheduled for the afternoon after you're with Nyske. What? She didn't formally ask, and I can't just balance a schedule off of non-concrete requests now, can I?" The pink-haired nymph huffed.

"How about Kelly's pack?" I continued through the list of people who might be affected.

"Last I heard, they were throwing a big banger of a party. I think everyone involved at least filled their pockets with some gold. Before you ask, T is using his to open up a barber shop near us."

I snorted.

"He said the shop would always serve the Dragon King's children free of charge." Pixie raised an eyebrow. "Do we really have no concern that T is going to use the kids' hair for something nefarious?"

"No. T is trusted, even if he is a lich. He's approved to watch any future kids," I answered.

Pixie tapped on her tablet, making a note. "Great. And he's taken care of a lot of the corpses. He's gotten them out of the city and made graves for the basilisks. The rest he left in a pile that has since disappeared."

She didn't want to talk about dragons eating the dead.

"Jadelyn?" I asked.

"Her mother put her on house arrest," Pixie snorted. "She went home and showed her parents her new invulnerability. They did not like the surprise, and I think there are a number of siren doctors checking her over before they let her go."

"Can we get copies of their findings?" I asked.

"Who do you think I am? Of course we are. Besides, I like Claire. She came to talk to me about it after and give me an update," Pixie answered.

I raised an eyebrow.

"The GODs—I don't like the name either—are still meeting. But they like me, mostly because I have access to everyone and everything."

Rubbing a hand over my face, I remembered the Grandmothers of Dragons group. "It is a terrible name."

"Agreed, but they aren't changing it. Secretly, I think those old biddies are having fun waiting for their grandchildren. More than a few of them are trying to schedule visits before and after the first wave of births."

"I can imagine. Honestly, let them. We'll be nesting as a giant family, so make sure each of them knows that I will only tolerate them if they do not stress out the harem. No arguing with the new mothers and no trying to force anything."

"I'll let the GODs know. Some won't like it," she warned.

"Tell them the Dragon King is going to be extra protective, and if a single one of them ends up yelling or making one of my wives cry, I'll probably start removing heads." I smiled, earning a glare from Pixie. "What? It's a very stressful time. I know I'm not going through childbirth, but if you think I won't be wearing a rut into the floor, you have some surprises in store."

"Aww. You are a big softie." Pixie grabbed my arm and pulled it down to her flat stomach. She wasn't showing yet, and she hadn't tested, but we knew she was probably pregnant given how easily all the nymphs were getting pregnant. "I bet she'll be a little dragon."

"Either way, they will be lovely," I promised Pixie, sharing a passionate kiss with her for a moment.

We broke apart as a new thought popped up in my head. "Oh. We need to have Sabrina, Ikta, and maybe T work on something so that we can bring a few kids down to Tartarus."

Pixie made a sound of understanding and nodded. "So you can see your father."

"And The Dreamer," I clarified.

Pixie pursed her lips. "Should I schedule your funeral for when Nyske finds out?" she teased.

"No. Nyske should see it, and we'll work through it. She and her mother are at each other's throats, but they aren't throwing punches. I think it is an opportunity. And she said she'd bring them down just to rub it in her mother's face how much better of a mother she'll be."

Pixie chuckled. "Okay. Good luck with that." Pixie worked away on her tablet.

Goldie set the house up and let out a big sigh. "I'm tired. These are heavy. Going to take a break." She snapped back to the bracer. Even if she was a powerful gold elemental, it cost her mana just to move, and we had been doing quite a bit the past two days.

"I think we'll call it then today." I shielded my eyes and looked into the sky, seeing the sun well on its way down.

"Prudent," Pixie answered. "Dinner is in half an hour. Just enough time to take a shower."

"No magic?" I teased, opening a portal to the baths in the mansion.

"Sometimes a shower is best." Pixie swayed her hips and looked at me over her shoulder, her bright blue eyes begging for me to chase her and encouraging the predator inside of me.

***

Satiated from the bath, I knew I was going to be late for dinner.

Pixie giggled, wrapped in a towel.

"We should really stop getting dirty," I told her.

"But getting dirty again was the best part," Goldie spoke from where she was standing behind me, toweling my back off.

"Oh, it was." Pixie had a mischievous gleam in her eyes. "Maybe we could do it again." She teased her towel.

"Didn't you just say we should stop?" I leveled a look at her.

"It's my nature, don't blame me. You keep falling right into my arms." Pixie giggled. The nymph assistant was having fun, and I had no problem joining her in her antics.

Despite the large number of women in my house, it didn't make anything tense. Instead, the mansion seemed even more full of love. It was magnified and multiplied rather than divided. We had become one giant family, and the Plushies had really cemented a sisterhood.

"Because they are very soft arms and you put my head between your breasts and make me a very happy dragon." I flashed her a smile and was about to pull out clothes but paused. "Goldie, would you rather just clothe me?"

Rather than answer, Goldie poured over me and made gold sweatpants and sweatshirt for me.

"Fitting." Pixie smiled and leaned over the bench, giving me a full view of her tempting chest.

Goldie still moved slightly, like she was rubbing against me just to remind herself that she was touching all of me. The rubbing was not helping me be ready for dinner.

"I guess I get to look like a dragon even in my sweats." I shrugged. "Take your time, Pixie. I'll see you downstairs."

Pixie blew out a breath. "I guess that's all you are going to give your poor little nymph."

"Oh don't be like that." I had to pause.

Scarlett came in, her tails flitting behind her. "There you are." She spotted Pixie. "Ah. Now I see the cause of you being late. Glad you got some time squeezed in, Pixie." She shot the nymph a wink that was returned by the nymph who stood up straight and had her clothes on in an instant.

"He was quite ravenous. Without Goldie, I'm not sure I would have survived." Pixie tossed her bouncy pink hair over her shoulder. "Let's go get dinner."

I shook my head. "It wasn't that bad."

"You can get a little worked up," Scarlett answered. "Pixie seemed uniquely adept at pushing your buttons."

"That's because she likes it rough," Goldie spoke up. "Likes it when he loses control and pins her down."

I chuckled and wisely didn't join the conversation because Pixie tended to do just that. She had my consent to play with glamors too.

We made our way downstairs.

"There he is." Morgana, led by her nose, saw me coming first. "You know, my dear husband." Morgana blurred over to me. "Your little whelp is hungrier and hungrier every day."

"Didn't I donate some blood this morning?" I asked Morgana.

"Yes, but fresh is best."

Hoisting her up by her thighs, I cradled her as I went to take the seat at the head of the table.

"Having fun?" Nyske had the spot on my left. Jadelyn, it appeared, had escaped her house arrest to take the seat on my right.

"He looks like he's having fun," Jadelyn teased.

Morgana stopped for a moment. "He always has fun when he's with me. Now that you are invincible, you should try some new things."

"I should get that gold dress back out." Jadelyn tapped her chin. "Maybe... Sabrina, would you join me tonight for some fun?"

The succubus looked down the table. "Of course. I had to turn him down before the fight, and I've had an itch that only he can scratch." Her smoldering look did something to me.

Jadelyn giggled. "This could be fun."

Morgana pulled off my neck with a sigh. "It is a little fun when he goes wild. How was Pixie?"

"Dirty while I was trying to get clean," I joked.

"Sounds about right." Nyske shook her head and glanced down at the table where Pixie was demurely taking a seat and striking up conversation with Yev.

Morgana gave me a parting kiss and stepped away to join the table a few seats down.

"Oh, my lord," a nymph tsked, seeing my empty plate. "That will not do. You need to keep your strength up." She had come in with a tray of steaks and quickly put a few medallions of beef on my plate.

I checked who was serving, noting that it was Petal. She giggled, giving me a kiss on the cheek before moving to replace the empty meat tray that had gotten stuck over by my dragon mates.

"Oh no. Just meat won't do." Helena's nymph stopped next to me and started putting some grilled vegetables on my plate. "I wanted to thank you, my lord. Helena has been much happier these last two days."

"She should be." I glanced down to the table to see her chatting with Maeve, with a smile on her face.

The smile was a rarity in itself, and I felt a warmth spread seeing her happier.

"Yes. She's been much lighter." Then in a whisper that barely entered even my enhanced hearing, the nymph leaned down. "You should go see her latest art. The subject has changed." She gave me a wink and wandered off.

Nyske raised an eyebrow.

"Sworn to secrecy on the last part. Ask Helena. Though, one of these days, I need to go steal something from her place." I would love the look on her face if a few of her pieces appeared in the hallway of the mansion.

Helena really was a wonderful painter, but I would honor her desire to not share with the rest of my harem that she was the painter.

"The place on the river?" Jadelyn asked. When I gave her a questioning look, she continued. "We all know about it. There really aren't secrets among the Plushies. Speaking of, since you are going to be missing tomorrow night, Nyske, we should talk about a few things that are including Mr. Growly here."

I gave her a playful growl at the name. "You know, now that you are invincible, that means I can nibble on you."

"I bite back." Jadelyn snapped her pearly white teeth playfully. "But I bring this up because it involves you. With the pregnancies and everything else happening, we are thinking about utilizing the Plushies more and letting you stay in reserve for only the big things."

"I'm being benched?" I teased.

Nyske gave me a look. "Unless you want to wander in Tartarus and pick fights with dead things, what's going to touch you? Not to mention, in a few years, you'll have a small army to take care of. I don't think settling down and nesting a bit is a bad idea."

"In a few years, you'll only be that much stronger," Jadelyn agreed. "So, let us handle the small stuff. That's what the court sessions are about right?"

I nodded. "We probably need to find a few angels to fill that session out. I should go to Heaven, actually."

Helena perked up down the table.

"After dinner, do you want to go to Heaven? We need to rope them into the morning court sessions," I spoke down the table.

"Be sure to pick out some really pretty angels to fill out all three seats," Ikta spoke up.

"Oh. If we can make sure the new Archangel of Justice is really pretty, that would be good," Pixie answered. "Maybe find one that's really delicate, and gentle. Opposite of Helena."

"Hey now. I like Helena as she is." I rolled my eyes. "But a nice gentle angel would be nice too."

Helena did the unexpected and started laughing. "I'll see what we can do. No promises. They are all probably scared shitless of the Dragon King."

"As they should be." Kelly raised a glass of sparkling grape juice.

The harem laughed and raised their glasses.

"Really, they should be shaking in their boots at the name of The Golden Plushie Society," Chloe added.

"Cheers to the Plushies." I raised my glass. "They are pretty fucking awesome."

"Damn right!" Jadelyn clinked her glass to mine enthusiastically before turning to me in a normal tone. "I can join you when you go to Heaven, right? Now that I'm invincible—"

"We all know!" Scarlett threw her hands up in the air. "Don't need to repeat it every time."

Jadelyn looked a little sheepish. "It's an adjustment. And I want to go see Heaven."

"Sure. But you still need to be careful. Something could still hurt Levi. So you'll just have to treat your invincibility as a last resort, I still want you to be careful," I teased her, even as she bloomed a smile at the chance to come on the trip.

CHAPTER 31

I stepped through Morgana's portal to Heaven with Helena, Jadelyn, and Pixie in tow.

"Wow. This is a shit hole," Jadelyn blurted out as she looked around.

The plane had ground as light, fluffy clouds, and tall, white marble buildings trimmed with silver. I imagined that it was once beautiful, but at the moment, it was all ruins. The landscape was uniform across the domain.

Angels flit about, toiling away at fixing their homes and businesses.

"It really has gone downhill," Helena muttered, watching impassively as the angels worked to rebuild. "Let's see if we can't find the archangels."

I let my aura rip through the plane and watched angels dive out of the sky.

"Like a doorbell," Jadelyn laughed.

"A very aggressive doorbell." Helena shook her head. "But it'll work."

Four figures shot into the air and headed our direction. I stood there with my arms crossed as they came and landed in front of me.

The four remaining archangels had even smaller wings than Helena. Two of them were male and two were female, but one in particular caught my interest. "Blindfold. Isn't that a bit much?"

Justice was a tall, busty, blonde-haired angel with a white cloth over her eyes. "Tell Aphrodite that," the woman sighed. "I'm not actually blind, but a very light-sensitive angel. It is painful without the cloth. Aphrodite found it amusing to promote me."

"She doesn't like Aphrodite, so that's a big plus for her." Jadelyn grinned.

"None of us do," another of the archangels spoke up. "She was controlling, and she only picked those of us to fill the 'lesser' archangel roles if she thought she could exert enough pressure on us."

I clapped my hands. "She's gone. Let's just forget about her. So, your place is a shit hole at the moment. Which wouldn't normally bother me, but it is connected to my own plane, so I need it to at least be presentable."

My statement took them aback.

"What do you mean?" Justice asked.

"Well, since I have control over your plane, two of you are going to attend my court sessions. You'll report in and we'll work together through a number of issues. The first one would be how you are going to be allowed to come and go from your plane so that you can restore it."

"Given your... proclivities..." The archangel that looked like an old man hesitated.

"I'll go." Justice stuck her chin out proudly. "So will you, right, Joy?"

Joy looked short standing next to Justice. "Sure. It would be an honor to serve the Dragon King. I can feel the strength of two Archangels in him, and Helena has taken over Aphrodite's power."

"Perfect." I clapped my hands together. "We meet to-morrow morning. You can use Morgana's portal, and we'll have someone let you out of that room."

"Long term?" Justice asked tentatively.

"Don't know. We'll figure that out in court; that's kind of its purpose. Now, let's do a lap around the plane and see if there aren't any cracks in the plane that I need to seal up before they get worse." I pulled off my shirt, noticing Joy's eyes lock on my body. But I ignored her, spreading my two dragon wings from my back.

"What? Don't want to go back and see your mother fawning over the nymphs?" Jadelyn teased and held out her arms for me to carry her.

"Right. Very thorough inspection. Don't want any problems later." I grinned back.

***

We were waiting for my court to start, Ikta was in my lap cracking jokes, but Helena was seriously conflicted.

"Do you sit with the FBI, or with the angels? Hmm?" Ikta teased her, noticing her apprehension.

"Both?" Helena hesitated.

"Unless you can split yourself in two, I don't think you can do that," Ikta continued, but her voice broke off, and I could tell she was considering ways to split my angel in two.

"Cut it out." I swatted Ikta on the rear.

The Spider Queen turned to face me, lust in her eyes. "Do that again."

"No. Stop taunting, Helena. She can sit in both or either. It doesn't matter to me. There is no rule about three seats per group. I have no idea why we always have three."

"Three is the best number," Ikta giggled.

Jadelyn walked into the room. "It is a good number. What's wrong with Helena?"

"Can't decide where to sit." Pixie didn't look up as she typed away on her tablet.

"Oh. I see the problem." Jadelyn nodded and took her seat in another cluster of three.

Ikta tilted her head back until she was looking at Jadelyn upside down. "Don't you have to decide if you want to sit with Hell?"

"Huh? No. I have no connection to Hell; I simply got Levi's personal power," Jadelyn answered quickly.

"No fun." Ikta looked back up at me. "So, do we have two beautiful angels coming?"

I shook my head at her antics. "Justice and Joy. Though, Justice wears a blindfold."

Ikta's eyes practically shined. "No way," she whispered. "Did you blind Justice?"

"He did not blind her, and she's not blind. Aphrodite found an angel that had some sort of light sensitivity and promoted her as a joke," Jadelyn explained and cut off when Morgana came in, escorting the two angels.

Ikta laughed with glee when she saw the blindfolded angel. "This is gonna be great." She jumped off my lap and scampered across the room to her own seat and picked up the basket of silk thread and needles to work on little pants for our kids.

"Alright, that is everyone. Let's kick off today's session. We have two new members I'd like to introduce." Everyone turned to the two angels. "Joy and Justice. Um, do you two have other names?"

Helena chose to sit with Rebecca, crossing her legs and casting looks at the two angels repeatedly.

"Our names were taken from us by Aphrodite," Justice answered, her tone clipped.

"Great, then we'll stick to the obvious. First up is the repairs from the angel attack. Pixie, do you have the total damages?"

"Right here." She handed me a tablet that I passed on to the two angels.

"What's this?" Joy asked.

"Reparations to the basilisks for what your people have done. The leaders that did it are gone, but we know you have plenty of resources through the Church. The sum you see is what they want, and what you will give them. Once that is arranged, we will be moving Morgana's tree and portal to a location where angels can enter Earth, but passage will be monitored. We will also be limiting how long angels can be on Earth. I won't have any more angels of hate."

Joy's smile faded as she stared at the list and her shoulders slumped. "This will be difficult."

"But not impossible," Helena answered sharply. "Get it done, or I'll just sweep Heaven and let it reset."

Joy swallowed around a lump. "Yes."

"Other news." Pixie pushed along the meeting's agenda. "Plushie meeting tonight, and everyone but Nyske will be there."

Pixie waited for any questions before she moved on to the next item. "We are in construction of another spatial shipping lane down to El Dorado, then making simpler lanes to each of the seven golden cities from there." She glanced at Jadelyn.

"I already had people start the purchases while we were preparing for the invasion. One is already a bunker, so it will be nice and easy to get it fortified and set up. We can get started on the spatial enchantments in a few days." Jadelyn started into several potential plans for how to structure the enchantments in South America.

I zoned out, knowing I wasn't really needed for the current discussion. Instead, my mind wandered back, thinking about how far I'd come since being the kid that had rushed to help Scarlett after she'd been hit by a clumsy biker on campus.

Back then, I had been happy, in a normal life, completely unsuspecting of the world that lived underneath my own. Now, I was the king of that world. I ruled multiple planes, and with each heartbeat, I was growing stronger along with making each of my planes better.

It had been such a short time. Part of me wondered what the future held. I wanted to reach forward and know. But at the same time, I was content to live in the moment with each of my mates.

Sabrina, Morgana, and Ikta were the most vocal as the meeting continued. I scanned the room, my eyes landing on Summer who was making bedroom eyes at me.

She raised an eyebrow now that our gazes were locked. I waffled my head and glanced at Nyske, quietly reminding her that she had me tonight. Summer rolled her eyes and pointed at herself and then the floor of the chamber before subtly hooking her finger at me.

She wanted me to come attend her court session after mine wrapped. I nodded, the two of us quietly communicating while others talked magic. Summer gave me a big grin and a wink.

She enjoyed playing me up during her court session and then being a seductive little minx once everyone left the room. That, and I was fairly sure she was trying to get pregnant. I was happy that she was beginning to show interest, and I knew she'd be a fantastic mother.

Summer caught my mind wandering and raised an eyebrow at me, as if asking if I was enjoying her before giving me a slow lick of her lips.

"Zach. If you'll stop eye fucking Summer, we have the next item on the agenda," Pixie sighed. "Really, you are insatiable."

"What?" I stuck my tongue out. "It's Summer's fault. She was taunting me."

"I can't help that my beauty draws my husband's eyes." Summer sighed and leaned against her hand in a playful pout.

"Uh huh." Pixie noted something down on her tablet. "Next up. Hell's envy territory is currently unclaimed, and the demons are fighting amongst themselves, Jadelyn has turned down the claim and we are monitoring, but we might need to step in to settle disputes."

"Anything at the moment?"

"Nope. This happens from time to time," Sabrina spoke up. "Like when the titan used to eat the princes. The demons will fight, and one will stand on top eventually. No idea what that'll do to Jadelyn or her new power."

"Shouldn't do anything," Ikta answered. "Doubt the titan was losing anything every time a new prince was crowned. But we should go lock them down, make sure they are on our side, and give them a seat here so that we can keep a balance in Hell."

"Good point." I nodded in agreement. "I'll go down with Goldie and we'll do a brief reminder of who's in charge."

***

Nyske walked ahead of me, holding my hand and leading me deeper into my mansion.

"And where are we going?" I asked, my eyes never swaying from her.

She was wearing her normal white blouse and black pencil skirt, but I could see hints of gold lingerie under the blouse. And her normal stockings had been replaced by ones that looked especially soft and were a soft gold color.

Nyske turned, her eyes dilated. I almost swore there were a pair of hearts floating in her pupils.

"Dinner," she breathed and stepped up next to me and ran her hands across my chest. "Tonight you are all mine, which means you need your strength." She pushed at my chin to keep my head still and slowly, tenderly kissed along my neck.

I groaned at the sensual touch as Nyske ran her nails gently through my hair. "I'm just a little eager."

"Good." She stepped back and started forward again, a serious sway to her hips. "Goldie, you have the night off," she reminded my elemental.

Goldie bled off my arm, forming a woman who waited in the hallway with a pout. "I will be back at 5 AM sharp."

"I expect nothing less." Nyske opened the door to a candlelit room.

Stepping in, I surveyed the room. There was a four-poster bed with silk ribbons coming off the side posts, and a lovely table set for two with a bottle of wine in the center and two steaming bowls.

"Soup?" I asked.

"Tiger and turtle soup." She grinned. "It helps a man stay vigorous. That, and eating tiger is cool as shit."

Before I got to the table, Nyske pushed herself up against me, staring up into my eyes.

There was a deep need in them that nearly swallowed me. "Zach." She ran a hand over my cheek. "I need you."

There was a deep obsession in her eyes as she pulled me down for a sloppy and long kiss that had me turning her against the door. Both of us were groaning in each other's mouths. The embrace was familiar, and my anticipation grew. We were both panting with need when we finally broke the kiss.

"Do we really need to eat?" I teased.

"Absolutely. Sit." Nyske pushed me over to the chair and into it. There was a tension in her as she was clearly holding back the desire to just jump me. She didn't wander off to her own side, instead lingering by me, waiting for me to take a bite.

I picked up the spoon and scooped up a bit, bringing it to my lips. The soup was salted and the meat surprised me. "This is actually really good."

"Eat up." Nyske slid around to the other side of the table and flowed gracefully into her chair, staring at me over the candles.

I took another few sips of the soup, but Nyske didn't touch hers. Instead, she stared at me longingly, candlelight flickering in her eyes.

"Going to eat?" I asked.

"Oh, you are going to feed me just fine. You'll need your vigor." She slid her bowl over to me. "The wine is for when we finally have a break."

"Nyske, you are being a little odd," I told her.

She shook her head slowly. "No, Zach. I'm showing you the real me. The me that is obsessed over you. I have been for a long time. It is so bad that, as a nymph, I haven't even touched myself, let alone touched someone else since you broke up with me."

I raised an eyebrow, and she slid out of her chair.

"Eat up. But you can go quicker if you want." She came behind me, running a hand over my shoulders and kissing my neck again. "I'm right where I want to be, and you are never going to escape me again. Understand?"

"Why would I want that?" I lifted one bowl after the other and drained them before tilting my head back. "I'm going to mark you tonight, and I never give up my mates."

Nyske kissed me upside down, her lips crushing into mine before her tongue battled with mine for a long minute. Her hand creeped down my chest and started to play with the button to my pants, popping it off in one swift motion before she broke the kiss.

Her strength showed as she spun my chair around in one motion, scraping it against the floor and falling to her knees, cupping my very erect member and bringing it to her lips for a soft sensual kiss.

"Nyske," I groaned. "Everything is on the table tonight. Let's just have fun."

She licked her lips, wetting them and making lewd slopping kisses along the shaft, running her tongue over me like she just had to taste the whole thing.

"Oh, Zach. What you don't understand is that I'm all yours, now and forever. I crave you." She swallowed my cock in a swift motion, plunging her head over the head and running her tongue up and down the underside.

I held onto her hair, seeing it glow faintly a myriad of colors as I guided her over me. "Nyske," I moaned.

She looked up at me, her blue eyes sparkling through the dark hair hanging down in her face. Her eyes were glazed like an addict was finally getting her fix. She really was a nymph, and if what she said was true, then she had been denying herself.

Her soft pink lips were spread around my cock and suckling on me with love. Nyske continued to swallow me until I was sheathed in her throat, then she started to moan around me.

I took a sharp breath as she worked me over, mumbling something incoherent around me before she started to bob quickly.

Grabbing her hair, I started to thrust her over me roughly, controlling her head. I knew she wouldn't mind, and my body was craving a faster speed. Her eyes met mine, filled with satisfaction as I pushed her deeper and deeper down onto myself.

"My dirty nymph. Are you getting off just giving me head?" I teased and she bobbed in a yes as a slightly sticky hand came up and started to play with my balls.

My orgasm came quickly, and she made a happy noise, sucking me dry like she was trying to get every last drop before she came off me with a sigh and leaned against my leg. "I needed this. I need you."

Running my hands through her hair, I enjoyed the beauty of my mate. "You can have as much as you want."

She slowly shook her head. "No, I cannot. Because if it were up to me, you'd be in bed with me from now until the sun grew cold." She grinned and crawled into my lap, hiking up her skirt and popping a few more buttons of her blouse. As the buttons came undone, I got a good view of the gold, lacy, crotchless lingerie she was wearing.

"Is that so?" I teased, reaching down and plucking one of the gold elastic strings holding the lingerie in place.

Nyske's eyes were fixed on me as she held my head back. "I'm going to fuck you from now until 5 AM, and then when that's done, I'm going to pretend to be normal. But the truth is, I *need* you." She drew out the word as she sank herself down on me.

She gasped with every inch as I penetrated her, moving slowly as she savored the feeling of having me inside of her again. Just penetration had her sex quivering with a small orgasm.

"Was it this bad before?" I asked.

She grinned. "Oh, yes. But this is so much more delicious, knowing that you'll never get away. And I might get a little dragon in me." Her eyes flashed greedily as her sex that felt like liquid velvet fully enveloped me, perfectly wrapping around me. "I'm greedy for you and you alone," she whispered in my ear as she started to rock slowly on me.

I didn't need any prompting to cup her chest and begin to play with her, fishing her nipple out of its cup and gently kissing it, before leaning down to run my tongue over the peak.

Nyske wrapped her arms around my head and pulled my face into her bosom as she started to slip and slide over my cock. She smacked against me, incredibly wet and nearly panting with desire.

Each ride over me squeezed some of her slippery fluid over my balls and she groaned in pure ecstasy as she steadily rode me. Suddenly, she moved her hips up high, catching me off guard as she flipped around and caught me in her sex before sinking down in one fluid motion again.

"Fuck. I needed this." Nyske reached around her back to run her nails through my hair, scraping my scalp as she rode me.

The new position made her chest stick out, and I played with her soft chest as she had the time of her life riding me. When she glanced back over her shoulder, her eyes were half lidded and glazed over while her face was flush.

"Come in me. Mark me," she breathed.

I was hit by emotion, and it wasn't based in glamor. I was lost in the sheer sexy beauty of the nymph losing herself on me as I twitched hard inside of her.

"Yes," she breathed, sliding over me, and suddenly, I felt far more sensitive. "Give it to me. Give it to your favorite. I'm the only one for you tonight. The only one." She rode me, begging me for my seed for a minute before I finally succumbed and poured my hot seed into her.

Nyske fell back against me, panting and nuzzling into me as she sighed, a giant smile spreading across her face.

My jaws shifted, and I marked her from behind, the magic in my bite searing a thin scar across her neck while she messed my hair and mewled. I didn't need her to tell me what she needed. I knew.

I picked her off my lap and threw her on the bed, holding her down and ripping her skirt off before plunging back into my rightful place.

"Yes!" She looked up from the bed, her face that of a nymphomaniac who was exactly where she wanted to be. She was flush and her breath was so hot, I swore I could see it as I pushed into her, spilling my seed of the last round out of her.

"Fuck me. All night. Always," she panted.

***

Five in the morning hit, and I felt completely drained.

Our time was up, and Nyske stood firm to the plan. It was almost like a switch flipped as we came out of the shower.

Nyske became the professional assistant and sweet girl-friend. "I'm a little hungry if I'm honest." She smiled.

"I'd say we worked up an appetite," I grunted and pulled on a pair of pants. The lack of sleep was getting me a little, but I had done worse. "Let's go see if we can't scrounge up some pickles."

"You are a smart man." She gave me a lingering touch, the only small sign of the nymphomaniac I had just seen for hours on end.

We left the room that reeked of sex and walked into the kitchen. The fridge door was open, and I could hear the familiar sound of pickles crunching.

Nyske gasped, her eyes narrowing. All we could see were the tight black pants around the corner. Nyske came around the fridge door with the fury of a thousand suns.

"You!" she hissed as she stopped short.

Morgana had her eyes closed and was softly snoring between large bites of pickles.

"Is she asleep?" I asked.

Nyske nodded and walked in a slow circle around Morgana. "And sleepwalking to eat all of my pickles?" Nyske held up two empty jars.

We were both stunned at the pickle-devouring vampire as she reached into the fridge and twisted off another lid, then pulled more pickles out of the jar.

"You aren't supposed to wake sleepwalkers," I cautioned.

"Torn between strangulation and just watching," Nyske said softly and sat down. "It's kind of cute."

Morgana's blue face had a light, sleepy smile as she ate another pickle.

"Think she's dreaming of your dick every time she eats one?" Nyske randomly asked, taking an untouched jar and sitting back down to watch Morgana tear through the stock of pickles.

"Dear god, I hope not. She has fangs, Nyske. Never should she bite like that." I shook my head rapidly.

"Doesn't she fang you while giving head?" Nyske's curiosity showed.

"Yeah, but that's like the pelvis, not the dick," I explained as Nyske scooted her chair closer and leaned against me.

I felt the cold metal of Goldie slither up my chair and quietly reclaim her place on my arm. Petting the bracer, I told her I knew she was there and welcomed her back.

"Still can't believe the pickle thief is Morgana," Nyske sighed. "Oh well. The pickle fridge will be installed tomorrow."

"Maybe we can lock it at night." I watched Morgana down three more jars of pickles before the main fridge ran out and she wandered off.

"Probably not the worst idea. I can leave the key out for anyone who comes after Morgana for a late-night snack." Nyske had her single jar clutched protectively as she crunched down on another. "So. Ready for this again in a week? Maybe we can add Sabrina and see what her tail can do." Nyske spoke as if we hadn't just finished a ten-hour marathon session.

I glanced at her, seeing Nyske in a new light. "You could go again right now, couldn't you?"

"Yep. I don't think I'd stop until my heart gave out if you let me." She smiled as she popped another pickle into her mouth.

CHAPTER 32

I walked through the mansion, which had continued to expand with the added mana from my new planes. And given that my children would soon start to arrive, one of the expansions had been turned into an entire hospital wing.

"Everything looks healthy." Trina sat on her egg and was reading charts while a pregnant nymph in a sexy nurse uniform sat to the side of the ultrasound machine. Another nymph lay on the exam table and held my hand.

The nymph let out a relieved sigh. "Thank you, doctor."

"No problem. Send in the next one." Trina put the clip board down. "Okay. I'm going to go over a few things. Let me know when the readings are ready." The copper dragon picked up her egg, planted a kiss on my cheek and left the room as another pregnant nymph entered.

"Husband." Petal smiled, taking the spot on the exam table and picked up my hand the same way the other nymph had. "Are we sure this is safe for the baby?"

"Perfectly safe," I reassured her.

"I'd like to hear from the nurse," Petal huffed.

"He's pretty much an expert at this point," Cinnamon chuckled, pushing her vibrant red hair over her ears. "This is your twenty-eighth ultrasound this week, right?"

"I lost count," I admitted. "But this is special for Petal. It's the last check up before nymphs start popping."

"Yev is sitting on her egg like a broodmother," Petal commented as Cinnamon started squirting gel over her stomach. "I think she's getting a little competitive."

"Dragon eggs take longer. That's just nature. Besides, nymphs are best, right?" Cinnamon knew I was in a tight spot.

"Don't share, but nymphs are my favorite." I winked at the two of them, but my mind drifted off to what had become of Nyske's nights. They had become a sort of debaucherous gathering of some of the more wild members of my harem, which included more than a few nymphs.

"He's thinking of Pixie, I bet." Petal puffed her cheeks out. "Hear she drives him crazy. He lets her glamor him until he's nothing but a wild beast, taking all three holes until she's satisfied."

I tried not to shift in my seat. This conversation was normal for nymphs, even if it did make me a little uncomfortable.

The past few weeks had been simpler. Just like they'd promised, my harem had picked up a lot of the work to run all I controlled. And I'd gotten a chance to settle down.

Part of me thought I'd run out of things to do without chaos everywhere, but with my harem, there was always somebody wanting my time.

Sometimes that meant sex, but sometimes it was daily household moments. Sometimes I went grocery shopping with a few of the nymphs, hearing about their day while people stared at the group of us with their jaws hanging loose.

I also enjoyed working on my enchantments with Sabrina and watching her geek out as she told me about her latest experiments. And Scarlett always welcomed me on her security checks before I'd meet with Jadelyn for any required business meetings.

It had been interesting to watch the two of them settle into a new type of relationship. Scarlett had lived most of her life working to protect Jadelyn, but now Jadelyn was invulnerable. It had changed their dynamic.

But behind the arrangement of their parents, they had always been close friends. And they'd each found their role.

Scarlett had taken on a bit more of the business, having watched Jadelyn for so many years that she was far more than capable. And Jadelyn was enjoying her new freedom. Scarlett had also begun spending more time leaning into being my first mate and running our harem. As it grew, there was more and more to be managed.

The hour of Petal's ultrasound went quickly, and I was able to point out most of the body parts at the same time as Nurse Cinnamon.

"That's it." Cinnamon printed out a series of black and white pictures, handing them over. "Good luck with the birth. We have a rotation, so not sure which nurse you'll get. Send the next one in."

Petal was engrossed in the ultrasound picture, and I wasn't even sure if she heard Cinnamon as she waddled out.

"Well, if there is a lull..." Cinnamon pulled out a set of gloves and snapped them onto her hands. "Maybe I can give you an examination. A thorough one."

The door opened and Cinnamon's shoulders drooped. Kelly waddled in, guided by Taylor who was struggling to help her maneuver through the room.

"I'm going to punish you somehow for putting twins in me." Kelly held her back while Taylor moved, a little clinking of glass jars coming from a backpack.

I raised an eyebrow at Taylor's nurse uniform.

"Well, since Kelly has been having trouble, I have full approval. The pack has been out for a week, and we can't have that." She pulled out one of the jars. "This is a sterile environment, so it is the best place."

I glanced at Cinnamon. "Well, in that case, I probably need the help of a trained nurse too. I'm sure between the two of you, you can get at least a few sterile samples."

"Okay. Wake me when you are done." Kelly rolled on her side. She'd become fairly sleepy and bedridden towards the end of her pregnancy. I was sure that at least one of them would be a dragon based on how worn down she'd become.

Taylor put four jars out on the window sill. "Cinnamon, I have this one chance to show Alpha-alpha just how well the pack's head bitch will treat him. So, help me make this memorable."

***

I paced up and down the hall. Kelly had asked for me to step out while they cleaned her up.

It was all hands on deck. Even some of the pack bitches were here helping out. Right now, many of my women were in hospital beds. Thankfully, they were either in the early stages or had already given birth.

Kelly had just finished; the twins were beautiful.

"Alright, you can come in." Cinnamon had a sleeping child strapped to her chest as she waved us into the room.

"How is she?" I rubbed Charles' cheek and kissed the top of his head. He was a week old, and I had come to learn that with dragon magic and all of the paranormal, they bounced back quickly.

"Good. Everything looks good. She's just tired, and the two of them are already hungry." Cinnamon's smile was warm, bordering on heated when I looked back up. "When you are done, why don't you come to the break room and cuddle with the two of us?"

"No sex," Scarlett reminded her. "Seriously, aren't you sore?"

"A little. But he's the father of my child and hopefully many more." Cinnamon kissed my cheek and moved on.

My eyes didn't linger as I went in to check on Kelly. "How are you?" I kept my tone soft.

Kelly cracked open her eyes. "Meat. I need meat. Also, I feel great. They are finally out." She sniffed the top of their heads and closed her eyes like she had just taken a hit of a strong drug. "Fuck, they smell amazing. Like... like... sex, meat, sunshine, and rainbows all at the same time."

"I think she's getting high," Scarlett chuckled.

"Maeve was like that too." I remembered the new Winter Queen melting all over her children after they were born.

Kelly pulled back the covers. She was naked, and honestly, everything looked normal.

"Damn. I hope I bounce back that quickly," Scarlett mumbled.

Jadelyn came rushing in, huffing. "Did I miss any of them?"

"Hi, Jade," Kelly said from the bed. "No, you are just in time to greet Brent and Madison." We had agreed to name the boy after her father.

"They are so cute." Jadelyn melted. "Don't worry, Auntie Jade is going to spoil you two so much." She leaned over them but didn't touch.

Both of them were latched to Kelly's nipples, and she seemed very content with the current situation.

"Well, you'll have to have your own soon." Kelly winked.

Jadelyn glanced at Scarlett. "I think we'll plan to have them together in not too long."

Cinnamon came rushing back into the room. "Zach, Trina has an egg hatching. We are moving her into room twenty-eight."

I started to move and Kelly cleared her throat. "You forgot something."

Moving back, I kissed her and then leaned down to kiss the twins before wrapping my arms around both of them and waited a moment, gently squeezing them. "I almost need multiple bodies."

"At least you aren't gallivanting across the globe anymore." Scarlett smiled.

"No, that would not go well," Kelly snickered. "Go check on Trina. She's going to be overthinking everything."

I nodded, kissed Kelly again, and got moving.

***

I was standing at the changing table, having just finished up with Charles before he was taken off the table and Lewis was put in his place. Thankfully, Lewis was a champion sleeper and would sleep through the changing.

Wiping my brow, I hurried up, noticing Petal coming over with Sarah. The nursery had three nymphs and me on duty at the moment.

"You're a pro." Pixie laughed and kissed at my neck as a hand wrapped around my waist.

"Really, in here?" I swatted her hand away. "Morgana is coming to replace me in an hour. I think I could use a little lunch break and have a hankering for some pink-haired nymph."

"Damn right you do." She laughed and swatted my rear.

"I'm sort of terrified as round two starts," I answered honestly, changing Lewis out for Sarah. I held baby Sarah sweetly for a moment as her big eyes stared up at me. "Hi, sweety, your mother will be by in an hour."

The lightly blue-skinned girl gripped my finger with surprising strength. There wasn't a hint of vampirism in her, and though she looked like a dark elf, she most certainly had the strength of a dragon.

Pixie moved on now that the large bottle warming tub had finished, and fished out two before moving to feed two babies at a time. I snagged one that had Sarah's name on it and picked her up, holding her gently as she suckled on the bottle.

"You are just so cute," Petal cooed to another baby in the room.

The nursery was always so filled with love. Even if the love each of them got was varied, they seemed to adapt well to it.

I turned to see Pixie cradling Alicia with her short, fuzzy pink hair starting to grow from the top of her head. Moving over, I kissed Pixie and then alternated between giving the two baby girls attention.

***

Yev, Pixie, and I were taking the kids to get their haircut. All of them. How I thought that was a good idea, I wasn't sure. But the portal to the salon was established, so it was game on.

"Oh. Welcome." T got out of his chair and grabbed some scissors. "Who wants lollipops? I bet you kids can't guess what the mystery flavor is."

He waggled a jar of them in front of the young dragons, nymphs, and more. Only a lich would be brave enough to make that move without fear of losing his arm.

"It's when they change the flavors on the machines. So they are all a mix of two flavors," Alicia, one of my oldest, proudly stated.

"Then you'll have to guess the combination." T didn't miss a beat. "So, how much do you want cut, Alicia?"

The pink-haired dragon looked to her mother, and Pixie held her fingers apart.

"This much." Alicia mimicked her mother.

T grinned and spun her around in a barber's chair. "Alright, let's get to work."

Several other skeletons moved the other children into chairs and clacked their teeth, making some of the younger ones giggle.

"Free barber services have been nice." Yev leaned against me. "And he's actually really great with kids."

"Yeah. Doesn't even try to turn them into undead." Pixie rolled her eyes.

"Oh, he's like a grandpa to them all. Besides, when Trevor caught that weird magical disease from that leech thing, he was more than happy to work on a cure," I answered, watching T with the children.

"This is why you don't let kids play in the Wilds," Pixie sighed.

"The older dragon ones always look out for them. And Alicia killed that minotaur that caused problems the other day. Anything much bigger than that knows to stay the fuck away from my children." I crossed my arms.

Several skeletons were playing with any of my children that were waiting for a chair. Simon was climbing up the rib bones of one of them and I had to step forward, hovering to make sure I could catch him if he fell.

"Simon won't even feel it if he falls. Besides, he's a great climber. He has that tail for balance." Pixie watched as Simon's single foxtail stuck out far from his body and wavered trying to keep the three-year-old steady.

"Let him dote." Yev sighed. "It's cute. Besides, he's done this dozens of times already."

"Freddy." Alicia grabbed her younger brother who was trying to join her in the chair and forcefully pulled him into her lap. "You have to be careful. Grandpa T has sharp things."

A few more nymphs came through my portal after the last of the children had been herded in. There were so many of them; it was easy to feel overwhelmed. The mansion often felt like a zoo.

Luckily, all the nymphs really liked having kids around because the household kept growing. And I was having an oddly large number of dragon children if the odds were supposed to be fifty-fifty.

My mass of children had created a few other complications as well. The local school district had called again, followed by social services. Both of them were shut down when the FBI showed up for the house inspection.

My influx into the local community had raised a few eyebrows, and there were people who were absolutely sure that I had women chained up in my basement. Georgia, normally shaking her head the whole time, came and explained the situation without mentioning the paranormal, which honestly had been a bit amusing to watch.

It also helped that I'd made some very generous donations to the elementary school a few years before my kids had started flooding in. A whole new wing was added on.

Thankfully, after the first two waves of children, some of the wives had calmed down, realizing there was no rush to get out as many as they could. The Pendragon Clan would exist for many, many years to come.

Pixie was wandering to the side of the salon, talking to someone on the phone while keeping a watchful eye on all of the children, nodding several times as the conversation continued.

"Little ones!" Tia burst in the door. "Come to grandma!"

Tia shouted with glee and picked up four of them in a single armload, squeezing them tightly before dropping them and picking up another set. The kids loved Tia and her zany appearances.

Yev was scowling, though, because she had asked Tia multiple times to tell them when she was coming over. Truthfully, I didn't think Tia gave it any forethought. Something told me she'd decide to see her grandkids on a whim and then a moment later show up.

"Mom." I hugged her as she finished up with the little ones.

"So good to see you. Got any more little whelps coming?"

"I think Nyske's eggs are the last sure whelps," I answered.

Tia frowned. "It's been, what, ten years?"

"We are pretty sure at this point that they are titan or titan adjacent." I shrugged. "Who knows how long they'll take. We are both very content with them. Do not say anything."

Tia bobbed her head quickly, staying quiet for once.

We had all freaked out a little when they weren't hatching, but Trina and Sabrina had spent no small amount of time looking them over. Something was growing in Nyske's eggs, and we were checking in with my father and The Dreamer to make sure that none of those sealed in Tartarus were using them to get out.

At this point, we had just settled in. According to Trina, they might very well take fifty years to hatch. Some of the nymphs joked about making sure there was another large wave of children to go with them.

But that was far in the future.

"Zach. Georgia is asking for your help with something in London," Pixie spoke up, covering the phone's microphone.

"Does it need to be me?" I asked. It had been a few years since something needed my direct attention from the FBI.

"Helena is stumped. Asked if we could bring Sabrina too. Nothing too dangerous, but very strange. Apparently, there's a group in London that is in the know and are holding him until they can get some answers."

"Sure. Pencil it in for tomorrow after we get back from Tartarus. We found a way to bring down Nyske's eggs, and The Dreamer has convinced Nyske to let her see them."

"Good. About time those two stop fighting."

"I'm not sure that's going to happen. You should expect them to fight the whole time. That's just how they are. But Nyske will be smiling at the end. That's the important part." I was settled into my new, wild life.

Problems with the supernatural were either swept up by the Plushies or our partners in the FBI and the various councils. I was just the guy who held all the planes together and enjoyed my wives and our budding family.

Yev grabbed my hand and pulled me over to one of the couches as the children were occupied in a rare moment. She curled up on my lap and rested her head on my shoulder. "We live a wonderful life."

"That we do." I held her as Pixie plopped down on the other side of me, claiming my other shoulder.

Letting out a content sigh, I just closed my eyes for a moment of rest.

CHAPTER 33

T he sun on my wings and the wind rushing over my
scales was making me happy. I pumped my wings as
I flew forward, smiling to myself. Our big family vacation
was literally on the horizon.

I soared over to the island off the coast of Dubai that was
conveniently off any maps.

I wasn't alone.

Dragons from all over the world were gathering. Normally dragon conclaves were far and few between, but
there had been requests for another given several changing
situations.

Not only was the FBI now equipped with a paranormal
investigation division, but similar divisions were budding
up around the world.

The age of surveillance was too great even for magic
to match. Our paranormal teenagers were no better than
human teenagers in terms of the decisions they made, and
any wrong decision was documented through the internet.

Originally we were going to hold the opening of the
conclave at Brom's home, but after Tia announced her
attendance, Brom had quickly pivoted to suggesting we
meet at the island.

The thought of Tia stomping through his gorgeous estate and breaking everything made me snicker.

"What's so funny?" Scarlett asked from my horns. Her six tails, developed far earlier than they should have been, batted the top of my head as I flew through the wind.

"Thoughts of my mother storming through Brom's estate." I chuckled again.

"Well, that, and you probably couldn't shift in that courtyard of his anymore big guy." Scarlett laughed.

"What can I say? I've grown." I glided closer to the island, happy for the flight to be over soon.

Goldie had made what were essentially four school buses on my back to ferry everyone.

"Dad!" Alicia raced out of one bus as the island closed in below us. My pink-haired daughter was already well into being a teenager. It baffled me every time I realized it. "We are going to get flying lessons here, right?"

"I don't know..." I started, not even wanting to think about the chaos that might bring.

"But Mom said that Auntie Jade was giving swimming lessons to the little ones, and you were going to give flying lessons to the older ones." Alicia joined Scarlett on my head, but she was much less gentle. My daughter gripped my horns and shook them like the little brat she was.

I tried not to roll my eyes.

"I wanted it to be a surprise... but now that it's not, it isn't fun. Go tell your mother that." I blew a raspberry as a dragon which sounded more like a jet engine firing up sounded above me.

"Daaad." Alicia whined.

"Don't 'Dad' me. Scar, what are your thoughts?" I played along. I did plan for the kids to get flight lessons, but I wasn't sure if I was going to be doing all of them. After all, I could only handle them crashing so many times before I died of heart failure.

"Sounds like a wonderful reward for the kids who can behave themselves at the conclave. There are a bunch of old dragons that can be prickly at best." Scarlett pretended to ponder the situation.

"We'll be good!" Alicia rushed to agree.

"I guess if you behave yourself today, we can talk about flight lessons tomorrow." I rumbled in agreement, feeling Scarlett's approval as her tails thumped on my head.

"Oh. My. Gosh! I'm going to be flying!" Alicia jumped in the air while I was going fast enough that the wind pulled at her, starting to lift her off my back. Goldie had to snag her before she was ripped into the air.

The moment of danger did nothing to dampen my daughter's spirits. She ran back into the bus structure and started chattering with the other older kids.

Goldie formed a humanoid body next to Scarlett. "I guess that cat is out of the bag."

"Blame Pixie. She spoils Alicia. Either that or it was on a schedule while Alicia was using her mother's phone." I sighed.

"Better this way." Scarlett shrugged. "At least now they might hold themselves back. The Pendragon family is going to be a little bit of a shock to the system for all these old dragons."

She teased me with her tails. "You've only added more new dragons in the last two decades than the previous thousand years. No big deal." Scarlett teased. "We have a very busy husband."

I sighed as the island below gave me an excuse to be quiet. Smiling, I pulled my wings in and dove. It took little to go down anymore. My full weight sent me hurtling downwards, only for me to turn up out of the dive just above the treetops of the island.

After almost twenty years, I was happy that green vegetation had returned to the island after we'd burned much of it in our fight with Ikta.

My father's tower still stood, and I recognized the beach that held my mother's now empty hoard. I'd worked on a plan for her hoard now that Tia was back.

My wives and children clamored from the structures on my back as I beat my wings and hovered for a moment before settling down on the island.

It felt much tinier than I remembered.

"It feels like you were smaller than me only yesterday." Brom landed beside me, not even making it up to my chest. I was truly massive.

"Time passes so quickly." I agreed.

"Son! Grandbabies! Come to grandma!" Tia shifted through her colors like a rainbow as she arrived and stole the show.

Her display caused more than a few of my kids to ooh and ah as they reached for their grandmother.

Tia landed less gracefully than me, making the island shake.

When she stood tall, I had a big goofy grin on my face.

"What?" Tia's brow pinched down at me.

I held up a claw to the top of her head, then lifted it slightly to the crown of my own head with an even bigger grin.

"Oh hush. Give me my grandchildren. Taken you long enough to grow taller than your old lady." She made grab-by claws at the golden structures on my back. "Maybe when I'm back here, I should show you my hoard. It's big enough to make you jealous. Absolutely huge."

I did my best to hide a reaction. "Goldie, let the kids loose."

The elemental made curly slides off my back, and my kids almost immediately threw themselves into the familiar Goldie slides they had all come to know and love.

My mother shrank down in an instant and tackled the first little one off the slide.

"That was a close one." Scarlett breathed a sigh of relief. "Don't worry. We have several nymphs on full 'distract Grandma Tia duty'. There's a full rotation. Pixie planned it."

"Of course she did." I chuckled. "Am I clear, Goldie?"

"I'll hold the structures until everyone is out. You can shift." Goldie confirmed.

Shrinking down, the island suddenly felt bigger than a stone in a river. I rolled my shoulders as I watched Morgana sail out of the bus with her silver wings and a kid in each arm.

She mimed falling with them; the impact stretching out as she used spatial magic without concern. Ever since her pregnancy was over and her bloodlord traits of being able to store far more mana in her system, she had begun using that half of her ability set more freely.

And it was certainly coming in handy for stopping the children from falling and hitting their heads, which they seemed to do constantly.

She still went out on some missions, but her focus on her children had grounded her enough that she expanded her businesses in other ways.

Paranormals needed more safe places to congregate, especially as it was harder to hide among humans.

She now had eight bars around Philly and another three along the east coast, along with two hospitals.

Ikta made her own appearance a moment later, jumping through several portals with four of her little ones cradled in her arms. "Wee!" She appeared before Brom, who took a cautious step back. "Oh, don't be a big baby. I won't pick on you." The spider queen held her youngest close to her chest and glared at Brom while the other children clung to her.

"Uh. Welcome to the island... Spider Queen." Brom hesitated, glancing at me to make sure this was all okay. Ikta hadn't exactly made friends with the dragons on her last visit.

"Ikta, don't provoke anybody." I sighed.

"It's fun though." She stuck her tongue out and put down the kids, who started running around with all the new things to explore. Only one stayed and cuddled into Ikta.

It was pretty obvious who each of them took after.

"Alright." Morgana clapped her hands. My children's presence was like a tidal wave over the place. The older dragons had no doubt heard the rumors but were shocked with the reality when faced with the utter chaos they all brought. "Who wants to carve targets into trees and do some shooting practice?"

Several of our children started clamoring to join.

"Scar, would you be so kind as to make sure that they learn proper gun safety?" I asked my first mate.

"And I'll make sure Jade doesn't let them use her for target practice again. Seriously, you'd think she had lost all sense of self preservation!" The kitsune threw her hands in the air but bounded over to the kids and Morgana, weeding out a few that were too young for guns.

"Swim lessons this way!" Jadelyn called out, ready to entertain the younger kids before they threw a fit.

Alicia slid up next to me with a few of the other older children. "So... are there rules for drinking?"

I turned and narrowed my eyes at her. "No drinking. Or at least, don't let your mother catch you. And I am not giving you permission. Remember, good behavior for flight lessons tomorrow."

Alicia gave me a quick salute before she and the other girls that were seventeen and eighteen scurried off.

I rubbed my head. They had just gotten through driving lessons, and now they wanted flight lessons.

"Don't worry." Nyske rubbed my shoulders. "We'll have Trina on deck for the lessons."

"That doesn't make it better, because that is practically inviting injury." I grunted.

"We'll have Helena and Morgana on deck?" Nyske tried again. "Or you could stop it all."

"Last time I babied Trevor during driving lessons, I was scolded that they don't learn if they don't make mistakes." I sighed. Watching my kids make mistakes was one of the hardest parts of parenthood.

The nymphs who weren't taking part in shooting or swimming lessons were already helping unpack several large spatial trunks that we had brought with us. Meanwhile, some dragons were unloading large packs and others were fishing around the tower for what furniture survived the battle with Ikta and her driders.

My dragon mates were herding their whelps into the tower with promises of a game finding furniture. I stepped up and worked with several other dragons who were knocking down some of the larger trees and carving them up into rough picnic tables and benches.

When you could shave the bark off with a swipe of the claw or split a tree in two with a magical ice wedge, it was easy to make basic shapes.

More than a few dragons had come with nails to make it even easier, moving around and pounding pieces together.

The smaller kids raced around the group, making the atmosphere lively while the ones old enough to have some dragon strength worked with the dragons, learning to make tables.

The younger, unmated dragons from outside my family were wide eyed, taking in my older daughters and sons.

I already felt a headache brewing from them. I narrowed my eyes, noting a few dragons who might need to be put in their place if they tried to make a harem out of my children.

"You are growling husband." Pixie came up and kissed my cheek to break me out of my thoughts.

"Was I now?" I blinked innocently as I saw one of the younger male dragons back away from Sarisha's daughter.

"Yes. And you are going to have to let them date eventually. You know Alicia has a boyfriend back home that she's been too scared to introduce you to."

"Wh-wha-what?!" My voice boomed.

"This is exactly why she didn't tell you." Pixie chided me.

Maddie zipped up next to us with Frank trailing behind her. My friend had put on a few years, but then Georgia sent us to that homunculus in London. The guy had enchantments that even stumped Sabrina and her mentor was brought in to study them.

Out of all of that, Frank had a litany of enchantments under his shirt, and one of my scales embedded over his heart. The combination had stopped his aging, so that he and Maddie could be together properly. Maddie was eternally thankful, but nothing was owed between friends.

"Dragon King." Thuun put a hand on his shoulder and shifted it green before bowing. "It's wonderful to see you and your lively family." He glanced over at all the dragon children.

A few saw his greeting and started mimicking him, trying to just shift their hands. It was cute to watch. Many failed, instead shifting into their little dragon forms and immediately tussling on the ground.

Helena picked up a silver youngling as the little girl shifted back, staring up at her mother with big doe eyes. "What have I told you about fighting with your brother?" Helena asked.

"Go for the throat and win quickly?" Hailey sounded like she was unsure if that was the correct answer in the current context.

"Good girl." Helena rubbed our daughter's head.

Hailey beamed under her mother's praise and hugged her tightly.

I loved seeing them so warm together.

"I see they are all doing well." Thuun commented, pulling my attention back to him.

"Yes, they are. There are a lot of them, but we also have a lot of hands in the mix. That, and when you get so many of them together, it is a lot easier than dealing with them individually."

Thuun nodded sagely. "The mural we'll paint for this conclave will be one to be remembered. I hope you don't mind being the subject for it again."

"Not at all." I was trying to keep up the conversation with Thuun but also pay attention to the surrounding kids.

I turned away for a moment but heard Tia's voice call out. "Flight lessons? Sure!"

My heart raced as I spun back around. "Mother, no!"

But Tia already had Alicia by the waist and wound up. Whirling around, she launched the pink-haired teen into the air faster than a jet takeoff.

Alicia screamed the whole way up.

"That's the way we used to teach them back in my day." Tia dusted her hands off as my daughter flailed in the air.

Morgana was already shooting up into the air, followed swiftly by Helena.

"That's not how you teach them to fly!" I charged over towards Tia.

"What? It's not like I pushed her off a cliff. Honestly, that might have been more effective." Tia shrugged, and I knew there would be no getting through to her.

My heart continued to pound until Alicia erupted into a gold dragon and started pumping her wings.

Helena was up next to her a moment later, and I managed to breathe again, knowing she would help the young dragon.

"See. Look, she's flying." Tia was grinning ear to ear when I glanced down at her.

I was about to berate my mother when a furious Pixie stormed up. "Mother-in-law." Pixie punctuated each word like it was a slap.

"Gotta go. Come on, little ones! Let's race to see who can get to the beach first!" Tia hurried away.

Pixie puffed as she stopped next to me. "You let her get away with that?"

"Oh no. She won't get away with it." I smiled at Pixie. "But managing Tia is in degrees, not trying to stop her. If you put a wall up, the first thing she wants to do is smash it." I pointed at the other older kids. "Besides, none of them are going to ask Grandma Tia for flight lessons anytime soon after watching that display."

The three others that had been with Alicia were literally shaking as they watched Helena and Morgana try to get Alicia out of the sky safely.

"Point." Pixie agreed.

"Besides, we let them do summer camp with Tia last year and that went okay."

"By 'went okay', you mean they all survived? Rick is terrified to go back next year." Pixie crossed her arms.

"He'll be fine by the time next summer comes around. The rest of the kids are excited to go back. He'll be infected by their excitement." I argued.

Pixie rolled her eyes. "We'll see. Seriously, you need to tone your mother down."

"I'll work on it." But I wasn't all that confident that anything could be done to contain Tia. The threat of less time with her grandkids might work, but if I pushed too far, she'd steal them away.

I turned, meaning to go back to my conversation with Thuun, but he had already wandered off.

So instead, I went back to helping the dragons set up for the party that would shake the little island in the evening.

Maeve was helping split the trees into workable logs. She had one of the biggest transformations among my harem. Now she had a stately poise to her as she settled into being queen. Flicker and Frost stood by her, the summer and winter fae half-sisters were inseparable. Maeve's first was a boy and a white dragon, who at eighteen was quite popular in the winter court. But her second was Frost only a month older than Summer's daughter, Flicker.

The two stayed together and split their time between the two fae courts. Their bond gave us hope for lasting peace in Faerie.

Tyrande was by the tables, waving her finger over the wood and sanding it down while two of my more magically inclined children sat with her trying and mostly failing to do the same.

Maybe after, I could sneak away with a few of my mates.

Sabrina and Helena came to mind for a moment. Despite their quips back and forth in public, in private they were fun and something in my brain enjoyed the two of them.

"What would have you so pent up?" Speak of the devil and she shall come. Sabrina leaned over the tree I was splitting. Ralph was sitting on her shoulders and holding onto her horns. The little angel had a troublesome streak, and because Sabrina was the opposite of an angel, he liked to spend time with her.

That and because she bickered with his mother.

"Thoughts." I looked into those eyes that were still stuffed full of golden grains, a faint pink spot appearing from time to time. "How to celebrate tonight. I thought that you should join me."

"Tia is actually trying to round up some of the other grandparents to watch the kids. Brom and his wives, Trina's parents and Ikta might even portal in the Grandmothers of Dragons. They'll take them off our hands tonight."

"All of them?" I asked, shocked.

"Yep. Tia wanted to show them something." Sabrina shrugged.

The idea of having all of my mates free on the same night was... well... unheard of. The idea was beyond tempting.

But then I realized what Tia was going to show them. "Shit."

"Shit." Ralph echoed with a giggle from atop Sabrina's head.

"Don't say that. It's a bad word," Sabrina chided him.

"Shit." Ralph called out louder, making Sabrina roll her eyes.

"We need to hurry down to Tia's cave. Goldie, do you have everything?" I asked my bracer.

The elemental made a small humanoid form on my wrist. "We loaded everything up. It's not all she had, but it is a good portion."

I nodded and led the Ralph toting Sabrina around the island to Tia's little spatial portal in the cliff face at the dueling beach and stepped through.

"Wow!" Ralph's head was on a swivel. "Where are we?"

"Grandma Tia's hoard." I answered, raising my hand and Goldie poured out gold and jewelry we had gathered for this occasion. It had been harder than I wanted to think about to turn my stocks back into gold.

Sabrina bent down with Ralph still hanging onto her horns and started forming several large enchantments around the piles that we had made.

One was to 'age' the gold. We weren't sure if it would work, but it would accelerate several reactions on the metal so it would smell like it had sat here far longer. Another was one to make them all seem larger than they actually were. The enchantment was sort of a magnified perception. Finally, another to make them shine brighter. That was my creation and was certainly not in my own hoard...

Goldie finished pouring out another pile, and I went to work putting the enchantments in place.

I wiped at my brow. "I think we are all done."

"Good thing Tia is distracted with the grandkids." Sabrina smiled.

"Why is that good?" Ralph asked.

"Because she loves you all so much." Sabrina tickled the little angel, who squealed and flapped his wings.

"Stop it!" He giggled along as we headed back out of the portal.

Tia was on the beach playing with some kids and looked over, spotting us. "What are you two doing?"

"Oh. I noticed the enchantment over here and wanted to make sure it was safe for the kids." I gave her a partial truth. I had technically noticed it, just not recently. And I did genuinely want to make sure the area was safe for my kids.

Tia narrowed her eyes.

"Ralph, I bet you and Grandma Tia would get into some trouble if you teamed up." Sabrina added.

"Grandma!" Ralph launched himself from Sabrina's head towards Tia.

Tia forgot whatever she was thinking and grabbed him. "Want flying lessons?"

"Yes!"

"No, Tia!"

Whoosh.

Ralph, luckily, was a consummate flier at four. Perks of being an angel. He shouted into the wind before his little angel wings caught the air and he glided back down.

Several of the young dragons jumped up and down for Tia to give them flying lessons, too.

I rubbed my face. "Make sure they can form wings, and maybe make sure they can glide before you throw them. They are a little young to push off cliffs."

Tia glanced down at them and then up at me. "I don't know. Do you all want to go to that cliff and see the beach from there? It's really pretty." Tia jumped away, and they all followed.

"She's going to push them off the cliff, isn't she?" Sabrina asked, looking concerned.

"Yeah. But it's only like a thirty-foot drop into sand." I thought about the impact and decided that it was better than her launching them several hundred feet up in the air. "Going to pretend I was never down here. They always come back alive after spending time with my mother, and I'm just going to leave it at that."

Sure enough, a little while later, Tia came back with all the children in one piece, but Fleur came back talking about how Tia healed her boo boo. I looked at my mother, who seemed to look anywhere else than me after that statement.

The party got going and Ikta portaled in the Grand-mothers of Dragons.

Claire took the lead. "Why don't you all enjoy your-selves? We'll make sure the kids get to bed. It's been a while since you've all had time alone." She shooed me off, but she didn't have to push hard.

Sabrina took the drink out of my hand and put it down before claiming that arm and Helena grabbed the other, raising an eyebrow at me. "She said you wanted us?"

"He's getting all of us." Morgana was carrying two bot-tles of bloodwine as she swayed her hips with every step. "We are just bringing the party back to the room for a more private evening."

I kissed each of them in turn and then started heading to what would be a wonderful evening and a fantastic week away with the family.

***

A few weeks later. Beneath the tower, the mural room had been swept clean. The damages from Ikta's plunder of one of her pieces of power had been removed, but the wall left broken as a sign of what had occurred.

The dragons had all left the conclave and a new mural was painted on the wall, far cheerier than the ones before.

From one dragon, half gold, half red, dozens more bloomed, spiraling out like a beautiful flower filled with hope and life.

Beneath that mural, there were children's drawings of a very large and happy family, with many depicting their first flight.

Afterword

That is the end of Dragon's Justice. Most things are wrapped up and Zach has entered a new phase of his life. The dragons as a species are saved and while Zach isn't fully in retirement, I'm sure he has his hands full and he's not getting out to adventure unless it is a dire, world ending threat.

We'll stop his story there.

As always, I have more ideas than I have time to write. We will see if I return to the Dragon's Justice world or not. One things is for certain, that I have plenty of books left to write and I'll keep on going as long as people keep reading.

Please, if you enjoyed the book, leave a review.

Review Dragon's Justice 9

I have a few places you can stay up to date on my latest.

Monthly Newsletter

Facebook Page

Patreon

ALSO BY

Legendary Rule:
Ajax Demos finds himself lost in society. Graduating shortly after artificial intelligence is allowed to enter the workforce; he can't get his career off the ground. But when one opportunity closes, another opens. Ajax gets a chance to play a brand new Immersive Reality game. Things aren't as they seem. Mega Corps hover over what appears to be a simple game. However, what he does in the game seems to effect his body outside.
But that isn't going to make Ajax pause when he finally might just get that shot at becoming a professional gamer. Join Ajax and Company as they enter the world of Legendary Rule.

Series Page

A Mage's Cultivation – Complete Series
In a world where mages and monster grow from cultivating mana. Isaac joins the class of humans known as mages who absorb mana to grow more powerful. To become a mage he must bind a mana beast to himself to access and control mana. But when his mana beast is far more human than he expected; Isaac struggles with the budding

relationship between the two of them as he prepares to enter his first dungeon.

Unfortunately for Isaac, he doesn't have time to ponder the questions of his relationship with Aurora. Because his sleepy town of Locksprings is in for a rude awakening, and he has to decide which side of the war he is going to stand on.

Series Page

The First Immortal – Complete Series

Darius Yigg was a wanderer, someone who's never quite found his place in the world, but maybe he's not supposed to be here...Ripped from our world, Dar finds himself in his past life's world, where his destiny was cut short. Reignited, the wick of Dar's destiny burns again with the hope of him saving Grandterra.

To do that, he'll have to do something no other human of Grandterra has done before, walk the dao path. That path requires mastering and controlling attributes of the world and merging them to greater and greater entities. In theory, if he progressed far enough, he could control all of reality and rival a god.

He won't be in this alone. As a beacon of hope for the world, those from the ancient races will rally around Dar to stave off the growing Devil horde.

Series Page

Saving Supervillains – Complete Series

A former villain is living a quiet life, hidden among the masses. Miles has one big secret: he might just be the most powerful super in existence.

Those days are behind him. But when a wounded young lady unable to control her superpower needs his help, she shatters his boring life, pulling him into the one place he least expected to be—the Bureau of Superheroes.

Now Miles has an opportunity to change the place he has always criticized as women flock to him, creating both opportunity and disaster.

He is about to do the strangest thing a Deputy Director of the Bureau has ever done: start saving Supervillains.

Series Page

Dragon's Justice

Have you ever felt like there was something inside of you pushing your actions? A dormant beast, so to speak. I know it sounds crazy.

But, that's the best way I could describe how I've felt for a long time. I thought it was normal, some animal part of the human brain that lingered from evolution. But this is the story of how I learned I wasn't exactly human, and there was a world underneath our own where all the things that go bump in the night live. And that my beast was very real indeed.

Of course, my first steps into this new unknown world are full of problems. I didn't know the rules, landing me on the wrong side of a werewolf pack and in a duel to the death with a smug elf.

But, at least, I have a few new friends in the form of a dark elf vampiress and a kitsune assassin as I try to figure out just what I am and, more importantly, learn to control it.

Series Page

Dungeon Diving

The Dungeon is a place of magic and mystery, a vast branching, underground labyrinth that has changed the world and the people who dare to enter its depths. Those who brave its challenges are rewarded with wealth, fame, and powerful classes that set them apart from the rest.

Ken was determined to follow the footsteps of his family and become one of the greatest adventurers the world has ever known. He knows that the only way to do that is to get into one of the esteemed Dungeon colleges, where the most promising young adventurers gather.

Despite doing fantastic on the entrance exam, when his class is revealed, everyone turns their backs on him, all except for one.

The most powerful adventurer, Crimson, invites him to the one college he never thought he'd enter. Haylon, an all girls college.

Ken sets out to put together a party and master the skills he'll need to brave the Dungeon's endless dangers. But he soon discovers that the path ahead is far more perilous than he could have ever imagined.

Series Page

There are of course a number of communities where you can find similar books.

https://www.facebook.com/groups/haremlit
https://www.facebook.com/groups/HaremGamelit

And other non-harem specific communities for Cultivation and LitRPG.

https://www.facebook.com/groups/WesternWuxia
https://www.facebook.com/groups/LitRPGsociety
https://www.facebook.com/groups/cultivationnovels

Made in the USA
Monee, IL
04 January 2024

51203571R00223